AND BABY

"Ross," I said, as he began to unpack a bag marked New Wine and Spirits. "I have something to tell you."

I perched on the edge of the couch. Ross followed with a glass of wine and settled comfortably next to me.

"It's nice to come home to you after a long day at the office," he said. "It's very relaxing."

Well, I thought, it won't be very relaxing for much longer.

And then I told him that I was pregnant. The expression on his face was impossible to read. He turned from me, reached for a coaster, and carefully set his wineglass on the coffee table.

"Ross?" Gently, I touched his shoulder. "Ross?" I repeated, ready for the worst.

And then he completely surprised me.

He leapt up from the couch, lifted me up after him and hugged me like he'd never hugged me before.

"This is the most amazing thing that's ever happened to me!" he cried.

"So you're not upset?" I asked.

"Am I upset? Anna, I'm kind of in shock, but it's going to be great!"

Books by Holly Chamberlin

LIVING SINGLE

THE SUMMER OF US

BABYLAND

BACK IN THE GAME

Published by Kensington Publishing Corporation

babyland

Holly Chamberlin

KENSINGTON PUBLISHING CORP.
http://www.kensingtonbooks.com

STRAPLESS BOOKS are published by

Kensington Publishing Corp.
850 Third Avenue
New York, NY 10022

All Kensington titles, imprints and distributed lines are available at special quantity discounts for bulk purchases for sales promotion, premiums, fund-raising, educational or institutional use.

Special book excerpts or customized printings can also be created to fit specific needs. For details, write or phone the office of the Kensington Special Sales Manager: Kensington Publishing Corp., 850 Third Avenue, New York, NY 10022. Attn. Special Sales Department. Phone: 1-800-221-2647.

ISBN 0-7582-1087-6

First Trade Paperback Printing: July 2005
First Mass Market Printing: June 2006
10 9 8 7 6 5 4 3 2 1

Printed in the United States of America

As always, for Stephen;
and this time, also for Joanie.

ACKNOWLEDGMENTS

The author would like to thank all the people who so warmly welcomed her to a new life in Maine, especially Kit and Carrie. Their friendship has become invaluable.

She would also like to acknowledge all the wee ones who bring such joy to her life—Lucca, Ella, Madison, Kimberly, and Colleen.

Welcome to the world, Kathryn Elizabeth Donner!

Thanks to the artist Judith Sowa.

Last but never least, the author would like to thank her editor, John Scognamiglio, for his expertise and encouragement. Every writer should be so lucky.

Part One

1

Mysterious Ways

Think about a trauma, like a car crash, sudden and unexpected. Or think about having your purse snatched. You're walking down the block, minding your own business, when out of the blue some creep grabs your purse and makes off with it while you stand there gaping and gesturing wildly. People stare, some might even stop to ask what happened, but no one can really help. The deed has been done. The car crashed; the creep stole your purse.

Nothing will ever be the same. Your perspective has been radically changed. You have been radically changed. And suddenly, life is wrought with consequences you never imagined because you never imagined the inciting incident.

You ask yourself: Why didn't I ever imagine that I could be in a car crash? Why didn't I ever imagine that my purse could be snatched? Why didn't I ever imagine that I could get pregnant even though I was on the pill?

I was thirty-seven and a half years old the morning I discovered I was pregnant. Going to have a baby. Knocked up. In the family way. The morning I learned I had a bun in the oven.

Thirty-seven and a half years old the morning I found out that I was expecting a blessed event—in other words, the end of my life as I knew it.

My name is Anna Traulsen, and this is my story. At least, the part of my story during which everything just exploded.

Back to that auspicious morning.

My first thought after dropping the pink plastic stick into the white porcelain sink was:

Oh, my God, this can't be happening.

My second thought, after retrieving the stick to give it one more hard look, was:

Of course this can be happening. I had sex. I missed my period. So of course I'm pregnant. This is what happens.

My third thought, after tossing the offending stick into the brushed-aluminum trash can was:

What will Ross say!

Ross Davis was my fiancé. From the day I met him he'd declared pretty strongly that he did not want children. And when we got engaged, Ross reminded me that a family of two—Ross and me—was all the family he wanted.

And I'd gone along with that.

Except for maybe a dog, I'd suggested. A small dog, one with short hair so the shedding problem would be minimal.

Ross had agreed. Maybe a dog. A small, nondestructive dog. The kind you can train to pee on newspaper.

Well, I thought that awful morning in April, a baby most certainly isn't a dog, and although it is small, it most certainly is destructive. It spits up on your best silk blouse; siphons your bank account in an alarming way; and puts a firm, wailing, pooping end to your sex life.

The thing that had gotten you into trouble in the first place.

Sex with a man.

I remember thinking that I should call Ross right away. I assumed he hadn't left the condo for his office yet; Ross is never his best in the morning. I belted my robe more tightly around my middle and hurried from the bathroom.

With a practiced motion I snatched my cell phone from the kitchen counter where it had been recharging for the past eight hours.

The number was loaded; I hit the proper button.

A woman's voice answered on the first ring.

"Alexandra," I said. "I need to talk to you."

2

All Eyes Upon Her

I checked my watch for the third time and wondered why I was bothering. Alexandra was always twelve minutes late. Never eleven or thirteen, always exactly twelve minutes late. Alexandra claimed this was just a bizarre coincidence, and she teased me for even noting it.

"I'd say you're the one with the problem, honey, not me. Sure that watch isn't bolted to your wrist?"

Well, it's no secret that I'm a bit anal. That would be Alexandra's term. I call myself disciplined. Orderly. Focused. I'm certainly not obsessive in any way. I do not suffer from OCD.

Anyway, I don't know how I made it through the day without spilling my dread secret. I swear I came close to grabbing the server behind the counter at Bon Marche, where I stopped for a cup of coffee, decaf of course, and shouting the news in his face.

Being a highly disciplined person, I refrained from attacking the poor server and even avoided telling Ross when he called at eleven to see if I could have lunch with him. I begged off, claiming a disgruntled client, and though I hated to lie to the man I was to marry in a few months, at the time it seemed the right thing to do.

How could I not have seen the signs? How could I have been so blind to the truth?

"Another soda water?"

I forced a smile for the too-pretty male bartender. Bartenders used to look like normal people, like your favorite grizzled sweetheart of an uncle, or your bland-faced third-grade science teacher who somehow made the task of memorizing the names of the planets come alive. Now, too many bartenders look like models. I have a hard time sharing news of my pedestrian life with a person too pretty to have a care that can't be alleviated by batting an eyelash.

"Thanks, no," I said. "Not yet. I'll wait for my—"

"Anna! What on earth is the matter?"

I swiveled on the bar stool to see my friend striding toward me. Alexandra can't help but stride; her legs are quite long.

"Nothing's the matter," I whispered as Alexandra slipped onto the bar stool next to mine. "I mean, everything is the matter. But we don't have to announce it to the world."

"Honey," she replied, "look around. The collective ego in here, apart from yours and mine, of course, is so overinflated it could sail us to Portugal. Relax. No one cares about you."

Alexandra had chosen the bar at Bodacious. It isn't one of my favorite places—the clientele is tragically hip—but Alexandra loves it. She enjoys, as she puts it, "mocking the ignorant."

I couldn't help but smile. "Well, that's comforting. I guess. Look, go ahead and order. I've waited all day to talk to you, I can wait another few minutes."

"If you say so." Alexandra hailed the bartender; he came dashing over and gave her a gorgeously flirtatious smile. She returned it mockingly; as she knew he would, the bartender clearly misinterpreted and began to fawn.

Alexandra is my closest friend although I've known her

for only about four years. She's one of those people who seem completely comfortable with herself. It's as if she looked in the mirror one day long ago and said, "Okay. I got it." And from that point on, she's been unapologetically and wholeheartedly Alexandra Ryan Boyd.

The Ryan came from her father. Disappointed to learn his firstborn child was a girl, he insisted on staking at least some claim by branding her with the name of his favorite uncle, long since deceased.

Good thing, too, as Alexandra turned out to be his only child and, therefore, his last chance at immortality, of a sort. It's Alexandra's opinion that her declaration of remaining forever child-free—that is, that there would be no grandchildren forthcoming—led to the massive heart attack that killed Mr. Boyd on the spot.

"Literally," she told me not long after we met. "I was on the phone with him, and the second the words were out of my mouth I heard this terrific thud, and then my mother was screaming, and the next thing I knew I was on a plane for Cincinnati. It was a very nice funeral, by the way. My aunts put together a very respectable party afterward. I always thought they should have opened a catering business."

Alexandra Ryan Boyd—she uses her full name professionally—is an interior designer. Her business—Alexandra Ryan Boyd, Inc.—is primarily focused on private homes, although on a rare occasion she accepts a corporate gig. And once in a while, for certain large budget, high-profile events I'm coordinating, I invite Alexandra to team up with Anna's Occasions. We do it partly for the big money and partly for the fun of working together. Clients want satisfaction, and that's what they get from us. Satisfaction and an inevitable photo in the *Boston Globe*; once, we even got a mention in a popular home-decorating magazine.

Not bad for two girls from families who reared us with all the attention usually reserved for an afterthought.

The bartender was still fawning over my friend. I rolled my eyes to the painted tin ceiling. It was almost always the same. Nine out of ten times, men greedily zeroed in on Alexandra and ignored every other woman in the room, even those at least as attractive. Like me. Although since I'd become engaged to Ross, being ignored didn't bother me. Much.

Alexandra isn't a conventional beauty, but I think she's the most attractive woman I've ever met. Clearly, I'm not alone in that assessment. Her face is challenging, planes and angles rather than round and welcoming. Her skin is superpale, very evenly white, like alabaster or marble. I swear not even a freckle mars her face. Her eyes are a very deep blue, almost the famous violet of Elizabeth Taylor's eyes.

Alexandra wears her thick, super-dark-brown hair slicked into a chignon, which serves to emphasize the angularity of her face. It's a conscious design decision, of course, as is the unusual shade of lipstick she wears. She mixes it herself and applies it from a 1950s gold and mother-of-pearl compact with a skinny-handled brush. The shade is a little like crystal with a touch of lilac, like a Cape amethyst.

Unlike me, a self-proclaimed jewelry addict, Alexandra owns only a few pieces and wears each piece consistently. On her left wrist she wears an antique watch she bought at an auction somewhere in France. Diamond studs sparkle fantastically on her earlobes; the earrings are a college graduation gift from her grandmother. And on the fourth finger of her right hand she wears a slim silver band with the inscription "vous et nul autre," an early version of French meaning "you and no other."

I often wondered who gave the ring to Alexandra; it isn't the sort of thing a person buys for herself. But something kept me from asking. I figured that if Alexandra wanted to tell me about the giver someday, she would.

I watched as the bartender slid the largest martini I've ever seen across the bar to Alexandra, all the while not so subtly trying to peer down her crisp-collared blouse. Alexandra doesn't need to dress like Adriana from *The Sopranos*. I swear she could wear a nun's habit and still be a knockout. In reality, her wardrobe is based on a few simple, signature pieces. A white tailored, long-sleeve shirt; black slacks; a few bright, silk scarves; a few fitted jackets in leather, suede, and lightweight wool; and sleek black pumps my mother would call "smart." On the coldest days of the year, Alexandra appears in a vintage fox fur inherited from the same grandmother who gave her the diamond earrings. (That grandmother, Alexandra told me, was the family's infamous wild child; no wonder she and Alexandra were so close.) On the hottest days of the year, the black slacks are replaced by a pencil skirt in Schiaparelli's hot pink; the pumps give way to stiletto-heeled slides.

Alexandra says she was born with her signature style, and while I know she's exaggerating for the sake of a good story, I want to believe her. Stylish, fiercely independent Alexandra sprung, fully formed, from the forehead of a tyrannical, pale-blue-polyester-wearing father. Why not?

That same polyester-clad man had told his daughter that he thought what she did for a living was frivolous; he suggested she get a real job, like "a secretary or something."

Alexandra had commented, "I think my father's notion of a 'working girl' was cribbed from a 1950s Technicolor movie, you know, dozens of wasp-waisted women wearing cat-eye glasses, corralled in a typing pool, longing only for a handsome husband and a kitchen full of shiny appliances. Not," she'd added, "that there's anything wrong with the handsome husband part."

Mr. Boyd, wherever he is, might be interested to know that Alexandra's professional reputation has been well established for a long time now. Her reputation is due partly to hard work, partly to an uncanny ability for knowing what the client needs even if the client doesn't know he needs it. I've seen her create a lush, opulent apartment, something completely the antithesis of her own sleek, art deco-ish home, for a fifty-year-old corporate lawyer, newly divorced, who practically burst into tears of joy when it was finally revealed to him.

"Did he ask for something so Oriental?" I remember asking Alexandra when she'd triumphantly finished the job.

"Of course not," she'd told me. "He had no idea what he wanted. So I had to tell him."

Alexandra, I have to admit, can be frightening.

"So?" she said now, fixing me with her violet, appraising gaze.

I took a deep breath. It was the first time I'd speak the words to anyone other than my reflection in the bathroom mirror.

"I'm pregnant," I said. "I bought a pregnancy kit, and it says I'm pregnant."

Alexandra calmly took a sip of her massive martini, set the glass down on the bar, and then looked right at me.

"Who's the father?" she said.

"My God, Alexandra," I cried, "Ross is the father!" I glanced around to see who was staring at me. No one.

Alexandra nodded. "Good. Just checking. I don't like to make assumptions. No one is perfect, my dear."

I needed a moment to get past whatever it was I was feeling right then.

"I wouldn't cheat on my fiancé," I said finally. "I'm not a cheater."

Alexandra sighed. "Honey, I know you're not a cheater. By nature you're a good, moral person. You're ethical, upstanding, all of that. You're a downright Girl Scout. But sometimes passion takes a person by surprise and—"

"Not me," I insisted. And then I wondered if that was something to brag about. Never having been swept away by overwhelming feelings. Never having committed a crime, not even a misstep, of passion.

"I don't understand why you're so surprised," Alexandra said, matter-of-factly. "I mean, you bought the pregnancy kit, right?"

"Well, yes."

"So you must have had an inkling that something was wrong."

"But I've never been pregnant before," I said. How could I explain my puzzlement? "I've always been so careful. How could this have happened? I'm almost thirty-eight years old, I've been on the pill for years, and every gynecologist I've ever been to has told me I'm a perfect candidate for intensive drug therapies and artificial insemination and all that other awful stuff. God."

"They say He works in mysterious ways."

"Meaning what?"

"Meaning that maybe He wants you to be a mommy. I don't know. I don't believe in God. Your hands and feet are going to swell, you know. You probably won't be able to wear your engagement ring."

I shot a glance at the three-carat emerald-cut diamond on my left hand. Not be able to wear that gorgeous piece of jewelry? It was unthinkable.

"Who says I'm still going to be engaged once Ross finds out that I'm pregnant," I said plaintively.

Alexandra opened her mouth and closed it again almost immediately. She frowned. She folded her arms across her chest. She unfolded them. She leaned forward.

"Oh, come on," she said, "you don't really think . . ."

"See? Even you think he's going to be mad and walk out on me."

"Or suggest that you have an abortion."

I didn't know what to say. I'd been avoiding using the *a* word even to myself. It isn't that I'm against the idea of abortion. I've always been staunchly pro-choice; there are certain circumstances where an abortion is simply the wisest path.

It's just that the word is so ugly.

Abortion.

It sounds like war. It sounds like a man's word. More accurately, it sounds like an aggressive man's word. Abort the mission. The enemy has found us out. Abort, abort, abort! It makes me think of characters played by actors like James Coburn and Steve McQueen and Arnold Schwarzenegger—

faces I personally don't care to associate with the image of a cooing bundle of joy.

"How can I get an abortion?" I said, lowering my voice, though I, too, was convinced nobody in Bodacious cared at all about two women over thirty-five talking about babies. "I'm financially stable, I'm certainly old enough to be a parent, and I'm engaged. At least for the moment. What's my excuse for not going through with the pregnancy?"

"You don't want children?"

"There is that," I admitted.

Alexandra took another delicate sip of her martini and swallowed.

"Perfection. And by the way," she added, "if Ross has the nerve to be mad at you for something he helped make happen, kick him. Hard. In the ass."

"I don't think he'll be mad," I protested. "Ross is rarely ever mad. He's rarely ever anything but—"

"But what?" Alexandra smirked. "Bland?"

"No," I corrected with some annoyance. "I was going to say he's rarely ever anything but pleasant. And let me tell you, a pleasant disposition is a good quality in someone you're going to spend the rest of your life with."

Alexandra shrugged. "If you say so. Look, why do you even have to tell Ross right away? Why not take some time and think things through."

Really, I thought, I wonder if she thinks about what's coming out of her mouth.

"Alexandra," I said with great patience, "human gestation is only thirty-six weeks or so. With maybe three weeks down I don't have much time to hide the fact that I'm pregnant. Anyway, I have to tell Ross right away. He is the father."

"So?" she said.

"What do you mean, so? He's my fiancé. We're getting married. Husbands and wives are supposed to be honest with each other, about everything."

And yet, when Ross had called earlier that day I'd chosen not to tell him he was about to be a father.

"Besides," I went on, "he'll figure it out on his own soon enough."

"Men can be dense," Alexandra pointed out.

"Not that dense. Anyway, Ross is very body conscious."

Alexandra popped a gin-soaked olive in her mouth and chewed. "He keeps track of your eating habits?" she demanded finally.

"No. But he notices a change in my weight." I shrugged as if Ross's uncanny attention to weight gain didn't bother me, but it did. Sometimes. "It's just the way he is."

"Neurotic," Alexandra suggested. "Controlling. Shallow."

"He cares about appearances. So do I. There's nothing wrong with that."

"Assuming you're not contractually obligated to undergo liposuction every five years."

Really, I thought, Alexandra can be such a drama queen.

"I'm not saying Ross would leave me if I gained a few pounds. He's not horrid. Would I be engaged to him if he were?"

"I don't know," Alexandra shot back. "Would you?"

"What's that supposed to mean?"

"It means that there's nothing wrong with marrying for reasons other than romantic love. Women have done it since the dawn of time. Well, you know what I mean. Since it was prudent for them to ensure their future by marrying up."

It took me several moments to reply. "I should be furious with you," I said, "for suggesting I'm marrying Ross for his money and his looks and his social connections. I really should. But for some reason I'm not."

Alexandra shrugged. "Because you understand that marriage is a legal contract at bottom. And within the bounds of that legal contract every couple has another contract, a private contract, their own rules. For example, I support you financially and you keep your mouth shut about my mistresses. That's a popular one. Just look at Tony and Carmela Soprano."

"Do I have to? That's such a depressing marriage."

"Do you really think so?" Alexandra said. "I think it's

kind of sweet in a way. But here's another private deal: I take care of your aging mother and do all the housework and the maintenance of our upscale social life and you don't ask me for sex. I'm sure that deal has its fans."

"I'm not one of them," I assured my friend. I wasn't even sure how that deal would work. Was the husband supposed to go elsewhere for his sexual pleasures?

"How about this?" Alexandra said now. "I call this the Arm Candy Deal. You do everything within your power to keep your looks—diet, exercise, Botox, surgery, bulimia if necessary—and I'll take you to Europe every summer and buy you diamonds from Tiffany for every little occasion."

"Where did you get such a jaundiced view of marriage?" I asked, wondering again what life in the solidly working-class Boyd family must have been like for a rare orchid like my friend.

"I keep my eyes wide open. The sanctity of marriage exists only in a storybook, if there."

I sighed. "You'll never get married with that attitude."

Alexandra put her empty martini glass on the bar with more force than strictly necessary. "Have I ever said I wanted to?" she snapped. "Really, Anna, it's dangerous to assume everyone wants the same happy ending. It makes one a very boring person."

"One?" I smiled ruefully. "Don't you mean it makes me a very boring person?"

"Now, I didn't say that."

But she'd implied it. And I really couldn't argue. Sometimes I did worry that I was becoming more of a bore with every passing year.

I shrugged, took a sip of seltzer, and wondered if I was wild and crazy enough to order a glass of wine. I wasn't.

"Did I mention that I'm happy for you?"

I looked closely at Alexandra. I was suspicious.

"Are you trying to make up for the boring remark?"

"No."

"You don't even like children."

"I like you, and I'm happy for you," she said. "Assuming of course that you're happy for you, and clearly your jury is still out. So maybe I should say that if you decide to be happy about this pregnancy, I'll be happy for you."

I sighed. "Will you be nice to my baby?"

"Of course I'll be nice to it. The kid. Although to be honest it would be easier if the kid turns out to be intelligent. I'm not very good with dumb people."

"Mentally challenged. Differently abled people."

Alexandra's expression remained bland. "That's what I said. Dumb."

"You're incorrigible," I said.

"And you're the only one I know who uses that word. Outside of a romance novel, I mean."

"You read romance novels? I find that hard to believe."

Alexandra smiled coolly. "I might not have great faith in marriage, but I'm not immune to chocolate hearts, chilled champagne, and violins singing in the background."

"You left out the most important element of romance," I chided.

"I mentioned the champagne."

"The man, silly. What about the man? And by the way, who are you dating at the moment? You've been oddly silent about your own life."

"That's because you've been oddly talkative about yours."

"I'm sorry."

"Really, it's okay, honey. What you've got going on is big news. Me? I'm just passing the time with some tax attorney."

"Don't you ever get tired of Mr. Right Now?" I asked.

I'm not a prude; I didn't care how many men Alexandra slept with as long as she played it safe. It's just that I was concerned my friend might miss a window of opportunity and never find someone nice with whom to settle.

"Ah, but that's the beauty of Mr. Right Now," Alexandra explained. "He's always changing, and change is always exciting."

Let me be honest. I've never been a huge fan of change.

Generally speaking, I crave stability. It takes people like Alexandra to force me beyond the comfort zones I so readily establish.

"I don't like change for its own sake," I told Alexandra, unnecessarily. "I think that's why I've never had a roving eye. Monogamy seems very natural to me."

"I'm not abusing loyalty to the familiar," Alexandra pointed out. "Necessarily. In fact, honey, I'm not even preaching here. I'm just telling you that I'm just fine not settling down. At least for now. Who knows what will happen in the future? The future, my dear friend, is deliciously uncertain."

I frowned. Deliciously?

"Of course the future's uncertain," I said. "Everybody knows that. It's just that suddenly it seems more uncertain than it ever has. Like, I don't know, like a big raggedy question mark ready to explode at the slightest inquisitive poke."

"Hmm. The future as pendulant piñata. Very interesting, if a bit of a stretch. But seriously, Anna, with a baby you're going to have to learn to deal with change. You're going to have to learn to expect the unexpected. You're not going to be in control of your life. Not for a while, anyway. So say goodbye to your current routines and habits, honey. Life is about to get weird."

"Thank you," I said, "for being so gentle with the truth."

3

He's Got It All

Let me tell you about Ross Davis. He's the dream catch of every single woman over the age of thirty. At least, of every urban-based, professional, well-dressed, single woman, and there are an awful lot of them about town.

People say Ross looks like a younger Pierce Brosnan, and that's true to some extent, but Ross's features are a bit more pronounced. His eyes are pale gray and quite pretty for a man. His hair is thick and dark and wavy; he has it expensively and expertly cut every three weeks at a salon on Newbury Street by a petite, stylish young woman he considers his grooming guru. I was jealous of the grooming guru until I learned that her husband is even wealthier than Ross. My fears were immediately put to rest.

Ross is in perfect physical shape. Some of that perfection is due to good genetic stuff; the rest is due to regular trips to the gym and a diet low in both fat and carbs. Ross appreciates good looks in others, too. I wasn't at all surprised to find that every one of his male friends is as well groomed if not as naturally handsome as Ross. No need for a visit from the Fab Five for that crowd. Ross is a born metrosexual.

Oddly, in those early days, Ross didn't care quite as much about my appearance as he did about his own. Sometimes I wondered if he saw me all that clearly, in detail, or if he was satisfied that I presented an overall attractive appearance. Ross might notice a change in my weight, but he often failed to notice things like a new blouse or highlights in my hair.

No one can argue the fact: Ross is self-focused. He's not selfish, exactly. I think of selfish people as mean spirited, and Ross is nothing if not generally pleasant.

Anyway, there's no doubt that one of the reasons Ross was drawn to me was because of my physical attributes and my personal style. And he liked the fact that I have my own small but successful event planning business. He liked the fact that I'm on a first-name basis with just about everybody who is anybody in Boston, even if most of those people are not my friends but my employers.

Ross is drawn to glamour like a moth is drawn to a flame.

Actually, that's not quite right. At first I wondered about the fatality of his attraction, but after a few weeks together I realized that while Ross might like certain accoutrements of glamour, like his XJ8 Jaguar, he's not interested in glamour's dangerous aspects, like drugs and high-stakes gambling and driving that outrageously expensive Jaguar over the speed limit. A healthy degree of caution is a good quality in a husband.

Overall, Ross is a nice guy—the right guy for a lot of women. But was he the right guy for me?

Here's what I told myself about two months into the relationship: Every man has his faults and flaws. What does it matter if Ross rarely reads a book and grumbles every time his accountant suggests he make a substantial charitable donation to one of the city's homeless shelters? He dotes on me to the best of his ability, and he's generally fun to be with.

I had no complaints. At least, none of the magnitude I'd had with former boyfriends. Ross isn't a cheater, and I knew this because before getting too involved with him I'd asked around. He isn't a drunk. He isn't a mama's boy. Well, he isn't too much of a mama's boy. He isn't homophobic or racist or ultra right-wing conservative. He went to college and graduated right in the middle of his class. More, he swears he never belched the national anthem, something a surprisingly small number of male college graduates can say. He doesn't chew tobacco.

Most people like Ross Davis on sight. He's not intrusive. He's friendly and remembers names and knows how to act at parties. He compliments women without being disrespectful. Men find him unthreatening; they want to hang out with him, have a drink with him, cheer along with him at a ball game.

Most men, that is. There is one man I know who never succumbed to Ross Davis's charms. But more on him later.

I met Ross at a party. We were drawn to each other right away and left the party early for more private conversation at one of the last surviving cigar bars in town, quiet even on a Saturday night. Neither of us smokes; Ross told me he was thinking of buying a leather chair similar to the one this bar featured and was curious to know my opinion of the chair.

We were engaged after about nine months.

Before the age of thirty-five I never would have dreamed of getting engaged to a man I'd known for less than a year. But when Ross popped the question—along with the cork on a bottle of very expensive champagne—I told myself I was old enough to know what I wanted. Why wait? What was the benefit of passing up a real, in-the-hand option for a phantom opportunity?

I asked myself, What if no one else eligible ever comes along? Where will I be then?

I was fast approaching forty, and for the first time the idea of spending the rest of my life alone seemed unappealing. I liked my independence (which could be why I waited so long to accept a marriage proposal), but I'd come to believe that personal independence could exist alongside healthy mutual dependence. At least, I hoped it could.

So I said yes to Ross's proposal of marriage. I put that three-carat emerald-cut diamond ring on my finger—rather, I let him slide it on for me—and I set my face in the direction of a bright and shiny future as Mrs. Anna Traulsen-Davis.

A bright and shiny future that was not supposed to include a baby.

4

Goodbye to All That

I got home that evening at seven. There was a message on voice mail from Ross, saying that he was sorry he'd missed me. "Knowing you," he said, "you're working late, again. Well, I suppose that's what makes Anna's Occasions the success it is. I'll try you on your cell."

I pulled my cell phone from my purse; I'd turned it off just before meeting Alexandra. There were no messages, but there was one other message on voice mail. It was from Mrs. Beatrice Kent's personal assistant; in a somewhat pained voice, Ms. Butterfield informed me that Mrs. Kent had chosen my "little company" to put together a small party at Mrs. Kent's home for the surviving members of her high school drama club.

I should have been thrilled. Mrs. Kent is well known, well connected, and well heeled. Landing the job was quite a professional coup. But my excitement was tempered by the disconcerting fact that I was unexpectedly pregnant just six months before my wedding to a man who didn't want children.

I walked into the kitchen and took a bottle of water from

the fridge. Rarely has anything gotten in the way of the enjoyment I derive from work. Alexandra calls me a workaholic, but I don't like that term. Besides, I cherish downtime; I know how to relax. It's just that work is for me what tennis is for professional tennis players. It's what I do; it's who I am.

I got my first job the summer I was fourteen; it was at the local branch of the public library. The salary was abysmally low, but I loved having a job; it appealed to my sense of structure and routine.

After that there were stints as an office assistant, receptionist, and checkout girl; for a few summers I was a waitress, then hostess, at a local Friendly's. My parents were thrilled at my industriousness. They stopped giving me an allowance when I turned fifteen; any spending money I needed from that time on, even through college, I earned.

After college I took a job with a mid-sized event-planning company where I worked hard and learned the ropes. And after ten years, I left that company to start Anna's Occasions. When I think back to those first arduous months of planning and financing, I can hardly believe I had the nerve to take such a risk, albeit a calculated one. Walking away from the safety net of a steady paycheck and a corporate-sponsored insurance plan took a lot of courage; I'm not bragging, just being honest. The only arena in which I've ever been bold is my career. Well, maybe I am bragging.

In the early days of Anna's Occasions, I worked from home to keep overhead low. But before long I found that it was virtually impossible to maintain any sense of private life when my office was down the hall from my bedroom. So I rented office space in a small commercial building on Tremont Street. The rent was high, but in the end my sanity was worth it.

Still, anyone who runs her own business—whether she be a freelance editor or a personal financial advisor, whether she has a staff of one or twenty, whether she works from home or an outside office—will tell you that her business is her life, her life is her business. It has to be that way if the business is to survive; the business never would have been born if she hadn't been super-dedicated in the first place.

Remember: It's Anna for Every Occasion.

I know. But one line hooks like this work, sometimes too well. It's hard to manage a long weekend, let alone a real vacation, when your business is thriving. But over time I learned how to better structure and, most important, how to say no. A girl needs her downtime. I don't need worry lines and crow's feet before I'm forty.

One more point: From the start of my solo career I declined to venture into the wedding-planning business. Twice I was made enticing offers: the first, by a bride-to-be whose imagination was as blank as her budget was limitless—imagine the possibilities!—and a year after that by a bride-to-be who had always dreamed of a Moulin Rouge–style wedding; but I stuck to my original plan and gave the hopeful brides a referral instead of my signature on a contract.

Here's why: Familiarity breeds contempt. I didn't want to become so jaded by the arduous process of arranging weddings that by the time my own wedding came along I opted for a quick civil ceremony at the courthouse, no big dress, no lavish reception, and no champagne toasts. I wanted my own wedding to be special, unsullied by an insider's view of the industry. It's reported that weddings are something like a sixty billion dollar industry in the United States. With that kind of money changing hands, it can be difficult for someone in the business to preserve any sense of romance about her own wedding.

The decision paid off. Now it was time for my wedding, and I was happy and excited; it all felt fresh. And things were going swimmingly. The vendors to whom I gave lots of business were coming through for me without a hitch. The florist, the caterer, the agency that booked bands (no DJ; Ross and I were in agreement on that). One of my regular clients recommended a makeup artist and a hairstylist she hired for all the charity galas she attended in Boston and

New York. Another hooked me up with a private masseuse who would be available for a stress-reducing massage the morning of the wedding.

Anna's big wedding. The wedding that might not be happening. Because once I told Ross that I was pregnant . . .

Well, I told myself with false cheer, look on the positive side, Anna. With no wedding to plan you'll have plenty of time to spend on Mrs. Beatrice Kent's project. That is, until you have to start converting part of your bedroom into a nursery, interviewing daycare agencies, and figuring out how you're going to support yourself and a child for the next eighteen years.

I put the empty water bottle in the sink and went into the living room. Although no one piece was spectacular, the room was pleasing. Good taste can take you far, especially when your decorating budget is modest. Now, I tried to imagine a Pack-n-Play in place of the coffee table, a baby swing where the ficus tree stood, a heap of brightly colored toys strewn across the couch. I tried to imagine those things, but I just couldn't.

I looked then to the fireplace. (Were you allowed to make a fire with a baby in the house?) Several framed photographs were displayed on the white marble mantel. I reached for the one of Ross and me on the beach in Puerto Rico earlier that year. One of the resort's employees had taken it for us, after he'd delivered two tall, frosty glasses of rum punch. With no false modesty I noted that Ross and I looked good together, both of us trim, healthy, and stylish. I didn't want to lose Ross. I didn't want to lose future opportunities to laze in the sun on foreign beaches with my handsome, well-behaved fiancé.

With a shaky hand I replaced the framed photo, and in spite of Alexandra's suggestion that I put it off, I decided to tell Ross about the pregnancy that very night. Why prolong the agony of not knowing how Ross would respond to my big news? Why put off the agony of being abandoned?

Because I just knew that Ross would dump me like the

proverbial hot potato. Ross isn't an irrational hothead. On the contrary, his basic rationality would be the cause of our split. He'd say that we had a deal and that I'd broken it. I'd argue that it had taken two to break the deal and besides, I—we—hadn't broken it on purpose.

But my arguments would fall on deaf ears.

I picked up my purse and headed out again. At the corner, someone was just getting out of a cab, and I slid in—amazing luck in Boston. The loft was only about a fifteen-minute walk from my apartment, but I'm not comfortable on certain fairly isolated South End streets after dark. The driver took off, and I continued to anticipate the scene to come.

It was an accident, Ross, I'd plead. All just a horrible accident. It's nobody's fault. Neither of us is to blame.

But Ross wouldn't listen. He'd shake his head, tell me how keenly disappointed he was in me, and suggest I remove my belongings from his place of residence.

Being pregnant brought out my hitherto undetected penchant for drama.

The driver sped up to make a light, and I gripped the edge of the seat. I'll be a single mother, I thought wildly, if I don't die first in this cab. I'll be alone for the rest of my life. Me and little Trevor or Emily, traveling the country in a beat-up old Ford, waiting tables at Denny's for loose change, stealing day-old loaves of bread, turning tricks in exchange for a warm, dry place to sleep.

Face it, Anna, I told myself. You'll never be able to run the business with the demands of motherhood. The cost of child care is astronomical, and you can just forget about asking your parents for help. They're far more interested in their time-share in Florida than in babysitting their grandchildren. So you'll have no help from that quarter. Within a year all of your clients will have abandoned you for someone who can actually meet a deadline and show up for a meeting without spit-up stains all over her blouse.

"Lady? Lady?"

The driver was scowling at me over his shoulder. The cab

was not moving. I mumbled an apology and stuffed a few bills into his hand.

"Don't you want change?" the driver called as I scooted from the back seat.

"Keep it," I replied, wondering just how big of a tip I had given him. Budget-conscious Anna Traulsen tossing away her hard-earned money?

Such was my state of mind when I arrived at the condo where Ross and I were to begin the rest of our lives.

5

And Baby Makes Three

Ross wasn't home. While I waited for him I surveyed the two-thousand square foot space and yearned in vain for the worries of the day before, the worries that only twenty-four hours before I'd found so monumental.

The contractor was two months behind schedule. (I later learned that this is par for the course.) The tile supplier had sent the wrong tile for the bathroom floor. The Ralph Lauren paint technique we'd chosen for the front hall was a disaster, impossible to achieve. Someone or something had dinged the hood of Ross's Jaguar (I'd told him not to drive it in the city), which required that it be in the shop for several days. The dry cleaners had failed to get out a stain in my favorite silk blouse, a stain they'd assured me they'd remove, and they'd charged me for the so-called service anyway.

Such were the tragedies Ross and I faced as two well-paid thirty-somethings with little or no responsibility to anyone but ourselves. I wonder if we knew just how good we had it.

Ross arrived at about eight-thirty. I greeted him with the

traditional kiss on the cheek. I waited with false patience for him to take off his jacket and empty his pockets of change.

"Ross," I said, as he began to unpack a bag marked New Wine and Spirits. "I have something to tell you."

"Okay. Hey, do you want a glass of wine? I found a fabulous bottle of Australian Shiraz this afternoon."

I was increasingly a nervous wreck. Ross didn't seem at all aware of that. Maybe that was a good thing. "Um, no, thanks," I said. "Let's sit down, okay?"

I perched on the edge of the couch. Ross followed with a glass of the Shiraz and settled comfortably next to me. He sighed, smiled pleasantly, and sipped the expensive, jewel-toned wine.

"It's nice to come home to you after a long day at the office," he said. "It's very relaxing."

Well, I thought, it won't be very relaxing for much longer.

And I told him. The expression on his face was impossible to read. He turned from me, reached for a coaster, and carefully set his wineglass on the temporary coffee table. He didn't turn back.

"Ross?" Gently, I touched his shoulder. He continued to stare straight ahead, at the wall against which we'd decided to place Ross's seventy-inch flat-screen television.

"Ross?" I repeated, ready for the worst.

And then he completely surprised me.

Ross leapt from the couch, lifted me up after him, and hugged me like he'd never hugged me before.

"This is the most amazing thing that's ever happened to me!" he cried, and I heard his voice break. "Anna, I can't believe this!"

Ross let go of me—thankfully, as I was beginning to gasp for air—and held my hands up to his chest.

"This is unbelievable," he said, eyes glistening with tears. It was the first and last time I saw Ross cry. "Just wait until my mother finds out she's going to be a grandmother! She's been dreaming of this day ever since I graduated from college and got a job. Ever since I established myself. Ever since Rob broke his engagement to that horribly boring woman from Florida and she thought she'd never have a grandchild. Anyway, she's going to be thrilled."

I resisted pointing out that Rob's horribly boring fiancée had been, in fact, a brilliant chemical engineer. Instead, I focused on the positive. Two people were thrilled about my pregnancy, Ross and his mother. It was a start.

"So, you're not upset?" I asked, daring to believe Ross's joy. "I mean, we talked about children and, well, we said we didn't want to have any."

Ross laughed. Yes, I heard joy in that laugh.

"Am I upset? Anna, I'm kind of in shock, but it's going to be great. I can't believe this! How did it happen, anyway? Did you forget to take the pill?"

"No!" I cried.

Here it comes, I thought. His seemingly enthusiastic reaction is just a cover for his fury. Maybe he's having a fit of some sort. Maybe this unbridled joy is a kind of psychological breakdown.

"No," I went on, my voice calm and, I hoped, soothing. "I'm very careful about taking the pill. I guess I'm just that one-in-a-million woman . . ."

Ross grinned. There was still no sign of fury.

"Or maybe," he said, putting his hands around my waist and pulling me in, "maybe I'm just that one-in-a-million man who's so virile your girls don't stand a chance against my boys."

I smiled. There it was, the ego. Ross was just a man like every other man. Cleaner, maybe; neater; and more stylish than the majority of men, but a man all the same. "You'd like to think that, wouldn't you," I said teasingly.

Ross kissed me. "I've got the proof."

6

The Other Road Traveled

Decaffeinated tea isn't so bad, I lied to myself heartily. And in only eight months or so you'll be able to have a normal cup of tea or coffee.

It was no use. The absence of caffeine in my diet was taking a toll in the form of a nasty, dull headache. Everyone said it would go away in a few days, but it was four days and counting. What constituted a "few" in the general opinion?

I dumped the cup of so-called tea into the sink and reached for my address book. I opened it to the section marked *T*. Under the number for my parents' home and the one for their time-share, under my brother's number and the number of his ex-wife, was the one I was seeking.

I met my friend Kristen Tremaine when we were sophomores in college, back when her name was Kristen Rivers. We were both enrolled in a course on the great mistresses of European history. The class's raging debates—such as, were these mistresses truly powerful players or merely victims of an abusive paternal regime—inspired us in more ways than one. For Halloween that year I dressed as Madame du Pompadour and Kristen dressed as Nell Gwyn. We were the hit of every party and fast friends from that night forth.

Still, in the second half of our twenties, our lives took very different paths. The last thing on my mind was marriage. But for Kristen, it suddenly was the first. When she was twenty-six she met and fell in love with a guy named Brian Tremaine, an Arlington local who'd gone to only one semester of college before realizing he could make a pretty decent living working for his uncle's mid-sized construction company.

Brian is friendly and hardworking, an all-around stand-up guy. There's nothing odd about him except for his being so very different from all the other guys Kristen had ever dated—highly educated professional men who wore dark suits to work, drove Mercedes, and took ten-day vacations to Cancun every February. Men you were supposed to date when you came from a home in which both parents were professionals, when you had gone to Harvard Law, when you were well on your way to partnership in a small but prestigious law firm. Men like, well, men like Ross.

"But what do you guys talk about?" I'd asked Kristen when she and Brian had been together for about six months.

"Plenty of stuff," she replied easily.

"Like what?"

"Like camping," she told me. "We both love to camp. I bet you didn't know that about me."

"No," I admitted.

"And we both love Dave Matthews. Do you know that between the two of us we've been to nine concerts? And we talk about the family we're going to have some day."

Kristen had made up her mind. Her decision to marry Brian came as a shock to me and our other friends from college. An even bigger shock was Kristen's decision after the birth of her first son, Robbie, to quit her promising position at the small law firm to be a stay-at-home mom.

Eleven years into their marriage, Brian is owner of his retired uncle's construction firm and Kristen the mother of three children ranging in age from nine to two. They live in a big, yellow, Victorian-style house in Wakefield, a house they bought as a fixer-upper and will probably still be restoring on their twenty-fifth wedding anniversary. It's obvious Kristen and Brian have little money to spend on luxuries like European vacations and jewelry and fancy cars. Each year they rent a cottage on the Cape and take along a grandmother or two; Kristen wears a simple gold wedding band without diamonds; Brian drives a Honda Accord; Kristen chauffeurs the kids in an old Jeep. And from what I can tell, they're really happy. Things could be far worse for the woman who saw her future in an unexpected place and had the courage to reach for it.

Anyway, after her wedding I continued to keep up with Kristen, but until recently our very different lifestyles precluded the possibility of spending a whole lot of time together. We exchanged cards at the holidays and e-mails every few weeks, and whenever Kristen could sneak away we'd meet for lunch, an event that Kristen says is "better than a day at a spa." I think Kristen has forgotten just how good a day at a spa can be; she hasn't been to one since the day before her wedding eleven years ago. (Note to self: For Kristen's next birthday, a gift certificate to Belle Sante on Newbury Street.)

Anyway, about two months after I met Ross I felt ready to introduce him to Kristen. I was a little apprehensive; I knew Ross might be a difficult sell to someone as down-to-earth as my college friend. Kristen came into Boston for the occasion; Brian was supposed to join us but an emergency on one of his jobs prevented him from coming. Kristen hired a babysitter at a last-minute bonus rate rather than cancel a meeting she knew was important to me.

Well, the meeting didn't go very well. No one threw a drink in anyone's face, but the conversation was forced and awkward. Kristen hadn't seen any of the gallery exhibits or movies Ross and I had; she hadn't gone to Cancun for a long weekend like Ross and I had; we didn't have first-tooth or first-day-of-school stories to share like Kristen did.

Just before we left the restaurant to walk Kristen to the

train station, Ross excused himself to say hello to a business associate he'd spotted at the bar.

"Well," I asked, with some trepidation. "What do you think?"

"He seems nice," Kristen said quickly, avoiding my eye. "His suit is very, um, beautiful."

I smiled half-heartedly. I certainly couldn't tell Kristen that Ross's suit had been purchased at Louis' of Boston for not much less than it had cost her and Brian to buy their house.

After that I knew there was no way the two couples were ever going to become close friends. I just couldn't picture Ross hanging out with Brian on a Sunday afternoon drinking beer, eating sandwiches from Subway, and watching football on Brian's twenty-inch television, kids tumbling in and out of the family room clutching sippy cups and Barbies and soccer balls.

Anyway, Kristen might not be a big fan of Ross but she is a big fan of motherhood. I called her one afternoon around two o'clock when I knew she'd be home between delivering one child to toddler gymnastics and picking up the older kids at the end of their school day.

"Anna, I'm so happy for you!" she cried when I told her the big news. "You're going to make a great mom."

I laughed nervously. "I don't know about that," I said. "I'm an absolute wreck about the whole thing."

"Well, of course you're a wreck. Every mother-to-be is nervous, that's natural. It doesn't mean you're not going to be just wonderful!"

"Do you really think so?" I asked. I needed to hear Kristen's warm support. I needed to believe it.

"I know so. Oh, Anna, really, this is just great. And anything I can pass on, I will. Of course, some of B.J.'s clothes have already been through Robbie and Cassie so they're not much good at this point. But maybe you'll want everything brand new! Have you registered yet?"

I was suddenly overwhelmed by the practical realities of

being a mommy-in-waiting. Mommies were responsible. Mommies were reliable. Mommies were dependable. Okay, no one would deny that Anna Traulsen was responsible, reliable, and dependable. But at the Mommy level?

"Oh, Kristen," I said, "I haven't done anything yet. I mean, besides tell you and Alexandra."

"And your family?"

I sighed. "Actually, I haven't told the families yet. I kind of want to wait, just to make sure everything's okay with the—with the baby."

How strange those words sounded! The baby. My baby.

"There are two ways of thinking about this, Anna," Kristen replied promptly. "One is to keep the pregnancy a secret until the initial danger period is over. That way if you lose the baby you don't have to make all those sad phone calls and listen to everyone's disappointment. Okay?"

"That's what I was thinking," I admitted.

"But there's another way. You can tell everyone, share your happiness, and then, God forbid, if the pregnancy fails, you have all those people to support you and pray for you. Right?"

"Right," I said, not because I was sure Kristen was right but because I was touched by her happiness for me.

We chatted for a few minutes more and then Kristen had to run off. I asked her to give my love to Brian. It was only after I'd hung up that I realized she hadn't once mentioned Ross's name.

7

Adjustments

"So, can you meet for lunch someday soon?" I asked. "Just something quick."

I imagined Tracy flipping through her date book, highlighter in hand; she's super-organized, even more than I am. "Sure," she said after a moment. "How about tomorrow at eleven-forty-five. I've got a client at one o'clock so that should give us plenty of time to chat about wedding plans."

Or about another big event, I thought as I hung up the phone.

I met Tracy at a book group I tried to be part of five or six years ago. Tracy was trying, too, but we both dropped out after only two meetings when the hostess handed out a quiz she'd devised. Reading groups are supposed to be about lightly intelligent conversation, fancy appetizers, and good wine. They're not supposed to be about tests and reports and grades.

Tracy, the daughter of an Irish-American father and a Japanese-American mother, is a physical therapist associated with the department of orthopedic surgery at Beth Israel Hospital. She's forty and in fabulous shape, which is only partly due to genetics. She works out and eats right and basically makes me feel like a fat slob when I'm with her. I'm not a fat slob, I know that, but it's hard not to have a doubt when you're with a person who wears a size two. I can't help experiencing a tingle of guilty pleasure when I show up for an event in a more stylish outfit than my petite friend. It's horrible of me, I know.

A few years ago Tracy married a very nice, very smart man twenty years her senior. His name is Bill Lomas and he's an engineer with a large construction firm. Bill became her patient after he injured his knee while playing a Saturday afternoon game of touch football along the promenade.

Tracy and Bill live in a small condo in Bay Village, a tiny six-block enclave of eighteenth-century houses between the South End and the Back Bay. Together, they have no children. But Bill has two children from a former marriage, which makes Tracy a stepmother. Bill's daughter is in graduate school; his son is married and the father of a two-year-old, which makes Tracy a step-grandmother.

To that point in time we hadn't talked much about Tracy's domestic situation. Sometimes I wanted to ask her how she felt about not having children of her own, and about her relationship with her stepchildren, but I never did. I guess I never sensed a true conversational opening. I wish I had just made the opening myself.

The next morning I met Tracy at Green, a small, casual café that specializes in power drinks, salads, and other healthy fare. (It's a nice enough place, but I prefer restaurants that aren't afraid of butter.) As soon as we'd settled at a table for two with our trays, I broke the big news.

"I'm pregnant," I said.

Tracy's face tightened just a bit. "If it's what you want," she said carefully, "I'm very happy for both of you."

You could at least pretend to be enthusiastic, I chided silently, and then I felt silly for being upset. What did I want, a parade?

Maybe Tracy was just tired. Or maybe she wasn't feeling

well. Really, I thought, is Tracy ever wildly enthusiastic about anything? In some ways she's the opposite of Alexandra, low-key, pensive, certainly more reserved. Really, I thought, I can't expect everyone to be all excited about my news when I'm not even sure how I feel about it.

"Thanks," I said brightly. "And don't worry about the wedding," I added. "This won't change anything for you as matron of honor. Everything's going to happen as planned." I don't know why I said that. I knew, deep down, that nothing would ever again happen as planned.

"Okay. So, is this what you want? To have a baby?" Now Tracy's face was flushed. Clearly, she was upset but for the life of me I couldn't understand why. Was she that worried about my happiness?

I reached across the table and patted her arm. "Of course it is," I assured her. "I know I said that Ross and I weren't going to have a family but, well, you know. Things have changed."

I wondered, Why have things changed? Because we wanted them to? No. Things changed because they just did and here we are, stuck with the change.

"Then I'm glad for you, Anna, really." Tracy raised her glass of Evian in a silent toast, and I raised mine in return.

"I'm glad for me, too," I said. I was only partly lying.

"So, when is the baby due?"

I considered. "By my nonprofessional calculations," I said, "early December. Which means that I'll be approximately six months pregnant when I walk down the aisle."

Finally, Tracy smiled. "Don't worry," she said. "I'll be there to help you waddle along."

"Oh, no, will I really be waddling by then?"

"I don't know," she said. "I've never had a baby. I don't really know much about anything."

Something in the tone of Tracy's voice prompted me to change the subject. "So," I said, "let me tell you about working for the infamous Beatrice Kent."

8

Domestic Bliss

Boston's South End is an eclectic neighborhood, combining a large and fairly affluent gay community, a long-term and less affluent Hispanic community, people now in their seventies who've been loyal to the neighborhood through its seriously crime-ridden druggie days of the sixties, a healthy-sized Chinese community, and people like me and Ross. We're the upwardly mobile types, the ones who frequent the finer restaurants with regularity, the ones who buy their breakfast at pricey little cafés and their clothes at chic little boutiques, the ones who abandon their expensive urban lifestyle for an expensive life in the suburbs within a year of having their first child.

I live in a renovated brownstone on Roland Street. There are three units in my building; I own the top floor condo, which is about eight hundred square feet, and the roof rights that go along with it. There are two bedrooms, one of which I use as a guest room and place for those artifacts of early days I just can't bring myself to throw away or relegate to storage. (Ross, it should be said, was not very happy about the notion of my bringing some of those items to the loft. He particularly objected to the badly gilded horse with a clock in its stomach that had once belonged to my father's favorite aunt. Helpfully, Ross suggested a storage facility in South Boston and gave me the phone number of the Salvation Army's nearest drop-off center, just a few blocks away, in Roxbury.)

Soon after moving to Roland Street, I had a cedar deck erected on the roof. Someday, I thought, when the final nail was hammered, I'll buy a grill and actually learn how to use it. But at the time of my pregnancy the deck was several years old and still without a grill. There were, however, two lounge chairs and a small table with an oversized umbrella.

On the first floor of the building lives an odd duck of a fellow named Arthur Audrey. He could be anywhere from eighty to a hundred; all I know for sure is that he served in World War II (on occasion he wears bits and pieces of his old Navy uniform), which makes him the oldest person I know.

I've never been inside Mr. Audrey's apartment, and I'm not sure I'd want to be invited in. Although he seems personally quite clean and spiffy, a variety of odd odors waft into the common hall whenever he opens his door just wide enough to slip in and out. On more than one occasion I've detected a whiff of sulfur, causing me to wonder if he's conducting dangerous scientific experiments in a homemade lab. On other occasions the distinct odor of patchouli permeates the hallway. Is Mr. Audrey a closet hippie?

Between Mr. Audrey and me there's Katie Ford and Alma Rodriguez and their adopted son Emilio. Emilio is one of those preternatural children who are four going on thirty-five.

Katie was born and raised in the tough working-class Boston neighborhood known as Southie. Alma was born in the Dominican Republic; she became a U.S. citizen when she came to live with her grandmother at the age of twelve. Katie and Alma have been a couple for close to eight years; before that they worked together for one of the neighborhood community action groups.

During the day, when I'm at work, Katie and Alma make good use of the roof deck. Alma likes to sunbathe. Seeing her all bronzed and glowing while my own skin remains unspectacularly pale all year round does on occasion make me regret my prudence. Maybe someday I'll throw caution to the wind and leave the apartment without my sunblock #45. Maybe.

Katie is a gardener, the gifted green thumb kind. I was happy to have her take over the roof deck; now from early spring through late autumn it's alive with color.

"How do you do all this?" I asked once, indicating the round pots of bright green basil and the rectangular planters filled with bright pink and purple pansies.

"The key to my success," Katie replied solemnly, "is that I become one with the plants."

"How can you become one with a thing that isn't sentient?" I asked stupidly.

"Ah. This is why you can't even grow a weed."

"I'm not sure I would know a weed from a legitimate plant," I admitted. "Until just last week I thought dandelions were something you planted."

"But you choose flowers for events, don't you?"

"That's easy. All I have to know about are color and shape. The florist does the rest. I know. I suppose I could learn."

Katie grinned. "Or you could leave the world of flora to the experts and just enjoy our results."

The Saturday morning just after my lunch with Tracy, I called my neighbors and asked if I could stop by. "You don't need to call first, Anna," Katie said. "But I know you always will. Come now. I'm making scones."

Five minutes later I was sitting at their kitchen table, enjoying the enticing smell of baking pastry.

"So," I said without preamble, "I'm pregnant."

The spatula Katie was holding slipped from her fingers and clattered onto the stovetop. "What! Since when?"

I laughed. "Since about a week ago, I guess. Don't look so shocked."

"I'm not shocked. Well, maybe I am. I thought you said you and your fiancé—"

"Ross. And yes, I did say that we weren't planning to have children."

"So?" Alma took a seat at the kitchen table with me. "What happened? I mean, okay, I know how babies are made. But was it the old-fashioned way, by accident? Or did you change your mind and get yourself inseminated or something."

"The old-fashioned way," I admitted. "It was completely an accident. Ross's boys slipped right through my girls' defenses."

"Wow." Katie whistled. "This is big."

"I know," I said. "I'm . . . I'm pretty shaken up by this turn of events."

Alma eyed me closely. "I'm not hearing exuberance, Anna. Are you happy?"

"I don't know," I admitted. "Maybe. I'm definitely scared. I have absolutely no faith in my parenting skills. The innate ones, I mean. I think I can learn from books, and I hope my doctor will give me some advice, but as for what's inside me already—I just don't know."

Katie placed a plate of warm-from-the-oven scones on the table. I couldn't remember. Did Katie bake before she became a mother? "You'll be a fine parent," she said. "Everyone doubts herself at first. It's normal."

"Well, what if I do turn out to be a fine parent?" I argued. I knew I was being silly, but I couldn't help myself. Would I have to learn to bake? Would I have to learn how to make meat loaf and chocolate pudding? "Isn't saying someone is 'fine' at something really saying they're 'okay' at something? That they're just mediocre? That they're just average? If I'm going to be a parent, I want to be an excellent parent."

Alma laughed. "I'm not sure anyone is ever an excellent parent, at least for more than a random moment or two. You'll be a good parent, Anna. A good parent is someone who continues to learn as she goes. And that's something I know you can do."

I wondered, Could I learn? When was the last time I'd really learned something new? Baking would require leaning. Cooking would require cookbooks and new utensils and a spice rack. I would have to learn how to install a spice rack. I would have to buy a hammer and a box of nails.

"You know," I said, further shaken by those frightening thoughts, "you two are the epitome of good parents." Katie waved her hand dismissively, modestly. "No, I mean it. I look at you with Emilio, and I look at how you treat each other and, well, I think there's no way I'm ever going to achieve that kind of success."

"There's no doubt," Alma said, "that it's easier to be a good parent when your relationship with your partner is strong."

"Of course," I replied automatically. And I wondered. Was my relationship with Ross strong, really strong in the way it would have to be if we were going to pull off being good parents, raising a well-adjusted child, building a happy family?

Suddenly famished, I reached for a scone. "I just wish," I said, "that the pregnancy was the result of a conscious choice. I hate the idea of accidents. I hate doing things on the spur of the moment. I hate when people say, 'oh, let's play things by ear.' I wish I could have planned this pregnancy, like you did."

Katie gave me a funny look. "Anna," she said, "of course bringing Emilio into our lives was a conscious decision. Let's face it, kiddo—it wasn't going to happen any other way."

"Oh," I said, stupidly. "Right."

"Look, Anna," Alma said, patting my hand, "getting pregnant accidentally is not a crime. It's a fact of nature."

I frowned. Nature. There was never a way to get around nature entirely. If it wasn't cicada plagues every seventeen years, it was monsoons and tornadoes and earthquakes and heat waves and ice storms and flash flooding. Central air-conditioning and gas heating were fine, but you had to leave the house at some point.

"Planning isn't necessarily all it's cracked up to be," Alma went on. "Don't you like anything about surprises?"

"No," I said shortly. "I don't like surprises at all. I like things neat and orderly and planned. I like to control what I can control and what I can't control, well, I don't like things I can't control."

Katie laughed loudly. "Poor Anna! Motherhood is going to be a terrible shock. It's one big surprise after another, kiddo. Better get used to it now. Forget about your old favorites. The next time you're at a restaurant, point blindly to the menu. Take what you get and learn to tolerate it if you can't enjoy it."

The thought was horrifying. "What if I pick something that makes me sick?"

"So you'll cough or break out in hives or throw up. But you'll survive."

Would I?

I glanced around the well-used kitchen. The room was warm and soothing. The scones were warm and soothing. The entire apartment was warm and soothing. It would be nice to live here, I thought suddenly. I wasn't ready to be a mother. I wanted a mother. Or two.

"Why can't you adopt me, too?" I said. "I promise I'll keep my room clean and I won't have boys over without permission and I'll even help out with Emilio."

Katie grinned. "So we won't have to give you an allowance?"

"Nope. I'll be the best daughter ever."

Emilio called out from the bedroom, waking from his nap. Alma stood from the table and patted me on the shoulder.

"Childhood is at its end, Anna," she said. "Now it's time for you to raise the best daughter ever."

"What if I have a boy?" I said.

Alma grinned. "Then you must promise to introduce him to nose hair trimmers immediately."

9

Old Ladies Having Babies

I shoved hard on the door to the building. Something was definitely blocking it. With a final burst of effort I managed to open the door just enough so that I could slip inside, where I found an enormous cardboard box. I peered down at it; it was from Kristen.

Ah, I thought. The promised books on pregnancy, childbirth, and child rearing. Mr. Audrey must have signed for the box while I was out and then not have been able to shove it aside. How I would get it up two steep flights of stairs to my apartment was the next puzzle to solve. The answer: I opened the box in the hallway and carried the contents upstairs in small quantities.

"It was difficult letting those books go," Kristen told me when I called to thank her. "It made me truly realize I'm not going to have any more babies."

Except for those accidental ones, I thought. But maybe Kristen knew something I didn't about controlling pregnancy. Maybe Brian had had a vasectomy after their third child was born. Maybe Ross should have had a vasectomy.

Later that evening I opened the books with trepidation. I

knew virtually nothing about pregnancy, let alone about the actual birth process. Child rearing? That could wait. There were plenty of scary new experiences to deal with first.

By the end of the evening I knew more than I'd ever wanted to know. Here are some of the things that I, as a pregnant woman, had to look forward to.

An increase in hair growth. That sounded positive until I read on and learned that the hair referred to was not only the kind that grew on my head. I could anticipate longer and more lustrous hair not only on my head but also all over my body.

An increase in nail growth. That sounded like something I could handle, although having to get more pedicures and manicures would definitely eat into my work schedule, not to mention my budget.

Hemmorhoids are quite common during pregnancy. So is intestinal distress.

Water retention. According to several sources, I'd begin to show water weight gain even before I'd begin to show actual baby weight gain.

And before my belly began to protrude, my waist would widen. My skin might break out; I might be plagued with broken capillaries. There was a good chance I would suffer morning sickness, which could strike at any time of day or night, and the accompanying sense of vertigo. The very smell of something as innocuous as broiled chicken might cause me to gag. Dizziness might cause me to fall down and hit my head on the coffee table.

Which—who knew?—might cause a miscarriage. Because according to one source, something like ten percent of pregnancies end within three months. That was only twelve weeks. Another source stated that approximately one out of every five pregnancies ends in miscarriage, the mother's age being a significant factor in predicting failure.

That particular piece of information made an impression. I was thirty-seven. Three years away from forty. Forty! I'm too old for this, I realized. I'm just too old to go through all these exhausting changes, even the relatively good ones, like thicker head hair and larger breasts. Besides, I thought petulantly, I never asked for thicker hair or larger breasts. I was perfectly content with my appearance. Why did it have to change?

I read on.

The very next source informed me that a woman over the age of thirty-five is considered to be of Advanced Maternal Age. That makes her baby more at risk for certain birth defects like cerebral palsy and Down syndrome.

I wondered, Did my being of Advanced Maternal Age also mean that my emotional capacity to bear and raise a child was less than full strength? Was there an age limit on maternal feelings and capabilities? Would I have been a better, more loving mother at twenty-one than I would be at thirty-seven?

The same source now talked about all the hype women have been fed for the past years about how easy it is, what with "modern science," to get pregnant well into their forties. Well, the source informed me, for most women it's hard to get pregnant at forty. For a lot of women it's expensive. And the author of another, purportedly humorous book ranted on—could I blame her?—about how exhausting it is to be the caretaker of a totally helpless little being on a totally random schedule when you're lugging around some forty-odd years of wear and tear, when all you want to do at the playground is sit on a bench in the shade and read the paper, not hoist a thirty-pound toddler to the highest bars of the jungle gym.

I closed the final book, exhausted. I couldn't read another word. Not that evening. But I could do some thinking.

First, I got a glass of juice and settled on the couch. In truth, I'd never felt a maternal urge, not even when Kristen's first was born; I hadn't really understood what all the excitement was about. Over the years, whenever friends asked if I wanted children, I told them that I was postponing serious thought about a family until I was married.

Well, here I was, just about as good as married. And together with my fiancé I'd given the notion of a family some serious thought and decided it just wasn't for me. And then I'd gotten pregnant.

What was I supposed to do? End the pregnancy and do some more thinking? But there wasn't much time left on my biological clock. Anyway, for me, ending the pregnancy just wasn't a viable option. And pregnancy isn't really something you can "put off," like a visit to the dentist or a trip to the Department of Motor Vehicles to renew your driver's license. Pregnancy isn't a chore. And pregnancy isn't a theory to be considered. It's a fact.

If not now, I wondered, then when?

I'm not a religious person, but I'm not without spiritual sensibility. I couldn't help but wonder why I had gotten pregnant, and why at that particular moment in my life, and why with Ross. Was some Power or Spirit sending me a message? And if so, what was that message? That I should "choose life" and become a mother?

I finished the juice and went off to bed. I turned out the lights, but my mind didn't get the clue that it was time for sleep.

Maybe, I thought, maybe the pregnancy isn't a message. Maybe it's a test. Maybe the Universe wants me to discover the kind of person I really am.

I stared into the dark and wondered, Would I discover the answer to that question in the coming months? And would I like what I discovered?

10

Orange Blossoms, Sugared Almonds, and Thou

Why do we choose to marry the ones we choose to marry? Why are we so often wrong in our choices?

Sometimes good choices go bad, and there's no way to know that up front. Some choices are wrong from the start, and everyone seems to know that but the one who made the choice in the first place.

I chose to marry Ross because he made me feel safe. Our life together was ordered and unchallenging. It was as calm as life can be for two urban-dwelling businesspeople. We were buffeted by the accoutrements of financial success, unencumbered by sick or poor parents, and blessed with good looks and health.

I've said that I'm not an impetuous person. I've never had a one-night stand. I never wrote a college paper at the last minute. I've never made a major purchase without running the numbers, twice, through my budget. I'm not comfortable with spur-of-the-moment social events; I've never, until recently, committed the crime of a drop-in; I don't call people after ten o'clock at night.

I suppose it was no surprise to anyone that the man I

chose to marry was consistently mild-mannered and nonconfrontational.

I'd hear women on talk shows chatting on about how their husbands were so inspirational and challenging, always pushing them to be all they could be, and I'd think, Why would you want to marry someone like that? It seemed to me that always being challenged by the one you loved meant always being on the defensive. I didn't want to be always fighting. I didn't want to be always changing.

I just wanted to be me. And I wanted a husband who would accept that. Ross seemed to be that husband. Supportive without crowding me; soothing without treating me like a helpless child.

And right then, I needed some soothing. It had been days since I'd taken the home pregnancy test, and we still hadn't broken the news to our parents. I'd made Ross promise not to tell them until I'd seen the doctor.

"Why? Do you think maybe you're wrong?" Ross asked, confusion clearly stamped across his handsome face. "Do you think you're not really pregnant?"

"No, no," I assured him. I knew I was pregnant. The sudden onset of morning sickness was indisputable evidence. "I just . . . I'm just a little bit afraid, you know. That everything's not all right and—"

Ross interrupted. "Everything's going to be fine, Anna. You're healthy and I'm healthy and we have the money for the best doctors, the best hospitals. Nothing can go wrong."

"Anything can go wrong, Ross," I said. I reached for one of the books Kristen had sent me. They were never far away. "Listen," I said. "This says that most miscarriages that occur within the first three months—that's the first trimester—are the result of a 'genetic malformation of the embryo.' And that's not something I can control, Ross."

Ross put his hands lightly on my shoulders. "You shouldn't spend so much time with those books, Anna. They're making you too upset. Listen to me, okay? Nothing will go wrong. I promise."

Why, I wondered, do people promise what they know they can't deliver? And then I realized, looking up into Ross's earnest, matinee idol face, that he really did believe he could deliver on his promise of perfection.

Was it hubris? An overdeveloped ego? Or a sort of innocence? Ross had lived a life in which he'd never really known hardship, a life in which his parents or their money could solve most problems handily.

In the end, did it matter why Ross felt so sure? No. Because I wanted to believe his promise of a perfect life.

"Thanks," I whispered and went into his arms.

11

Family Ties

"Hi," said Ross. "It's me. Ross."

After almost a year together, Ross still felt the need to identify himself by name every time he called my cell phone. Even though he knew his name came up on the screen and that, of course, I would recognize his voice.

"Yes," I said, "I know. What's going on?"

"Nothing much." I pictured Ross at his desk, legs crossed elegantly, phone between his ear and shoulder.

"Okay," I said, glancing at my watch, thinking of the work piling up on my desk as I did.

"I just wanted you to know that I told Rob about the baby. Now, before you get upset, he promised not to tell Mom and Dad."

Well, we hadn't promised not to tell our siblings, had we? Still, I felt a twinge of annoyance. Ross worshipped his older brother although he'd deny it heartily. Really, it was a sort of self-worship. Rob was simply a forty-two-year-old version of Ross, as well groomed, well dressed, and uninspired. No wonder Rob's relationship with the brilliant chemical engineer hadn't lasted.

Anna, I scolded silently. Don't be mean. Not for the first time it occurred to me that I might be a wee bit jealous of the close relationship Rob and Ross shared. My own brother and I weren't exactly the best of buddies, although there was no hostility between us. There wasn't much of anything, really. The Traulsen family could never be described as closely knit.

I took a deep breath and said, "How did he take the news?"

Ross laughed lightly. "He was happy for me, of course. He gave me some advice on getting into the best private preschools and—"

I didn't hear much else of what Ross had to say. I was glad Rob was happy for Ross. Really.

Maybe, I thought later, as I got ready for bed, maybe I should tell my own brother the big news. But why? The truth was it didn't matter to me whether Paul learned about the pregnancy now or later.

I slipped beneath the covers and reached for one of the several books on my nightstand. A favorite Agatha Christie mystery? Or maybe the Robert Hughes book on Goya? Finally, I opened the Goya tome, but after reading the same paragraph three times without comprehension—please note that my inability to focus had nothing to do with the quality and clarity of the writing—I closed the book. My mind was not on the eighteenth-century painter. It was on the Traulsen family dynamic.

I suppose it was nice growing up with an older brother. Paul did all the expected, big brotherly things like threaten the bully who taunted me in second grade, and warn me against certain boys when I began to date, and even, on occasion, give me little treats like barrettes for my hair. But then Paul went to college and then on to business school in Virginia, and then he got married to a woman I have very little in common with, and the inevitable happened. We began to see each other only a few times a year, mostly on holidays, and to talk on the phone only when there was important information to relate, like the death of our sole aunt, or my engagement, or Paul and Bess's divorce.

Today Paul lives out in Lincoln, a few miles from the Weston house he gave up in the divorce. Paul and Bess have two children, an eight-year-old boy named Matthew and a six-year-old girl named Emma. Paul is a devoted father; no matter the circumstances he would never have moved far away from his family. But in this case his presence is even more of a necessity. Matthew has a fairly severe form of autism, one that seems to be worsening as he ages. Emma is, as far as anyone can tell, as unencumbered as her brother is burdened.

I often wonder, If Paul and Bess had known then what they know now, that their marriage wasn't going to stand the strain of Matthew's caretaking and all the attendant stresses, would they have had another baby?

As far as I can tell neither Paul nor Bess has much of a personal life. Things seem to have gotten even more hectic and financially strained since the divorce, and how could they not have? Sometimes—like when my brother got bronchitis twice last winter and still had to go to work and fulfill his duties as dad, and there was no one to take care of him when he collapsed into bed each night—I think that maybe it would have made more sense for Paul and Bess not to get divorced.

But what do I know of my brother's life, really?

I called Paul at his downtown office the very next afternoon. He works on State Street as a financial analyst.

You can see again why Paul doesn't have much time for himself. Virtually all the hours not spent commuting—about two hours daily—and working—ten-hour days are common—are spent with the kids.

"Hi," I said, when his assistant had put me through. "It's me."

"I know. Peg told me. What's up?"

He sounded distracted, busy, remote.

"Can I come out for a bit this Saturday? Maybe for lunch. I'll bring something."

"The kids will be there you know," he said.

"I figured. That's fine."

"Then sure. Come around noon. Emma's got swimming lessons at two-thirty and Matthew has physical therapy at three o'clock, so that gives us about two hours before I have to get on the road."

I thanked Paul and hung up. I'm sure he was already deep into the next task or demand or crisis before I did. It exhausted me even to think about his life.

Sometimes, too, I wondered how much my decision not to have children of my own had been informed by the example of Paul and his family. Maybe my choosing not to have children was like dodging a bullet pretty sure to shatter at least some aspects of my life.

Dodging a bullet. How grim. And how ridiculous to think I'd protected myself from harm by deciding not to have children. Because now I was pregnant in spite of that decision, and if my life hadn't exactly been harmed it certainly had been disrupted.

Face it, Anna, I told myself. There are no guarantees in this world. You'd have to be dumb not to know that.

But you didn't have to like it.

12

Sympathy for the Devil

I called Michaela and suggested we meet for a drink one evening.

"This week is hell for me," she said briskly, "but I can give you half an hour on Wednesday. Meet me at six at the bar at Leopard."

Michaela Newman seems to have everything. Sometime in her early thirties, she left the financial services firm where she'd been a bond analyst since graduating from business school and started her own financial consultant business. If her designer clothes, spectacular apartment at the Marina Bay condo development, 7 Series BMW, and twice yearly trips to Canyon Ranch are any indication of financial success, Michaela is a winner.

To boot, she's also stunning, tall, and voluptuous, with dark, glossy hair that falls just below her shoulders. Michaela is the woman every other woman hates on sight. And there's some reason for women continuing to hate her after that first impression. The truth is that Michaela can be brash and self-serving and even, on occasion, cruel.

I met Michaela about the time I met Ross, at a small

women-in-business seminar I hadn't wanted to go to in the first place. Neither, it turned out, had Michaela, but she'd been offered a nice honorarium to speak. Michaela, I was to learn, didn't do much of anything without a self-serving motive.

I was never really close to Michaela, not in the way I'm close to Alexandra, Kristen, and Tracy. We had no common history and no shared interests other than owning our own businesses. I'm not quite sure why we called each other friends; maybe we never actually used that term.

So, if we weren't friends, what were we? Circumstantial urban acquaintances? Or maybe Michaela was something like an unexplained rash. There seems to be no cause for it; it's just suddenly there, and it itches, but after a while you learn to live with it, and one day you notice with surprise that it's gone, and you realize there's only a faint memory of irritation and you miss it, sort of, for about a minute.

Whatever the case, Michaela was in my life at the time I met and got engaged to Ross. And at the time I found out I was pregnant. And the reason this is significant is because, for reasons I still can't fathom, Michaela wanted a child.

All right. I admit to being judgmental. Just because Michaela doesn't seem the motherly type doesn't mean she isn't potentially the motherly type. The fact is she's responsible and intelligent, and responsibility and intelligence are two good qualities for a parent to possess. Right?

There I was passing judgment on my friend's maternal capabilities when I myself wasn't at all sure I would make a good parent. At least Michaela wanted a child. At least she was actively pursuing adoption, having given up on the possibility of marriage and having declared quite emphatically that she would never be so insane as to go through a pregnancy without a husband, and at the age of forty-something.

It's also true she had stated quite definitely that the very idea of childbirth disgusted her. To be fair, I wasn't exactly looking forward to childbirth, either. Why, I wondered, couldn't it be like it was in the old days? Why couldn't the doctors just knock you out completely? It seemed a civil way to do things. And when you woke, all bathed and stitched and wearing a pale pink, satin bed jacket tied with a bow, a nurse would hand you your baby, all clean and pretty and already preferring a bottle to a breast, and you hoped, once you were home, you'd have no drug-addled memories of the actual birth.

Anyway, there I was, engaged to a wonderful man and pregnant with his child. And there was poor Michaela, wading through the bureaucratic red tape of legal adoption, spending large amounts of money to no avail, and going home every night to an empty, albeit luxurious, apartment.

And I had to tell her that I was going to have a baby.

"She'll find out," Alexandra told me. "You don't owe her information."

Alexandra never liked Michaela. In fact, it was mutual loathing at first sight.

"I don't loathe her," Alexandra once protested after a particularly acid exchange between the two women over cocktails at the Four Seasons. "I just distrust her. And I despise her. I don't know why you're friends with that woman. I don't know why you keep asking her to join us."

Frankly, I'm not sure why I continued to include Michaela in our social plans. I guess I began to suspect that in spite of—because of?—her beauty and arrogant bearing, Michaela was a lonely person. Maybe I was her only real friend. Maybe she felt it was better to spend an evening sparring with Alexandra than to sit home alone.

"Sit home alone?" Alexandra had laughed. "Michaela? She's out with a different guy every night, you can be sure of it."

"I'm not so sure you're right," I'd protested. "A lot of men are intimidated by gorgeous women."

"That's a myth perpetuated by average-looking women to help them deal with their killing jealousy. Besides, I have my spies. I hear things about Michaela."

"You're so suspicious!"

"And you're such a bleeding heart. But, it doesn't matter what I think. I tolerate her for your sake, honey."

"Barely. You barely tolerate her."

"I'll try to be good. I'll try to be better. Okay?"

"Okay," I said. I knew that for my sake my friend would try to control her strong feelings of dislike for Michaela, but I had absolutely no hope for her success.

Anyway, Wednesday came around. I got to Leopard a few minutes early and took a small table away from the already crowded bar. I wanted some privacy when I told Michaela my news.

At precisely six o'clock, Michaela arrived. She looked spectacular, as usual. Both men and women stared as she made her way to where I sat. I wondered if it bothered Michaela that people were so blatant about their interest in her. Unlike Alexandra, she didn't seem to enjoy the attention.

"Hi," I said. "I love that jacket." I tried to keep the rabid envy out of my voice. "Chanel?"

Michaela dropped gracefully into the seat across from me. "It's horrid. I'm throwing it out when I get home."

I almost fainted. I almost asked if I could have the Chanel piece. But I did neither.

Michaela ordered a glass of champagne. She made no comment when I asked for a glass of seltzer with lime.

"I've got some news," I said when our drinks had arrived. My tone was tentative, gentle. "I'm pregnant. Isn't that funny? I wasn't even planning it and—"

The look on Michaela's face stopped me cold. "Well, isn't that just wonderful for you," she said, with full sarcasm.

I felt as if I'd been slapped in the face, hard. I felt nauseous.

"Sorry, Anna," Michaela said briskly. "But you really can't expect me to be thrilled for you when I've been going through hell with this adoption process."

I attempted a smile, which, I suspect, came out a little wobbly. "Could you at least be mildly pleased? Neutral even?"

"I thought Ross didn't want a family," she replied.

"He didn't." I was a bit thrown by Michaela's non-answer to my question. "But now he does."

"Now he says he does." Michaela's words were murmured but I heard them. And I decided to steer the conversation away from me.

"So," I began tentatively, "is there any good news about the adoption?"

Michaela's answer came firing back. "Everyone I've been dealing with is an ass. I had to fire my attorney for doctoring his bill and the so-called professionals at the agency are just incredibly stupid. I swear I want to bitch slap them all, and I would if it would shake some sense into them but all it would do is get me arrested. But once I get the kid, those bitches are going to hear from me."

I attempted a sympathetic smile. "Oh," I said. "I see."

Michaela left shortly after that, claiming another appointment. She hadn't left any money for her drink. She was probably too rattled by my news to remember that she'd consumed nine dollars worth of bubbly.

Poor Michaela, I thought, watching her leave the restaurant, Prada bag over her arm, Manolo Blahniks tapping smartly against the Italian marble floor. Life can be so unfair. She has so much but not the one thing she really wants.

13

Foray into Suburbia

Paul met me at the train station that Saturday at noon, which was very nice of him considering my visit was probably ruining his well-honed schedule.

"Where are the kids?" I asked as we pulled out of the parking lot and onto the highway.

"Hello to you, too."

"Sorry. Hello." I leaned over and pecked my brother's cheek. Paul didn't seem to notice.

"The neighbor's watching them for a while," he said. "I had to make a few stops before meeting you."

"Thanks for picking me up."

"No big deal. The station's between the dry cleaners and home."

"Oh," I said. "Good."

Ten minutes later we were in the kitchen of Paul's small ranch house. It was clean, but kids' toys and backpacks and sports equipment were strewn everywhere. I removed a pink sneaker from one of the kitchen chairs and sat. Paul opened the fridge and took out a half-empty plastic jug of orange juice.

"It's all I have to drink," he said, unapologetically. "This and coffee."

"Juice is fine," I replied. "I'm off coffee for the duration. I'm pregnant."

"Huh." Paul poured two small glasses of juice and handed me one. "Congratulations. I thought you and Ross decided to pass on the kid thing."

"We did decide to pass on the kid thing. But things happen, you know."

"I do know. So, how's Ross handling it?"

Better than I am, I thought.

"Great. He's thrilled. He's acting like a kid on Christmas morning."

"That must be a big relief."

"It's a lot better than his leaving me," I replied.

Paul looked at me closely. "Have you told Mom and Dad yet?" he asked.

I shrugged. "No. I'm going to, though. Soon. I want to see my doctor first and all."

"Why are you putting it off? Mom's going to be thrilled. And even though Dad's not overly fond of Ross—"

"He isn't?"

Paul grimaced and put the plate of gourmet sandwiches I'd brought on the scarred, wood table. He'd gotten it at a yard sale after he'd moved out of the beautifully decorated house he'd shared with Bess.

"Oh," he said. "Sorry. I thought you knew that."

Well, the truth was I did sort of know that. I mean, my father isn't exactly subtle, or a good social liar. And he and Ross are so different in so many ways. It dawned on me then that for all I knew Ross might not like my father all that much.

"It's okay," I said.

"Well, what I was going to say is that Dad will be thrilled he's getting another grandchild. I'm sure of it."

I wasn't so sure, but I didn't argue. Neither Dad nor Mom is much in the grandparent department. They prefer golf vacations in North Carolina with other comfortably situated couples to family trips to Disney World and Sunday dinner en famille.

"Will you tell Bess?" I asked.

"Sure, if you want me to. Or you could call her yourself."

"I'm kind of uncomfortable doing that," I admitted. "Since the divorce, things have been a little awkward between us. I'm sorry."

Paul shrugged. My delicate feelings were the least of his worries.

"She's a good mother," he said, blandly. "She might be of some help along the way."

"Okay," I said, a bit ashamed. "Thanks."

Paul and I ate lunch in relative silence, and at two o'clock I helped him herd Matthew and Emma into the family's requisite truck-like car. Paul drove me to the train station; he kept the motor running while I said goodbye.

I leaned over the back of the seat and blew the children kisses. Neither seemed particularly sorry to see me go. Matthew was staring out the side window; Emma was playing with a lavender-haired doll. I climbed out of the monster truck.

"Good luck, Anna," Paul said, as he pulled away.

I waved half-heartedly.

What my brother didn't say but what I know he was thinking: You're going to need it.

14

Do No Harm

"I made an appointment to see my gynecologist this Thursday," I said. Ross and I were at the condo; we'd met there after work to discuss color choices for the master bathroom. "Her office is in Chestnut Hill."

Ross looked up from the paint samples he was studying. "Good. I'll send my car service to take you there and back. I don't want you dealing with the T. There are too many deranged people in this city, and God knows how many germs are floating around those filthy cars."

I didn't want to take the T, either. A car service was a better option, but . . .

"I was kind of hoping you would come with me," I said.

"Anna, I can't." Ross handed me the stack of paint samples. "Take a look at these. I'm leaning toward Seashell for the master bath. We'll need an accent color, of course."

"Why can't you?" I asked. I put the stack of paint samples on the unfinished kitchen counter. One slid off to the floor. Ross picked it up and straightened the pile.

"Because I've got meetings all day Thursday," he said. "Maybe Cocoa Cream instead of Seashell. See what you think. And remember the tile we chose. There's a sample in my office."

I didn't care about tile and paint color. Not right then. I cared about me.

"Couldn't you reschedule something?" I asked sweetly. "My appointment is at ten o'clock. I guess it should take about a half hour. We'll be back in town by eleven. Eleven-fifteen." And, I thought, most days you're hardly in the office by ten. You'd never schedule a meeting before eleven. I know you, Ross.

Ross put his hands on my shoulders and squeezed gently. "Anna, I'm sorry, I can't. Why don't you ask one of your girlfriends to go with you?" Ross dropped his hands and stepped away from me. "I mean, it is a woman thing, after all."

Nurturing another human being inside you for approximately thirty-six weeks? Ejecting that human being through your vaginal canal? Oh, yes. It was a woman thing.

"Don't you want to be involved in the pregnancy?" I asked. The books all said that today's fathers were involved. Today's fathers were supposed to be involved whether they liked it or not.

"Well, sure," Ross said amicably. But his eyes showed he was losing patience for the conversation. "Of course. But let's face it, Anna. There are certain things you'll have to do all on your own. I can only be there for you up to a certain point."

I realized I could forget about Ross's being my labor coach.

"Okay." I smiled gamely. "I'll be fine."

Ross planted a tiny kiss on my forehead. "I know you will. Call the office when the appointment is over and let me know how it went. Leave a message with Tad if I can't be disturbed."

Poor Tad, I thought. I hope Ross pays him well. The young man officially worked for the company, but as far as I could tell, Ross used him pretty heavily as a personal assistant.

I went back to my apartment soon after. It was only nine, but I was bone tired. I got into bed, eager for oblivion, but sleep didn't come easily. I was getting used to lying awake and staring at the ceiling, my mind whirring busily with worries.

I thought about the fact that I'd been on my own for a long time. I thought about the fact that I'd done pretty much everything on my own, from building a business to buying an apartment, from taking a vacation in Jamaica to going to the hospital for a cervical biopsy. I thought about the fact that I was good on my own, strong and competent.

But as I watched the light of the street lamp outside my window flicker across the ceiling of my bedroom, none of those facts mattered. The truth was I did not want to go to that doctor's appointment alone and I did not want to go with anyone but my fiancé.

Sometimes we don't get what we want. On Thursday morning I took Ross's company's car service out to the medical building in Chestnut Hill. Maybe, I thought, as I rode the elevator to the second floor, maybe after this I'll ask the driver to take me to the mall; Bloomingdale's might be having a sale, and I could use a new pair of navy pinstripe slacks.

And then I remembered that I was pregnant and that any pair of pants I bought right then might never be worn. With a sigh I got off the elevator and walked to Suite 206.

There were two obviously pregnant women in the waiting room. Both were with men I took to be the fathers. One man wore a UPS uniform; his arms proved the workout he got every day on the job. The other wore a sober dark suit; I guessed he was in finance or law. The women looked calm, relaxed. Uniforms inspire confidence.

I smiled awkwardly at everyone—they smiled awkwardly back—and walked up to the receptionist's desk.

Observable social truth: Women who aren't pregnant go to the gynecologist alone. Women who are pregnant go with their mates. That is, if they have mates. That's the rule. Even the receptionist knew this.

"Is your husband with you Mrs.—uh . . ." The overweight but pretty girl scanned the screen before her. I wondered if the doctor scolded her about her weight. I wondered if she encouraged her to embrace herself just the way she was.

"Ms. Traulsen," I said. "And it would be my fiancé. Ross Davis. And no, he's not here. He's—he's out of town on business." I looked at the blandly pleasant face of the receptionist, and then the ridiculous lie came bursting out. "There was some really important meeting he just couldn't miss," I said. "In Europe. Switzerland. Basel, in fact."

"I bet you can't wait until he gets home!" she enthused. "I hope he brings you some chocolate."

I thought, What? Why chocolate? And then, "Oh, sure," I said. Switzerland. "Yes. I can't wait until he gets home. With chocolate. Of course. Yes." And maybe a watch? And a cuckoo clock? I was mortified.

The receptionist suggested I take a seat. The doctor, she said, would be with me soon. I took a seat at the other end of the waiting area from the two couples. Liars, I thought, should be segregated from good and decent people.

Twenty minutes later I was flat on my back, my feet in cold metal stirrups.

Dr. York, my gynecologist, could never be described as a warm and fuzzy person. At least not in the context of her professional life. Who knows what she's like at the end of the day when she hangs up her speculum and stows away her swabs.

But I can do without a great bedside manner in medical personnel as long as they've got education, experience, and expertise. What I don't care for is a tendency some doctors have to judge a patient. A symptom might indicate a particular illness, but it doesn't describe a person's character.

Dr. York got up from her swivel stool and carefully stripped off her latex examining gloves.

"You're fine," she said briskly.

"Good," I said. "I mean, I'm glad that I'm fine."

Dr. York looked down at my chart and scribbled a note. "I see many women like you," she said.

"Like me?" I asked.

"Yes." Dr. York closed the manila folder and placed it on the counter behind her. "Women who decided to wait a while before having children."

"I didn't decide anything," I blurted. "Well, actually, I did. My fiancé and I decided not to have children."

The doctor raised her eyebrows in the most obvious way.

"Oh. I see," she said. "The pregnancy is unplanned."

If I'd been deaf to the tone of judgment in the doctor's voice, or blind to the arched brows, I still couldn't have missed the disdain displayed by the flair of her right nostril.

I wondered, Does getting pregnant accidentally make me a bad person? Does it mean I'm going to be a bad mother? Irresponsible? Self-centered? Emotionally unavailable?

And by the way, how do people flair just one nostril?

"Yes," I said hurriedly, the awful paper crackling under my naked thighs. "But we're going through with it. The pregnancy. That's why I'm here, of course. We want the baby. Really."

I prayed, Please like me now. Please. And let me get dressed.

"Okay."

That was all? I thought. No praise for my noble act?

"I've read that lots of pregnancies end in miscarriage," I blurted.

"That's true."

What had I expected to hear?

"Am I at risk?" I asked. "I mean, because of my age."

Dr. York tapped my chart with her pen. "As your doctor of several years, I'd say you're no more at risk than any other thirty-seven-year-old woman going through her first pregnancy."

That news wasn't particularly heartening.

"Should I schedule an amniocentesis?" I asked, not entirely sure what that was.

"Well, it's far too early for an amnio. We do one at the end of the fourth month. I wouldn't worry about that now. Let's see you through a few more weeks. If everything's going well—"

"You mean if I'm still pregnant."

My interruption didn't throw Dr. York at all. "Yes," she said matter-of-factly. "If the pregnancy is still in place, then we'll schedule an amnio and whatever other tests seem wise."

"And then?" I asked.

"Then we'll analyze the results, and then you can decide what to do."

I shook my head. "I don't . . . What do you mean, decide what to do?"

Dr. York looked at me as if I was deeply stupid.

"Decide whether or not to let the pregnancy continue," she said slowly, with more than a hint of condescension, like an embittered college professor speaking to a particularly dense undergraduate.

"Oh," I responded.

Again with the eyebrows.

"Can I decide not to have those tests?" The question came out in a thin, high-pitched voice I didn't recognize as my own.

"Of course," the doctor snapped. "But at your age it wouldn't be wise."

What she meant to say was at my Advanced Maternal Age. I was long in the tooth, over the hill, downright moth-eaten. I was old.

"You don't want to spend months worrying, do you?" Dr. York went on. "Not knowing is not a healthy thing. Information is good for you and your baby. I'm going to strongly recommend you do everything I tell you to do. I'm going to give you prescriptions for vitamins and dietary supplements, and I'm going to want you to take them, every day. Okay?"

"Okay," I said. I heard the pitiful weakness in my voice. "Can I get dressed now?"

15

The Parents

There was no putting it off any longer. The doctor had confirmed the pregnancy. Now Ross and I had no choice but to make the announcement to our parents. That would make it all official.

"Do you think," Ross asked, "that we should tell our parents in person?"

"Isn't that making too big a deal of it?" I countered after a moment's reflection.

"Well, it is a big deal."

"The pregnancy or the telling? I think we should just tell our parents over the phone. We'll see them soon enough after that."

At least, I thought, we'll see Ross's parents. Mine aren't exactly the emotional sort. I used to wonder why they even had children. Then, of course, I realized that Paul and I were more than likely "accidents." I wondered now if Ross and my announcement—that we were having an "accident"—would cause even a mild emotional response.

Reluctantly, Ross agreed to telling our parents over the phone. So one evening we called first my parents—Ross said that's the way it should be done—and then his. Here's what they said.

Mrs. Traulsen: "Well, congratulations. When are you due, dear? Because your father and I have already booked a trip to Florida for late November and it's nonrefundable, so you'll understand if we're not around for the birth."

Mr. Traulsen: "Have you started a college fund? It's never too early to start a college fund."

Mrs. Davis: "That's wonderful, Ross! Oh, I have so much to do! I've got to call Aunt Aggie right away and tell her the good news that our little Ross is going to be a daddy! And I'll talk to Pastor Keats first thing tomorrow and see about booking the rectory basement for a party. But I'm jumping ahead. Oh. Anna. Are you there, too?"

Mr. Davis: "Good work, son. You didn't forget that meeting we have tomorrow with the auditors? Nine o'clock sharp."

When we finally hung up the receivers, Ross looked exhausted. "I'm going to pour myself a scotch," he said. "I'm sorry you can't have one with me."

"Me, too," I said, patting his arm. "I'll just inhale your fumes."

16

Between the Sheets

My sex life with Ross was undemanding, pleasant, and routine, and that was all right with me. I enjoyed sex as much as the next woman, assuming the next woman was basically normal and not damaged by an early prudish religious training or a horrible case of sexual abuse. But in all honesty I could take or leave sex.

I wanted to be wanted; I just didn't want to be wanted all that often or in unusual ways or at inconvenient times.

When I met Ross I seemed to have met my perfect sexual partner. Undemanding, pleasant, and routine. And when Ross asked me to marry him I thought, So what if I'll never know really over-the-top passion? There's more to life than sex. There's certainly more to marriage. Every married woman I knew had confirmed that truth.

And then when I got pregnant I thought, With a baby in the next room—or, if Ross got his way, in a crib by our bedside—how could we possibly have a passionate sex life even if we were the passionate types? There was a good chance that with the baby's arrival our sex life would disappear entirely.

But the baby hadn't yet made an appearance and already our intimate life was a thing of the past. I've read that some men are turned on by their wives' pregnancy, but that wasn't the case with Ross. After that first night of victory sex—in actuality there was nothing triumphant about it—he made no further sexual advances and repulsed the few I worked up the nerve to make.

The first time we were in Ross's fabulously expensive bed. It was about 10 p.m. Ross had just turned out his reading light; I put aside the *Bazaar* I'd been studying.

"So," I said, nestling against his shoulder, "do you, you know?"

Ross didn't respond; I knew he was awake, but I thought that maybe he hadn't quite heard me.

"Ross?" I said. "Do—"

"I'm not sure that's a good idea, Anna." His tone made his answer final.

"Why not?" I asked.

Ross shifted away from me and yawned. "It's been a long day. I'm going to get some sleep. Good night, Anna." He turned toward the door, his back to me.

"I'm not sick, Ross," I said, trying to keep the annoyance from my voice. "I'm just pregnant. Ross, are you listening to me?"

His answer was a slight snore. And within minutes, I, too, was asleep.

The next day I felt bad for being annoyed with Ross. I remembered reading that a father-to-be might be a bit nervous about sex. If Ross harbored fears of hurting the baby or me, it was my job to put his mind to rest.

A few nights later we were sitting in the living room of the loft. It was about eight o'clock. Ross was reading the latest issue of *Vanity Fair*. I, with a copy of *The Girlfriends' Guide to Pregnancy* in my hands, was on a mission.

"This book is really informative," I said brightly. "It's really putting my mind at ease about so many things. For example, did you know that having sex won't hurt the baby? Unless the doctor orders me on full pelvic rest, which would mean she thought I was at a particular risk for miscarriage, we can have sex without any worries."

"That's great, Anna." Ross smiled at me fondly and then looked back to the magazine.

I waited a full five minutes before picking up another book from the stack by my chair and trying again. "Huh," I said. "Well, this is reassuring. This book also confirms that sex can't hurt the baby. The baby's perfectly safe in the womb. My uterus."

Uterus. Blah. Why do female body parts have such ugly names?

There was no response from my erstwhile lover. He continued to read—or pretend to read—*Vanity Fair.*

"Ross?"

"Huh?" He looked up from the magazine, eyes wide and slightly startled. "What did you say? I'm sorry, Anna, I didn't hear you. I'm reading this very interesting article about Michael Jackson's legal woes."

Okay, so he had been reading. And, it seems, concentrating.

"Nothing." I smiled and shrugged. "Just thinking aloud."

Ross smiled and once again resumed reading.

Okay, I thought. Maybe my timing is bad. Maybe Ross is too tired to fool around at night. Maybe now that the baby is coming he's working extra hard at the office to build up that college fund my father is always talking about.

So, I decided to abandon the idea of sex at night and apply my feminine wiles in the morning. Ross isn't a morning person, but we all know what men wake up sporting. They can't help it. It just happens. Ross might be groggy, I considered, but his required effort would be minimal. I was sure he could handle the job.

The next morning Ross's alarm clock went off at seven o'clock. I'd been awake and ready since six. With a groan he turned off the pulsing machine. I rolled against his back and slipped my hand over his hip. And before anything at all could happen, Ross shot from the bed and was in the master bathroom, door closed, shower running.

One more option remained. Afternoon delight. Admittedly, it was a long shot. Ross and I rarely—had we ever?—made love at odd hours. Sex was associated with bed, which was associated with sleep, and neither of us were big nap takers. But I was determined.

So, when one Saturday Ross and I found ourselves at loose ends because the architect had cancelled his visit at the last minute, I thought, Perfect. Two hours before our next appointment, which was at a high-end furniture store in the Back Bay, and nothing to do in the meantime but flip through decorating magazines together.

I looked hopefully at Ross. He was standing at the kitchen counter, ever so carefully peeling a grapefruit with a paring knife. His face wore a slight frown of concentration. Or was it distaste? Ross didn't like grapefruit. He was peeling it for me. I hadn't asked for a grapefruit, but Ross said he wanted me to eat more citrus.

I opened my mouth. Ross flicked a grapefruit seed into the sink with a finicky flip of his manicured fingers. I closed my mouth. A girl can only take so much rejection.

17

The Inimitable

I stood on the sidewalk four houses down from Mrs. Kent's home and checked my watch. If I began walking right that moment I'd reach her door precisely two minutes before my appointment. I knew this because I'd done a few practice runs the day before.

With each step my heart beat a little faster. I'd gotten the job planning Mrs. Kent's party solely on the basis of my resume and portfolio; this was our first meeting. What if I blundered badly? I'd lose the job for sure. I'd never been fired and wasn't keen on going through the experience.

I checked my watch again. Two minutes early. I counted out thirty seconds and then lifted the knocker—was it really brass?—and rapped three times. A moment later the door opened, and I was face to face with a man dressed like a butler straight from a movie about life in an English country house.

"Yes?" he inquired, with only a hint of impatience.

"I'm Anna Traulsen," I said, with only a hint of panic. "I have an appointment with Mrs. Kent."

The butler allowed me entrance, where I was immediately

accosted by the most formidable woman I'd ever encountered. She was at least six feet tall with shoulders usually found on professional basketball players. Her chest was propped up so high and so firmly she seemed more like the bow of a ship breasting its way through choppy waters than a woman walking across a carpeted floor. Her eyes behind her metal-framed glasses were severe. Her mouth was incongruously tiny and pursed.

In short, Mrs. Kent's personal assistant made Mrs. Danvers of *Rebecca* fame seem like a ball of fluff. I don't think I've ever been so intimidated in all my life as I was by that estimable woman.

"I am Ms. Butterfield," she said. "Mrs. Kent's personal assistant."

I put out my hand to shake hers; she frowned at it before giving me a brisk shake that almost broke my bones.

"Nice to meet you, Ms. Butterfield," I squeaked. I was sure I was going to slip and call her Mrs. Butterworth, and just as equally sure she would have no reference to the popular maple syrup.

After a piercing scrutiny she pronounced, "You'll do, I suppose. Follow me."

Ms. Butterfield led me into a room straight out of a Henry James novel.

"Miss Traulsen is here," she intoned, as if announcing a disaster of massive proportion.

"Mrs. Kent," I said, with an automatic nod.

She was a tall woman still; she must have been at least five foot nine in her youth. Her hair was thick and white and piled on her head in a charming, early twentieth-century fashion. No old lady haircut for her. She was dressed in a suit that consisted of a high-necked white blouse, a boxy jacket in powder blue, and a straight skirt that fell just below her knee when she sat. I noted that her legs were in fine shape; I thought of the old slang "gams."

A magnificent brooch sat close to her left shoulder; at her ears were pearls; on her wrists were several gold bracelets;

and on her fingers were no fewer than three gorgeous rings, two obviously Victorian in style. And her pale blue eyes, although dulled by age, were still keen with intelligence and, I was to discover, an almost macabre sense of humor.

"Thank you Ms. Butterfield," she said, with a fixed, unnatural smile, "that will be all."

With a parting glare at me, Ms. Butterfield left the room.

Mrs. Kent's fixed smile relaxed into a grin; she rolled her eyes in the direction of the door through which Ms. Butterfield had just passed. "Oh, and don't mind her, Miss Traulsen. She's congenitally displeased. Between you and me, I call her Mrs. Butterpat. Not to her face, of course."

I allowed myself a small, tentative laugh. What, I wondered, would Mrs. Kent be calling me behind my back?

Mrs. Kent invited—commanded?—me to sit in a chair facing her perch on an overstuffed couch and after a few preliminaries—we agreed the weather was fine—the talk turned to the business at hand.

"There were eight of us girls in the drama club, all friends," Mrs. Kent informed me. "And we were quite the free spirits. Always breaking into laughter at inopportune moments and getting into all sorts of trouble. Well, what was trouble in those days would be seen as mere high jinks today. But oh, we had fun. We all went our separate ways after school, of course, marrying and raising families. Still, we always managed to keep in touch with a letter or occasional phone call."

"That's wonderful," I said politely. "That you keep in touch."

"Yes, yes," Mrs. Kent said brusquely; I wondered if she was embarrassed to have offered me a peek at her personal life. "Today there are only five of us still alive."

"I'm so sorry," I said.

Mrs. Kent looked at me with some wonder. "What are you sorry about, my dear? We all die. It's just a matter of time. Which is why I want to give this little party, because

Marion is not long for this world. Of course, she's been telling us that for the past three years, but I have a feeling that her time really is close. I'd love to see the old dear one more time. She owes me a game of poker. I caught her cheating last time, though of course, she swears she wasn't."

I made a note to self: Try not to sentimentalize the elderly.

"Yes, well," I said, just a bit nervously, "I have some preliminary ideas, of course. Still, I'd like to ask you some questions so I can get a better idea of what you had in mind for this event."

I looked questioningly at Mrs. Kent, who nodded.

"For example," I went on, "we might work with a theatre theme, in which case I'd like to know the names of some of the plays your club performed. We might also choose to recall your alma mater, in which case it would be helpful to know the school's colors and to have a copy of its crest. Or, we might go with a seasonal theme. You mentioned the event is scheduled for June 15th?"

"June is the month for weddings," Mrs. Kent said, not quite answering my question. "I see that you are engaged."

I glanced down at my left hand. Was my ring too big, too ostentatious? I looked back to the massive diamond brooch on my employer's shoulder and felt reassured. Even if my ring was too flashy for some, it was probably just fine for Mrs. Kent.

"Yes," I said. "I'm not getting married until September, though."

"Ah." Mrs. Kent sank in her seat; suddenly, she seemed tired. "About these questions, my dear," she said. "Why don't you write them down for me and let me think about them for a day or two. I'll have Ms. Butterfield call you when I've finished."

I left soon after, ushered out the front door by the peerless Ms. Butterfield. Once on the tree-lined, shaded sidewalk, I took a deep breath. I'd survived the first meeting with Mrs.

Kent, and if her unexceptionable assistant was professionally intimidating, at least the lady of the house was surprisingly down-to-earth.

The sun was shining, the breeze was light, and forsythia bushes were in bloom. There was a bounce in my step as I walked back toward the South End. I might just enjoy this job, I thought happily. I think it's going to be fun.

18

The Last Vestiges

"Anna," Ross said, "would you like something to drink?"
"No," I snapped, "thanks, I'm fine."

It had been a trying day. The printer had delivered the right invitations on the wrong paper; proving they were the ones who'd screwed up the order took half the morning. And dear, eccentric Mrs. Kent, through Ms. Butterfield, of course, had further compounded my problems by twice misplacing the list of questions I'd faxed to her. (Although Mrs. Kent wasn't one for any device more complicated than the telephone, her matchless assistant was fond of communications technology.)

All I wanted to do that evening was watch a mildly amusing sitcom and drift off to sleep. But I still had some bills to review; my accountant was expecting a variety of papers the following day. Ross, probably thinking I wanted his company, had stopped by after what seemed to have been a stress-free day at his family's successful construction business.

Why, I wondered with some impatience, as Ross nibbled a small piece of Manchego cheese, didn't he ever bring work home with him? True, he often worked late, but I'd come to learn that "working late" meant drinks and dinner with clients, potential clients, and his father's cronies.

Suddenly, every little noise my beloved fiancé made shredded my nerves. Ross cleared his throat, and I wanted to scratch his eyes out. He slit open an envelope, and I wanted to scream. He poured himself a glass of wine, and the sound of the liquid filling the glass was enough to force an "EEErrrgghhh!" from my lips.

Ross looked up, startled.

"What's wrong, Anna?"

"Nothing's wrong," I snapped. "I'm just trying to work."

Ross raised his hands in the universal gesture of surrender. "Okay, okay, I'm sorry I asked."

I thought, He's thinking, "Uh, oh, here come the mood swings." And I needed to set him right. I tossed aside the account book and got up from the couch. "Okay," I said, "do you want to know what's wrong? I'll tell you. It's just that there's so much to do. There's always a phone call to make or an order to pick up or a client to appease. It never ends, Ross. And I'm so on top of things, it's not like I'm negligent. I just . . . I just don't know how I'm going to handle running the business and caring for a baby. I just don't know."

Ross was calmness personified. Calmness and neatness. He'd been home from the office for two hours and was still wearing suit pants, a white shirt, and a tie. He was barely wrinkled.

"Well," he said easily, as he sat in an armchair and folded his legs, "you can always close the business for a while. It would be like a sabbatical."

I swear I thought I would pass out. I sank back onto the couch heavily. Breathe, I told myself. Just breathe. And then, try to explain that what Ross has just suggested is impossible.

"That would be career suicide, Ross," I said, more forcefully than I'd intended. "Once I'm off the scene, I'm off. Do you have any idea how hard it would be to win back my former clients, let alone woo new ones? I'm in a business that's all about relationships and relationships have to be maintained. If I shut down Anna's Occasions, my regular clients will see it as abandonment and find someone else to take care of them. And then, when I'm ready to start up again, it will be that much harder to—"

"Calm down, Anna. I'm not—"

"—make new connections. I'd have to relearn the social scene, who's hot, what's not. Besides," I said, looking at Ross pleadingly, wanting so badly for him to understand, "I like my business. I like working."

Ross chuckled. Since when had he taken to chuckling? Since I'd told him we were going to have a baby, that's when. Next thing I know, I thought, he's going to be wearing argyle cardigans and loudly sucking hard candies.

"You'll be working with the baby, believe me," Ross said all-knowingly. "My mother and my aunts tell stories. You know, why don't you talk to my mother, and to your friend Kristen, the one with all the kids."

"Three kids," I said. He hadn't understood.

"Okay, so talk to her. And talk to your sister-in-law, too. What's her name again? She must have her share of stories. Anna, I think you'll see that you're in for a huge amount of work right here at home. And honestly, if we can afford to live on one salary, and we can, why kill yourself keeping Anna's Occasions alive?"

Because it's my creation, I answered silently. In a way, it's my first child.

Ross abandoned the armchair and joined me on the couch. I fought the impulse to scoot away.

"Come on, Anna, promise me you'll at least think about giving up your business. Hey, I could help you negotiate a sale of your client list. Well, my lawyer could. Just think about it, okay? You don't have to make a decision right away. You still have some time."

I didn't reply. Ross seemed to take my silence for acquiescence.

"Besides," he went on, "everyone says the minute the baby is born you're not going to want to spend one minute away from him. Ross, Junior. Think of how much easier it will be to have sold off the business before the baby's born so you can concentrate on what really matters."

"What really matters," I repeated dully.

Not me, not Ross, not our marriage, not my career.

Ross squeezed my shoulders in a fatherly way. "Good girl," he said. "I know you'll do the right thing."

April, I thought, truly is the cruelest month.

19

Of the Flesh

An entire morning without nausea and vomiting. This bodes well for the entire day, I thought, as I locked the front door behind me and headed out for the office. Maybe the morning sickness phase is over. Maybe for the rest of the pregnancy I'll feel just great, rested and strong. Maybe this gloriously sunny day is the start of a brand new phase of my life!

I made it an entire two blocks before it hit. My mouth filled with saliva, and before I could make it all the way to the fence surrounding the community garden, I vomited. Trembling, I tried to take a deep, slow breath, but the torment wasn't over. I continued to gag for what seemed an eternity; mercifully, my stomach was now empty.

This is what my life had become. Puking on a public street. I desperately hoped no one watching me thought I was drunk. I desperately hoped no one watching me thought I was a drug addict going through withdrawal.

"Disgusting." The voice came from behind me. Automatically, I turned and saw the retreating back of a young man with a shaved head.

"You could at least have tried to find a toilet." This voice belonged to a woman pushing a high-end stroller that looked more like a vehicle for three armed soldiers than transportation for a sleeping baby.

I was too mortified to protest. What next came out of my mouth was perhaps the most humiliating thing of all. "I'm sorry," I croaked.

Not something sarcastic like, "Gee, thanks for the help"; not something angry like, "You bitch"; not something explanatory like, "I'm pregnant."

I found a tissue in my purse and used it to wipe my mouth. If the concrete sidewalk could have split just then and allowed me to slip into the rat-infested depths of Shawmut Avenue, I would have been pleased. Rodents be damned. I was mortified.

As soon as possible I turned around and headed home. I wanted to run, to bolt, but I felt too woozy to risk more than a slow and careful pace. And while I walked I thought about The Body.

The Body, I had come to understand by the age of twelve, betrays you. You're going along just fine, largely oblivious to the internal working of The Body, when suddenly, for no apparent reason, once every month or so you bloat, cramp, and bleed for five or six days. Your face breaks out, your mood swings wildly, and the craving for sugar reaches outrageous proportions.

Discovering I was pregnant at the age of thirty-seven was like revisiting that adolescent awakening. Pregnancy was serious, incontrovertible proof that The Body could rise up and surprise you at any time. The Body was unreliable.

The Body was life.

I don't remember how old I was—I must have been quite young, maybe four—when I first saw an image of an angel that was basically a pretty, blonde head with pretty, pale blue wings. I think it was a painting; maybe it was on display in a museum. Maybe I saw this odd image in an art history book at a relative's house. Or in a bible at the home of a Catholic neighbor, I don't know.

But I do know that I was fascinated by that image. And years later, at eight or nine, I remembered that curly blonde head and pale blue wings and thought, That's what I want to be. The brain is in the head and that's where my thoughts come from, so I want to be all thoughts—all thought and feelings and spirit—and a pair of filmy wings. Because The Body, I thought, is not really you. You are what's inside The Body—your thoughts, feelings, and spirit. Your soul is you.

Or something like that. I was, after all, only eight, not exactly at the age for serious philosophical thought.

Of course, I soon grew up to learn that heads got colds and aches; there was hair to maintain and style. Worse, there were diseases that were attributable to chemical imbalances in the brain—depression, both manic and chronic; schizophrenia; multiple personality disorder; obsessive compulsive disorder; attention deficit disorder. The list went on. Eventually I just had to face the fact that when you're human there's just no way around The Body. Without it, we're nothing. Spirit needs a residence, at least here on planet earth.

When I finally reached the safety of home that awful day, the first thing I did was scrub my teeth. Work could wait a few hours. The office would be fine sitting there all on its own. My cell phone rang. It was Ross; I didn't answer. He, too, would be fine all on his own. Propped up in bed, I reached for one of the books stacked on the nightstand and opened it randomly.

"Pregnancy," the author of *The Girlfriends' Guide to Pregnancy* writes, "is a great time to learn the life lesson of surrender."

20

Panic in Babyland

Sometimes too much information is a very bad thing. Here's how I learned that lesson for the second time in a matter of weeks.

My mother called me at the office one afternoon.

"What's wrong?" I asked immediately.

"Nothing's wrong. Why, are you too busy to talk?"

I shook my head, confused. How had she made that leap? Anyway, my mother never calls me at work. She rarely calls me at home. Why wouldn't I think something was wrong?

"No," I said. "I can talk."

"Well, I only have a minute. Anna," she said, "you'll want to take a subscription to a parenting magazine. Let me know which one you want, and your father and I will pay for it. It was his idea."

Gee, thanks, Mom, I thought. I don't know if I could afford the twelve dollars a year.

"Thanks, Mom," I said. "But you don't have to do that. I—"

"You already took a subscription? I told your father as much. Okay, then. I'll talk to you next week."

My mother's half-hearted offer—I was sure my father knew nothing about it—annoyed me but it also got me thinking. I supposed I should find a parenting magazine I could rely on, something that was both enjoyable and informative.

I took a break around one o'clock and walked to the Barnes and Noble in the Prudential Mall. And I stared stupidly at the colorful selection spread out before me. Three rows of glossies. Approximately thirty titles. How to decide which magazine to buy?

In the end I bought them all: *Parent*; *Parenting*; *Parents*. *Good Parent; Better Parent; Best Parent. Traditional Baby; Modern Baby; Today's Baby. Infant Infatuation; Totally Toddler; Cherished Child. Family; Families; EveryFamily*; *Your Family. Family Funtime; Family Mealtime; Family Learningtime. Mommy's Little Helper* . . .

Okay. That last one is a joke. But really, who expects mothers to have the time or energy to implement every fantastic craft and "easy" fifteen-step recipe without a little help from her friends?

"Doing some research?" the clerk at the checkout counter asked pleasantly. Her hair was worn in two long braids; her face was flat and smooth like a slice of potato. She looked about eleven. "Are you a writer?"

"Research, yes," I said shortly. "Writer, no."

"Oh. So, like, you just want to know about stuff."

"That's it exactly," I replied, handing her my frequent buyer card.

"So—" she began, handing me the bulky plastic bag filled with information.

"I'm sorry," I said, cutting the poor girl off. "I'm in a hurry." And I dashed off as fast as my burden would let me.

That night I spent almost two solid hours reading articles from the various publications. Here are some of the fascinating facts I gleaned:

Approximately eight thousand children each year are born with some form of autism, from Asperger's disorder to

Rett's disorder. (My brother and his family are not alone in their pain.)

Thousands of children are killed each year by childhood cancers and other deadly diseases.

Pedophilia is on the rise; at least, it's being reported more often than it ever has been, which is both a good and a bad thing. Good if you consider that victims are speaking out. Bad if you consider that there are so many victims in the first place. Teachers, neighbors, clergy, family members—everyone was suspect.

Every year in the United States alone, 700,000 children are reported missing. Three to five thousand of those children are snatched by strangers from the sidewalks just outside their home, from their schoolyards, from the mall. Most of them never come home. Some people advocate the implantation of microchips in children at birth so that if the child goes missing he or she can be tracked. Kiddie LoJack. Pretty much everyone agrees that you'd be crazy to let a child walk to school on his own. Pretty much everyone agrees that children needed to be chaperoned 24/7.

A seventh-month-old baby could roll right off her changing table, even a changing table with a lip. A two-year-old could get his hands on a peanut and suffer a severe allergic reaction and maybe even die. An infant in his crib could be alive one minute and dead the next, a victim of SIDS. While his negligent nanny's back was turned, a three-year-old could fall from the top of a jungle gym—where he shouldn't have been in the first place—and land on his head.

There were, I realized in a state of growing panic, no end to the disasters that could befall an innocent baby in arms. A toddler could grab a fork from the dinner table and poke his own eye out. He could swallow a penny or stick his finger in an electric socket or break away from his father's grip, dash out into a busy street, and be hit by a passing bus. The other kids in his daycare center could infect him with all sorts of nasty bugs—including lice!—and there was not much even the most careful and concerned parent could do about it. Nobody could baby-proof the world!

I looked at the tumble of glossy pages on the dining table and shuddered. Helping? The parenting magazines weren't helping one bit. Instead they were causing acute anxiety that couldn't even be appeased by the photos of chubby-cheeked Asian-American babies in ladybug Halloween costumes; or curly-haired, blonde toddlers in pink velvet dresses; or roly-poly African-American infants in the latest Ralph Lauren styles.

I addressed myself sternly: Face it, Anna. You are going to give birth to a child and subsequently drop her on her head. You are going to nurture her inside your own body for nine long months only to roll over on her in your sleep when she is no more than a week old.

Disaster, it seemed, was inevitable.

I picked up one of the many postcards I'd ripped from the glossies. "Would you like to place a subscription?" the postcard asked.

"No!" I said to the room, tearing the postcard in two. "I most certainly would not!"

And I reached for *Vogue*.

21

Arrevederci, Anna

Alexandra and I were at the bar at Suede. She looked impeccable, as always, in her simple white blouse and black slacks. I wore a vintage Diane von Furstenberg wraparound dress with knee high Kenneth Cole boots. Since I'd discovered I was pregnant and learned that my body was about to undergo several alarming changes, I was mad to wear every piece in my extensive wardrobe.

For the last time? I wondered if after the baby I'd ever fit into the fabulous Missoni skirt I'd scored at Filene's, or the silk halter-top Prada dress I found at a high-end resale shop on Newbury Street, or the slinky dove-gray Armani evening dress I'd bought—on sale—to wear to a gala event at which Ross's father was receiving some kind of award from the Chamber of Commerce.

I complained about this impending problem to Alexandra. "It's such a waste, really," I said finally. "I've spent so much time and money on these beautiful clothes. And now . . ."

"Do you even like children?" she asked bluntly.

What, I wondered, did children have to do with my wardrobe? And then, of course, I understood.

"Of course I like children," I said, although I realized I'd never really thought about liking them or not. "It's just that I don't really know many children, and I haven't spent much time with the ones I do know."

"What about Kristen's kids?" Alexandra asked.

"What about them? I've never even babysat for them. I wonder if I should be insulted that Kristen's never asked me."

"Have you ever volunteered?"

"No," I admitted. "I'm not really comfortable with the notion of babysitting. It's such a huge responsibility. I don't trust myself to keep a child safe and sound."

"Anna," Alexandra countered, "you're one of the most responsible, cautious people I've ever met. You'd be a fine babysitter."

"I lack experience with children."

"Well then why don't you get some?" she suggested reasonably. "Why don't you ask Kristen if you can watch one of the kids while she's busy with the other two. Start slowly. And what about your brother's kids? You've spent time with them, haven't you?"

"Some," I said guiltily. "But mostly on special occasions. You know, on Christmas Day or at a birthday party. Come to think of it, I've never even read a bedtime story to a child, or given a bath to a baby, or warmed a bottle. It's hopeless, Alexandra. I'm going to be a terrible mother."

Alexandra patted my hand. "Poor Anna. You'll be fine and you know it. You're just panicking. Let's talk about something else, all right?"

But I couldn't let go. "Pilots are required to log a certain number of hours in the air before they can fly solo or get their license. Hair stylists have to practice on wigs before they're allowed to cut real hair on live heads. Serious jobs require training. So why aren't prospective parents required to spend a certain amount of time with children, learning all the basics like how to properly perform CPR, and how to safely use a Q-Tip, and, I don't know, even how to change a diaper. Let's be real. Prospective parents should be required to pass a battery of tests—psychological, experiential, and emotional—before they're allowed to reproduce."

"Okay," Alexandra snapped. "Now you're just being silly. Look, no one can deny that lots of parents are totally unqualified to be caretakers. The world is full of idiots. But you're not an idiot, Anna. You know that. You're just experiencing a degree of very normal anxiety. Idiots don't feel anxiety; they don't understand self-doubt. They just blunder through life, and their successes are as much accidents as their failures. You're different, Anna. You—and okay, even Ross—have a conscience. And you're self-conscious, maybe too much so, but still."

"That's all well and good," I said, "but am I really qualified? I mean it, Alexandra. I'm going to be entirely responsible for the life of another human being. What makes me qualified for that job?"

"The fact," she replied, "that you're educated and intelligent, and if anyone I know is qualified to be a competent, loving caretaker, it's you. So, enough pretending to be an incompetent. I don't want to hear any more self-indulgent whining from you."

"Okay," I said. I'd keep my mouth shut but that didn't mean my mind was going to stop its anxious racing.

"Okay. So, what about Italy?" Alexandra asked.

I shrugged. "What about Italy?"

"Is the honeymoon still on? You planned on being away for a month, right?"

I took a tentative sip of steaming herbal, decaffeinated tea before answering. "Of course it's still on. Why wouldn't it be?"

Alexandra shrugged. "I thought pregnant women weren't supposed to fly."

"Only very pregnant women aren't allowed to fly. I think."

I was suddenly aware of just how much knowledge I lacked. Add to my To-Do list: Go home and read, cover to cover, Kristen's copy of *What to Expect When You're Expecting*. And then go to Amazon.com and purchase every book Dr. Spock ever wrote.

Alexandra raised her glass of merlot to the light and sighed.

"I can't imagine spending a month in Italy and not being able to drink wine!"

"Italians aren't as rabid about the alcohol thing as Americans," I pointed out. "Lots of pregnant women have a glass or two of wine. Now and then. Once in a while."

But I'd better not, I thought. Just to be safe.

"Okay," Alexandra said, "I'll admit Europeans on the whole are more reasonable about health than Americans. A glass of wine won't kill you or create a horror show of a baby. But what's Ross going to say?"

Alexandra's eyes narrowed to slits, although maybe that was in my imagination. Sometimes it seemed that one of Alexandra's favorite hobbies was to pick on Ross. And what had he ever done to her but ask me to marry him?

"He'll be fine with it," I said evenly.

"You're deluding yourself. If I know Ross at all, and I think I do, he sees this baby as his investment. Why don't I just say it? He sees this baby as his property. And like any smart businessman, he's going to do whatever it takes to protect that investment. To keep trespassers off his property."

"I thought I was his property," I said, lamely attempting a joke.

"You are." Alexandra pointed first to my face and then to my midsection. "You and the baby. You better believe he'll be ready to whack any guy who comes within ten yards of you."

"Ross is not violent."

Alexandra shrugged. "You're right. But he is the jealous type. And he won't stand for anyone imposing on his turf. He'll hire someone to whack the intruder."

Now Ross was a member of the mob?

"You're horrible," I said. "You have such a warped idea of Ross. Why can't you try to like him, for my sake?"

"Aren't I always nice to him in person? I bet he doesn't even know I don't like him. Unless you've ratted me out."

"No," I admitted, "I haven't ratted you out. Ross is under the impression that you adore him. He's under the impression that everyone adores him. It's just the way he is. He doesn't have a lot of imagination."

And at the time I considered Ross's lack of imagination a good thing. Ross was stable, rooted. He didn't make me roar with laughter, but he didn't make me cry.

"Maybe I should suggest we postpone our honeymoon," I said miserably.

"So you can take it with a bawling baby in tow?" Alexandra demanded.

"No." I hesitated. "Maybe we should just plan to go to Italy on our fifth anniversary or something. By then the baby won't be a baby and we can leave him, or her, with my parents. Better yet, with Ross's parents. Maybe we'll have a live-in nanny by then. I don't like the idea, but Ross thinks it's smart."

I felt miserable. I'm sure I looked worse.

Alexandra put her hand on my arm. "Anna," she said, "you've been dying to go on this trip! And every bride deserves a honeymoon. Especially you."

Why especially me?

"But not every bride gets a honeymoon," I said glumly. "It won't be the end of the world if I'm one of them. I mean, what if we go to Italy now and I'm sick every morning and can't eat spaghetti carbonara, which is one of my favorite things ever, because Ross won't let me near raw eggs? I'll be miserable. Ross will be miserable. Maybe it will be better if we just stay home."

Alexandra sighed. "How much money will you lose if you cancel now?"

"I'm not sure, exactly. A lot, I imagine."

"It is a shame to waste money," my friend murmured.

I wondered, What kind of person would value a trip to Italy over her own baby? I shouldn't care a bit about my honeymoon. Alexandra was wrong. A person like me didn't deserve a honeymoon.

"Now I'm thoroughly depressed," I said. "And it's all your fault."

"And I can't even buy you a drink to make up for my bad behavior."

"You could buy me an appetizer. I'll have the grilled calamari."

Alexandra gestured to the pony-tailed bartender, busy at the other end with a gaggle of young blondes.

"There is one more thing I wanted to ask you," she said, turning back to face me.

"What?" I asked. "Do you want to know if I have hemorrhoids? Do you want to know if I'm constantly peeing? If my extremities are swollen? If my waistline has widened yet? Do you want to know if I've grown hair on my chest? What? What else can you possibly ask me that will bring me any lower than I am at this very moment."

Alexandra looked at me steadily.

"Have you told Jack?"

22

What Makes a Man

Jack was—is—Jack Coltrane, professional photographer. I'd known him for close to six years at that point and worked with him on maybe twenty events. His massive loft, which served as both studio and home, is in the Sowa district on Harrison Avenue near East Berkley.

Jack Coltrane and Ross Davis are polar opposites. Ross is sophisticated; Jack is rough around the edges. Ross is clean shaven; Jack is often scruffy. Ross is a businessman; Jack, although he owns a successful business, is an artist first. Ross watches his diet and works out at the gym three times a week. Jack eats whatever he's in the mood to eat, whenever he's in the mood to eat it. And the last thing he'd do is waste his time on a treadmill walking away his day like a hamster on his wheel. The "waste" is Jack's term.

In some ways Boston is more like a small town than big city. Sometimes it seems that everybody knows everybody, at least within certain geographically and socially defined circles. Jack knew of Ross through some of the larger corporate and charity events he photographed. Ross knew of Jack through some of the larger corporate and charity events he attended. And they both came to despise each other through me.

Consider the afternoon I showed up at Jack's studio for a shoot wearing for the first time the three-carat emerald-cut diamond and platinum engagement ring. Jack pointed at my left hand, which, I admit, I was waving around rather conspicuously.

"That thing is monstrous," he growled.

"I know. I like it that way. And thank you for the heartfelt congratulations."

"I didn't offer congratulations of any kind."

"I know. And I don't care."

Jack grunted. "That Davis idiot?"

My good mood could not be broken by a grumpy old man. Okay, Jack was only forty-five, but I swear there were times when he masqueraded as a nasty old coot. I wondered what he got out of the act. The pleasure of pissing people off? The satisfaction of being considered a genuine curmudgeon? Was keeping people at arm's length really his desired result? If so, he was doing a fine job of it.

On another afternoon I stopped by Jack's studio to review the layout I'd completed for the twenty-first birthday of a bimbo-esque socialite. In my bag was an article from the business section of that morning's *Globe* mentioning Ross as one of the city's up-and-coming, and handsome, entrepreneurs.

"Did you see this?" I said, sticking the article I'd clipped in his face.

Jack squinted at it then pushed my hand aside. "I think your taste in husbands is lousy."

I felt the tiny pinpricks of blood vessels popping just beneath the surface of my skin. Jack Coltrane, I vowed, was not going to make me break out in a rash!

"Haven't you ever heard of the white lie?" I asked rhetorically, smiling nicely. "Wait, of course you haven't. You've never been introduced to the social graces."

"He's not as smart as you are."

Yes, it seemed Jack Coltrane was going to make me break out in a rash. Most infuriating, his own demeanor was bland, unruffled.

"How do you know that?" I cried. "And even if he isn't as smart as I am, so what? What does it matter? Where do you get off making that kind of judgment? Ross owns his own very successful business!"

"It's his father's."

"It was his father's," I corrected. "Now it's his. Mostly."

What's wrong, I thought, with a parent helping his son get a start in life? The family business was a venerable tradition. Jack, I decided, was just jealous that nobody had handed him part-ownership in a successful business. Jack was just pissed that he'd had to do everything on his own. Jack was a bitter, self-made man, that's what he was.

I crossed my arms and waited for Jack's comeback.

"You're right," he said simply. "Hand me that Exact-O knife?"

Jack might have been willing to let the subject drop, but I wasn't. I grabbed the tool and thrust it at him.

"You're just jealous," I said, all self-righteous.

Jack carefully took the sharp instrument from my hand and looked at me with mild amusement. "Yeah," he said, "that's it exactly."

I was instantly mortified. Of course Jack wasn't jealous of Ross. The truth was self-evident, at least to me. Ross was jealous of Jack and he didn't even know it.

"Let's just drop the subject," I said, fully aware I was the one who'd refused to let it go. "Let's just agree to disagree about Ross."

Jack didn't answer; I left soon after.

And now Alexandra wanted to know if I'd told Jack that I was pregnant.

23

The Lion in His Den

When you think about a couple, you don't usually think about the details of their intimate life together. Usually, you assume they have an intimate life, and that's really all you need to know. And unless one member of the couple decides to share an intimate detail—say, a medical problem like dysfunction—you remain blissfully ignorant of private matters that are really none of your business.

And then someone gets pregnant.

Pregnancy, as everyone knows, is proof of sex. It's proof of the intimate life your friends assume you have; it's proof of the intimate life your family would like to pretend you don't have. When someone announces her pregnancy, you're forced to imagine her having sex; even for a split second, the thought flashes into your mind. You can't help it, can you? Announcing a pregnancy is like inviting a person into your bedroom, if only for a moment.

That was why I was not looking forward to telling Jack Coltrane I was pregnant. Because telling him I was pregnant was telling him that yes, I definitely had sex with Ross Davis. My fiancé. The man Jack disdained.

Of course, I argued with myself about this. Anna, I wondered, why do you care if Jack doesn't approve of Ross? Ross doesn't approve of Jack and that doesn't bother you in the least. Well, it doesn't bother you that much.

And here's what I told myself: I care that Jack doesn't like Ross because I want all of my friends to like each other. It's the same thing with Alexandra and Michaela; I'd like them to like each other. That's all.

Maybe, I thought, Jack will hear about my pregnancy from someone else. Maybe I can go the whole nine months without ever mentioning it at all.

Like that could happen.

Finally, I determined to just spit out the news like I was spitting out news of a sale on toothpaste at CVS. Matter-of-fact. No big deal. No emotional content.

I dropped by Jack's studio late one afternoon, unannounced. Was this my first ever drop-in? I believe it was; it certainly wasn't my last.

"What are you doing here?" he asked with a scowl.

"Hello to you, too." Anna, I thought, maybe this is a bad time. Maybe Jack is too busy.

"Look," I blurted, "there's something I have to tell you. Actually, I don't have to tell you, I want to tell you . . ."

Jack looked to the ceiling and then walked away, right across the room, to a row of shelves. I stood there with my mouth open, like a fool.

"Hello?" I said loudly, to his back. "I was talking to you. You don't just walk away when someone's in the middle of a sentence."

Jack looked over his shoulder. "You were?" he said. "Sorry. I'm a bit involved here."

"You're socially inept," I declared, once again to his back.

"Uh."

"See? You grunt instead of forming an answer with words. An adult answer. A normal person's answer."

"Hmm."

"It's like you were raised in a cave. Were you?"

"Was I what?" Jack, having found whatever it was he was looking for across the room, rejoined me at one of the cluttered worktables.

"Raised in a cave! And there's another thing. You don't listen."

"Is there anything at all about me you find acceptable?"

"Yes," I admitted. "Your work. I find your work more than acceptable."

I saw a tiny smile play at the corner of Jack's mouth.

"Howie Manowitz's bar mitzvah photos?"

"No. Well, that too. I mean your work. Your own. Jack Coltrane's photographs. The few I've seen of them, anyway."

"Jack Coltrane, artist, retired some years ago," he said evenly. "Sorry to disappoint you."

"You didn't disappoint me," I said inanely. I wondered how the conversation had gotten onto the subject of Jack's work and so far away from what I wanted to talk about.

Just tell him, Anna. Just say it.

"What's wrong?" Jack asked. "You look like you ate a bad clam."

My stomach lurched. It wasn't bad clams; it was nerves. I felt as nervous as I had just before going onstage as a lineless member of the shabby crowd in my senior year's production of *Les Miserables*.

"Amendment," I said, archly. "You were raised in a cave with a big pile of bat poop for a playmate."

"Guano. Bat poop is called guano."

"I know what it's called. I just like to say bat poop."

"And I'm the one with no social graces?"

"By the way," I blurted, "have you heard my big news?"

Jack was busy now cutting a mat. "You got the job doing Beatrice Kent's reunion party?"

"Yes, but that's not the big news." Not the really big news. "I'm pregnant. I mean, Ross and I . . . We're going to have a baby."

"Congratulations," he said evenly. "Is that what you're supposed to say in a situation like this? You know I'm lousy when it comes to social graces."

"Congratulations is an appropriate thing to say," I told him. To myself I added, It's even nicer when you mean it.

Jack looked up from the mat. "Hand me those gloves, will you?"

I did. I felt like crying.

"What?" he said. "What's wrong?"

"Nothing's wrong," I lied, eyes wide. "It's just that, I don't know, you could be, I don't know—"

"Jumping up and down with excitement? Calling the neighbors to tell them the big news?"

I shrugged. I felt like a total fool. "No. I mean—"

"Anna, your big news doesn't change anything in my life. There's a limit to what I can be excited about." And then he laughed. "Come on, what did you expect me to say?"

I was stunned. I'd never heard anything so cruel. "Nothing," I said. I tried to sound cold, but my voice shook. "I don't expect anything from you. Because you are the most self-centered person I have ever met. And there's no reason to be such a jerk."

"Don't cry, Anna."

"I am not going to cry," I said, although tears had gathered in my eyes, "and I am not a hormonal wreck, so don't even think about cracking jokes at my expense about female mood swings and ridiculous cravings and swollen ankles."

Jack had the decency to look slightly ashamed. "I wouldn't stoop to quoting the stereotypes," he said. "Look—"

"I'm leaving," I said, cutting off whatever lame apology he might be considering. "I don't know why I'm here anyway."

I practically ran back to my office so great was my anger, and my embarrassment. Why, why, why, I wondered with every step, did Jack have to be such a jerk? Worse, why had I made such a big deal of telling him I was pregnant? What,

what, what had I been thinking? Why should Jack care if I was pregnant? Why should he care about me at all?

And then a sneaking, sly, and seductive voice in my head whispered, Because you want him to.

24

Peas in the Pod

Ross's slim, manicured fingers traced an invisible line across the tablecloth. "Can we request a creamier tone?" he said. "This is a bit too harsh for my taste."

The Tuxedo Hotel's wedding coordinator, a dapper man in his midthirties named Walt LaFond, frowned in a practiced sort of way. "No, Mr. Davis, I'm sorry. The linen is non-negotiable."

Ross looked to me, then back to the sample table Walt had set, and frowned.

"Well," he said finally. "I suppose they'll do."

"They'll be fine, Ross," I said consolingly. "The centerpieces will look lovely against the white, I'm sure."

Ross had helped design the lush centerpieces that included snapdragons and freesia. You see, unlike the majority of men—or so I'm told—who want nothing to do with wedding preparations, Ross assumed an active role immediately after our engagement. I thought it was sweet, and given Ross's excellent taste, I found his input very welcome. Especially now that I had a pregnancy to endure and a baby to plan for and a business to run. I hadn't even asked Ross to come with me to this tasting; he'd offered to go along all on his own.

"Shall we discuss the vegetable dishes?" Walt said.

Ross frowned. "No saucy preparations for the vegetables. There's too great a risk of spillage."

Walt nodded seriously and looked to me as if for confirmation of Ross's dictate.

"Absolutely no saucy vegetables," I said, imagining with horror buttery grease stains on the bodice of my gown.

Again, Walt nodded. He was very solemn for a wedding coordinator. I rather liked that about him. "Noted," he said. "No sauces on the vegetables. Next we'll try the roasted rosemary potatoes and the grilled asparagus."

"Actually," I said, "I'd like to forgo the potatoes in favor of the risotto you mentioned earlier. Ross?"

"Exactly what I was thinking," he said. "And, of course, you do understand there'll be no shellfish and nothing remotely raw." Ross winked at me then, and I noted just how pretty his eyes were. If I didn't know better I would have sworn he'd applied glycerine drops before he left the condo.

"Of course," I agreed. Ross was always looking out for the baby.

The waiter cleared the table and left to bring out the final course. Dessert! I'd requested that we sample several types of cakes, including, of course, a triple-layer chocolate and hazelnut cake and, for those who preferred something lighter, an apricot-filled white cake with a fondant icing. As a treat, I'd also ordered plates of tiny marzipan fruits for each table. I hoped mightily that the kitchen had procured some for the tasting.

When Walt's beeper sounded and he excused himself to take a call in his office, Ross and I shared a smile of content. "We're so in sync, Anna," he said, taking my hand and squeezing it gently.

I looked up at my handsome, mild-mannered fiancé with fondness. "We are, aren't we?"

"Oh," he said, releasing my hand, "I almost forgot to tell

you the big news. I booked us into The Palace Hotel in Rome, very close to the Spanish Steps. It's amazing that I even got a room only six months before the honeymoon, but I talked to some people and, well, I think you're going to love it. Of course it's wonderfully high-end."

Of course. And to be honest, wonderfully high-end sounded, well, wonderful. And I hated to put a damper on what had turned out to be a very pleasant afternoon. But someone had to do it.

"Ross?" I said softly. "I'll be so far along in the pregnancy by then. Six months along. I'm not even sure I'll be allowed to fly. Oh, Ross, I'm so sorry."

Ross's expression remained neutral. "Anna," he said, "don't worry about a thing. Why don't you check with your doctor and see what she says. We can always postpone the honeymoon until after the baby is born. My mother can watch the baby, or we'll look into hiring an au pair. There's plenty of time and we have plenty of options."

"But you've gone to so much trouble planning it all," I said, genuinely sorry for being the unwitting cause of Ross's wasted efforts. "And it all sounds so lovely!"

"It does," he agreed. "An entire month in Italy. But it will still be lovely when we finally go. And just think. It'll be a celebration not only of our marriage but also of our family. Besides, after a few months you'll need a break from the demands of little Brockland or Boundary."

I didn't bother to point out that if I was still breastfeeding little Brockland or Boundary—shudder!—I wouldn't be going anywhere without the baby for quite a while. I didn't want to further spoil the plans for what would have been our life. Besides, Ross was being so wonderful about the pregnancy.

"You're a very good man, Ross Davis," I said, sending him an air kiss. Ross doesn't like lipstick anywhere near his collar.

"So I've been told. Now, come on. Smile. We still have a

cake to taste. But remember, only one bite of each. We don't need the sugar."

My smile faltered just a bit. The truth was I had been fighting off an intense craving for chocolate all morning. I was so looking forward to wolfing down several pieces of rich, gooey wedding cake. And if I were at the tasting alone or with Alexandra, I would have gone right ahead and done so.

"Right," I said to my perhaps overly fastidious fiancé. "Just one bite."

25

The Elephant in the Room

I couldn't avoid Jack entirely; we were in the middle of two projects. So I was determined to act as if I'd never told him I was pregnant. As if he'd never been so horrible. As if I'd never been so wounded.

I arrived at Jack's studio out of breath. I wondered, Had I already gained so much weight that I was reduced to huffing and puffing? By the end of the pregnancy would I be getting around town in an electric scooter intended for the elderly and infirm?

"I've got the seating plan for the Gotts' party," I told him when I'd caught my breath. "And the essential shot list. Absolutely no photos of Mrs. Gott with her in-laws. I didn't ask why, of course, but I got the feeling—"

Jack cut me off. "Those are for you," he said, nodding toward one of the many worktables. This one was made of an old wood door atop two sawhorses, and on top of it stood a magnificent arrangement of Blue Moon roses and glossy greenery.

I darted over to the flowers. "They're gorgeous! Who are they from? That's strange. I can't find a card. I guess I can call the florist . . . Wait a minute. Why would flowers for me have been delivered here?"

"They're from me."

I whirled around, not sure I'd heard him correctly.

"From you?"

"Yeah."

"Why?" I asked, none too graciously.

Jack looked back to his work.

"I think you're supposed to give flowers to pregnant women."

"You're supposed to give flowers to all women," I amended. Oh, how cool and flip I sounded! How tumultuous I felt inside! "That is, of course, if you're a man of culture."

Jack shrugged. "Sorry it took me so long. But what can you expect from a cultureless man."

"Thank you, Jack. Really."

He didn't reply. And I didn't dare bring up the fact that Blue Moon roses are my favorite flower. Whenever they are available, which isn't often, I choose them for special events like twenty-fifth wedding anniversaries. Unless Jack was entirely deaf or entirely uninterested in anything I had to say, he had to have heard me express my love for the roses the color of blueberry ice cream.

I glanced over at Jack and wondered. My prickly colleague, my grumpy occasional friend, had given me a stunning bouquet of my favorite flowers. What did it mean? Were the flowers simply an apology for his having been such a jerk when I'd told him I was pregnant? If so, Jack's apology was a mighty sincere one, especially if money equaled sincerity, and for Jack, I doubt it did. So maybe the bouquet wasn't an apology after all.

"You're still here? What do you need?"

Jack's harsh voice broke my reverie into shards. He was staring at me with as much enthusiasm as he'd show a smelly bike messenger who was lingering unnecessarily after dropping off a package. "Yes," I said. "I mean, I'm just going. I don't need anything."

He nodded and turned back to his computer. I'd been dismissed.

"Thanks, again," I said, about to wrestle the arrangement out the door. "For the flowers."

Jack didn't reply.

26

Three's a Crowd

"Lovely," a woman in head-to-toe couture murmured as I made my way down the carpeted hallway of the Ritz lobby. I blushed—I know I did—and smiled graciously at my admirer. Rather, at the admirer of the dozen Blue Moon roses I carried in my arms like a beauty queen's winning bouquet.

I spotted Alexandra the moment I passed into the bar. She's never hard to spot.

"Where did you get those?" she asked. "Here, put them on this chair." She got up and pulled a third upholstered chair away from the small table. "Magnificent. Who's the florist?"

"Alfonzo's. They do beautiful work."

Alexandra sat back down and peered at me. "You haven't answered my first question. But maybe I should rephrase it. Who gave you the bouquet? I've never seen roses so blue."

"Jack gave them to me," I said with a nonchalant toss of my head. "You know, because I'm having a baby. And maybe because he's sorry he wasn't more excited when I first told him I'm pregnant."

Alexandra's expression remained neutral, but something in her tone was not. "That's a mighty big apology. And a bit personal from a colleague, don't you think?"

"Not at all," I lied. "Lots of people have given me little gifts since they've learned I'm pregnant."

"Gifts for you or for the baby?"

I considered. "Well, mostly for the baby. I've already gotten three packs of onesies, and I'm not even sure what they are. But Ross gave me a gold bracelet. See?" I held up my right arm to display the glittering bangle.

"That's appropriate," Alexandra said, unimpressed. "He's your wealthy fiancé."

I looked at the stupendous bouquet propped in the chair like a third person at the table. A third, troublemaking person.

"Are you saying that Jack's gift is inappropriate?"

Alexandra laughed. "Everything about Jack Coltrane is inappropriate. That's only one of the reasons I like him."

"That's only one of the reasons I find him infuriating."

"Ah, so he does arouse some passion in your breast."

"I wouldn't call it passion," I protested.

"Strong feelings then," Alexandra concluded. "That's a start."

The conversation was not going at all as I'd hoped. Or was it?

"A start of what?"

Alexandra took a sip of her drink before answering. "I don't know. That's up to you."

I let that remark sink in for a moment. And then I said, my voice low, "Are you suggesting I have an affair with Jack?"

"Absolutely not. What an imagination, Anna. Pass the cashews, please."

Yes, I thought, what an imagination, Anna. I passed the dish of cashews.

"Well, what do you mean?" I asked.

"I just think it's good for you to know someone who

makes you really feel your feelings. Someone who shakes you up, challenges you, someone who makes you think."

I looked at my exotic friend. The style. The attitude. The intelligence.

"That someone is you," I replied.

"I'm not a man."

"Well, I've got Ross."

I've got Ross. It sounded like I had a disease. I've got the flu, I've got eczema, I've got shingles.

Alexandra reached for her bag. "Yes, indeed, you have. And I've got to get going. You'd better put those flowers in water soon."

"Each stem is in a little tube of water," I said. And then I thought, That must have cost a pretty penny.

Alexandra leaned into the bouquet and breathed deeply. "Lovely fragrance. Are you sure you have a big enough vase?"

"Of course. Don't be silly. The bouquet isn't that monstrous."

But I wondered, Did I have a large enough vase?

Our waiter appeared, and Alexandra asked for the check. Until then, he'd been entirely impersonal and professional. "Ma'am," he said now, "that's the biggest bouquet I've ever seen. And working here, I've seen a lot of flowers given to a lot of women. Whoever he is, he knows he's got someone very special."

The waiter walked off, and Alexandra grinned mightily.

"You look like the Cheshire cat," I said. "That's not necessarily a compliment."

"I think the Cheshire cat is quite fetching. Admit it, Anna. Flowers are a romantic gift."

"Not always," I said. "I send my mother flowers on Mother's Day."

"Don't pretend to be obtuse, Anna. It's very annoying."

The waiter reappeared. Alexandra grabbed the check and signed, and off went the waiter with a grin as wide as Alexandra's had been. Alexandra is a notoriously big tipper.

"Okay," I admitted, "maybe Jack's gift is romantic. But this is a romantic occasion. I'm having a baby. I'm bringing a new life into the world."

I knew how lame I sounded. I didn't need Alexandra to roll her eyes so dramatically.

"I need to leave," she said.

"Do you really have to go?" I said suddenly wanting very much not to be alone.

"I do. I've got work to do."

Alexandra headed off but was back within minutes.

"You changed your mind?" I asked hopefully.

"No. But I forgot to mention that I heard a name today you might want to consider. You know, for the kid."

"Oh."

"Wait, I wrote it down." Alexandra flipped open her wallet and extracted a yellow Post-It note. "Here."

She handed the note to me. It read: Mnuple.

"Um," I said, handing the note back to her, "where did you hear it?"

"Some show on NPR. I don't know if I got the spelling right. Anyway, keep it." She stuck the Post-It note to the table. "I'm off."

You're off, all right, I thought, watching Alexandra negotiate her way past a table at which were crammed two beefy middle-aged men in gray suits.

I left the bar a few minutes later. The Post-It note remained stuck to the table.

Later that night I lay in bed and thought. The whole thing, which at first had made me feel oddly excited, now was beginning to make me uncomfortable.

Jack Coltrane might have feelings for me. And instead of being repulsed or unconcerned, I was enticed by the possibility. Enticed and now disturbed. The idea of Jack's having feelings for me was one thing, but the idea of my having feelings for him in return was quite another.

But I didn't have feelings for Jack; I wasn't interested in

him romantically so there was no problem, was there? But there was a problem.

Be honest, Anna, I told myself. Jack's feelings alone have no power. What gives them power is your having feelings in return. For some horribly incomprehensible reason, you have feelings for Jack. Tiny feelings. Just the hint of feelings. But even those miniscule feelings are too much.

I remembered then something that Alexandra had said to me months earlier. I'd complained that I'd badly scuffed the toe of my pink suede pumps on the way back from Jack's studio that morning.

"I don't know why you spend so much time running over there," she'd said, looking innocently at her new manicure and not at me. "Most of your correspondence with Jack can be done by e-mail or fax."

I'd opened my mouth to respond and realized I had no response. No good one, anyway—nothing that made sense. And now, alone in my darkened bedroom, I wondered, Why did I spend so much time face-to-face with Jack when it wasn't strictly necessary?

I shivered with embarrassment. It didn't matter that there was no one who knew what I was thinking; my own conscience was ashamed of itself.

Why, why, why, had Jack given me those flowers? And for one wild moment I wondered, Had Jack tried to outdo Ross's gift? But Jack didn't know about the gold bracelet, he couldn't; I'd never mentioned it to him. Of course, he might have assumed that Ross had given me an expensive bauble; men like Ross are very skilled givers of high-price-tag gifts. But would Jack stoop to such a macho tactic? And to what purpose? To impress me. To offer his sincere apologies. To get me into trouble with Ross.

With a loud groan I tossed back the covers. If I couldn't sleep at least I could do something productive like read a book, rather than obsess about Jack and his damned flowers. And about my having happily accepted them. Because accepting those flowers was the closest I'd ever come to doing—to feeling—anything illicit. I wasn't so hormonal that I failed to realize a woman engaged to one man ought not to be titillated by another man's gift of flowers.

Even if the flowers were given in apology of rude behavior. Even if they were given by someone who was nothing more than a friend.

27

Practice to Deceive

The following night Ross stopped by on his way home from a late meeting with his accountant. The meeting, I learned, had been held at Morton's. Ross loves their beefsteak tomatoes; he forgoes the football-sized baked potatoes and passes on the bread.

"Alfonzo's."

I finished pouring hot water into my teacup before turning to him and saying, "Excuse me?"

Ross walked over to the bouquet of roses sitting on the dining table. "Those flowers must be from Alfonzo's. I recognize the style."

"Oh." It was all I could say. Please, please, please, I prayed, don't ask who gave them to me!

You've done nothing wrong, Anna, I told myself. But I didn't quite believe it.

Ross touched one of the blossoms with a perfectly manicured finger. "When did you get them?"

I felt faint. I didn't know if the truth was the best answer or the worst. I set the cup of tea on the countertop, afraid my hands would start to shake.

"What?"

"When did you buy them?" Ross looked from the flowers to me. "They're amazingly fresh. Alfonzo's has the freshest flowers. Of course, the prices are insane. But you know that. You've worked with Alfonzo's for a few events, haven't you?"

Was it possible I would be able to avoid both lying and telling the truth? Was it possible Ross didn't care to press me on the matter?

Was it possible I was such a coward?

"Um, yes," I said. "I have."

Ross looked at me with head cocked. Was it concern on his handsome face? Or suspicion?

"What's the matter, Anna? Do you feel sick? You look pale."

I laughed lightly and crossed my arms. It was a gesture of defense, or maybe one of avoidance.

"No, no," I said, "I'm fine. Just tired. I'm always tired these days."

"Promise me you'll try to get some sleep. Your clients can wait. Your health is more important right now."

I wondered, Only right now? Because I'm carrying your baby?

"I promise," I said.

Ross gave me a kiss on the cheek and hugged me gently. "I can't say I particularly like the color of those roses," he said, pulling away. "There's something strange about it."

"Mmm," I said, noncommittally.

When Ross left I fell onto the couch and breathed a troubled sigh.

28

A Rose by Any Other Name

When it comes to names for a baby, everyone and her sister has an opinion. And no one is shy about voicing it.

My mother, not usually the type to interfere in my life—some might say, in fact, that the day I moved out of the house and went off to college she heaved a huge sigh of relief at her newly empty nest—suddenly had several interesting suggestions to make.

"I've always loved the name Myrtle," she told me one afternoon during my weekly call to my parents. "You know, the myrtle has lovely fragrant flowers. Pink and white. Very pretty. I'll never forget the myrtle bushes I saw when your father and I took that package tour to Greece."

I repressed a groan. My mother hadn't been able to offer any advice on recovering my sanity when my high school boyfriend left me for my so-called best friend, or when I was starting my own business, but she could serve up suggestions for naming my unborn child.

"Mom," I said, quite calmly, "if I wanted to name my

child after a plant I'd choose Rosemary. Or Sage. Or Fern, or even Daisy. Not Myrtle."

"Now why do you just dismiss the idea of Myrtle?" my mother snapped. "Is it because you're thinking of one of those weird names, like, I don't know, Mergatroid or something?"

Mergatroid?

"No weird names, Mom," I assured her. "Ross doesn't like out of the ordinary names, and neither do I. We're sticking with the classics. Like Elizabeth or Catherine. And if it's a boy, then Stephen or William."

There was a moment of silence, and I dared to think my mother had dropped the subject.

"Mom?" I said, when the moment had gone on freakishly long.

My mother said, "Have you considered Hazel?"

That evening, I discovered that Ross had had an alarming change of heart.

After dinner we settled in my living room. I put on a Madelaine Peyroux CD and got comfortable with *Vogue* and a cup of tea. Ross stretched out on the couch and put his hands behind his head.

"I've been thinking," he said, musingly. "I want my son to stand out. I want him to be a take-charge kind of guy so he's going to need a take-charge kind of name. You know?"

"Sure," I said, innocently flipping through *Vogue,* sipping tea, paying only partial attention to my fiancé.

"And if she's a girl, well, I want the same thing. I want her to be a real standout. But not aggressive like a boy, of course. I want her to command attention but in a feminine way. I want her to be beautiful and strong but not bitchy. I see my daughter as a Bodecia or maybe an Anastasia."

I choked and reached for a napkin with my free hand. Had I heard Ross correctly? "Sorry?" I said brightly, dabbing my lips.

"Wait a minute," Ross replied, still more to himself than to me. "Didn't that Russian princess Anastasia wind up getting murdered? Or going insane? Something bad happened to her. No, I think a warrior princess makes a better role model after all." Now Ross looked directly at me and smiled. "Bodecia Davis. That has a nice ring to it, don't you think?"

"Um," I said, closing the magazine, "yes. It has a—ring. So, what names are you thinking about for a boy?"

"Caesar is my first choice," he replied, looking back to the ceiling. "But I have considered Thor. Or Attila. Attila Davis. King seems a bit much, a bit obvious. I don't want to throw my son's superiority in the faces of the lesser kids. Besides, someone might make a comparison to Elvis, and I really don't want that happening. No son of mine will die fat and on the toilet."

I thought I might be sick. Carefully, I took another sip of tea and wished it were a vodka tonic. What's next? I wondered. Famous historical battlegrounds? I could see it now: Meet little Waterloo and his sister Iwo Jima. Life isn't hard enough so we wanted to burden our offspring with provocative names that would hang around their wee necks like a big stinky albatross.

More important, we wanted everyone we meet to know how clever we are!

"Ross?" I said. "Maybe we should just wait on choosing a name, you know? I've heard stories of parents having a name all picked out, and then the baby is born and they take one look at her and realize the name is all wrong. And then they come up with another name. A brand-new name."

A nice, normal name like Robert or Marianne.

Ross smiled indulgently and rose from the couch. "All right. We won't make any decisions yet. No use in your getting upset and upsetting the baby."

I smiled faintly.

"But that doesn't mean I won't be thinking," Ross promised, planting a kiss on my forehead like a daddy. "You know me. I'm always thinking."

29

Green-Eyed Monster

How could I say no to what might be the last opportunity to wear my navy blue Ralph Lauren pants suit? Worn with a few strong gold accessories it would be just right for the party Ross and I were invited to at the home of a power couple he had met while vacationing with his brother in St. Barts. Ellen and Martin Mountjoy lived in a four million-dollar penthouse in the Four Seasons.

Everyone, Ross told me as we rode the elevator to the Mountjoys, was going to be there. Just about everyone was. Including my interesting colleague Jack Coltrane. I spotted him as soon as Ross and I came through the front door. He wasn't alone.

"Ross," I said, "why don't you go on in. I think I saw the Casablancas over by the buffet. I'm going to visit the ladies' room."

Ross looked down at me, puzzled. "But you went just before we left the apartment."

I smiled stiffly. "Yes, I did. But—"

"Of course." Ross nodded. "Right. I'll be—"

"I'll find you."

Ross melted into the crowd, and I walked right over to Jack.

"What are you doing here?" I asked by way of greeting.

A slow grin came to Jack's face. "Nice to see you, too."

"I just saw you three hours ago," I snapped. "I didn't think there was a need for niceties."

Let me explain why I was acting like a social cretin and Jack like a polite, civilized fellow. Next to Jack stood a woman no older than thirty. She was tall and statuesque with long brown hair I can only describe—begrudgingly—as flowing. At first glance it seemed as though she was swathed in an unwound bolt of gauzy fabric. At second glance I saw she wore a chiffon gown similar to something the female characters in *The Lord of the Rings* trilogy wear. Around her head was a thin circlet of what looked like gold but what was, I was sure, gold-plated silver.

My mood was not generous.

I had no desire to be introduced to this creature, but perversity won out over mature restraint. "Aren't you going to introduce us?" I asked, sweetly.

Jack eyed me with some amusement. It annoyed me. "Anna, this is Rowena. Rowena is an artist. She shows at JAW Gallery. Rowena, Anna."

I stuck out my hand. "And I'm an event planner."

Rowena stared at my outstretched hand for a full fifteen seconds—it felt like an hour—before giving it a limp little shake. I noticed she wore a chunky ring on every finger.

"Oh," she said, with barely a flicker of interest. Then she turned to Jack. "Darling, there's someone at the bar to whom I just must give greetings. I shan't be but a moment."

Shan't?

Rowena glided off toward the open bar, her dress flowing in her wake.

"Does she have a last name?" I asked. I didn't really want to know that bit of information either, but the woman's affectations must have rattled my brain.

Jack took a slow sip of his drink before answering. "Not that I know of."

Not, then, a serious relationship. And not a friend. Friends know each other's last names.

"You," I said, "are on a date with a woman and you don't know her last name?"

"That's right. As a matter of fact, I don't even know if she has a last name. You know how artists can be. And by the way, what makes you think I'm on a date? Rowena could be my cousin for all you know. My out-of-town-visiting-for-the-weekend cousin. From Milwaukee. Or Timbuktu."

"I know how artists can be," I shot back. "I'm dealing with one right now. And I think—no, I know—you're on a date because of the way Rowena—" I hesitated, suddenly embarrassed.

"Yes?"

"The way she touched your arm," I blurted. Please, I prayed, don't let me be blushing.

"Excellent observation." Jack's tone was laconic. "But why do you care?"

"I don't."

"Oh."

"You don't believe me?"

"Of course I believe you. Anna Traulsen never lies. Not even to herself."

"What's that supposed to mean?" I snapped, although suddenly I knew exactly what he meant.

"Hmm. Maybe I should join my date at the bar. My drink could use some freshening."

I just couldn't let it go. I just couldn't let him go.

"She looks like an actress in a cheesy summer Renaissance fair," I blurted. "Is she really an artist? What does she create? Mock-medieval pottery shards?" The moment the words were out of my mouth I regretted them. Were the hormones, I wondered wildly, making me regress to childhood? Not that I'd ever spoken nastily about anyone when I was a child. I was far too shy and repressed for that.

"That's not very nice," Jack said, although clearly he was half-amused.

"Well, you say mean things about Ross all the time."

"That's different."

"How?"

Jack's bantering tone changed instantaneously; suddenly, he sounded impatient, almost angry. "Do I really need to explain it to you? I hardly know Rowena. She's just my fairly amusing date for this fairly amusing party. But you're marrying Ross. You're having his baby."

Rowena chose that mortifying moment to return, a glass of champagne in each hand. She smiled at Jack seductively. I scurried away.

I found Ross staring up at a three-dimensional piece made of paint and found objects on canvas, mounted on the wall. His face was a mask of incomprehension. Or maybe fear.

I took a deep, steadying breath and tapped his shoulder.

Ross turned and smiled. "There you are," he said. "I thought I'd lost you."

"You didn't lose me." I slipped my hand into his.

"Where were you?"

"Talking to Jack. And his date."

"Jack Coltrane?"

"Yes." I heard an unanticipated note of defensiveness in my voice. Did Ross hear it, too? "Why?" I asked.

Ross's small frown indicated distaste. "I don't know how you tolerate working with that guy. He's just another pitiful wannabe. A whining artist. Who does he think he is?"

Blood rushed to my cheeks, and I let go of Ross's hand. Ross was being unfair. He was making himself feel superior by cutting down someone different from him. Someone not as fastidiously dressed or as neatly coiffed. Someone he couldn't understand.

Someone he considered a rival? The thought flickered across my mind and was gone.

I kept my mouth shut. I was mad at Jack. I certainly wasn't

going to defend him to my fiancé, the man who was the father of my child.

Father. Mother. Parents. Adults.

What a pair Ross and I are, I thought, suddenly ashamed of our immature behavior. Were we really such emotional idiots?

A sudden screech followed by a prolonged wail caused Ross and I—and every other guest—to turn. In the dead center of the room, a little boy was wrangling with a well-dressed woman in her early forties. The little boy was throwing what my mother used to call a temper tantrum but what is now generally referred to as a meltdown.

"I can't believe the Geils brought their two-year-old to this event," I whispered to Ross self-righteously. "What were they thinking?"

Ross shrugged. "Maybe they couldn't get a sitter."

Then, I thought, one of the Geils should have stayed home. I watched in horror as Johnston Geils, the now recovered heir to the Geils impressive car dealership fortune, dashed across the living room and hurdled into the legs of a waiter bearing a tray of drinks. Miraculously the waiter kept his balance and his tray. Johnston continued on his way, deftly avoiding the outstretched hands of well-meaning guests, and tore off into the hallway.

"That child is a disaster waiting to happen," I said, sotto voce.

Why, I thought, isn't he better behaved? Why aren't his parents better disciplinarians? And, I thought, it's an insult to the hostess to unleash a hellcat in her well-ordered home.

Where had Mrs. Geils disappeared to, anyway?

Ross shrugged. "I think it's fine. We're going to bring little Chestnut or Badger everywhere. Parties, vacations, concerts."

My stomach sank. We were? And it occurred to me then that Ross and I had never discussed parenting styles. Why would we have? We had decided we weren't going to be parents. As a consequence I knew absolutely nothing about my fiancé's views on, for example, corporal punishment or breast-feeding or homeschooling. And he knew absolutely nothing about mine. Ross and I were virtual strangers when it came to the basics. And when it came to choice of names. Chestnut? Badger?

"So," I said, oh-so-casually, "you'll watch the baby while you're talking business with a major broker?"

"Sure, why not?"

"Ross," I asked, struggling to keep the panic out of my voice. "Have you ever even held a baby?"

"No, but what's to learn?"

I didn't know. Maybe there really wasn't much to learn. I tried to remember the times I had held a baby. The number wasn't impressive. We were both so inexperienced.

Ross's voice called me back to the moment. "Anna," he said, "I have to talk to this guy. He's a friend of my dad's."

Ross strode off. I watched as he shook hands with a man about fifty dressed in a lightweight, pale gray, suede blazer; within a minute they were deep in conversation.

Ross was going to bring a baby to events like these? Ross was going to talk business with a squirming, drooling, ten-pound baby strapped to the front of his Armani suit?

Not likely. I knew as absolutely as I knew I was wearing Ralph Lauren that Ross would routinely be handing off the inconvenient baby to me at parties, restaurants, and concerts.

Because Ross wanted me to close down Anna's Occasions. He wanted me to be entirely employed in a new venture. He wanted me to be a full-time professional mother.

"Aaahh! My Judy Sowa! It's worth a fortune!"

I whirled around to see Johnston Geils smirking up at our hostess, clutching in his grimy hands a fistful of colored markers. Behind him, on the wall, hung a beautiful painting almost seven feet tall. A beautiful painting now marred by thick marker squiggles.

Your Judy Sowa was worth a fortune, I commented silently. The party was over. It was time to go home. And when I got there, I was going to dump those damn roses.

30

Woman to Woman

Kristen wanted to know if I was up to meeting for lunch. "Sure," I told her. "I'm usually done throwing up by ten o'clock."

We met at The Cheesecake Factory. Kristen loves their pizzas. For the first half hour she shot me questions about the state of my belly. Finally, I exploded. It was Kristen's obsession with my insides and the fact that all my troublesome insides could handle at the moment were dry bread sticks.

"You know," I snapped, "I'm not just a womb."

"I know, honey, I know," Kristen said soothingly.

"I'm still Anna," I said. "I'll always be Anna."

Kristen couldn't hide the look on her face that said, Poor, naive thing.

"I will," I repeated stubbornly.

"Anna, having a baby changes you forever. You're never just who you are. You're never just you. You're always someone's mother. I can't really explain it but . . ."

"But everything you do changes you forever," I argued. "Going to a particular college, moving to a particular city, marrying—or not marrying—a particular guy. Even seeing a particular movie or reading a particular book can change you forever. I swear I've never been the same since I read *Wuthering Heights*."

"That's all true," Kristen admitted. "But I don't know. Becoming a mother changes your identity so radically. At least it did for me. Maybe not every woman has that same experience."

Something deep inside told me they probably did. I looked at my friend and suddenly saw her as she was when I first knew her, still in her teens, her cheeks plump with health, her hair in a long fat ponytail, a pair of nerdy glasses hiding her wide eyes.

"Are you sad you aren't you anymore?" I said.

"I'm not sad," Kristen said readily. "Exactly. Sometimes I feel a bit wistful about the young girl I once was. The truth is I can hardly remember her. But Anna, believe me when I say I don't want to be who I was before I became a mother."

"I believe you," I said.

"There's just no point in dwelling on the past." Kristen paused before going on. "Still, sometimes I feel kind of burdened. Kind of encumbered. Maybe I'm just tired. I'd love a nice long nap! But I don't think I'm going to get one until B.J. leaves for college. Only sixteen more years to go."

Suddenly, I felt terrified. "Oh, Kristen, how do you do it? Please, tell me how to be a parent!"

"Anna," she said, "I have no idea how to be a parent. No one does. When you're a parent, there's no time for ideas or theories. You just act. You just do what comes naturally and hope it works."

"Sleeping comes naturally," I said, desperate. "How can I handle not sleeping?"

"You just will."

"I'm not so sure."

"I am. Look, Anna, I know I complain about being tired and overworked, but honestly? I'm really happy. Being a mother is great. It's the best. You're going to love it, and you're going to be wonderful. Really."

What was the point of arguing? "Okay," I said, resigned

to my friend's unfailing optimism. If Kristen didn't want to entertain the notion of my failure, why should I?

And then the conversation took the inevitable turn.

"Oh, by the way," Kristen said, leaning in as if about to impart a juicy secret, "I know I shouldn't butt in, but I heard the cutest name the other day and I thought you might want to consider it."

Et tu, Kristen?

"Oh?" I said brightly.

"It's Alchemy. You know, as in the ancient science of trying to produce gold. Or something like that. Isn't that adorable!"

Adorable? What, I wondered, was up with this rage for idiotic baby names? It had affected even my sensible, suburban, attorney friend.

"Uh, is it a boy's name or a girl's name?" I asked.

Kristen shrugged. "Either. That's one of the great things about it, it's so versatile."

I fought to turn an involuntary grimace into a smile. "Thanks, really. I'll, um, mention it to Ross but he's kind of conservative when it comes to names . . ."

Was there no end to my lies?

We parted soon after that. Kristen headed back to her husband and children, the people who largely defined her. I went back to my office, to the business I'd so carefully created and built. And on the way I wondered:

Was there any way to be in a loving, committed relationship and still remain in your own possession? Or did intimacy—true love—render that impossible?

I asked myself this question: Do I feel as if I'm in Ross's possession? The answer was: No.

I asked myself another question: Do I want to be in Ross's possession? Again the answer was: No.

And I had no idea if those answers mattered.

31

Babies 101

As far as future mothers-in-law went, Theresa Davis was promising. She called her son at home only once a week (although later I learned she called him at his office every day), treated me with respect (although later I learned she had hoped Ross would choose a younger bride), and to that point had largely kept her opinions about the wedding plans to herself (although later I learned she had tried to convince Ross to have the reception at the Davis's country club).

Mrs. Davis was very good at being almost invisible.

That is, until she found out I was carrying her grandchild. Then, suddenly, my future mother-in-law came roaring into plain sight. Suddenly, I was common property, someone to call every other day, someone to cuddle like a puppy. She touched me every time she saw me, my arms, my face, even my belly.

I'm not a touchy-feely sort of person. I'm not comfortable being grabbed and hugged and kissed and squeezed. But what could I say to my future mother-in-law? She was just so happy. She just wanted to be involved.

Mrs. Davis called me one evening at my apartment. She wanted us to have lunch sometime that week. She'd been to my office a few times so I suggested we meet there. Having lived in well-tended, well-policed suburbs all of her adult life, Mrs. Davis wasn't entirely comfortable traveling around the city on her own.

I'd just ended a call from a whiny client when Mrs. Davis appeared at the door. She was carrying a large monogrammed bag more appropriate for a weekend at the beach than a two-hour lunch at an upscale restaurant in the city. I wondered if there was a prettily wrapped wedding present inside.

After the requisite mauling, I retreated back behind my desk. Mrs. Davis dove into the depths of the bag and produced a sheaf of glossy pages obviously ripped from a magazine.

"What's this?" I asked, taking the pages.

"Information about the latest models of car seats. You know, it's never too early to be thinking about a car seat."

"A car seat?" I repeated idiotically.

"A starter car seat. For an infant. You know they won't discharge you from the hospital unless you have a car seat. Then, of course, as the baby gets older, you'll need a bigger seat, and you don't want to accept a hand-me-down because of the safety issue."

"What safety issue?" I asked, feeling for the first time in my life seriously stupid and uninformed. Ignorance is not bliss, I thought. It's embarrassing.

"The standards improve all the time, Anna," Mrs. Davis explained. "One year a car seat meets code and the next year, poof! A child has shot through a windshield and the seat's no good."

I felt slightly nauseous. The baby was still months from making his or her appearance and already I was forced to consider its safety accoutrements. And in the meantime, there was something else monumental I had to think about. My wedding.

"I was thinking," I said, "that maybe we could talk for a moment about my bridal registry?"

"Oh." Mrs. Davis looked truly surprised. "What about it?"

"Well, um, I noticed that not many items have been bought yet. I was wondering—"

Mrs. Davis laughed a fond, motherly laugh. "Oh, silly Anna! Of course no one's been buying from your bridal registry! Everyone's waiting to see your baby shower registry. I mean, what's more important now, right? The baby, of course! A baby is much more exciting than a wedding!"

What she meant to say was that a baby is much more exciting than a bride.

"Oh," I said.

I thought, I want my wedding. Am I a bad person to want the wedding I planned even if I am pregnant? I want to be a bride. I have a right to be a bride!

Don't I?

Mrs. Davis dug in the massive bag once more. But any thoughts of a wedding present—perhaps something from Tiffany?—had already been crushed.

"And by the way, Anna," she said, "I want to give you this."

Finally, Mrs. Davis extracted a carefully folded piece of yellow, lined paper and handed it to me.

"What's this?" I said, unfolding the paper with trepidation. What other piece of basic safety information was I lacking?

It was a handwritten list of names.

"Well," Mrs. Davis explained, "I knew you'd want to consider some of the Davis family names for Ross's child so I thought I'd save you some time by making a list of the most important ones."

Ross's child? Ah, I was simply the vessel, the receptacle, the human tote bag.

"Important?"

"Yes. Like, for example, Temperance. See? At the top of the list."

"Temperance?" I repeated senselessly.

"Temperance was Ross's great-great grandfather's wife's third cousin." Mrs. Davis lowered her voice conspiratorially. "She died in childbirth. The poor thing was only eighteen. I always thought it would be nice to honor her memory, but as you know, I just had the two boys."

No, you certainly couldn't name a boy Temperance, I thought stupidly. But what was I giving birth to, a pilgrim?

I smiled weakly, and when Mrs. Davis once more stuck her hand into the depths of her bag of tricks, I slipped the paper into the trash can under my desk.

"We'd better get going," I said.

Mrs. Davis didn't seem to have heard me. She smiled triumphantly and held up what looked exactly like a wad of dirty dreadlocks. "Don't you love it!" she cried. "It's a sweater. I had it made especially for the baby by one of the ladies at the nursing home where I do volunteer work. Isn't it gorgeous!"

"I think," I said, fighting a sudden gag response, "that if we don't leave now we'll lose our reservation."

32

Anna, Supersized

It's one of the miserable truths of life: When you absolutely can't be late for something, like an important meeting or your best friend's wedding, something will rise up and try its mightiest to make you late.

I had a meeting at nine o'clock with a disgruntled client; said client owed me two thousand dollars for services already rendered. I hoped to solve the dispute without the assistance of a lawyer, so it was important I be on time, cool, calm, and collected.

Of course, my alarm failed to go off. When I woke with a start, it was already five after eight. Frantically, I showered, gulped my vitamins, and sloshed down a glass of fortified juice. And then I reached for a pair of my favorite pants, stylish, reliable, confidence-inspiring navy pants. In went one leg; in went the other. And then . . .

It was bound to happen sooner or later. It happened sooner. It happened overnight. The dreaded widening of the waistline. Just one more confirmation of the fact I was still struggling to accept. The fact of pregnancy. As if breast swelling and tenderness weren't enough; as if morning sickness wasn't enough.

One last time I tried to close the pants, but it was to no avail. With a groan of disbelief and frustration, I tore the pants off and tossed them onto the floor. I swear it was the first time I'd ever mistreated a piece of clothing.

I looked at the crumpled trousers and felt pity for them. It wasn't their fault they didn't fit. It was my fault. My body's fault. The baby's fault!

Anna, I scolded, calm down. Don't blame your unborn child for your sudden girth spurt, even though it is her fault. No, his fault. The baby was probably a boy. This was probably his idea of a joke.

Deep breath, Anna. If your thickening middle is anyone's fault it's Ross's. And he'll look spectacular at the wedding, trim and fit in his custom-tailored tuxedo while you, the bride, the person supposed to be the most beautiful center-of-attention woman at the wedding, will look ludicrous and hairy and swollen.

I picked up my poor navy pants and hung them carefully in the closet.

It was an impossible situation. If the pregnancy progressed normally there was no way I would fit into the dress by the wedding. And no, the dress couldn't just be let out. It would have to be completely redesigned and that would cost money and would there be enough time? I so loved the dress as I'd designed it.

Dieting, of course, was out of the question. The baby's growth might be stunted, and I'm far too mature and responsible to do anything that might harm a child. My child.

Besides, I thought grumpily, tossing yet another pair of useless pants onto the bed, these days you could get arrested for child abuse simply by looking at your son or daughter with a scowl. Discipline was now equated with criminality.

And then it began. I was taken over by a demon of irrational discontent and random pissiness. I proceeded to stomp around my bedroom—I am not a stomper by nature—a not very coherent rant roaring through my head. It went something like this:

Here I am giving birth to a baby who will be an American citizen because I'm an American citizen—and I'm certainly not getting on a plane until said baby has safely landed!—and that's fine except that, unbelievably, certain school districts in this great country of ours have outlawed the Honor Roll because it makes some kids feel bad about themselves.

I yanked a cotton cardigan from the closet and asked myself, Well, what kind of sense does that make? Everyone is good at something; everyone is bad at something. Better to learn that lesson early; better to find your talents, develop and hone them, and eventually learn how to make a living with them.

That's what I would encourage my child to do, anyway. My child who was making me late for a very important meeting! Didn't he understand I would need every cent I could make for his private education?

How, I wondered, rejecting silk knit top after silk knit top (silk knit does not work well with bulge), how does eliminating the Honor Roll gel with the notion of democracy and all it implies about personal freedom, individuality, and self-reliance? America was supposed to be a melting pot, a country that celebrated diversity. Right?

I turned to the linen blouses hanging at the far end of my closet and wondered crazily if it was too early for linen. Of course it was too early for linen! It was spring in New England. Had I already lost my sense of style and appropriateness? And how, I wondered, did eliminating the Honor Roll coincide with a parent's favorite feel-good message: "You are special. You are unique. There's no one else in the entire world just like you. No one else has your face or your thoughts or your talents."

I reached for a now defunct Ann Taylor black leather belt and wondered, Whatever happened to the notion of healthy competition? What ever happened to those inspiring slogans like Be all you can be! Just do it! Reach for the stars!

No, I thought, tossing the belt onto the floor of the closet, which I now thought of as the donation pile. Some parents and so-called child-care professionals now believe it's better to level the playing field, pretend that everybody's the same, no better or worse than anyone else. Of course that's never worked and it never will, but people—entire cultures!—will never learn from their mistakes!

My shoes. My beloved shoes. I stared down at my slippered feet. Had my feet started to swell? I'd read that feet tend to grow half a size or more as a result of pregnancy and that they never return to their pre-pregnancy size. I already wear a size nine. I wondered, Would I become a regular Bozo the Clown?

I scanned the three racks of shoes crammed into my bedroom closet. The strappy pink sandals. The lime green, patent leather pumps. The faux crocodile skin slides. The gray suede pumps. Was it all over for them?

I thought about my boots. All five pairs of them. My precious boots, from ankle to thigh-high, doomed now to a dusty life at the back of my closet or tossed in a bin at some secondhand shop in Somerville.

I walked over to the blond wood dresser across from my bed and slid open a drawer of bras and panties. How long would it be before I transformed into a female version of the Hulk and all that lace and silk was ripping at the seams?

I slammed the drawer. No wonder, I thought, the American educational system lags behind that of other developed nations. No wonder there's so much drug abuse among preteens. No wonder kids are having oral sex with multiple partners at the tender age of thirteen.

I walked back to my closet and scowled at my size 8 blouses.

Being fat really stinks, I thought. Where did the myth of the jolly fat person come from, anyway? And now the experts were saying that obesity is at epidemic proportions in the United States. Would my own child fall prey to that awful disease?

Hordes of fat children squeezing themselves into school bus and movie theatre seats too small for their giant butts. Everywhere you went there were children. The world was lousy with them. Why was I bringing another child into the already overpopulated, war-torn, poverty-blasted, and disease-riddled world?

Because the pregnancy was thrust upon me and I didn't have the heart—or the guts—to end it.

I grabbed another pair of pants from the closet and wondered, Was depression a common problem pre-partem, too?

33

Epiphany

I sat on a bench in the Public Garden, a book closed on my lap. It was a beautiful day but I saw nothing of the flowers and the newly green leaves.

The tumult of emotions I'd experienced the morning before while dressing had frightened me. The panic and rage, the hints of desperation and despair—who was I? Not Anna. At least, not the Anna I'd known for thirty-seven years.

What was happening to me? Who was I becoming?

A mother and her little girl were walking along the paved path. I watched as they detoured onto the grass and went down to the water. The mother took a clear plastic bag from her purse; it was filled with small chunks of bread. Together they began to toss the bread to the ducks. Both mother and daughter had bright blonde hair; I wondered how many other traits they shared.

And I wondered about my own child. Would she have my auburn hair and blue eyes? Would she be tall like me, or would she favor Ross's family and have to shop in the petite section? Would my child have perfect eyesight, like Ross, or would he have to wear glasses or contacts like my brother and me? Would my child be interested in art or politics or sports or business or all of those? Who would my child be all on her own?

And suddenly, I wanted very badly to know the answers to those questions. Suddenly, I couldn't wait to meet the little boy or girl growing inside me.

I watched the mother and her daughter and thought, I can have that. I am going to have that. Someday, before long, I'll be feeding scraps of bread to the ducks with my own child and cherishing every moment of it.

Wow.

I am going to have a baby. I whispered the words aloud. I am going to have a baby.

And it was wonderful. I was flooded with joy, and it was pure. It wasn't colored by stress over the wedding plans, or Mrs. Kent's sometimes unnerving behavior, or the contractor's latest blunder at the condo. The joy I felt had nothing at all to do with anyone but the baby and me. Not even with Ross.

So what if I swelled to gigantic proportions? So what if my honeymoon was postponed for months or years? What did it matter that I might have to put my business on the back burner for a while?

All that really matters, I realized, is what exists between my child and me. And what exists is love.

Suddenly I became aware, really aware, of the world around me—the slightly chilled April breeze, the squawking ducks, the giggling girl, the bright red of the early tulips. And I felt a deep sense of peace along with a great sense of excitement. Oddly, the feelings were thoroughly compatible. It was an epiphany, the moment at which I really accepted the fact that I was going to be a mother—a rare moment when I was still, quiet, and alone.

But not really alone, I thought. Never really alone again.

34

Hauntings

There was no reason to mention the night of the party when I'd been so nasty about Jack's date. Personally, I was hoping to forget my immature behavior; I hoped Jack already had. Because I'd realized in a calmer moment that I must have been experiencing a flash of jealousy due to a silly, passing crush probably brought on by hormones—the bane of my existence!

Did I really want Jack Coltrane as a boyfriend? Did I really want rude, grumpy, smug Jack Coltrane as my lover?

Absolutely, positively not. Besides, I was marrying Ross in September.

"There you are," I said. "I've got the sketches for the Gott party space."

Jack tromped into the studio. His hair was wild. I noticed he must have been in the sun since I'd seen him last; his face and neck were bronzed. Jack was not a man for sunblock. I worried about his contracting skin cancer—can we be any more paranoid about the sun?—but I also thought he looked very attractive with a tan—very Mediterranean; his dark brown eyes seemed even darker and more liquid.

"I got held up by traffic."

"Your unspoken apology is accepted," I said, shaking off the entirely inappropriate thoughts of Jack's sun-darkened body. "Besides, I've been keeping busy." I held up the oversized glossy magazine I'd been reading.

"What's so fascinating?"

"I'm reading an article on the latest developments in digital photography. I'm not sure I understand it all but it's kept me occupied."

Jack tossed his bag onto one of the worktables. "Since when do you read *Photo-Op*?"

"Since you were late, and it was either read this magazine or snoop through your files. And I know how you hate people who snoop."

"Fair enough. So, anything else worthwhile? I haven't looked at that issue yet."

"Well," I said, flipping back a few pages, "there's an interesting piece about this photographer named Leslie Curtin. I can't say I like her work very much. What's shown here, at least. But she's certainly provocative. Do you know her?"

Jack turned away. It was a moment or two before he answered. "I knew her."

I waited for more, but there was nothing.

"Are you going to tell me how you knew her? I mean, did you work together back in the olden days, when I was still a schoolgirl?"

Jack turned back to face me. The black look on his face told me that my lame teasing had not been a good idea.

"It was a long time ago," he said shortly. "I've forgotten most of what went on."

Ah, I thought. So something had "gone on." But what? And I wondered, Had Jack really forgotten what had happened long ago or had he blocked it out?

"I'm not asking for details," I said. "But if you don't want to talk about it . . ."

"I don't."

"Okay," I said. I closed the magazine and tossed it aside,

as if I didn't care. But I did. In spite of the promise I'd made to myself after that awful party to put all questions about Jack's personal life out of my head, I was curious. What had gone on between Jack Coltrane and Leslie Curtin in the dark and distant past? One thing seemed abundantly clear. It had to have been a romantic relationship. One that ended badly.

I snuck a look at Jack; he was frowningly absorbed in work. I realized that he'd never mentioned a serious relationship to me, but why would he? Most men don't easily open up about their personal life, especially about their past romantic relationships. And Jack, I reminded myself, was primarily a colleague, not a friend. A sometimes churlish colleague. What did I expect from him? A tearful confession of youthful heartbreak, offered as casually as a comment about the previous night's Leno show?

There was really no reason for me to be hanging around Jack's studio, so I stopped pretending to read e-mail on my Blackberry, stuck it back in my purse, and walked to the door.

"Anna?"

Jack was looking at the screen of his computer, his right hand on the drawing wand.

"Yes?" I asked, my hand already on the doorknob.

Without looking away from his work he said, "We were involved."

"Oh," I said, casually. "Okay." And I left.

35

Curiosity Kills

Before going home that afternoon I detoured to the Barnes and Noble in the Prudential Mall. In the extensive magazine collection I found the current issue of *Photo-Op*. I pulled it from its slot, and with a quick glance to the left and to the right, I opened to the table of contents.

As I stood there pretending to be a casual reader I wondered crazily if my true motives were obvious. Reason quickly assured me that for all anyone knew I was interested in learning about zoom lenses. Only I knew that what interested me about the magazine was the picture of Leslie Curtin that accompanied the feature article. It wasn't a very good picture. I wondered why a photography magazine would print something so dark and muddy. About all I could tell was that she was very thin and had long hair. Her clothes didn't give a clue as to when the photo was taken. Maybe this is an old picture, I thought. Maybe now she's fat and bald. It was an unworthy thought, but there it was.

I replaced the issue of *Photo-Op* and reached for another magazine about the world of photography. And then another, and another.

I scanned for every mention of Leslie Curtin. The mere mention of her name had rattled Jack. So, who was this woman? What exactly had happened all those years ago? Jack said they'd been involved. I wondered, Had Jack and Leslie been married?

And why did I want to know? Simple female curiosity, I told myself briskly. Women like to know the stories of their friends' lives. Women like to understand. Understanding some of Jack's past might make me better able to deal with him in the present.

The magazines didn't tell me much. Leslie Curtin lived in Los Angeles; she summered in Martha's Vineyard. From that information I surmised she was doing quite well as a photographer. Or maybe she had another source of income; maybe she was independently wealthy. There was no way to know. She'd gone to the University of Chicago undergraduate and had gotten a Masters in Fine Arts from the Rhode Island School of Design. All pretty standard stuff. Not the sort of information I was hoping to find.

For a moment I considered flipping through every other photography-related periodical on the racks—at quick glance there were about fifteen. And then sanity took hold. Really, Anna, I told myself, don't get crazy about this. Besides, there's a much easier way to get the information. You can Google her from the privacy of your own home.

I stuck the third magazine back into its slot on the rack and left the store. As I passed through the mall's revolving doors and into the early evening sunshine, I realized that a Google search might yield only the sort of information I'd already gleaned from magazines. Even Leslie Curtin's own web site was unlikely to reveal a list of her former lovers.

I wondered if I knew anyone who could tell me something about Jack's past. And if I did know someone, I wondered if I would dare to ask. Because he or she would inevitably ask why I wanted to know about Jack Coltrane's former love affairs. And what would I reply? What could I possibly say when I was engaged to another man and pregnant with our child?

I stopped on the corner of West Newton and Huntington Avenue to wait for the green light. Traffic was heavy; it's always heavy in Boston. No wonder Jack had been late. And while I waited I wondered if my interest in Jack's romantic past was mere curiosity about someone I saw almost every day of the week. No. I had no desire to know the intimate details of my mail carrier's life.

The walk sign finally turned green, and I crossed Huntington Avenue. Not far off the corner is my favorite nail salon. I decided to stop for a manicure. Sure, I'd had one just three days earlier, but sporting the three-carat rock made me obsessively concerned with the state of my nails. I took a seat on the brocade couch to wait my turn. A recent issue of *People* caught my attention, and I began to browse.

There was an article about a California boy who'd lost his arm to a shark. Even though he'd defied the lifeguard's orders to leave the water, the boy's family was suing said lifeguard for negligence. Several celebrity moms were taking up a collection for the boy's hospital bills.

There was a mention of a minor celebrity who had committed suicide after the half-hour comedy he'd starred in wasn't picked up for a second season.

There was a report that the wife of a major celebrity was undergoing a stomach stapling operation.

And there was yet another short piece about yet another May/male–December/female celebrity couple. Disgusted, I tossed the magazine aside.

Really, Anna, I chided myself, since when have you become so interested in gossip? Jack's personal life is his personal life. Not your property. Anyway, why do you need to know about his past? It's not like he's someone important in your life. It's not like he's Ross.

The smiling technician beckoned to me, and I rose to follow her.

36

Libido Limbo

We met at Velvet for a drink before going off to the Huntington Theatre to see a revival of *Cat on a Hot Tin Roof.* The outing had been my idea, but now I had little enthusiasm for light conversation or for dramatic performance.

The situation with Ross and the bedroom had really begun to worry me. I wanted to talk to my friends about the problem, but unlike Alexandra or Michaela, I rarely brought up the topic of sex; I never, ever talked about the particulars of my sex life. And whenever someone veered too close to sharing the particulars of her sex life, I found an excuse to leave the room. Some things are just meant to be private, like how much money you make, and what you eat straight from the carton when you're depressed and alone, and what you do or do not do when your clothes are off.

I looked at my friends: Kristen was trying to engage Michaela in small talk; Tracy and Alexandra were having more luck with each other. So far no one had commented on my silence. Being pregnant, I thought, somehow excuses you from having to be properly social at all times. "Oh, don't mind her. I know she's been kicking the leg of the table for the past ten minutes but, you know, she's pregnant."

The waiter brought us our drinks—a martini for Alexandra, champagne for Michaela, a light beer for Kristen, and a cranberry juice with sparkling water for me. Well, I thought, at least my drink is the prettiest.

Everyone took a first appreciative sip, and I thought, Maybe I'm being overly sensitive about Ross's lack of interest in sex. Maybe I have nothing to complain about in the end, as long as he isn't interested in having sex with some other woman, and I'm pretty sure he isn't. Anyway, I'm not even all that interested in sex.

Still, I wanted Ross to be interested. I wanted to feel wanted. I wanted him to want me.

"Is a man ever really too tired for sex?" I blurted. Kristen's eyes widened, and Tracy cleared her throat, but I was undeterred. "I mean, if a man says, 'Not tonight honey, I'm tired,' is he lying?"

Alexandra nodded. "I'd say there's a good chance he's lying. It could be he's having an affair and doesn't want to waste his energy on you. It could be that he's caught an STD from his mistress. Or 'I'm too tired' might really mean he's been traumatized somehow and has lost total interest in sex and just the sight of your naked body causes his penis to deflate. Which could also mean that he's finally realized he's gay."

Kristen shook her head, clearly amazed. "Where," she asked no one in particular, "does she get this stuff?"

"You should be writing for *True Confessions* with that imagination," I said.

"You asked my opinion."

"I think I want to hear another opinion."

"Well," Kristen said, "speaking as a woman who's been married for eleven years, I think it's perfectly valid for a man to be too tired for sex, just like it's valid for a woman to be too tired for sex. I mean, sometimes Brian has worked his usual shift and then overtime, and then he's had to take the truck to the shop or stop in to see his mother on the way home. She's not doing too well, you know; she's diabetic. Anyway, some nights he practically crawls into bed. Some nights he's even too tired to eat dinner! I can't expect him to make love to me when he's been working so hard all day. Can I?"

Alexandra sighed and looked at me as if to say, From what happy valley has this innocent sprung? "No offense, honey," she said, "but if you were Pamela Anderson he'd have the energy."

"That's mean," I said.

"That's reality."

Michaela, who had been silent until this point, now offered her opinion. "I don't believe the 'too tired' excuse is real for women, either. Be honest. When you say you're too tired to fool around, doesn't it really mean you're just not interested? I mean, how much energy does it take to just lie there? Which is really all you have to do to meet the minimum requirements."

I wondered, Did Michaela really just lie there? I couldn't see it, but then again, I really didn't want to.

Alexandra raised her eyebrows but wisely made no comment. "Anna?" she said. "What brought up this topic? Has Ross been failing to perform his marital duties?"

"We're not married yet," I pointed out. "And yes, Ross has been—failing to perform. Since I told him I was pregnant he's lost interest in sex. Sex with me, anyway. But he won't talk about it. He just avoids me, and when he can't avoid me he tells me he's tired. Really, how tired can he possibly be? He's not mining for coal twelve hours a day. He's not even in the corporate trenches. Not really. His poor assistant Tad does an awful lot of his work."

"And," Michaela drawled, "Ross is in peak physical condition. I'm sure it's not as if he can't perform."

I shot a look at Michaela, who shrugged elaborately. "What?" she said. "How can a woman help but notice that tight butt?"

"Just because you notice something doesn't mean you have to talk about it," Kristen said angrily. Then, she blushed. "Not that I've ever noticed Ross, you know, in that way!"

"Anyway," Michaela went on, "a man who spends as much time as Ross does on his appearance wants the attention." She looked at the others—not at me—as if for confirmation. "He's not spending hours at the gym and watching his diet just for his health. He's doing it for the admiring glances of the ladies."

"And for his fiancée," I snapped.

Michaela looked at me and seemed surprised to learn I was still there.

"Oh, sure. For her, too."

Why am I friends with her, I wondered, not for the first time. Can I retract the invitation to the wedding? Can I send an unvitation?

"Let's drop the subject," I said testily. It wasn't as if I was hearing any real and useful advice on how to deal with my libido-less fiancé.

"I'm sure everything will be all right," Kristen said with a knowing pat on my arm.

Her condescension annoyed me even more than Michaela's hitherto unknown familiarity with the shape of my fiancé's butt. "Of course it will be all right," I snapped. "Everything's already all right. I shouldn't have said anything."

"Has anyone seen the new Baz Lurhman film?" Alexandra asked brightly.

Tracy grabbed onto the new topic like a drowning woman grabbing for a life raft. "Yes, I have, have you? I've been dying to talk about it with someone."

They launched into an animated discussion about the movie; Kristen made small talk at Michaela, who didn't even pretend to listen; and I sulked. A fat lot of good it had done to ask for my girlfriends' advice. From now on, I vowed, I'm keeping my personal life personal.

37

Carpe Diem

What, I wondered, as I kneeled on the old but well-preserved Oriental carpet, can Mrs. Kent possibly find so fascinating in a scale drawing?

Earlier that morning I'd taken exact measurements of the room where Mrs. Kent wanted the party to be held. It was at the very back of the house and opened onto a splendid garden. And now, as I worked on the plan, I was aware of Mrs. Kent's unnecessary presence just behind me on that overstuffed couch. Every day was the same; Mrs. Kent was just—there.

Maybe, I thought, I should speak to the officious Ms. Butterfield next time I found her lurking in the hall and explain my discomfort. But I rejected that idea as potentially incendiary. Who was I to criticize the behavior of my employer? Besides, I wasn't sure I had the nerve to approach La Buttercup unless it was a matter of life and death.

I wondered as I drew in a center table, Maybe Mrs. Kent thinks I'm going to steal her silver. Anna Traulsen, supposed good girl, worms her way into the homes of the rich and famous only to case the joints and make off one night with the family jewels.

Or maybe, I thought, Mrs. Kent is lonely; maybe she just likes the company of someone else in the room. She wasn't really a bother, was she? It wasn't as if she kept up a stream of chatter; in fact, she never spoke a word until I asked a question. And it wasn't as if she was staring at me fixedly, watching for mistakes. In fact, she sat quite silently on the overstuffed couch reading a novel or book of poetry. Mrs. Kent favored Edith Wharton and Edna St. Vincent Millay; neither choice much surprised me.

"You seem like a nice young woman," Mrs. Kent said, apropos of nothing.

I almost tottered to the floor; it wasn't a long fall, but it would have been an embarrassing one. "Thank you," I murmured.

"Are you?"

My head shot up. I found Mrs. Kent staring intently at me from her perch on the overstuffed couch. I laughed nervously.

"I, uh, I think so. Yes. I'm a nice person. I try to be."

"Too nice," said with the air of a hanging judge pronouncing a sentence of guilty. "I sense you are too nice a person, Anna."

"Can anyone really be too nice?" I asked rhetorically, and against my better judgment. I wasn't there to discuss the flaws and foibles of my character. I was there to work.

Mrs. Kent showed her magnificently perfect teeth in what I thought might be a smile. "Absolutely," she declared. "There is a difference, my dear, between a kind and thoughtful person and a martyr. A difference between having a generous nature and allowing yourself to be taken advantage of by every grasping, needy specimen who comes along."

I was too stunned to be insulted. Besides, I sensed Mrs. Kent wasn't insulting me as much as she was trying to educate me. In her own interesting way.

"Yes," I said. "I suppose there is."

And then, in what I was to learn was a common habit, Mrs. Kent changed conversational directions without warning.

"You know, my dear," she pronounced, "there's nothing good about getting old except that you stop caring so much about lots of ridiculous things that used to occupy your precious time. When you're fifty, sixty, seventy, you realize—if you're smart, of course—that you just don't have any time to waste caring a damn about an extra pound, or the stray hairs that have been appearing in the strangest places since you turned forty, or the liver spots and skin tags that have been wreaking havoc with your complexion for the past ten years or so."

"Oh," I said. I was slightly horrified. Old people were monsters, and I would be one, too! I did a quick calculation: When my as-yet-unborn child was twenty, I would be almost sixty. Certainly, I would repulse my own child!

"But that's it, my dear," Mrs. Kent went on with a magnificent sigh. "There's nothing else good about growing old. Nothing. Except maybe not being dead. But even that's debatable."

I could see that. Who wouldn't rather be dead than, say, suffering a horrible, prolonged, and ultimately fatal disease? But still. I didn't want to accept Mrs. Kent's thoroughly negative view of aging.

"What about wisdom?" I countered boldly. "What about wisdom and a sense of peace that comes with experience?"

But Mrs. Kent was having none of it. "A myth, my dear," she said firmly. "Very few people learn from their mistakes. Most old people are as stupid and wrongheaded and prejudiced as they were in their youth and middle age."

"But surely some people achieve wisdom," I protested. An image of Katharine Hepburn came to mind. She was wise, wasn't she? I'm not a Catholic but I'm pretty sure the pope is wise, too, and he's quite elderly. The Queen Mother seemed wise. At least, she was always sporting that beatific smile. "Surely some people make it a point to learn from their mistakes." I almost added, "I do."

Mrs. Kent dismissed my silly notion with a wave of her bejeweled hand.

"Fine. So you're an eighty-year-old with wisdom to impart. Well, it doesn't matter at all. Nobody listens to the elderly. The young find us laughable. Our adult children find us inconvenient. That's when we're not being depressing reminders of their own mortality. The government would prefer if we conveniently died en masse. The drug companies would like us to linger on and get sicker."

"That can't be entirely true," I murmured. But how would I know? Aside from my neighbor Mr. Audrey, and now my client Mrs. Kent, I didn't know anyone over the age of seventy. Except for my parents, of course. But my parents were different. They were—well, they were my parents.

And would I come to consider them an inconvenience? Would I come to see them as depressing reminders of my own mortality? Was there something wrong with me that I was almost thirty-eight years old and hadn't yet come to recognize them as—old?

"The stink of decay lingers around us, Anna." Mrs. Kent's voice was sepulchral in its tone. Her face had taken on an expression of exaggerated angst last seen in a silent movie. What must the young Beatrice Kent have been like onstage!

"Why are you telling me all this?" I knew I sounded angry. I was.

Suddenly, Mrs. Kent was full of life and purpose. She scooted forward in her chair and pointed a bejeweled finger at me. Sapphire, I noted automatically. And diamonds. Many diamonds.

"Because life is short, my dear Anna," Mrs. Kent said, with force. "And you're dead a very, very long time. So, my dear, whatever it is that you're not doing even though you want to do it, whatever it is you're avoiding out of fear or laziness, do it. Face it. Seize the day, my dear Anna. Before it's too late."

I left Mrs. Kent's mansion at four that afternoon, completely exhausted. It wasn't the work that had tired me; it was my estimable employer.

I wondered. Mrs. Kent had lots of money and most of it old, not in any great danger of dissolving, as far as I could tell. She lived in a magnificent house on the corner of Marlborough and Berkeley. Her wardrobe was lovely and obviously expensive. How, then, could she be so negative, so bitter?

I reached Boylston Street just as the light turned red for pedestrians. Two women, probably in their seventies, stood arm in arm at the corner with me, waiting for the green light. They had the air of old friends, two people completely comfortable with each other. They seemed happy. At least, they seemed to be enjoying the moment.

I thought again of Mrs. Kent.

What did I know of her personal life? Not much, just a few facts. (Of course, I'd researched her when she offered me the job.) At the age of twenty-one she'd married Ambrose Williams Kent, whose family and fortune were both old and well established; not long after she'd become a society hostess to reckon with. For almost thirty years she had been on the board of the Isabella Stewart Gardner Museum; for forty years she'd been the chairwoman of a charity she'd established to help "wayward girls." She had two sons, both now in their fifties. I'd heard from one of Ross's friends that they had both established vanity businesses and that they lived in Cohasset. Ross had mentioned that the older son, Charles, owned a second home in Tortola. The younger, Francis, spent four months of the year in Europe. All together, Mrs. Kent had five grandchildren.

Not much information at all.

The light turned green, and I stepped into the street.

Maybe, I thought, Mrs. Kent had never been deeply in

love. Or maybe she had been deeply in love and betrayed by her lover. Maybe she'd resented having to be a mother; maybe her sons resented her for resenting them.

Maybe, although she looks healthy enough, Mrs. Kent is dying of cancer. Maybe Beatrice Kent was just born this way, able to cast a cold eye on the stark realities of life, unsentimental, unromantic, a pragmatist.

I was almost to the loft when something else Mrs. Kent had said that afternoon came back to me.

"Better," she proclaimed, "to regret actions you have taken than to regret not having had the courage to take them in the first place."

I wondered if I would ever know if she was right.

38

What's in a Name

Ross and I were spending a quiet night at home. Rather, at the half-finished condo that would be our home once we were married, once I had sold my own apartment on Roland Street. I'd told Ross that I'd spoken to several real estate agents about the listing, but that was a lie. I'd put off making it official; the idea of selling my home made me sad. Besides, I told myself, the apartment was sure to sell immediately once it was on the market. There was no rush in listing it when the wedding was still months away.

After dinner I loaded the dishwasher—that appliance had been hooked up the week before—and Ross leaned against the center island, watching me.

"I spoke to my mother today," he said.

"Oh? How is she?"

"Fine. She and Dad had dinner last night with the Cirillos. She was all excited about telling Mrs. Cirillo she's going to be a grandmother. Aggie Cirillo is one of those professional grandmother types. Mom says she's always pulling out photos and report cards and bragging about how her grandchildren are the most perfect little angels."

"Oh," I said. I poured liquid detergent into its compartment and closed the door of the dishwasher. "That sounds annoying."

"By the way, my mother wants to know what the baby will be calling her."

I shrugged. "I don't know. Grandma, I guess."

"Isn't that usually what a kid calls his mother's mother?"

Was it? I'd mostly grown up without grandparents. All four had died before I was five. And for the life of me I couldn't remember what I'd called any of them.

"I'll ask my mother about it," I promised. I pushed Start, and the expensive, almost silent, Bosch began its wash cycle.

"She was thinking maybe Nana."

My distaste must have been all too obvious.

"You don't like Nana?" Ross asked.

"Not particularly," I admitted.

"Well, my mother really likes it. It's what she called her father's mother."

Then why ask my opinion, I wondered. If Ross and his mother had already made a decision, why bother with me?

"Fine," I said. "It doesn't really matter to me." But it will, I thought, if my mother decides she wants to be called Nana.

"Good. I'll tell her right away. I think she's having something engraved."

Ross went into the study—really his at-home office; Ross hadn't studied in many a year—to call his mother. I put away the dishcloth I'd been folding and walked to the giant window overlooking downtown Boston, now glittering in the night.

And what, I wondered, would the baby call me? Mommy, of course. Maybe Mama. And later, when he or she grew older, Mom. Never, I hoped, Ma. Or Mother.

Mom. That was okay, wasn't it?

I wondered what Mrs. Kent's sons called her. Mater?

I thought back to my lunch with Kristen. I'll always be Anna, I'd told her. Just Anna. I wanted to believe that, but the truth was I was no longer sure that was possible.

Standing at the window, looking out over the darkening city, it occurred to me that I'd never been known as anything but Anna. I'd never even had a nickname, unless, of course, you counted Anna Banana, which some big bully had dubbed me in second grade. Thankfully, the moniker hadn't stuck. Even Ross rarely called me "honey" or "sweetie."

I was Anna. And now I was also going to be Mommy. The thought frightened me.

"She's thrilled." Ross was off the phone. He joined me at the window.

"Good," I said.

"How are you feeling, Mommy?" he asked, putting an arm around my shoulders and a hand on my stomach.

"I think," I said, "that I'm going to be sick."

39

The Lady Doth Protest

Ross was meeting a friend from the gym for drinks and dinner; far preferring the specialty bed at the loft, he planned on going there afterward, not to my apartment. I felt antsy; I just couldn't stay home alone. I called Alexandra, who happened to be in the neighborhood, having just attended a yoga class.

"Sure, I'll meet you," she said. "I've done a healthy thing; now I'll have a drink and ruin all my good work."

We met twenty minutes later at a small local restaurant called Poodle. It was early; the place was otherwise empty.

"I thought pregnant women are supposed to be tired all the time," Alexandra commented, placing her yoga mat on the floor against the bar. "But these days you're hardly ever home."

"I'm going out on the town while I still can," I explained to her. "Frankly, I'm exhausted, and I'd love to just curl up in bed with a good book and be asleep by eight. But these are my last days of freedom. I want plenty of memories to cherish when I'm knee-deep in dirty diapers and hooked up to a breast pump."

"Ah, that does sound like the life!"

"Be careful," I warned. "It could happen to you."

Alexandra pretended to shudder. "I'll have a martini," she told the bartender. "A big one. Dry, two olives."

"You got it. And you?" he asked me.

"I desperately want a cocktail," I said to Alexandra. "You know, before I couldn't drink I never felt that I needed a drink. Now, I feel like an alcoholic."

"It's all in your head," Alexandra informed me annoyingly. "We always want what we can't have."

"No kidding. I'll have a seltzer with lime, please," I told the smirking bartender.

When our drinks arrived, and after a toast that was half-hearted on my part, I said, "So, entertain me. Allow me to live vicariously. Who are you dating?"

"Who says I'm dating anyone?"

"You're always dating someone," I pointed out. "And that's not meant as a criticism. So, who is he?"

"Actually, at the moment I'm not dating anyone. It's rather a relief, really. Of course, the offers are still coming in, but I just don't have the energy to spare."

I shrugged. "The men will be there when you're ready to get back into the game."

"If I choose to get back into the game."

"What's that supposed to mean?"

"Oh, nothing. It's just that dating can be such a bore. And I'm not in the market for a husband, so what's the point of wasting all that precious time on someone who'll be in and out of my life—and my bed—within a month or two?"

"You're sounding cynical this evening," I commented. "Very world-weary, very fin de siecle, and it's only the start of the century. What about falling in love?"

Alexandra's answer was right on the tip of her tongue.

"I won't be falling in love."

"How do you know?"

Alexandra carefully sipped her drink before answering. "I just do."

"Aren't you the woman who declared that the future is deliciously uncertain?"

"Yes," she said, "I'm that woman. But our lives aren't entirely random. We do have some control over what happens to us."

"Like falling in love? But I thought you believed—"

"Let's change the topic, shall we?"

I shrugged. "Fine. I'll just have to read the tabloids for some vicarious excitement."

For a little while we talked about the mundane stuff of daily life. Which long distance phone carrier we'd switched to; interest rates; how hard it was to get in to see a dermatologist; recent changes in the tax laws.

And then I said, "I know I promised to drop the subject of your love life but—"

"But you're going to ask me something personal anyway."

"Just this. Have you ever lived with a man?"

Alexandra leaned back and eyed me warily. "Why do you want to know? And why now, after—how long have we known each other? Three years?"

"Four," I said. "I'm just curious. There's a lot I don't know about you. Maybe that's my fault. Maybe I don't ask enough questions."

"Maybe I like that about you."

"Why? Are you hiding some dread secret?" I joked. "In the distant past did you mastermind a sinister event resulting in the destruction of an entire middle-class suburban neighborhood? Are you on the run from the police? Is that your real face?"

"Yes, I lived with a man in college," Alexandra said without preamble. "Only he wasn't really a man. Oh, sure, he had the physical parts, but emotionally he was about nine years old. What can I say? I had to learn, too. Satisfied?"

"For now. You can ask me a question about my past life if you want. I'm sure there's still something you don't know about me."

"Okay," she replied. "Tell me something I don't know about your former love life."

"Like what? Be specific. But not too intimate. You know I don't—"

"Yeah, yeah, I know. But that narrows the field considerably. Can I ask if you've ever had a threesome?"

"No, you may not," I replied. "But if you did have permission to ask, the answer would be no. Most emphatically, no."

Alexandra sighed. "Well, that's all I've got. Your life, my dear Anna, has been rather—"

"Unexciting?" I suggested. "Decidedly not glamorous? Fairly dull?"

"Those are your words, not mine. But yes, that's about what I meant."

"It's true," I said. "I can't deny it." And, I realized, it's only going to get duller. Suddenly, I felt miserably old. I felt—over.

"I think I'll go home," I said.

"But it's only seven thirty!" Alexandra protested. "Stay for just a bit. After all, this was your idea."

I picked up my purse and sighed. "If I hurry I can be in bed by eight. Goodnight, Alexandra. Don't stay out too late."

40

Retrospect

Soon after I got my first apartment after college, my mother sent me three cardboard boxes filled with my childhood trinkets and toys. Report cards, too, and books, drawings done in kindergarten, a few tiny dresses and goofy hats, and the photo albums I'd kept in high school and college. She also included an envelope full of miscellaneous shots of my brother and me together, photos she'd never gotten around to putting in an album.

I've never checked my parents' attic or basement but I'd bet there's not a trace left of Paul or of me.

Over time I tried to forgive my mother for being who she is. After all, I reasoned, she'd kept the stuffed bear and the finger paint masterpiece in the first place. She'd taken the photos of birthday parties and Christmas mornings. What did it matter that as soon as I got my own home she'd shunted every trace of my past out the door? I couldn't stay a child forever, could I?

But my mother could want me to be her child forever. Couldn't she?

Anyway, by the time of my pregnancy I'd gotten over

being hurt by my parents' lack of interest, enough to vow that I was going to shower my own child with endless affection and concern until the day I died.

That evening, after leaving Alexandra alone at the bar, I went home and poked through those cardboard boxes. And while I picked through ragged dolls and crayon drawings, I wondered, Had I ever been young? Really young, wild and carefree and devil-may-care? Had I ever thrown caution to the wind and worn jeans without underwear and shown up for work with a hangover? Had I ever made out with a boyfriend in public or passed notes in class or snuck outside food into a movie theater? Had I ever shoplifted a piece of gum or walked on a lawn with a No Trespassing sign?

Of course not. I just wasn't a high-spirited, devil-may-care person. In fact, more than once I'd been called an old soul, but I'm not sure that was an accurate description. Didn't "old soul" imply a sort of ageless wisdom? I'd certainly never felt in the least bit wise.

I scanned the various photographs I'd spread out on the dining table. Anna in pigtails on her first day of kindergarten; Anna in an upsweep, heading out for the senior prom. Anna in her high school graduation portrait, all solemn-eyed and hopeful; Anna in her college graduation portrait, black mortarboard perched smartly atop her sensible head. Good, efficient, conscientious, law-abiding, status-quo-keeping Anna.

Looking at those pictures, I wondered, Is this all there is to me?

Yes. Maybe. No.

I swept the loose photographs into a messy pile. It's okay, I told myself. Nobody wants you to be other than who you are. Nobody but you even suspects there's something more to Anna Traulsen. Nobody but you suspects there's anything wrong at all.

41

Showers, Showers Everywhere

Alexandra and I met for a quick lunch the next afternoon at the Au Bon Pain on Newbury Street. I felt bad for having run out on her the night before; besides, there was a new worry on my mind.

"Good afternoon, dear Anna," she said when she swept into the storefront twelve minutes late. "I trust you got lots of sleep last night, although I must say you don't look very rested. And isn't it a beautiful day?"

"It's okay," I replied, stirring the broccoli soup I'd gotten while waiting for my friend to show up. Surprisingly, that week I could eat broccoli with no problem, but crackers made me queasy. "And no, I didn't get lots of sleep because the phone rang at eleven last night and I was stupid enough to pick it up."

"So, does this late-night phone call have anything to do with why you're so glum?" Alexandra took the seat across from me, undeterred by my grumpy answer.

"You don't want to know. Really, you'll be bored."

"Probably," Alexandra admitted. "But we're friends. Remember, we have the right to bore each other now and then."

"You've never bored me."

Alexandra unfolded her napkin and placed it on her lap. "I'm saving the boring stories for when we're creaky old ladies with blue hair and stockings rolled to our knees."

"If I ever wear stockings rolled to my knees, put me out of your misery."

Alexandra raised her right hand as if to pledge. "It's a promise. Now, what's going on?"

"My mother," I said, "assumes she's hosting the baby shower."

"What happened to the wedding shower?"

"That's what I'd like to know," I replied dryly. "It seems the bride has taken a backseat to the baby. But that's the least of my problems right now. Kristen has offered to host the baby shower, too. I can't have two baby showers. Well, I suppose I could, if my mother invited one group of people to her party and Kristen invited another group to hers, but I don't want to have to endure two baby showers. I can barely wrap my mind around one."

Alexandra shrugged. "So, tell your mother or Kristen thanks but no thanks."

"I can't do that," I protested. "My mother would be devastated."

"You mean she'd be pissed off and you're afraid of standing up to her and making her really listen to you for the first time in your life."

"Right." There really was no point in arguing that truth. "And I can't say no to Kristen because she sounded so excited, and I know she loves to host adult-only parties and hardly ever has the chance since having the three kids."

"Anna," Alexandra pronounced, "you're a wimp. You're putting your friend's feelings above your own."

"I prefer to think of myself as a generous person."

"Self-effacing," Alexandra corrected. "Remember, Anna, this is your baby shower. A party in your honor shouldn't be something inflicted upon you. It should be something you want and will enjoy."

"I suppose I could suggest they share the hostess duties," I said.

"You know as well as I do that won't work. Your mother and Kristen hardly know each other. And your mother, well, she's not the easiest person to get along with. Even Kristen might be tempted to strangle her."

"My mother is strong willed," I corrected, warningly. "That's all. Besides, you've only met her once and she wasn't in the best of moods that day. She'd only come into the city for a sale at Lord & Taylor, but when she got to the store she couldn't find anything she wanted to buy. It set her off."

"Did I say anything nasty about your mother?"

"No, not really," I admitted. "But you were thinking it. I just wish there was a clear, incontrovertible reason for choosing one hostess over the other."

"There is a clear, incontrovertible reason," Alexandra said. "Your mother comes first. She has priority. Why? Because she gave birth to you, and so until the day she dies you owe her your life."

I wondered, Years from now, would my daughter resent everything I said or did, no matter how altruistic my motives? Probably.

"Is there another clear, incontrovertible choice?" I asked.

"In my opinion, yes. You're an adult. Your mother treated you like a child, like someone who has no opinions or rights of her own, by assuming you'd want her to give you a baby shower. Kristen, on the other hand, treated you as an adult for whom she has respect. She asked if you would like her to host your baby shower. I'd reward the person who considered me an equal. I'd accept Kristen's offer."

Alexandra had a point. She always does.

"I'll think about it," I promised. "Anyway, I suppose I should be grateful my mother is showing any interest in my life at all. Generally speaking she's a devoted proponent of laissez-faire parenting."

"Let's talk about something else," Alexandra said brightly, suddenly. "How's the wedding shower shaping up?"

"You," I said, "are a troublemaker."

"And you're pathologically afraid of causing trouble. We won't have to eat cucumber sandwiches, will we?"

"At the wedding shower?"

"At either shower."

"I like cucumber sandwiches. But no, we won't. My mother hates cucumbers. They give her gas."

"Cucumbers cause gas in everyone over the age of thirty."

"They don't give me gas."

"You're special, I guess. So, what about the bachelor party?"

The question took me by surprise. "I don't know," I admitted. "Ross hasn't mentioned a bachelor party. I kind of forgot about the men."

"Of course you did. Weddings are all about women. The men are merely accessories."

"I'll ask Ross if his brother is organizing a party. I can't imagine the Davis boys at a strip club. They really are like the Crane brothers, you know. Maybe they'll go to a steak house for dinner."

"I thought Ross doesn't pollute his body with red meat."

"He doesn't," I said. "Not often. But I think most steak houses offer a broiled fish these days."

Alexandra grinned. "Well, maybe Rob will hire a private stripper to go along with after dinner cigars and brandy. Wait, does Ross drink brandy?"

Ross's drinking brandy wasn't the question. Ross's getting a lap dance was. He didn't seem at all like the type to appreciate a stripper, even a highly paid one. His father, on the other hand, did seem like the type. His brother, I thought, could go either way. If turning down a lap dance meant ridicule from the father, then Rob would say, "Bring it on!" and probably burn his trousers afterward.

"Anna?" Alexandra's voice startled me back to the moment. "Did you hear me? Does Ross drink brandy? Or is he on a strictly oxygenized water diet until the wedding?"

"Of course he drinks brandy," I snapped. "Sorry. I didn't mean to snap."

"It's the idea of Ross getting a lap dance, isn't it? Don't worry, honey. I'd bet my last dime against that ever happening."

"It's a good thing Ross would refuse a lap dance," I pointed out. "You make it sound like a character flaw."

"Not at all. I think with Ross there are certain things you can count on, like his being faithful."

Had Alexandra finally seen the light? "I've been telling you that Ross is a good person."

"It's not that he's a good person," Alexandra shot back. "It's that he doesn't like mess. Cheating is messy. It's too haphazard for his taste."

"You'll never like Ross, will you?"

Alexandra shrugged. "Probably not. But he'll probably never like me, either. Our mutual dislike cancels itself out."

"That makes no sense," I said. "Besides, have you ever considered how hard it is for me to live with the fact that my fiancé and my best friend hate each other? It's very awkward, you know."

"I know, and I'm sorry, Anna. I'd like Ross if I could. It'd be easier on me, too. We three could be all chummy and cozy and take vacations together and—"

"Don't be like that," I snapped. "There's no need."

Alexandra grimaced; she looked contrite but how could I be sure? "I'm sorry, Anna," she said. "Really. Sometimes I'm a jackass, I know. I wish I knew why."

I do, too, I thought. But I said, just a bit stiffly, "It's okay. Thanks for the advice about the shower."

42

Acid Bath

"You know who I think is cute?" Kristen looked around the large round table at Tiger with bright-eyed expectation. "Orlando Bloom. I know, I'm old enough to be his, well, his older sister, but I just think he's so adorable! Don't you think so, Anna?"

It was the last time the five of us—Kristen, Tracy, Alexandra, Michaela, and I—would be together at one table. Had I known what was going to happen, would I have put an end to that silly chatter right then? Would have, should have, could have. There's just no benefit to that kind of thinking.

"I'm going to be a mother soon," I pointed out. "I'm almost a married woman. I feel silly talking about what celebrity I have a crush on. It's, I don't know, unseemly."

"Well," Kristen replied briskly, "I don't feel silly and I don't think it's unseemly, and I'm a wife and mother. So there."

"Unseemly? Oh, please, Anna." Alexandra laughed. "Kristen's right, you don't always have to be Miss Propriety. Come on, tell us. Who would you like to fool around with? Who would be your free pass once you tie the knot?"

Kristen was looking at me eagerly now. Tracy betrayed a wry but amused smile. Well, I thought, what harm would it really do to engage in a little game with my girlfriends? As long as Ross didn't find out. "Hair Guy," I said promptly.

"Who?" Michaela inquired. Her tone suggested she'd been forced to pick up a particularly slimy worm with her teeth.

"Hair Guy," I repeated. "You know, from *Queer Eye for the Straight Guy*."

Alexandra shook her head. "Poor Anna. First and second and third: He's gay. You can't have sex with him."

"In my fantasies I can do whatever I want," I protested. "He's very good-looking. He has wonderful muscles. He's the only man I've ever seen who looks truly good in a sleeveless T-shirt."

"Well, I'll give you that," Kristen said, laughing. "Have you seen him doing push-ups? By the way, Anna, his name is Kyan Douglas, and I think he's called Grooming Guy, not Hair Guy."

Michaela grimaced. "Just how much time do you spend watching television?" she asked Kristen. "Well, I suppose when you don't have a job . . ."

"Personally," Kristen said, undeterred, "I'm partial to Ted Allen, the Food and Wine Guy. He's so sophisticated and witty. I mean, Brian's a wonderful husband, but he's hopeless in the kitchen. If he could just spend an afternoon with Ted he'd be perfect. Maybe he'd stop buying cheese in a plastic tube."

Not for the first time I thought, Yes, Ross and Brian are not meant to be friends.

Tracy laughed. "Enough with the men we really, really can't have. What about heterosexual men? What about the men we can't have because they're celebrities and we're nobodies? Nobodies with average bodies and no money for serious couture and daily visits to the spa."

"That's easy," Kristen said. My friend, I realized, had played this game before. "George Clooney."

Alexandra groaned. "Of course! Everybody says George Clooney!"

"Have you seen him in *Ocean's Eleven*?" Kristen demanded. "The scene where he and Matt Damon are breaking into the vault? Did you get a good look at those arms?"

Chris Noth was Tracy's hands-down choice, as Mr. Big or as himself, whoever that is.

"Michaela," I said, although the look on her face made it clear she thought our fluffy conversation beneath her. "What about you? Who would be your free pass?"

"Do I really have to pick just one? How dull. Leave me out of this." She took a sip of her drink and then said, "Alexandra, what about you?"

Alexandra leaned back and crossed her legs. "Oh, I don't know," she drawled. "Let me see. Russell Crowe is attractive. And I wouldn't kick Robert DeNiro out of bed for eating crackers. But if I have to pick just one I'll say Benicio Del Toro."

Michaela rolled her eyes magnificently. "He's far too bulky."

"Too bulky for what?" Alexandra snapped. "Your taste? Well, then it's a good thing he's my free pass and not yours."

"I prefer slim men," Michaela said, her voice suddenly husky. "The essential thing about slim men is that there's nothing in the way of what's important."

"What's that?" Kristen asked, without a trace of self-consciousness.

Michaela directed her words to Kristen, whose cheeks grew increasingly red.

"Isn't it obvious? When a man has a fat stomach or is too pumped, the package isn't quite as accessible. It's not as *pow*, right out there, in your face—or wherever—like it is on a man built like Ashton Kutcher or Brad Pitt or Jude Law. And let's be honest," she added, looking around the table. "Men are good for one thing and one thing only. Sex. Otherwise, they're entirely disposable."

"You're a bit of a freak show, you know that?" Alexandra's assessment came shooting like a bullet from a gun.

Michaela shrugged. "If it makes you happy to think so. I just know what I like. A slim man with a big package he knows how to use. A man who does his job and then leaves before he can open his mouth and bore me. A man who knows his place."

No one said anything for a moment. And then Alexandra opened her mouth. "If I were you," she said, "and thank God I'm not, I'd keep those particular ideas concerning the male population from the people at the adoption agency. They're not going to be real enthusiastic about giving a child to someone who considers almost half of the human race disposable."

Oh, no, I thought. Alexandra's gone and done it now.

Michaela seemed to morph from a human female into some magnificent beast. Honestly, it was like watching a cobra raising its jeweled head. I half expected to see a forked tongue come flickering from Michaela's mouth and venom spew from her jaws.

"I doubt," she said acidly, "that you even remember what a man looks like, you dried-up old bag."

Kristen hunched as if afraid of blows. Tracy shot me a look that begged, Do something! But I had no idea what to do. Except to wait for Alexandra's response.

"At least," she said finally, every word delivered with careful deliberation, "I don't have to pay for someone's love. How is the adoption process going, anyway?"

Suddenly, I felt nauseous. Angry confrontations always make me physically ill.

Michaela's face was flushed with what I assumed was rage. She grabbed her purse from beside her drink and stood. She glared down at me, and I could see her struggling to control a fit of trembling. "You might try to muzzle your friend when you let her out of her cage," she spat. And then she was gone.

No one spoke for a long moment. Finally, Kristen erupted. "That was horrid, Alexandra!"

"I know. I'm sorry I said it. Really. I just—Aargh! She makes me so mad! And how does she know anything about my personal life? It so happens I had a date just two nights ago."

"That's not the point." I said. "Okay, Michaela was way out of line, but that was no reason for you to retaliate the way you did. She's very vulnerable about the adoption."

"Are you saying I shouldn't defend myself?" Alexandra demanded. "That I should just turn the other cheek?"

"You should always try to take the high road," Kristen murmured.

Tracy folded her arms across her chest. Was she afraid she'd poke Alexandra? "Defending yourself isn't the same as offending against your enemy. Don't pretend you don't know that."

Alexandra sighed heavily. "Look, I promise to apologize the next time I see her. Which may be never because I can't subject myself to another girls' night out if she's included."

Not a problem, I thought. Because I'm going to make very sure you and Michaela are never invited to the same event.

"Can we salvage what's left of the evening?" Tracy asked briskly. "Or should we all just go home?"

There was a moment of silence.

"Well," Kristen said, finally, "Brian's not expecting me until eleven."

We all looked to Alexandra.

"I'll stay for another drink," she said, a bit sheepishly. "If you'll let me."

"Of course we'll let you," I replied. "But you're buying the next round. Pretend we sued for pain and suffering and won."

Alexandra smiled. "Deal."

43

Ashes

"I don't know why you just don't join Netflix." Alexandra handed me the DVD of Robert Altman's *Gosford Park*. "Keep it as long as you want."

"Thanks," I said, and put it on top of the TV, VCR, and DVD player setup. "And I don't join Netflix because I don't watch that many movies. It doesn't make economic sense for me."

Alexandra had stopped by my apartment on her way home from a meeting at a client's home in Brookline. It was a few days after the debacle at Tiger; neither of us had mentioned it since, although I'd been thinking about it all right.

Alexandra rolled her eyes dramatically. "Whatever, Miss SkinFlint."

"I'm not cheap," I protested. "I'm just cautious about spending my hard-earned money. Most of the time."

"Well, you're certainly not opposed to splitting a bill even if you've only had an appetizer and I've had a steak, so I guess I should keep my mouth shut."

"Thank you. I'd appreciate it. Can you stay for a drink?"

Alexandra checked her watch and shrugged. "Sure. Just

one, though. I've got *Prizzi's Honor* at home and I'm dying to watch it. I've never seen it, can you imagine?"

I fixed a vodka martini for Alexandra and a seltzer with lime for me and put out a bowl of cashews. Alexandra, I often thought, would be addicted to cashews if you could be addicted to a nut.

"There's something I've been meaning to ask you," I said as I sat on the couch.

"Shoot. Mmm. You do make a mean martini."

"Thanks. Anyway, why do you find Michaela's attitude toward men so personally offensive? I've heard you say mean things about men. About men and sex."

"Not mean things, Anna," she corrected. "True things. But to answer your question about why I find Michaela's opinions so offensive, it's because I like men. Not every individual man of course, but I like men the same as I like women. I can't write off almost half of the human race just because they pee standing up. That's sexism."

Yes, it was sexism, but I wasn't buying Alexandra's easy answer. Something else had to account for her genuine regard for men. She certainly hadn't gotten that from her father. And she had no brother. I wondered. There must have been a significant man somewhere along the line, someone special.

"So, who is he?" I asked. "Or who was he?"

"Who?"

"The man," I said. "There had to be someone special in your life, someone who, I don't know, made you forgiving of men the way you're forgiving of women." A kindly uncle, I thought. Or a dynamic college professor, someone who made men real, the way I suppose my brother had made men real for me.

"There was no man," she snapped. But Alexandra often snapped; it didn't scare me off at all.

"Oh, come on," I said, teasingly. "What are you hiding? Tell me about the mysterious man lurking in the shadows of your life."

"I'm not hiding anything," she said promptly. "There's something I choose not to reveal. Anyway, why should I talk about something that's been over for years?"

It was a challenge. I took it. I'm not sure why. "Because it's not really over?"

Alexandra's normally pale face grew red. She more than blushed; she flushed so dark I was almost afraid. What had I done? Why hadn't I kept my mouth shut? Why had I demanded she talk about something she didn't want to talk about? It wasn't like me to provoke.

"I'm sorry," I said, reaching across the couch for her arm. "You don't have to talk about whatever it is. I shouldn't have . . ."

But Alexandra moved away from my grasp and took a deep breath. I watched as her usual calm and paleness returned.

"Okay, Anna," she said finally. "You asked for it. You want the truth, you'll get the truth. Just know that from this point on you're going to look at me differently. You're going to see some sad, romantic fool, living among the ashes of her one great love. You'll lose all respect for me and then you'll start to pity me and before long, our friendship will be over. Dead."

"What are you talking about?" I said. What, I wondered, was happening in my living room? "Why would our friendship be over?"

"Because you won't want to spend time with a swooning, pitiful idiot, and I'll know you never understood what happened to me in the first place and I'll be too angry and embarrassed to want to spend time with you."

"For God's sake, Alexandra," I cried. "Just tell me what happened!" And then I took a deep breath. "Look, you know what, maybe you shouldn't tell me anything after all, okay? I'm sorry I pried. I didn't mean to bring up a sore subject. Really."

"It's too late for retreat," she said steadily. "Here it is, Anna. I'm in love with someone I can't have. Okay? I'm in love with someone I haven't seen in years. How's that? Wait, it gets better. I'm in love with someone I'm pretty sure loathes and despises me. I'm in love with someone I never wanted to hurt but who I wound up hurting very badly in the end."

"Oh," I said.

Alexandra took a long sip of her drink before going on. "And none of it will go away," she said. Her voice was tired now, resigned. "The memories bombard me every day. The dreams haunt me every night. You know, Anna, if I close my eyes I can still see every inch of his skin, just like he's right here in front of me. I can smell his sweat, just like that. I can hear his voice. He's very real to me, Anna. He's a living memory."

I sat back heavily. I felt slightly sick. "I don't know what to say," I admitted. "What happened? Why aren't you together?"

Alexandra laughed bitterly. "He was married, Anna. He's still married."

The notion of my self-respecting friend breaking one of the cardinal rules of self-respecting behavior stunned me. It must have been all over my face.

"I know what you're thinking," Alexandra said. "You're thinking I don't seem like the type to get involved with a married guy. I'm too strong and too smart."

"Yes," I admitted. "I guess I was."

"Love doesn't have a lot to do with intelligence."

Didn't it? I realized that I might not know.

"But didn't it bother you?" I asked. "Didn't it drive you crazy that he was going home to another woman every night? I know I could never handle that."

"When you're in love," Alexandra said, as if she were declaiming from a mountaintop, "you can handle almost anything as long as you can spend some time with your loved one."

Did love make you a superwoman? Maybe that was something else I didn't know a lot about.

"How did it start?" I asked. Visions of a smarmy, oily haired cretin leapt to mind.

"Did he come on to me in a bar?" she said, once again proving an uncanny ability to know what I was thinking but afraid to say. "Did he deliver some disgusting pickup line better associated with the Rat Pack?"

Did he, I wondered, tell you his wife didn't understand him?

"Well, yes," I said. "I mean, no. Just tell me how you met." This is all very confusing, I thought. I'm just not cut out for drama and intrigue.

"We met about ten years ago when we were both doing some volunteer work at the MFA. I knew he was married. He wore a ring, he made mention of his wife in conversation like any normal person. You know, 'My wife and I saw a great movie Saturday night,' that sort of thing. I liked him immediately, but I had no thoughts of falling in love. Who in her right mind would choose to pursue a situation bound to end in disaster?"

No one in her right mind, I thought. But someone desperate for love?

"I don't know," I said stupidly. "No one, I guess."

"Before long," she went on, "we found ourselves becoming friends. I knew it was a bit odd, becoming real friends with someone who supposedly didn't need any new friends because he had a wife, right? That's what people assume about the married, don't they? That they don't need any more friends of the opposite sex, but that's just stupid."

Was it? What assumptions did I have about marriage and its participants? Who was I going to be once I married Ross? Who would other people assume I was?

"How did things change?" I asked, although I wasn't sure I wanted to hear the answer.

"Naturally. Things changed naturally and imperceptibly. Honestly, Anna, at first I thought I could handle just being friends. So did he. But then, we just kept growing closer and closer, and then it was too late to walk away from each other.

We had to be together. That's as clearly as I can say it. It was inevitable, and it was wonderful. I'd met my soul mate, Anna. And he'd met his." Alexandra laughed bitterly. "Can you believe the rotten luck?"

I wondered, How could she have been so sure of his feelings? How could she have trusted anything he said?

"Rotten luck," I repeated stupidly.

Alexandra finished her drink and carefully set the empty glass on the coffee table. "We were happy together," she said, "but the entire situation was bad. It tore him apart to be cheating on his wife. And frankly, I felt pretty horrible being the 'other woman.' Finally, the guilt just ate us up. He couldn't leave his wife and the kids, and I couldn't bear being with him but not really with him any longer so . . . I ended it."

"I see," I said. But I didn't see, not at all.

"And I got married."

"You what?" I cried. I jumped to my feet, sloshing seltzer onto the hardwood floor. "I can't believe you never told me any of this! You're not still married are you? Are you keeping your husband a secret? He's not locked away in an attic in some creepy abandoned building in South Boston, is he?"

"Of course not," she said, testily. "It didn't work out. We got divorced. I wasn't in the marriage for the right reasons."

"Oh," I said, relieved. "Okay. I mean, I'm sorry."

Alexandra was silent for several minutes. She stared down at her hands, lying lightly on her knees. "So now," she said finally, "here I am. I married a man I didn't love and I'm in love with a man who's married to another woman."

"But you date," I said inanely.

Alexandra looked up at me. "I don't really enjoy dating, you know. But it does get me out to some good restaurants. And it keeps people from making assumptions about my sexual preference."

I opened my mouth to make some sound of protest. Alexandra cut me off.

"And don't," she said, "try to tell me that someday I'll get over him and fall in love again and get married and live happily ever after, because your telling me that would mean you have absolutely no understanding of who I am. Of who I really am. Okay?"

I thought, I'm not sure I do understand who you are. "Okay," I said. "I'll respect you for being who you are. I'll respect your love for this person."

"Who will remain nameless. So don't bother to ask. You wouldn't know him anyway." Alexandra sighed.

Was she relieved to have told me her secret? Or disappointed that she'd broken her vow of silence? I studied my friend without seeming to. Her black hair in a chignon. The signature lipstick. So familiar yet so foreign. Suddenly, Alexandra seemed a stranger to me. I didn't want her to remain a stranger.

"Alexandra?" I hesitated before going on. I wondered if I had the right to ask. And then I said, "What if, I mean, do you ever wonder what you would do if he suddenly showed up on your doorstep? If he said he was divorced and wanted you to be together again?"

Alexandra stood and gathered her bag and portfolio. "It will never happen," she said suddenly. "And if it did happen I know exactly what I would do. I would go with him. Now, promise me you'll never mention this whole thing again. I can't stand talking about it. I don't want it coloring my friendship with you any more than it already has."

I walked Alexandra to the door.

"Okay," I said. "But if you ever want—"

"I won't." Alexandra slipped on a pair of big black sunglasses. "But thanks. And listen. If you ever feel for someone one-tenth of what I feel for this man, don't let him get away, Anna. Don't. Oh. Enjoy the movie."

Before I could reply, Alexandra was gone.

44

Process

Later that night I woke in a cold sweat. I dashed out of bed and grabbed another blanket from the linen closet. Huddled back in bed under several layers, I took a few deep breaths.

The dreams had come back just after my engagement to Ross. I'd told myself then they were brought on by stress; the thought of planning a wedding in less than a year must have gotten to me. Since then the dreams had lessened in frequency if not intensity. Most nights I was able to sleep uninterrupted until morning.

And then the dreams had come again only hours after Alexandra left, as horrid as always, all about choking, and blindness, and fear. Briefly I wondered if I should talk to someone about them. But wouldn't talking about them only make things worse? Wouldn't it give the dreams even more of a reality than they already had?

I couldn't know for sure if the dreams had been brought on by Alexandra's story. But it had disturbed me. Lying there in the dark, I tried to figure out why. I didn't condemn my friend for being involved with a married man. I didn't judge her; I didn't find her morally decrepit.

Zebra Contemporary

Whatever your taste in contemporary romance – Romantic Suspense... Character-Driven... Light & Whimsical... Heartwarming... Humorous – we have it at Zebra!

And now Zebra has created a Book Club for readers like yourself who enjoy fine Contemporary Romance written by today's best-selling authors.

Authors like Fern Michaels... Lori Foster... Janet Dailey... Lisa Jackson...Janelle Taylor... Kasey Michaels... Shannon Drake... Kat Martin... to name but a few!

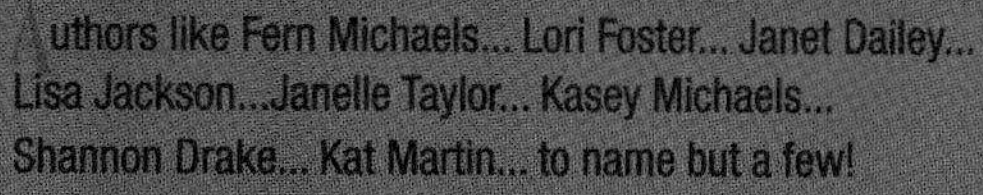

But don't take our word for it! Accept our gift of FREE Zebra Contemporary Romances – and see for yourself. You only pay $1.99 for shipping and handling.

Once you've read them, we're sure you'll want to continue receiving the newest Zebra Contemporaries as soon as they're published each month! And you can by becoming a member of the Zebra Contemporary Romance Book Club!

As a member of Zebra Contemporary Romance Book Club,

- You'll receive four books every month. Each book will be by one of Zebra's best-selling authors.
- You'll have variety – you'll never receive two of the same kind of story in one month.
- You'll get your books hot off the press, usually before they appear in bookstores.
- You'll ALWAYS save up to 30% off the cover price.

SEND FOR YOUR FREE BOOKS TODAY!

Still, I was a bit disappointed in her. Why? Because she had kept such an important part of her life from me? Or maybe because Alexandra wasn't the perfect person I'd made her out to be.

I asked myself, And whose fault was that? Not mine! It was Alexandra's fault for withholding a truth that would have helped illuminate her whole self.

I took a deep, slow breath. Really, my blood pressure was going to become an issue if people like Mrs. Kent and Alexandra and Jack kept smashing my expectations. What was happening to me? Why was I so affected by the words and actions of people who—of people who meant something to me? Where were my barriers?

And then I considered, more calmly. Maybe, I thought, I am partly responsible for the disappointment I feel. Maybe all along I'd just seen what I wanted to see. Why had I assumed that Alexandra's persona was all there was?

The truth was I felt torn between pity and admiration. To sustain such loyalty to a memory was impressive but it was also a bit creepy. My best friend was a bona fide, old-fashioned romantic heroine. Underneath her stoic veneer beat a passionately committed heart. What would the Brontë sisters have made of Alexandra's predicament?

And then I thought about the ring, the simple silver band that read "vous et nul autre." Of course it must have been from Alexandra's Mystery Lover.

Mystery Lover. For the first time in a long time I remembered the waking fantasies of my girlhood: misty moors and fog-shrouded castles, magical green forests and prancing white unicorns, dashing heroes and lovely princesses, places of intrigue and romance and danger, people of high dramatic aspirations.

Silly. Standard stuff. You're not very unique, Anna, I told myself for about the millionth time. But you like it that way, remember?

I curled up on my side and tucked my feet into my nightgown. And I thought about the child growing inside me, a total stranger and yet the person I would know most intimately in all the world. What did I want for that child? Health and happiness, of course. Success in her chosen career.

But what about in love? Parents were supposed to want the best for their children. And what was the best? The painful and often fleeting joy of ecstatic love? Or the temperate reasonableness of what I had settled for with Ross, something safe and comfortable. Something perfectly respectable. Something stable.

I burrowed down farther under the covers. I'd made my choice. I was not marrying my soul mate, and I was glad for it. I didn't want that kind of intensity. I didn't want messy passion. I didn't need it.

I didn't.

45

Retail Backfire

The following morning I felt groggy and disoriented, probably the result of a night of interrupted sleep and the lack of caffeine. The headaches were gone, but the habit was still strong enough to make me crave that first cup.

A little shopping might lift your spirits, I told myself. And in an uncharacteristic move I decided to take the morning off. Hormones again? Or simply exhaustion?

In the Prudential Mall, I found a cream-colored silk scarf at Ann Taylor Loft and a lightweight, taupe knit sweater at J. Jill, which would work nicely with the scarf on a cool spring evening and was loose enough to hide the beginnings of a tummy; at the MAC counter in Saks, I picked up a tube of Russian Red lipstick. Although I'd never worn red lipstick—it didn't really fit my personality and Ross thought it looked cheap—suddenly I wanted to know that it was in my make-up kit. Just in case.

Feeling far brighter than I had earlier that morning, I left the mall and emerged onto sunny Boylston Street. Why not, I thought, extend the spree? On Newbury Street, between the Nike Tower and Armani Exchange I came upon a high-end maternity shop called Mamma. I'd never noticed it before, but then again I hadn't been looking. In the window were two mannequins dressed in bright, attractive prints. Well, I thought bravely, why not? Just do it, Anna. Just walk right into that shop and pretend you belong. Wait. You don't have to pretend. You do belong. You're an official member of the mommies-in-waiting club.

I pushed open the door to the shop and was greeted not by a bell or buzzer but a recording of the classic nursery song "Rock-a-Bye Baby." There were no other customers and no salespeople in view.

The left wall of the shop was lined with shelves on which were stacked cotton tops in a variety of colors. I pulled a black one from the top of a pile; it was well-made and soft to the touch. And then I checked the price tag. Two hundred dollars for what was essentially a T-shirt? A T-shirt that would be useful for only a few short months?

"May I help you?"

I jumped. I hadn't seen or heard the saleswoman approach. I noted her extra-wide, extra-white smile and found myself mimicking it. Pregnant women are happy women, I reminded myself. At least they should be.

But the shining saleswoman didn't have to know I was pregnant, did she? I closed the smile.

"Yes, thanks," I said, returning the black top to the pile. "My friend is pregnant. Not me. I just thought I'd look through the summer selection and maybe buy her a gift."

The saleswoman's extra-wide, extra-white smile now moved to her eyes. They were high beams below her forehead. "How nice. Feel free to browse, and please let me know if you have any questions."

I did have a question. Do your teeth, I wanted to ask, glow in the dark?

The saleswoman disappeared as mysteriously as she'd arrived, and I began to flip through a rack of three hundred-dollar skirts. Thirty seconds, I figured. After thirty seconds I'd walk my lying, crazy self to the door.

"There you are!"

I jumped. The saleswoman was at my shoulder again, burning brightly.

"Now, isn't this cute?" she said, thrusting an armload of pale pink fabric at me. I focused. It was a dress, not a tent, and it was dotted with teeny white kittens.

"You won't even feel pregnant in this ensemble!" the saleslady bubbled.

But I will so look it, I thought unhappily. And why shouldn't I look pregnant? Why would I try to hide my pregnancy? I'm not insane. I suddenly remembered reading that Jackie Kennedy attempted to hide her pregnancy while in the White House. And everybody liked her. Everybody thought she was perfectly sane.

"She won't feel pregnant," I corrected the ever-so-helpful saleswoman. "My friend. The pregnant one. Not me. I'm not the one who's pregnant."

The saleswoman directed a not-so-subtle glance at my midsection and with an air of practiced condescension said, "If you say so, dear. By the way, the nursing bras are in the back."

I felt mortified. Was I showing already? Was my face exhibiting a telltale glow? Or was I just a lousy liar? The saleswoman walked off to accost a new customer.

The dress was exorbitantly expensive and completely hideous, but I bought it anyway. And then I scurried from the shop like the fraud I was.

46

Not So Secret Society

After the disastrous shopping experience in Mamma, I decided to treat myself to lunch at Stephanie's. Maybe, I thought, food is what you need. Maybe you're suffering from malnutrition. Malnutrition can trigger bizarre behavior and even hallucinations.

I ordered a nicoise salad. And the moment the waiter had gone off to place the order, I panicked. Should I have asked the chef to hold the tuna? Was all fish dangerous to pregnant women? Or was it only raw fish? Maybe it was shellfish that was deadly. And what about eggs? Should I be eating eggs? And why couldn't I keep my information straight? Was the malnutrition that advanced?

My panicked thoughts were interrupted by the arrival of three twenty-something salon blondes at the table next to mine. While their facial features were each quite different, almost everything else about them was in concert. Clearly they all went to the same hair cutter and colorist; clearly they shared a favorite style, something solidly between Talbots and Gap. I wondered if their husbands were carbon copies of each other, too.

But more important than their clothing and hair, like me, the women were pregnant. We were all going to bring babies into the world at approximately the same time; well, my child would be a few months younger than their children, but a few months wasn't much of a difference. Didn't that make us somehow related?

Our babies would cut their first teeth at approximately the same time. They would utter their first words within months of each other. They would enter first grade the same September. They would graduate from high school in the same year. And they would legally become independent, self-directing adults who might choose to marry one another, their birth mates, and live happily ever after.

A lonely woman could dream. I hadn't yet joined a Lamaze class. I didn't know any other pregnant women. Maybe, I thought desperately, these women could be my friends.

I must have been staring.

"Can we help you?" the blonde on the left drawled. I couldn't place the accent, but it was clear these women were from out of town.

"I'm sorry," I said, and I felt my cheeks redden. "I didn't mean to eavesdrop. Really. But I couldn't help overhear a bit of your conversation. See, I'm pregnant, too."

The blonde on the left cocked her head to get a look at my left hand.

"I'm engaged," I said, unnecessarily. I had the distinct impression she did not approve of single motherhood.

"How nice for you," the blonde in the middle said, in a tone that belied the slightest bit of interest.

"I'm so sorry," I said again, growing more flustered each moment under the smug stares of the three mommies-in-waiting.

"That's all right," the blonde on the right said, with a hint of an insincere smile.

The bulging shopping bag from Mamma squatted at my feet like a toad. I had a sudden, crazy urge to offer it to the three blondes.

But I was too late. The mommies-in-waiting were ostentatiously ignoring me now. Hurriedly, I ate my salad (except for the tuna), paid the check, and dashed out into the bustle of Newbury Street. I'm a crazy woman, I thought. I'm certifiable. First, I'm pretending not to be pregnant, then I'm telling total strangers about my interesting condition. Maybe it's not malnutrition. Maybe it's all the hormones. Hormones would explain the lunacy, right?

But there was no consolation in that. If I'm this crazy now, I thought, what am I going to be like at three months? At seven months?

As if possessed I strode to the corner and stuffed the shopping bag from Mamma into the stinking garbage can. Maybe, I thought, a drag queen will find the balloonlike dress and transform it into some slyly amusing costume for his stage couture collection. Certainly, only an over-the-top performer would be brave enough to wear it.

I gave the bag one last push and stepped away from the garbage can. I was breathing heavy; my sunglasses had slid down to the tip of my nose. I'm not sure, but I might have been muttering. A well-dressed, very normal-looking man was passing by only a few feet away. He gave me a funny look. The kind of look that said, "Okay, there's a woman on the very edge of sanity. I think I'll cross the street." And he did.

At that very moment, watching that no doubt well-adjusted man weave his way through traffic, I vowed to start a new savings account. No more unnecessary fashion accessories like scarves and sweaters and lipstick. Therapy was expensive. And I was sure my poor child was going to need a lifetime of it.

47

Thou Shalt Not Covet

"Oh, Ross," I said, "I'm really not in the mood for a party right now."

"It's not until Saturday."

"By 'right now,'" I explained, "I mean for the next eight months or so."

"Oh, come on, Anna," he said, "that's ridiculous."

"No, it's not ridiculous," I replied petulantly. I felt horrible. The day had started bad and gotten worse. The left heel of my favorite day pumps broke off. A client called to say she'd changed her mind about the theme of her fiftieth birthday party and asked if I'd mind starting the job from scratch. From a tropical paradise to an ice palace, in two weeks? I estimated another twenty or so billable hours, which was nice in one way and terrible in another. And the morning sickness had been particularly violent. I'd hardly been able to think about food since seven a.m., let alone eat it. I wondered if pregnant women could be fed intravenously for the duration.

"But you have to come with me, Anna," Ross said with a hint of a whine. "It's a very important party, and some very important people are going to be there. You just have to be there with me."

"But Ross," I began.

"You need to remember, Anna, that it looks good for me to be there with my wife. My soon-to-be wife. In my line of work, well, it's like being a politician. A politician needs his spouse at his side, doing and saying the right thing. He needs to know he can trust her. He needs to know she'll always support him and put on a good face even when things get rough. Do you understand?"

I understood. I understood that I was considered a piece of arm candy, an accoutrement, a tasteful accessory. What else did Ross consider me? His better half? The ball and chain? She Who Must Be Obeyed?

"Okay," I said, defeated. "I'll go."

"Great," he said. "Maybe you'll even grab a new client."

The last thing I needed at that moment was a new client. What I needed was another set of hands, a long nap, and a personal stylist to make me fit for public consumption.

Because although I wasn't really showing I felt as if I were. And in spite of what *InStyle* and *E!* tell us—which is that pregnancy is chic—I wasn't buying it. Sure, all the stars are having babies, and they all look fabulous doing it. But all the stars have huge clothing budgets and professional stylists to cover those nasty blemishes and broken capillaries, and to deal with those ever-changing curves in all the wrong places.

That Saturday night, in spite of having no personal Pilates coach or devoted makeup artist or live-in seamstress, I managed to pull together a decent outfit: a champagne-colored brocade evening coat (spring evenings in New England can still be quite chilly) over a simple pair of pearl gray silk pants and a matching tank.

The moment we arrived at the party Ross abandoned me to speak with one of the Important People he'd told me would be there. And there I was, vulnerable to the force who is Ginger Matthews, the suspiciously enthusiastic wife of one of Ross's business associates. The Matthews have one child, a boy. At the time of the party he was almost a year old and properly at home with the live-in nanny while his mommy was charging right at me, a squealing missile seeking its target.

"What's this I hear about you and Ross having a baby? Congratulations! Good work!"

"Thanks," I said. As if getting pregnant is a big accomplishment. Which, I guess, for some people it is.

"So," Ginger went on, poking me lightly in the arm, "I imagine you'll take a leave of absence from the business, right? I'm sure your partner can handle things while you're gone."

"I don't have a partner," I said.

"Oh, well, then, a fabulous assistant, someone who can keep things afloat in the office while you're home with the baby. Because, trust me, once you see that adorable little face you'll never want to go back to work."

I smiled and tittered, although what I really wanted to do was wipe the smug, mother-knows-best smile off Ginger's face. So what if I didn't have a business partner? So what if I chose to keep overhead low by not hiring a fabulous full-time assistant? Those were my choices. And I'd been doing just fine until . . .

Until I got pregnant.

What if Ginger's right? I wondered. What if I take one look at the baby and decide I don't want to go back to work ever again?

Wait a minute, I thought. Ever again? That's crazy! What happens when the baby goes off to college and I've got nothing to do but roam an empty house and make unnecessary care packages my child is only going to sell to her roommate or dump in the trash?

Calm down, Anna, I scolded. Take a deep breath. Maybe Ross's idea of a sabbatical is a good one after all. Maybe I should put Anna's Occasions on hiatus, just until the baby goes to school. Even if it means losing the clientele I've worked so hard to acquire.

"You know," Ginger went on, oblivious to my troubled reverie, "I heard the most fabulous name the other day and really, it could work for a boy or a girl."

"Oh?" I said blandly. If I had said, "I don't want to hear it," would she have walked away?

"MacNab. Isn't that fabulous?"

"Isn't that a last name?" I said, as if it mattered.

"It could be, I suppose, but isn't it just too wonderful as a first name?"

It was too something all right.

"I'll keep it in mind," I lied. "If you'll excuse me I—"

"Have to pee?" Ginger winked. "No need for apologies, Anna. Pregnancy is all about peeing!"

I grimaced and backed away. This party, I thought, cannot get any worse. And then, of course, it did.

Alexandra appeared from the crowd. She looked wonderful, but her expression was slightly tentative. It was the first time I'd seen her since she'd told me about her Mystery Lover. I'd vowed not to let that new information interfere in our relationship; I'd vowed never to say a word about it.

"There you are," she said. "I've been looking for you. I was beginning to think you were avoiding me."

"Of course not," I told her. "And I wish you had found me ten minutes ago. I was stuck with that awful Ginger Matthews. What's up?"

Alexandra nodded curtly toward the far end of the crowded loft space. "Honey, I hate to be the bearer of distressing news, but your so-called friend Michaela is flirting up a storm with your fiancé."

"Oh, come on!" I protested, although actually I had no doubt Alexandra was telling the truth. Alexandra isn't purposely cruel. And Michaela? Well, rumor had it she'd broken up a marriage or two in her time.

Alexandra gave me an appraising look, head to foot.

"What?" I challenged.

"I'd get over there now if I were you."

"I trust Ross," I said. And I did, as far as I'd ever trusted a man with whom I'd been involved.

"There's trust," Alexandra replied, "and there's stupidity. Ross is only human, Anna. And I'm pretty sure Michaela isn't only human. But hey, if you're confident he's got the stuff to repel the advances of a gorgeous woman, that's just fine."

I considered. I was moody and bloated. Ross and I hadn't had sex in weeks. And Michaela was wearing a pencil skirt that hugged every perfect curve and a pair of stiletto pumps that drew lots and lots of attention to her long, long legs.

"I'll be back," I muttered.

"Take your time," Alexandra said as I stalked off. "And don't damage the ring when you slap her across the face."

The fury built as I made my way through the crowded room. I don't know when I'd ever felt so angry. Easy, Anna, I told myself. If your blood pressure soars, the baby's will, too.

Michaela saw me coming and slipped away into the crowd surrounding the bar. I followed her as best I could but lost her almost immediately. I wouldn't have been surprised to learn she'd perfected the art of evading angry wives and girlfriends.

Fine, I thought. If I can't confront the temptress I'll confront the temptee. I found Ross staring longingly at the Hathaway's state-of-the-art home entertainment center. He looked like a worshipper at a shrine. I almost hated to bother him.

"Ross?" I tapped him on the shoulder and he startled.

"Anna," he said, "I didn't see you."

"I know. Ross, there's something I have to ask you." My voice trembled. Confrontation is not my specialty.

"Wait," he said. "I've got something to tell you, first."

"But—"

"Please, Anna," he said, taking my hand. "This is important. I don't want that Newman woman hanging around our house. She'll be a bad influence on the baby."

I struggled to hide a grin of pleasure. At least, I thought, I can trust my fiancé if not my friend. "Why?" I asked feigning innocence.

Ross frowned slightly.

He never frowns mightily, I thought. He never smiles broadly. He never laughs loudly. Okay, I've seen him cry, but only once. Only once in almost a year.

"She actually had the nerve to hit on me," he said, letting go of my hand and straightening his tie. Had Michaela literally hit on him? Knocked his tie askew? "Can you believe it? With the mother of my child in the same room. I'm sorry, Anna, I know you two are friends—"

"Not anymore," I replied firmly. "That bitch is dead to me."

"Language, honey. Look, try not to get too upset, okay?" Ross's face took on a practiced expression of mild concern. "It can't be good for the baby."

He really could have been a model, I thought. He's mastered the basic facial expressions. Standard concern. Standard pleasure. Standard interest.

I wondered why I was suddenly so mad at Ross. He'd done nothing wrong. Nothing at all. My feelings were irrational, misplaced. I should have been angry with Michaela, and I was, I was furious with her. But . . .

It's the hormones, I reasoned, although I didn't quite believe myself.

Ross's voice penetrated my troubled thoughts.

"Honey? You look like you're a million miles away. What were you going to ask me?"

I shook my head. "Oh, nothing. Never mind. Ross, I'd like to go home now. I'm feeling kind of tired."

Ross immediately hurried off to find my jacket and to say goodbye to the hosts.

Maybe, I thought as I watched him go, I should just run away.

After I confronted Michaela.

48

The Premarital Bed

Within minutes of our getting to the loft, Ross was stretched out in bed, sleeping deeply. But two hours later I was still wide awake and resenting him for the ease with which he could tune out the world and its woes.

I should have gone home, I thought grumpily, readjusting the covers for the millionth time. I would have been able to sleep in my own bed. My old, familiar, discount furniture store bed. Not the insanely expensive designer bed that Ross had picked out for its superior ergonomic qualities.

Why am I here? I wondered. It isn't as if Ross and I are going to have sex. No, I'm too fat and grotesque for that. I'm too precious for that. I'm too much of a mommy.

I turned on my side, hoping a change of scenery would lead to a change in mental obsession. It didn't.

I wasn't sorry I'd called Michaela a bitch. Michaela deserved to be called a lot worse. And after I'd opened up to my friends about Ross's lack of interest in sex! Oh, Michaela must have loved hearing that, I thought, fuming. What's she after? Ross's sperm? His money? His hand in marriage?

I looked over at my sleeping fiancé. My sleeping, oblivious fiancé. And then it came to me, just like that, why I was so angry with Ross. Something about his response to Michaela's attempted pickup was all wrong.

Was Ross really bothered by Michaela's flirtation or by the fact that I was in the vicinity of her sexual advance? The mother of his child. The vessel in which his precious seed had been deposited. The receptacle in which the fruit of his loins had taken up residence. If the mother of his child hadn't been in the same room, would Ross have gone off with Michaela Newman for a little on-the-side action?

Of course he would have. Of course he wouldn't have. It didn't make a difference. Because I didn't figure in the equation at all. Not really. It was all about Ross's baby, and only as the carrier of his baby did I count.

I took a deep breath and wished I knew some calming yoga techniques. Maybe, I thought, I am being oversensitive, a classic trait of the Hormonal Woman. Maybe to preserve my nerves I should stay away from parties and other large groups until after the baby is born.

I glanced at the bedside digital clock. Two-thirty a.m. I knew I should try to get some sleep. But the truth was I was afraid to close my eyes. The dreams would come that night, I just knew it. Choking, blindness, and violence.

Was there any way to avoid them?

49

Connections

Alexandra was more than twelve minutes late. I began to worry. Why doesn't she call, I wondered. Maybe she can't. Maybe she's sick. Or maybe she's just caught in a meeting. How would I know? She hasn't called!

In a momentary mood of high dudgeon I thought, I'll have to speak to her about this annoying habit of making people wait and not calling. But who was I kidding? Alexandra did what she wanted to do for her own unfathomable reasons, and nothing I said was going to make her do differently.

I hadn't brought along a book to pass the time, and the bar at Le Chat Noir was virtually empty so there was no possibility of people-watching. With nothing to distract it, my mind wandered back to a morning shortly after I'd told Jack that I was marrying Ross. I was in Jack's studio, where, it seemed, I spent far too much of my time. I must have mentioned the wedding.

"I'm not photographing this thing," he'd said.

"This thing?" I'd responded. "It isn't a cockfight, Jack.

It's an elegant wedding. And anyway, I'm not asking you to. I've already hired Don Rivers."

"He's a hack."

"No," I'd replied, trying to control my growing annoyance, "he's not a hack. Why would I hire a hack to photograph the most important event of my life?"

"He'll overcharge you."

"He'll try, but he won't get away with it. Are you forgetting what I do for a living?"

I remembered Jack turning away and tossing a stack of prints on the worktable. "Fine. I look forward to seeing his pedestrian documentation of the big day."

"You don't have to see the pictures if you don't want to. You'll have your own memories to enjoy."

Then Jack turned back to face me. "What?" he'd snapped.

I'd hesitated a moment before answering. Something in his eyes scared me but I didn't know why. "Well, you're invited, of course."

"Why 'of course'?"

"I don't know why 'of course.' " I'd raised my arms in the air like a cartoon of a frustrated woman. "Okay? Don't come if you don't want to. Don't even send a gift. I wouldn't want to discomfit you in any way."

Jack didn't answer right away. Finally, he said, "I don't know if I can be there." His voice sounded different somehow, lower, slightly strained.

And suddenly I felt disoriented. "Well," I'd said, looking away, "check your schedule. I've got to go. I've got another meeting. I—"

"Yeah."

And I went. And that was the last time either of us had mentioned the wedding. Now, sitting at the bar at Le Chat Noir, with only a glass of cranberry juice and seltzer for company, I wondered if I really cared if Jack came to my wedding. On the one hand, Jack was my friend, and my colleague, and it would be nice if all my friends were in attendance. Right? And on the other . . . Well, Jack was critical of anything remotely sentimental; if he came to the wedding he just might spend the whole time sneering, thus ruining what was supposed to be a happy occasion. Well, I thought now, taking a sip of my overpriced drink, the official invitations would go out in mid-June and soon after Jack would give me his answer. And I could worry about it then.

I spotted Alexandra making her way through the restaurant.

"Finally," I said.

"I'm sorry, Anna, really." Alexandra dropped into the chair across from me. "I dropped my cell phone this morning, and I didn't have one free minute to run to the store and get it replaced. Can you believe it just died? It's not like it fell from the roof of a skyscraper. What a piece of junk."

"That's okay," I said. "Sorry about the phone."

Alexandra shrugged. "Actually, it was nice not having it ringing in my ear all day. I'm sure I missed some important calls, but on some level I just don't care."

"The phone is an evil necessity. It's an incredibly rude instrument, don't you think? Yet how could we summon an ambulance without it?"

"Uh, right. Anna, really, you are so grim sometimes. Anyway, I've got some interesting news. I've been asked to be a godmother."

"What?" I blurted. "To whom?" Who, I wondered, associates the decidedly not warm and fuzzy Alexandra Ryan Boyd with children?

"To the as yet unborn daughter of Barbara and Mike Nugent, aspiring Internet moguls. You've read about them, I'm sure. They manage to get their names mentioned and photos taken almost weekly. They're quite their own PR machine."

Alexandra ordered a martini while I tried to place this interesting pair.

"Ah, I know who they are," I said finally. "She's a bit—solid—isn't she? And he has the worst haircut! It's like there's a raggedy, dead animal on top of his head. A raggedy, dead, red animal. Ugh. They've been at several parties I've done, but I've never had the dubious pleasure of being introduced. How do you know them?"

Alexandra took a sip of her cocktail before answering.

"I hardly do. We were introduced once. That's just one of the strange things about this situation."

"You're not Catholic."

"And that's another strange thing. Apparently, these days you don't have to be Catholic to be a godparent to a Catholic kid. I mean, officially I should be Catholic, but the Nugents assure me they'll 'fix it' with the priest. By which I assume they mean they'll write a sizeable check and my documentation will be forged."

"But what does this mean?" I asked. "What are you going to have to do for this baby?"

"Foster her Catholicism, I suppose. I'm a little hazy on the details. Anyway, I'm assuming I'm off the hook concerning all the religious duties. How can I support a kid's religious upbringing when I haven't been inside a Catholic church since I was a kid myself?"

How, indeed?

"Forgive me," I said, "but, why you? Why not someone Catholic? And who's the godfather?"

Alexandra smirked. "As for why they chose me, I have an idea. I hate to attribute less than noble motives to anyone, of course—"

"Of course."

"—but I suspect the Nugents, who have recently purchased a three-bedroom condo on Marlborough Street, would like some free advice from a well-known interior designer."

"No!"

"Yes. And as for the godfather, I believe he's Jewish. I'm not sure. But I do know he has some connection to the Patriots, so I'm guessing the Nugents are hoping for free tickets on the ninetieth yard line. Or whatever yard line is a good one. I don't do sports."

"How horrible of the Nugents," I declared. "If your theory is correct."

"Are my theories ever wrong?"

"Rarely," I admitted. "Anyway, being a godparent is a big responsibility, isn't it? Aside from the religious duties, I mean. You're going to have to send cards for every occasion and attend school plays and ballet recitals and write checks for birthdays."

Alexandra took a long, meditative sip of her martini before replying. "You know, maybe I should just say no to Barbara and Mike. I'm sure they'll understand."

I smiled. How disappointed they'd be when they found out they'd have to pay for an interior designer! "But didn't you already say yes?"

"Oh, honey, no! I told them I'd think about it and I have and I've decided I'm just not the right person for the job."

"Well, I don't know about that," I said. "Okay, you're not Catholic, but that doesn't seem to matter to the Nugents, and you'd make a great role model for a little girl."

"What!" Alexandra laughed heartily. "Oh, please, Anna. You've heard the stuff that comes out of my mouth. You've agreed I can be a jackass. Besides, it's too much pressure. Role model, mentor, inspiration? Ugh."

"You're intelligent and talented and hardworking and an excellent friend," I replied. "In spite of an occasional lapse into jerkiness," I added with a smile. "That makes you a wonderful role model for anyone."

"Thanks for the vote of confidence," she said. "Really. But my mind is made up, if only because I think it's hypocritical to promise to be a godparent in the Catholic church when I have no intention of doing so."

"I agree about the hypocrisy. But I want you to promise that when I ask you to be my baby's godmother—you know, godmother in a broad spiritual sense—you'll consider accepting."

Alexandra grinned. "Can I be a goddess mother?"

"Certainly."

"Not that I buy into the Goddess stuff, mind you. But I think I could pull off a toga-like gown better than a long white beard."

"You can be whatever kind of god-like figure you want to be to my child," I promised.

"Then I accept. Oh, by the way, I ran into Jack on the way over here."

"Jack?" I repeated inanely.

"Jack Coltrane. How many Jacks do we both know?"

"Just one, I think. So, what did he have to say?"

Alexandra began to speak but I didn't hear a word. As if he were right next to me at the bar, I saw Jack as he was that day we'd last talked about the wedding. I saw the oddly frightening look in his eyes and heard that strange, low tone in his voice when he'd said he didn't know if he could be there. I hadn't understood exactly what had happened in those few moments but now, suddenly, weeks later, sitting at a bar with Alexandra, remembering now those roses, too, it all came clear.

Jack Coltrane was in love with me. A crazy thought but . . . If it were true . . . If Jack was in love with me—and hadn't I suspected before now?—then the issue of whether or not to attend my wedding was huge. A thrill ran through my body at this disturbing thought. Would Jack stay away because he couldn't bear to see me marry another man? Or would he attend because—because what, Anna? The thrill in my body became a buzzing in my head. Would Jack be there because when the minister asked if anyone had an objection to the wedding he planned to leap from his seat and shout, "Yes, I have an objection. I'm in love with the bride."

"Anna?" Alexandra was shaking my shoulder. "What's wrong? You've got this awful spacey look on your face. I've been talking and you have no idea what I've been saying, do you?"

I felt my face flush in embarrassment. "No," I admitted, wondering if I were losing my mind. Jack Coltrane, in love with me? I didn't want that. I didn't want that at all. "I mean, I'm fine but no, I'm sorry, I didn't hear what you were saying."

Alexandra eyed me with curiosity. Or was it really suspicion? "I was saying that Jack had nothing to say. We just exchanged the usual amenities. You'll remember that I was late and in a hurry."

"Low blood sugar," I said. "That's all it is. Let's order."

50

Something New

"It's too bad your mother couldn't join us, Anna," Mrs. Davis said with a cluck of insincere sympathy.

Before I got pregnant, fittings at the Quadri Salon were all about fun; they reminded me of playing dress-up as a little girl, or of playing with Barbie dolls, except that I was now the Barbie in the pretty white veil.

But show up for a scheduled fitting with the news that the dress everyone's been slaving over is pretty much useless, and the fun rapidly turns to misery. Add your future mother-in-law to the mix and expect the imminent onset of an ulcer.

"Yes, well," I said, "she feels bad about it, but she just couldn't get out of—" Out of what? Mrs. Davis was watching me, waiting. "She just couldn't get out of her volunteer commitment," I concluded lamely.

I just couldn't tell my future mother-in-law that my mother had waved off my invitation to lunch and this dressmaker's appointment with nary a qualm.

"Oh, Anna," she'd said, "how many times do I have to tell you that I have my poker game on Wednesdays?"

"Oh," I'd said. "Sorry."

"What do you need me there for, anyway?"

"Nothing," I'd assured her. "I don't need you for anything."

Maybe it was better that my mother hadn't joined Mrs. Davis, Tracy, and me. The Italian-born dressmaker was muttering at me, clearly furious that all her marvelous work to date had been in vain.

"I'll come back when I'm alone," I promised the sophisticated, also Italian-born owner of the shop. "We'll work something out." She nodded curtly; her lips were pursed in annoyance. I smiled apologetically at the dressmaker, who returned the favor with a frightening scowl. "I promise."

The dressmaker stormed off into the back of the shop, followed by the owner, who seemed to be whispering apologies and placating promises to her resident artist. Either that or she was cursing me. I don't know; I don't speak Italian.

"Let's take inventory," Tracy said brightly. "Something old and something new, something borrowed and something blue."

"Okay," I said, "the something old is my grandmother's pearl necklace. The something blue is the embroidery on the handkerchief my mother carried on her wedding day. Which doubles as something old, I suppose. And the something borrowed is my handbag, which the designer is lending me for the occasion. It's free advertising for her and a gorgeous seed pearl bag for me. Now all I need is the something new."

"But you've already got the something new, Anna!" Mrs. Davis exclaimed.

"What do you mean?" I asked.

Mrs. Davis's eyes gleamed with grandmotherly pride. "The baby! You've got to carry something borrowed and something blue, something old and something new. And you've got the new! You're carrying Ross's baby!"

My baby, I amended silently. Our baby.

I shot a look at Tracy; her face was strained with disbelief. "Er," said my formerly articulate friend.

"A baby is hardly an accessory," I protested feebly. "What

I mean is, I think the new thing is supposed to be a gift from your future husband."

The second the words were past my lips, I knew I'd made a horrible, horrible mistake.

Mrs. Davis stiffened. "Well, dear, what greater gift could Ross have given you than the baby?"

How, how, how could I have answered that?

"I think Anna meant a more traditional gift," Tracy said quickly, starting to life. "Like a diamond tennis bracelet. That's very popular, you know. Bill gave me one on our wedding day. See?"

Tracy held up her right hand to show Mrs. Davis the piece sparkling on her wrist. Mrs. Davis glanced at the bracelet, then looked to Tracy's face.

"In this case," she said, evenly, "it might be more suitable if the bracelet contained the baby's birthstone. What would that be? Yes, I believe it's aquamarine for December. I'll have to check to be sure."

More suitable for whom? I asked silently. I imagined the kind of tacky birthstone jewelry I'd seen in the bargain basements of certain department stores in ugly strip malls along Route One. I remembered the time I'd agreed to accompany a particularly cheap client to Guy's House of Baubles in search of a hideous charm decorated with the birthstones of each of her siblings.

Mrs. Davis went off to "powder her nose" in the dressmaker's tiny but immaculate bathroom. And I found myself staring blankly at the shelves of sparkling bags and tiaras, of seed pearl chokers and rhinestone-encrusted hair combs, of satin-covered guestbooks and silk embroidered gloves.

"Well," Tracy said, "if Ross doesn't come through with a diamond bracelet we can always buy a C.Z. bracelet at Landau's."

"Oh, if he knows he's supposed to do something he'll do it," I said testily. "I'm not worried about that. After all, I am the mother of his child, and he'd do anything for her."

There was a beat of silence before Tracy said, "Do I detect a tone of bitterness?"

I turned my back on the display case of bridal accessories. "Sorry. No. I'm just feeling a little off, that's all."

Tracy frowned and took my arm. "What do you mean by off? Do you feel sick? Do you want to sit down?"

"No, no, I'm fine," I said. "Really. I guess it's just the stress and all. Planning the wedding . . ." I let my vapid explanation trail off. Truth: I wasn't fine. Everything was in place, plans were being followed, but something, something was just not right. It wasn't the dreams—not entirely; it wasn't the absurd notions I entertained about Jack—not really; it wasn't Ross's lack of desire; it wasn't anything I could name. And if anyone—even Tracy—told me the uneasy feeling was simply due to hormones, I was going to start screaming and never stop.

Mrs. Davis reappeared, and Tracy smoothly suggested we be off to lunch right away. Before Mrs. Davis could protest, Tracy took hold of her elbow and was leading her through the door. I followed, wishing the day were over.

51

Love Happens

"Coming, coming!" I flung open the door to the building, expecting to see my friend covered in blood or otherwise in distress. "Gosh, Alexandra, I can only run down so fast. What's the crisis?"

Alexandra wasn't covered in blood, but she did look different somehow. Was she taller? I looked down at her feet. No. The heels were her usual.

"I have something to tell you," she said, barely suppressing a giddy grin. "You're not going to believe it. I hardly believe it myself."

"Well come upstairs and tell me." I closed the door and followed her up to my apartment. "I'm guessing it's not something bad. That grin reaches from ear to ear."

"No, it's not something bad. It's something wonderful."

We went into my apartment, and I closed the door. "Let me catch my breath and then you can tell me."

"I have my breath. I'm telling you right now. The man I told you about. The one I was—"

I raised my hand. "There's no need to specify. How could I possibly forget?"

"He called me last night. I saw him this morning. We met for coffee."

"Wow," I said. It was the last piece of news I'd ever expected to hear. "That is a headline. So, where do I begin? I have a million questions."

"Start with the most obvious."

"Okay. Why did he call after all this time? No, wait," I said. "If we're going to talk about this I really need to know his name. I'm tired of thinking of him as your Mystery Lover."

Alexandra seemed to find this inordinately funny. When she finally stopped laughing, she said, "His name is Luke Romane. And he called because he's free. We can be together."

"He got a divorce after all?" I asked, shocked. "Oh, don't tell me his wife died."

"She didn't die," Alexandra replied impatiently. "I'm not a ghoul. I wouldn't be grinning over someone's untimely death. She asked Luke for a divorce."

"Oh," I said. Curiouser and curiouser. "And he said yes?"

"Yes. He moved out of their house last week."

And he immediately called Alexandra. There was something unseemly about the situation. "Well, he didn't waste any time, did he?" I said, trying to keep my tone light.

"Enough time has been wasted," Alexandra said shortly. "No more."

I wondered, Did I have the nerve—or the right—to ask my friend if she thought the love of her life had acted like a coward by staying in the marriage when he was in love with another woman?

"So, for all those years he couldn't leave her," I said tentatively.

"He wouldn't leave her," Alexandra corrected. "He made an active choice to stay with his family."

I didn't dare bring up the term *hypocrisy*. "Okay," I said. "But now when she decides to leave him . . ." I stopped. What was my point, exactly?

"What's your point?" Alexandra asked, her tone challenging.

I shook my head. "Nothing, I guess. I'm just trying to get my head around this. I'm stunned. I think I'm happy for you. I know I'm scared for you."

"I know you are. I would be for you, too. Happy but concerned. Thank you, Anna."

"You're welcome," I said. "But are you sure you don't want to think about this a bit before getting back together?"

"You don't turn away love," Alexandra said definitively. "You don't turn away your soul mate. It doesn't matter how we're together, Anna, just that we are."

Well, I didn't know how to argue that. Maybe Alexandra was right.

"You're in for a long haul of divorce and stepparenting," I said. "His kids might hate you. They might hate him if—when—they find out he cheated on their mother. Loyalty to the mother is a very strong emotion."

I automatically put my hand on my stomach and spoke silently to the baby: I will fight to the death for you, Little One. Just love me in return.

"I know, Anna," Alexandra said. "But nothing can be worse than being without him. Look, I thought he hated me. I thought I'd hurt him beyond repair."

"Didn't he hurt you beyond repair?" Had I not understood anything?

Alexandra answered promptly. "No. He didn't hurt me. Life did. His intentions were never bad. Mine might have been, when I married Gus."

"What do you mean?" I asked. Just listening to Alexandra's story was exhausting. How had she carried the burden of her past for so long without breaking?

"Nothing," she said. "I take that back. I never really wanted to hurt Luke. Not really. Maybe just a little bit. A therapist would say it was understandable, but I'm not proud of my behavior. I've forgiven myself for agreeing to marry Gus, but I'm still paying the price. Memory is a harsh reality."

"You could try to forget," I suggested stupidly.

Alexandra ignored the remark. "I have these flashes of memory," she went on, "just horrible blinding flashes, and I feel so deeply ashamed and humiliated."

"Humiliated?" My stomach sank. "Oh, Alexandra, Gus didn't hit you, did he?"

"No, no. The marriage wasn't abusive or even miserable, but it didn't have to be. It was just wrong. Let me tell you something, Anna." Alexandra pinned me with her eyes; I had no choice but to pay particular attention. "There are few personal experiences worse than waking up next to someone you don't love but have pledged to love. It's jail; it's a prison. It kills your soul. And it's completely unfair to both people."

"Oh," I said after a moment. "Okay." I suddenly felt defensive: Why did Alexandra think I needed to know that?

"I'm trying to understand," I said. "Why, exactly, did you marry this Gus?"

Alexandra sighed. "Because I wanted to save myself. After two years of torture with Luke, I wanted to give myself a normal life. Do you understand?"

"Yes," I said. I did understand. By marrying Ross I was hoping to embark on a normal, stable journey through the rest of my life.

I decided then not to ask Alexandra if she'd been in love with Gus.

"What was I thinking?" Alexandra now spoke more to herself than to me. "I must have been temporarily insane. But enough of the past. I've been given this chance—I don't know why I've been given it, but I'm thrilled—and I'm frightened—I could—I feel—"

"You're crying," I said. I'd never seen my friend cry. Not even at the funeral of a thirty-four-year-old colleague who'd died the previous year of breast cancer. It made me uncomfortable somehow. It made me feel that everything was suddenly changing. If I couldn't count on Alexandra to be who I thought she was, what could I count on?

And that selfish thought frightened me, too. Was I so immature?

"I'm crying," Alexandra said, and she sounded proud. "It's not the first time and it won't be the last. Welcome to the wonderful chaos of life!"

52

Betrayal

"I'm not sure why we have to do this," I said.

Ross was leaning languidly in the doorway to my bedroom; I was finishing dressing. Getting ready to leave the house had become a chore since my body started exploding. I looked again at my reflection in the full length mirror on the back of the closet door. Was there really a tummy bulge or was I imagining it?

"Because," he said, "we're all going to be related in a few months. We're going to be family. And with the baby coming, it's very important the grandparents get to know each other better."

I wasn't at all convinced it was important for my parents to know Ross's parents any better than they did. To date they'd met only once, right after Ross and I got engaged. Mr. and Mrs. Davis had hosted a small party at their home—Mrs. Davis had referred to it as an "elite gathering"—and in spite of the champagne toast and shrimp wrapped in bacon, the evening was less than successful. Some might even have called it a disaster. When Mrs. Davis proudly showed Ross's baby pictures, my father yawned loudly in her face. When

Mr. Davis gallantly complimented my mother's dress, she told him it was about to go into the garbage. ("Mom," I said later, "you implied that Ross's parents aren't good enough for one of your new dresses." My mother replied, "Whatever. I can't be responsible for how people interpret everything I say. You don't want the dress, do you? If not, it's in the trash.")

"Are you almost done?" Ross's voice broke through my unpleasant memories. "We'll be late if we don't leave in the next five minutes. And you know my father hates people to be late."

Four minutes later we were in the backseat of Ross's company car, being driven to the new and well-reviewed Cashmere.

On the way I told Ross about Alexandra and Luke.

Alexandra hadn't asked me to keep it a secret. But Ross was my fiancé, and there's an unwritten rule that between a husband and wife there should be full disclosure.

Still, I'd kept things from Ross in the past. So, why be open now? Because for the past few days I'd been feeling guilty. Guilty about having accepted those flowers from Jack; guilty about not having told Ross where they'd come from. Guilty about thinking Jack might be in love with me; guilty about my own disturbing feelings for him, about what could be called my "crush," even though I knew the "crush" was all just some crazy, pregnancy-related hormonal thing, not my fault, out of my control. Some crazy hormonal thing and, very likely, cold feet. Maybe, I realized, maybe that was why I found myself thinking about Jack when I should have been thinking about Ross. Cold feet. It was normal to feel scared as the wedding approached; it was normal to consider, for one last time, all the possibilities you were rejecting by choosing just one man, just one life.

Just one man. And if that one man were Jack Coltrane—what a ridiculous notion—what would I be choosing? Someone who charted his own course. Someone who took chances. Someone who made me feel.

Someone risky.

Cold feet. I tried to comfort myself with the fact that I'd

never once done anything that could truly be considered cheating; I'd never betrayed Ross by as much as a kiss on the cheek. Ross, as far as I knew, was completely oblivious to the absurd thoughts running through my head. And, I vowed, I would do anything to keep him in the dark because none of it mattered in the end. Nothing, I reminded myself, that I was feeling in those days was real. Nothing.

Still, for all the stupid stuff in my head I felt I owed Ross something, some gesture of solidarity. So, I told him about Alexandra and Luke.

Really, how had I expected him to react?

"That woman is a loser, Anna," he said, contempt dripping from every word. "You should spend less time with her and more time with—Well, frankly, I don't think any of your friends are up to par, but I suppose Tracy is the least objectionable."

There were so many things I wanted to say, so many, but I couldn't even open my mouth. I tried; I did. But I felt as though I had been heavily drugged into submission. It's like in my dreams, I thought, as I stared out at the darkening city. I'm being choked.

And maybe I deserved to be. I'd just betrayed my dearest friend. I betrayed Ross every time I listened to Alexandra trash his character. I betrayed Ross again every time I thought about Jack. What was wrong with me? Was I loyal to no one? Trustworthy Anna Traulsen could no longer be trusted.

We arrived at the restaurant, exactly on time. The Davises were already there, at a table in the bar. My parents, as usual, were late. When they made their entrance any shred of hope I'd had for a successful evening died an ugly death.

My mother was wearing what amounted to a cobalt blue running outfit, although she probably had bought it at a suburban store that featured "leisurewear" and "athletic chic" for the never-been-to-a-gym, over fifty-five set. Mrs. Davis, in her proper skirt suit, looked infinitely lovely compared to my mother, but somehow, amazingly, she seemed the one making the faux pas. My mother has that kind of power, an unshakeable self-confidence that bullies those around her into automatic self-doubt and timidity.

And my father, admittedly never the most elegant of conversationalists, was inordinately silent. I'd seen it before; undoubtedly he was furious with my mother—had she nagged him mercilessly on the drive into the city?—and was inflicting his bad mood on all of us.

It was an excruciating hour and a half. I tried, however subtly, to hurry things along; thankfully, and without consultation, Mrs. Davis joined me. We were partners in discomfort, and silently I forgave her for any minor crimes she'd committed against me. I was mad at Ross, annoyed with my parents' lack of social grace, dismayed by Mr. Davis's boorish recitation of his latest financial achievements.

Finally, the dinner plates were cleared. "Would you care to see the dessert menu?" the unsuspecting waiter asked.

As if we'd rehearsed, Mrs. Davis and I replied in unison. "No, thank you," we said.

"I'm afraid I have a bit of a headache," Mrs. Davis added, looking fixedly at her water glass.

"I'm afraid I'm feeling a bit tired," I said, looking fixedly at my fiancé. "I think we should go home."

My parents made no move to pay for dinner.

53

Making Sense of It

A few days after she'd broken the big news, Alexandra persuaded me to take a stroll through the Public Garden.

"Exercise is good for pregnant women," she said as we walked past the equestrian statue of George Washington on the Arlington Street side of the park.

"Exercise is good for every woman. I guess I should think about getting some."

"We are nearing forty," Alexandra pointed out. "We're losing bone and muscle mass as we speak."

"Gee, thanks for the upbeat reminder," I said wryly.

"Oh, Anna, don't be glum. It's such a beautiful day. A walk will be good for the soul."

Well, I thought, my soul could use some soothing. I couldn't forget the contempt in Ross's voice when I'd told him about Alexandra and Luke. From now on, I vowed, glancing at my friend's dramatic profile, my friends' lives are their own. I will not practice full disclosure with my husband. At least, not with the husband I've chosen.

"How are things with Luke?" I asked.

"Good. There's some strain," Alexandra admitted. "It's odd being familiar strangers."

"I imagine so."

"It's so odd to know nothing about his life for the past eight years. I mean, I love Luke and yet in a daily, mundane sort of way, he's a stranger. I know nothing about him anymore."

"You know he wants you," I said. "And that he needs you."

"Yes," Alexandra said. "I should be content with that but I'm not. I want it to be like old times, when I knew everything. I knew what brand of toothpaste he used. I knew how he took his coffee. I knew that when he was in the car alone he liked to listen to NPR. I knew everything."

Not everything, I thought. Not how he acted alone with his wife. Not where his comb rested on their bathroom sink. Not the color of the bathrobe she bought him or the way he looked at her while she was sleeping. Not what he felt the first time he saw her holding their firstborn child. Not those intimacies.

I said nothing, just nodded encouragingly. The sun was warm; the gardens were alive with color; the sound of a child's laughter reached my ears. My soul, however, didn't feel particularly soothed.

"Now," Alexandra went on, more to herself than to me, "I know nothing. I know nothing about what for the past eight years made him happy or sad. Are his parents still alive? What books did he read? What HBO series was he addicted to? Where was he on September 11th, 2001, when he heard about the attack on the World Trade Center? I know nothing."

Alexandra's words made me think. I knew virtually everything about the daily Ross. I'd been with him almost every day for the past year. And yet, what did I really know about him, beyond the habits and behavioral traits? What had I really learned about him during our time together? Why hadn't I asked some important questions?

"But you'll learn," I said. "You'll ask questions."

Alexandra gave a small smile. It looked pained.

"Oh, sure," she said. "But it's odd to know so very little about the life of someone you love so much. It's not like we were writing letters or e-mailing or talking on the phone. It all just—stopped. And I never knew what he was thinking about me. I never knew if he regretted ever having met me. I suspected he might. I doubted his love even then."

I don't know what made me say what I said then. "Maybe," I said, "maybe you didn't doubt his love as much as think you weren't worthy of it."

Alexandra paused over this. "Astute," she said finally. "You're right. I guess I couldn't imagine love that big."

"Though you felt love that big for him?"

Alexandra shook her head. "Inconsistent, aren't I?"

"Human."

We walked along without talking for a while. I looked for mothers with their children. And I wondered what their husbands were doing after hours.

"It's like he was a prisoner of war," Alexandra said suddenly, "or missing in action, and I was his lover waiting alone at home, waiting for some news. Except that I knew Luke was alive, and I wasn't really waiting, was I?"

I didn't know the answer to that question. I said, "You were living your life. You had your career and your friends and—"

Alexandra interrupted. "I think maybe I was waiting. After my divorce, anyway. Though I never would have admitted it, not even to myself."

"Maybe," I said, "you were in a state of renunciation. Or of resignation."

"Resignation masking an unconscious state of anticipation. Expectation." Alexandra laughed. "Boy, life is weird."

"Alexandra," I said gingerly. "What if it doesn't work out?"

"It will. We'll make sure of that."

"But—"

"No buts. I can't stand to think about another end. We've had our end. Now it's time for our beginning."

After a moment I said, "I'm happy for you, Alexandra. Really. But this is taking some getting used to."

"I am so hungry," Alexandra said suddenly. "My appetite has almost doubled since Luke came back. Let's get lunch."

"I guess I could eat something," I said unenthusiastically.

"Still battling nausea?"

"No, not really," I said. "I just feel a little off."

Alexandra didn't press the matter. "Look at us, Anna," she said musingly. "What incredibly divergent paths our romantic lives have taken."

"You've had adventures. You've taken chances. I've kept to the straight and narrow."

Alexandra gave me a close look. "I'm beginning to think," she said, "that the straight and narrow is kept to by very few people. I'm beginning to think that maybe the straight and narrow doesn't even exist."

I felt uncomfortable under Alexandra's scrutiny. "Are you saying life might surprise me yet?"

"I'm saying that you might surprise yourself yet. Far stranger things have happened, Anna."

We walked across the Commons to a small comfort food place called Pasha. I had little appetite but ordered a tuna salad sandwich.

"I'll have the cheeseburger and fries," Alexandra told the waitress. "And do you have real Coke, not diet?"

"Your appetite has improved," I commented when the waitress had gone off with our order.

Alexandra grinned. "I know. And I'm not even worried about gaining weight. How bizarre is that? Oh, and Anna, I need to ask you a favor."

"Sure," I said. "Anything."

"Would you not tell anyone about Luke and me? I had to tell you, you're my closest friend, but I want to keep Luke to myself for a while. I want to keep us private."

"Of course," I assured her, hoping my crime wasn't stamped across my face. "Your secret's safe with me."

"I'm not ashamed," she explained. "And I don't see a reason why when I do introduce my friends to Luke I have to reveal the whole tragic story."

"I understand," I said, but I wondered about the shame factor.

Our lunch came, and Alexandra tucked in like the proverbial truck driver. I took one bite and chewed unenthusiastically.

"So," I said, "if it's okay to ask, what really happened with Luke and his wife?"

"What happened is that his wife decided she didn't want to be married any longer."

"Just like that?"

"Well, according to Luke it was out of the blue. Right after dinner one night. He went out back to turn off the sprinklers and she followed him. Told him right there on the lawn that she wanted him to move out."

"Oh," I said. "What reason did she give for wanting a divorce?" Please, I prayed, don't let there be accusations of spousal abuse.

"She said she was leaving on grounds of incompatibility. I'm not even sure she needs a reason in the state of Massachusetts. I don't remember; I've blocked out most of my own legal experience. Anyway, I suspect her decision wasn't made on the spur of the moment. Can you imagine making such a monumental decision in the snap of a finger?"

"Not really," I said. My personality precluded the possibility of spontaneous decision making, even regarding something as insignificant as choosing a breakfast cereal. "But what about the children?" I asked. "Didn't Luke stay in the marriage for the sake of the children?"

"He did indeed. For the sake of the family unit."

"So," I asked, tentatively, "isn't he still trying to keep the family unit in place?"

Alexandra's mouth tightened just a bit. "Of course. He asked her if she'd properly considered how a divorce would affect the kids. And she said something like, Now that the kids are on their way to college and not lunatic drug fiends and basically well adjusted, I don't see a problem with leaving."

"Maybe she was just beating him to the punch," I conjectured.

"No. When Luke made the decision to stay in the marriage, it was for good. Not just until the kids were on their own."

"Ironic, isn't it?"

"That's one word for it."

Disturbing is another, I thought. There I was, on the cusp of married life, and suddenly I was spending an awful lot of time talking about infidelity and the dissolution of an almost twenty-year marriage.

"Do you think his wife ever knew about you?" I asked. And I wondered, Would it be better to know that your husband is having an affair? Or would it be better to live in ignorance? If you know about a problem you have the opportunity to fix it, or at least to try. But if you don't know about a problem, does the problem even exist?

Alexandra sighed. "I don't know. I've never understood how a person could not know she's being cheated on. Even if there's no damning evidence lying around, there's got to be less tangible evidence. Right?"

"Right," I said. But I didn't really know. I'd never been cheated on. Had I?

"Some people just don't want to see the truth," Alexandra went on. "As long as the wheels of the marriage are turning they can accept a few suspicious creaks and groans. And some people just can't see the truth because they're so wrapped up in their own version of reality. I suppose I could ask Luke if his wife ever confronted him about having an affair. I could ask him if he ever confessed."

"Confessing at this point would just open a huge, messy can of worms," I said. "And it would probably make a divorce a lot more costly for him. Besides, what purpose would that information serve now? What would either of them gain? Unless he told her in anger, like a slap in the face, punishment for her crime. You're leaving me? Fine. Well, I had an affair. So there."

Alexandra put down the fork with which she was spearing the last of her fries. "I don't think he would do something so unkind."

"Unless she knew all along," I mused. "Maybe she's punishing him now by walking out."

"This conversation has taken a horrid turn."

"I'm sorry," I said. "My point is that confessions are highly overrated."

Alexandra looked at me closely. "Is lying a better alternative?"

"Kinder, sometimes," I said. "Don't you think? Especially if a mistake was made only once. I know, it's pick-and-choose morality. I just think that sometimes confessions make the confessor feel noble or forgiven but leave the confessee feeling devastated. People should think carefully before they reveal their sins."

"I see you've thought carefully about this topic."

I laughed. "And yet I've never had something awful to reveal. Not that I'm perfect. But seriously, I guess I just fear being the confessee."

"What you don't know won't hurt you?"

"Ignorance is bliss. I know," I said. "How ridiculous."

"Well, there's definitely something to be said for self-restraint," Alexandra admitted.

"For knowing when to keep your mouth shut."

Alexandra raised her glass to mine. "For sticking a sock in it."

"For stuffing the pain way down into your gut!"

"For stoicism!"

For not acting on your impulses, I added to myself. For doing without what you want. For doing without what you need.

"Did you ever try to contact Luke?" I asked then. "I mean, after your divorce."

"No. Absolutely not."

"You have enormous self-discipline."

"It had nothing to do with discipline," she said. "It had to do with kindness. I didn't think Luke needed my poking into his life again. I'd already done enough damage, unintentionally, of course. Besides, I was afraid. I knew I couldn't handle his anger or disappointment. It was bad enough that I imagined it."

I picked up the sandwich I'd ordered and then put it down again. I made a mental note to talk to my doctor about more vitamins and supplements.

"I really can't imagine what you've been going through all this time," I said. "I mean it, Alexandra. I truly can't imagine."

"Your life hasn't been a complete lark," she pointed out.

"No, but I've never had my heart broken." And as soon as I marry Ross, it never will be. "It was selfless of you," I said then, "not to go to his wife and cause trouble."

"Selfless? I don't know about that. If I made a stink with Luke's wife it would have ruined any feelings he might still have had for me."

"Still," I said, "it was good of you to back away."

"Whatever. Maybe I'm not a total jerk. But I'm certainly not a saint. No one is."

I smiled. "Not even Mother Teresa?"

"I can't believe there wasn't something in all those good works for her. She was human, wasn't she? Maybe a bit more, but she was born from a woman after all. Isn't that the point of Jesus, too? Son of both God and Man?"

"I'm not religious enough to know," I admitted.

"It's not about religion," Alexandra said dismissively. "It's about human nature. But we're off the topic. And maybe we should be. You must be bored by my romantic travails."

I laughed. "Alexandra, how many times do I have to say this? If there's one word I never associate with you, it's *boredom*."

"My time will come. You know, when I've got the blue hair."

I shuddered and attempted another bite of the sandwich. Alexandra had ordered another Coke and piece of apple pie.

"Aren't you afraid he'll go back to his wife?" I asked tentatively.

"No," she said. "I'm not afraid. He won't go back. And even if he wanted to, which he doesn't, she wouldn't take him back."

"How can you be so sure?"

Alexandra looked at me steadily, as if to make sure I got the message. "I'm sure," she said. "Anyway, he's kind of in shock, of course. He never expected her to go. How well did he know her, after all?"

How well, indeed. Maybe, I thought, if Luke had paid more attention to the woman he'd married, then—What? Then Alexandra might never have met him. Would that have been a good thing or a bad one?

"But now, he's free," Alexandra was saying. "He feels liberated. He won't go back. What would he go back to?"

To the familiar, I thought. To the status quo. To the public face of respectability.

Who am I kidding, I thought. Marriage doesn't automatically confer respectability. Why should it?

"You have such faith in him," I said. "I'm impressed by that. I feel that you deserve this chance with your one great love."

"I don't know about deserving the chance," Alexandra replied promptly. "I don't think the world works fairly. I don't think anyone gets what she really deserves, good or bad. But the chance is here and I'm taking it, and if I don't take it wholeheartedly, what's the point in taking it at all?"

I laughed. "You aren't very good at doing things halfway. That's true."

"Love isn't half-hearted, Anna. It's like the song says, all or nothing at all. Love is either there or it isn't. Love is easy that way. It's not confusing. It's very simple. I like that about love."

Love, simple?

"I don't know how you can say that love is simple," I argued. "Maybe for some people it is, but for other people it's horribly complicated. What happens when you find yourself in love with someone you're not supposed to be in love with?"

"What does that mean?" she said, eyeing me curiously. "'Supposed to' has nothing to do with love."

"Of course it does," I protested. "You're not supposed to fall in love with a married man. You're not supposed to fall in love with someone so different from you he'd irrevocably disrupt your life and just make a mess."

"I gather you're not talking about Ross," Alexandra said, folding her napkin and placing it next to her empty plate. "The man probably never even made a mess in a mud puddle."

"I'm not talking about anyone in particular," I retorted. Of course, Alexandra knew I was lying. But I could pretend to ignore that fact.

What had she said about people who choose not to see the truth?

And then I thought, When you say you have to grab love when it shows up, even when it means hurting someone in the process—like a wife or a husband—aren't you just creating an excuse for selfish behavior? Aren't you just saying, forget willpower and self-control and sacrifice. Just take what you want and if someone gets destroyed in the process, well, so be it. That's life. That's the way the ball bounces and the cookie crumbles.

"So, it's okay to cheat on someone if—"

"I don't advocate cheating, Anna," Alexandra said firmly.

"I do advocate love. Anyway, what are we really talking about here? Not me any longer, that's for sure."

"Nothing," I said, with a dismissive wave of my hand. "I guess I'm just tired. I feel a bit confused. I haven't been sleeping very well lately."

Alexandra popped the last piece of apple pie into her mouth. "Maybe you need more exercise and fresh air."

"Maybe," I said, "I do."

54

Sur L'Herbe

"Look at those azaleas, Ross," I said. "Have you ever seen anything so beautiful? The pinks are so clear and clean."

On Alexandra's assertion that exercise and fresh air cure all ills, I pressured Ross to spend an afternoon with me at the Harvard Arboretum. Ross isn't much of a nature lover. Even a well-manicured path through a formally sculpted garden has little appeal for him.

"Oh," he said, "that reminds me. I picked up a few new shirts at Brooks Brothers yesterday. I thought my wardrobe needed a little more rounding out in the nouveaux classics department. I got one in a sort of dusty rose, which I think works wonderfully with my complexion."

"Good," I said.

And there he was. Jack, camera in hand, tripod on a strap over his shoulder, striding closer to a bank of white azaleas. I watched, heart racing, as he squatted then stretched out on his stomach to get the shots he wanted.

"So," Ross said, "I'm thinking of starting these special vitamins for people doing the low-carb thing. They're over-the-counter so I don't have to bother seeing my doctor first, which is great because I swear it takes a month to get in unless you have an emergency."

"Mmm," I said.

Maybe, I thought, Jack won't see us. Maybe Ross won't see Jack and I can pretend not to see him, either. Maybe, I thought, I can ignore him, cut him dead and explain later.

Explain what, Anna?

"This sun," Ross said, "is so strong. I'm glad I wore the SPF 45. Oh, did I tell you I made an appointment to see my friend Jason's dermatologist? He's doing some new kind of dermabrasion that's supposed to make you look ten years younger. If I like this guy maybe you should see him, too."

"Okay," I said.

Jack got to his feet and strode off, his back to us. I felt weak with relief. He hadn't seen us, I was sure of it. I didn't think he was that good of an actor; I didn't think he could fake anything at all.

"I think I'm allergic to these lilacs," Ross said. He wrinkled his nose as if their smell was truly foul.

"They do have a strong fragrance," I replied, without much sympathy.

"Anna, are we done here? I thought we could stop by that fabulous new furniture store over on Washington before we meet Rob and his date for dinner."

"Okay," I said.

"I saw a gorgeous occasional table in the window, and I thought it might go perfectly in the hall to the second bedroom. Ugh. We're not having lilacs at the wedding, are we?"

I never made it to dinner that night. As soon as we left the furniture store I knew something was wrong. Ross accompanied me back to my apartment, where I immediately got into bed. He went off to meet his brother.

I'd heard enough about migraine symptoms to know the headache was no ordinary tension headache. I wanted to fall asleep, but the pain just wouldn't let me go. I wanted to pass out. I wanted to die. And all I could do was lie on my bed and wait it out.

Lesson learned: Knowing the pain will eventually go away is no consolation to the sufferer.

55

Analyze This

"So, is the migraine totally gone?" Alexandra asked. We were having dinner at Cobra, yet another new hot spot she'd forced me to try.

"Yes, finally. It lingered for two days. I don't think I've ever felt so sick."

"Poor you. And not even able to take medication."

I sighed. "Frankly, even if I was allowed to take something I wasn't well enough to crawl into the bathroom to get it."

"You should have called me sooner. I know there's a phone right by your bed. I would have come by."

"I know. I should have. If there's a next time—"

"Don't think about a next time. Anna, my dear, you really need to learn how to think positively. Sometimes you're downright lugubrious."

Was I lugubrious? Maybe. "Then," I said, "you're not going to want to hear what I've been working up the nerve to tell you."

"Anna," she said, "I am your friend. I daresay I'm your dearest friend. If you can't talk to me, who can you talk to?"

Who, indeed?

"Do you ever have recurring dreams?" I asked.

Alexandra looked at me over the rim of her martini glass. "Besides the ones I have about Luke and me being torn apart by three-headed Godzilla-like monsters? No."

Three-headed Godzilla-like monsters? I'd never known anyone whose dreams were actually haunted by monsters, the kind with scales and claws and green skin.

"Oh. Well," I said, "lately I've been having recurring dreams. Not the same exact dreams every night, but they all share similar themes. It's kind of upsetting me."

"It shouldn't," Alexandra said. "If the constant themes are love and peace and sex with a gorgeous man. But I'm guessing they're not."

"Um, no," I said. "Nothing like that I'm afraid."

"Go ahead, tell me about them. I'm not a shrink so I probably can't help you interpret, but I can listen like one."

"That's awfully generous of you," I said sincerely. "Most people are bored to tears listening to someone else's dreams."

Alexandra grinned. "I'm in a generous mood. I just got a big job and I'm feeling expansive in every way. Plus, I owe you for all the hours you've listened to me go on about my extramarital affair and its extraordinary outcome."

"You don't owe me anything," I said. "And congratulations on the job." And then I began.

"Okay, here's one. I pick up a piece of paper. I know that it's a printed list of some sort. But I can't see any of the words. I try really hard to read it, but everything is a blur, nothing is in focus, not even the edges of the paper. At first I'm frustrated, and then I start to panic. I think, 'I'm going blind!' but nobody notices that I can't see or that I'm panicking. And I don't want them to notice. I don't want anyone to see that anything is wrong with me or that I need help."

"Huh," Alexandra said. "Then what happens?"

"Nothing. I mean, I wake up or the dream just ends."

Alexandra took another long sip of her drink before saying, "Okay. Is there more?"

"Yes," I admitted. "But this one is horrible, truly disgusting. Are you sure you want to hear it?"

"Yes. I think. No, go ahead. I'm brave."

"Well," I said, watching Alexandra closely for any signs of distress, "in some dreams my mouth is stuffed with a gritty, viscous substance. I don't know what it is or where it comes from. It's not like when you've got a cold—"

"Oh, ick." Alexandra grimaced. "Honey, that really is disgusting!"

"I'm sorry," I said. "I'll stop."

Alexandra patted my hand. "No, go on. Really. I'm fine. I think you should talk about these dreams. Even if they are disturbing. Especially if they are disturbing. I just won't order anything gooey tonight."

Friends. Really, where are we without them?

"Okay," I said. "If you're sure. Anyway, this stuff prevents me from being able to talk. I have to scoot away from whomever I'm with, find some private place, and pull the stuff out of my mouth. It comes out in clumps, or sometimes it pulls out like taffy. It always seems endless. I try to find a mirror so I can make sure I get it all out. I don't want anyone to know this happens to me. It's so embarrassing. And that's it."

Alexandra shook her head as if coming back to life and took a long sip of her martini. "That's enough," she said finally. "What a nightmare! Poor Anna. You must wake up in the morning completely exhausted."

"I wake up completely grateful that it was all just a dream."

"But still," Alexandra said. "Maybe you should see a therapist about these dreams. They don't seem very healthy."

"Dreams can't hurt you," I said with a dismissive wave of my hand. But of course I didn't believe that.

Alexandra leaned forward across the table. "Anna," she said, "the dreams might be an expression of hurt you already feel. Like the dream where you can't read what's written on the piece of paper. I think it's about your trying to communicate. I think it's about your trying to be part of the world. I think it's about your trying to see what everyone else is seeing."

Did that make sense? "Maybe," I said. "And sometimes I dream about having no voice. Sometimes I'm furious with someone for being cruel to me, and the more I try to scream at this person the less noise comes from my throat until all that's left of my voice is a scratch."

"That sounds like a classic frustration dream. You're trying and trying to do something but nothing is happening. Your efforts are in vain."

"My efforts are in vain." I repeated the words as if to try them on, see if they fit. "Anyway," I said, "sometimes I need to defend myself against a false accusation, and my voice is just gone. And sometimes I need to call out for help; sometimes someone is trying to rape me or stab me. And every time I try to shout, I can't. Nothing comes out of my mouth but pitiful, strangled gasps."

"No wonder you've got dark circles under your eyes," Alexandra said.

"I do?"

"You mean you haven't noticed? Boy, you are in need of a peaceful night's sleep."

"I know. So, what do you think?"

"I think that your dream self is essentially blind and dumb."

"At least I can hear," I joked lamely.

"What good is the ability to take in information if you can't actually put it to use? What good is hearing the question if you can't give an answer?"

"Do you want to hear about another dream?" I asked, ignoring Alexandra's rhetorical challenge. "It's not grotesque."

"Sure," she said. "I've got no place else to be. Tell on."

"I dream of being alone." And then I considered. "No, it's more like I'm unseen or forgotten. I dream that love has passed me by and I just don't understand how it happened.

t's like maybe I fell asleep and missed something. Do you understand?"

"Not really," Alexandra said. "Give me something specific."

"Okay. Well, in one of these dreams I'm at a beautiful tropical resort, and suddenly my dream self remembers that I was at the resort years before with someone. I vaguely recall that the person was someone important, a lover. I remember there was a violent hurricane blowing in. But I can't remember anything more, and it troubles me. Why can't I remember my lover's name or his face? Why can't I remember what happened to him? Why can't I understand how I wound up all alone? And then, suddenly, I remember that I'm engaged and that I haven't been left behind after all. I realize that I haven't missed my last chance and that I won't grow old alone."

"That sounds happy," Alexandra said.

"But it isn't happy," I said. I heard my voice shake. "In the dream I don't feel happy; I don't even feel relieved. And then I wake up, and my waking mind says, 'Anna, you have Ross, you're not alone,' and still I feel no comfort or joy in knowing that. I still feel utterly alone."

I watched Alexandra absorb what I'd told her. "Anna," she said finally, "dreams are significant. They might be random in one sense but in another sense they're meaningful. Have you really thought about what these dreams are expressing? In terms of the choices you've made. You know, like getting married . . ."

Like getting married to Ross. Suddenly, the conversation had gotten too close for comfort.

"Not really," I said. "Not much. I'm not sure dreams are all that important."

Alexandra gave a dry little laugh. "If you believed that you wouldn't have told me all about them."

"Maybe."

"Don't jump down my throat when I say this. But maybe the dreams are a product of pregnancy hormones."

"No," I said. "I've been having these dreams for qui some time now. It's just that they've intensified lately." Sinc Ross and I got engaged, I added silently. Since I learne about you and Luke. Since I can't help but compare Jack Ross and find my fiancé lacking. Since everything has gotte so complicated.

"That doesn't reassure me at all," Alexandra said gloomil

It didn't reassure me, either.

56

Necessity

"Who is this Charlie Nestrowitz?"

Ross called me at my office the next day to tell me he was adding someone to the guest list.

"He's a major player, Anna. Dad's been watching this guy for a few years now. We've finally made a move, and he bit. If we work hard enough we can reel him in before the end of the year."

Suddenly, I was so tired of Ross's corporate speak. Mr. Nestrowitz was a human being, not a fish.

"He comes with a wife, I suppose?"

"Of course."

"And we absolutely have to invite them to our wedding?"

"Yes, Anna," Ross said, "we have to invite them. Look, it's not as if we've done a seating plan yet. The invitations haven't even gone out. I don't understand why you can't get on board with this."

On board? Ah, yes, wedding reception as corporate maneuver.

"But I've never met him, Ross," I argued. "It's not like he's a friend or someone you've worked with for some time.

Weddings should be about friends and family. Why can't you just take him to dinner or to a show?"

"I have taken him to dinner, Anna," Ross explained patiently. "No doubt Rob and I will take him to dinner a few more times before September. But Dad thinks it's a tactical move to invite him to a family event."

Who does Mr. Davis think he is, I thought angrily. A don? He just wants to show off. He wants this Charlie Nestrowitz to see just how much money he has and how everybody adores and idolizes him.

When I said nothing, Ross went on. "Anna," he said. It sounded as if he were speaking more closely into the phone. "If we get Charlie's business we'll be able to sell the loft in less than a year and buy one twice the size. We'll be able to get an upgrade on the diamond. Trust me, being nice to this guy will pay off in the end."

I thought, Kissing his ass, you mean. I said, "Fine. Give me his address."

57

The Introduction

I walked into the restaurant at exactly seven o'clock and scanned the bar. There was a man seated alone at the far end. And although Alexandra hadn't described Luke in any great detail, I just knew this man was him. My friend's famous Mystery Lover.

He looked nervous. If he'd been lounging with an arm thrown over the back of his chair and a toothpick hanging out of his mouth, I would have been furious with him.

As it was, I was furious with Alexandra. I'll kill her, I thought. I'll kill her for being late and forcing me to spend time alone with this man I don't know and am not sure I want to know.

You could sneak out, I told myself. He hasn't seen you yet. You could wait around the corner until Alexandra arrives. Why did you show up on time, anyway? You know she always keeps you waiting!

Too late. The man had seen me and was giving me the same curious but tentative look I was now giving him. I took a breath and walked the length of the bar to where he sat.

"Luke?" I said.

"Anna?" He sounded a bit relieved.

"It's a pleasure to meet you," I said, and extended my hand.

"The pleasure," he said, taking my hand, "is all mine. Really. I know this must be awkward for you. It certainly is for me. Thank you for coming."

"Thank you for being straightforward."

Luke pulled out a stool for me. "Would you like something to drink?" he asked.

I ordered a seltzer with lime. And we looked at each other.

"So," he said.

"So," I replied.

"There you are!"

I whirled around to see Alexandra striding toward us, all smiles. "Why don't we sit at this little table? It'll be easier to talk."

Luke practically jumped from his stool to greet her. I lowered my eyes as they kissed hello. In a moment we were seated at the table.

"You were late," I said.

Alexandra grinned. "Luke hates the fact that I'm always late."

"Twelve minutes late." Luke and I said it completely in sync.

"He thinks it's passive-aggressive of me." Alexandra eyed us both, waiting.

"So do I," I blurted.

"So why didn't you ever say anything?" she demanded. "I've told you that I think your constantly checking your watch is obsessive–compulsive."

I smiled brightly and falsely. "Alexandra," I said, "I think your always being late is passive-aggressive."

Alexandra nodded, satisfied. "Thank you for sharing your opinion."

"She has control issues," Luke stage-whispered to me, and I laughed.

So far so good, I thought.

"I hear congratulations are in order," Luke said when we'd ordered drinks.

"Yes. Thanks."

"A wedding and a baby. You must be very busy."

I noted—how could I not?—that Luke hadn't said I must be very happy. How much had Alexandra told him about my increasingly disturbing dreams? How much of her low opinion of Ross had she shared?

"Not much more than usual," I said lightly.

Alexandra smiled at me blandly. I thought back to when she'd asked me to join them that night. She hadn't invited Ross. I hadn't even considered bringing him.

While the lovebirds caught up on their days, I surreptitiously—I hoped—examined Alexandra's beau.

He's handsome, I noted, but not perfect. His earlobes are a bit long. When he gets old they'll be sweeping his shoulders. Okay, his hair is great. And his eyes are dreamy. But he is a bit short for Alexandra. And his laugh is rather loud.

And then I looked at Alexandra's face and it was like watching Elizabeth Taylor gazing at Richard Burton; Heloise contemplating Abelard; Juliet swooning over Romeo. And I wondered why I was picking apart this man she so totally adored.

Because I wanted to understand why he was so special to my friend. But of course the answers wouldn't be found only in his appearance. And of course they could only be fully known to Alexandra.

But I could try to see some of what moved her. I needed to because I was still wary of this person who demanded such devotion from someone I had thought so impervious to love.

I wondered, Was Alexandra a weak person because she was in love? Or was she really far stronger than I had ever been? Love required sacrifice; it demanded selflessness; it needed unwavering commitment. Love, I thought, is very, very hard. For Alexandra it had involved years of quiet sacrifice for one unspectacular person. But maybe that's what true love is all about, I thought. Seeing the spectacular in an average human being and living accordingly for him.

Are we only fully alive when we're loved?

I suddenly felt parched and took a long drink of water. Sitting there with Alexandra and Luke, I was forced, one again, to face the truth that Ross, the man I was going to marry, the father of my unborn child, was not the great love of my life. And by accepting Ross's proposal of marriage I'd effectively eliminated my chances for a great love in my future.

That's okay, I told myself again while the lovebirds cooed on. Over-the-top, erotically charged romance simply isn't in the cards for you. It's simply not your fate to experience intense passion. You, Anna, are just one of those women who are unlucky in great love.

I wondered, Then what was I lucky in? Mediocre love?

And what, I thought, was wrong with that?

"Earth to Anna!"

Alexandra's voice called me back to life. I smiled embarrassedly at Luke.

"I'm sorry," I said. "Something I just remembered, about a job . . ."

"You really should try to relax," Alexandra scolded. "Here, honey, try some of this paté; it's fabulous."

Luke passed the plate of bread. The conversation turned to health insurance and then to the upcoming show at the MFA. I tried to participate, but one powerful thought kept nagging at my brain. What if—just think, Anna!—what if great, passionate love, the kind that's eluded you for all these years, is finally here, right in front of you, waiting to be embraced?

The thought was terrifying. Don't be an idiot, Anna, I chided. You've made your decision. And you'll stick with it.

But thoughts of Jack Coltrane would not go away.

58

Knock Down, Drag Out

I woke the next morning feeling as if I'd swallowed a watermelon whole. It wasn't just an average case of gas; it was Pregnant Woman indigestion. I defy anyone to be in a good mood with a giant hand grenade in her stomach, especially on an unseasonably warm day. Eight o'clock a.m. and the temperature was already eighty, and the humidity was seventy-six percent; The Weather Channel predicted thunderstorms that evening.

How, I wondered, toddling to the bathroom, am I going to survive being pregnant in August if I feel so bad in May? Briefly I considered working from home (my computers were linked) where I could turn up the air conditioning full blast and avoid the boiling streets. And then I remembered I'd left an important e-mail address on the desk in my office. And that I'd promised to drop off a book of Susan Sontag essays to Jack in his studio.

Of course, I could have called to postpone the visit. But I wanted to see Jack. I wanted to hear his critical take on the senator who'd just been indicted on racketeering charges. I wanted to see the pictures he'd taken that day at the arboretum, when I'd effectively hid from him. I wanted to talk with him about the Sontag book. I wanted to talk with Jack about everything.

I wanted to see his face.

"You don't look very good," Jack said when I showed up around eleven o'clock.

I gave him a patently false smile. "I don't feel very good."

"What's wrong? Do you feel sick?"

"Something like that. Trust me, you don't want to know."

Jack gestured toward the small refrigerator by his desk. "Do you want some water? Sorry it's not cooler in here. The AC is acting up. A service guy is supposedly coming this afternoon. Or next month."

"Yes," I said, "thanks." I hoped I could drink it without burping in his face.

Jack grabbed a cold bottle of Dasani, opened it, and handed it to me. "I see your fiancé got his name in print again," he said.

I took a long swig of water before saying, "Really? I haven't seen a paper today. I haven't even read the news online. Do you have the *Globe*?"

"It's not in the *Globe*," he said flatly.

I felt a trickle of sweat at my temples. I hoped I'd brought along my finishing powder. "Okay," I said. "What paper then?"

Jack picked up an oversized magazine from his desk and thrust it at me.

"Ross is in *Outrageous*?" *Outrageous* is a black-and-white weekly that chronicles the nightlife of Boston's wealthier swingers, aspiring socialites, wilder athletes, visiting models, and other dubious luminaries. "I didn't know you read anything so vapid. Do you know there are an average of five typos or misspellings or obvious grammatical errors per page? I've counted."

Jack grimaced. "I have to keep up on what my clients are doing on their off-hours. Believe me," he said, "I don't enjoy it."

The truth was I didn't enjoy the magazine much, either. It really was a rag, but it was an essential rag for those of us in the media-friendly professions. With some trepidation I opened the magazine.

"I'll save you some time," Jack said. "Page thirty-five."

I opened to page thirty-five; a trickle of sweat plopped from my brow onto one of the four pictures of my party-hopping fiancé. The photos were dated; they had all been taken over the past few weeks. Ross at dinner with a man I recognized as a celebrity defense attorney; Ross in a bar deep in conversation with one of the most infamous members of the Red Sox; Ross in a tuxedo, at a charity event, posing with several members of the unofficial club of wealthy Boston businessmen; and finally, Ross at a nightclub, dancing—Ross danced?—with an unnamed buxom blonde who might not have been of legal drinking age.

There really was nothing damning about the photographs. There were no babes sticking their tongues down Ross's throat; he and his dance partner were feet apart from each other. There was no suggestive copy. There was also no mention of Ross's fiancé.

"So?" I said, looking back up to Jack. "Socializing is an important part of Ross's business."

"It's an important part of your business, too, but you don't make a fool of yourself doing it."

"Ross doesn't make a fool of himself." I pointed at the four pictures. "Do you see him doing anything foolish in these pictures? Do you?"

Jack laughed bitterly. "I see him prostituting himself for his daddy's money, which it seems is all he's fit to do."

I stood there, sweating, trembling; I thought I would throw up; I thought I would pass out. Finally, I found my voice.

"Why did you even have to show me this stupid magazine?" I said. "So you could antagonize me? So you could try to embarrass me? Look, Jack, it's my life. Why don't you just let me live it?"

"Because you're not doing a very good job of it," he snapped.

"What?" I cried. "How dare you! What gives you the right to talk to me this way?"

Jack didn't answer. His mouth was tight; his eyes were black.

"Look," I said, "I don't want to hear another word about Ross. I mean it, Jack. I've listened to your obnoxious opinions for too long."

"If you really were listening," he began. "Forget it."

Jack turned away, and I did something I'd never done before. I grabbed his arm and yanked. He turned back; the look on his face was unreadable. I was horrified; I was furious.

"No," I said. "I don't want to forget it. What were you going to say? That if I were really listening I would have what? Reconsidered my marriage based on the opinion of a forty-five-year-old bachelor who knows nothing about what it takes to make a relationship?"

"Anna—"

"You're despicable," I shouted. "I hate you for making me feel so horrible!"

And suddenly, it was as if I'd slapped him in the face. He seemed to deflate from an angry, self-righteous jerk to a confused, penitent man. "I didn't want to make you feel bad, Anna," he said, voice low.

"Then what did you want?" I challenged. "How did you expect me to react to your so-called constructive criticism?"

"I didn't think," he said. "I shouldn't have said anything. I'm sorry. I'm sorry."

Oddly enough, I believed him. Jack isn't a liar. I believed he was sorry for hurting me. But at that moment, his apology, no matter how sincere, didn't mean a thing.

"Apology not accepted," I snapped. "I'm leaving. Here's the book I promised you." I flung the Sontag book on his desk and marched toward the door. Wisely, Jack didn't try to stop me by word or outstretched hand. Once on the sidewalk

I stopped to breathe; I sat for a minute on the stone steps of the building, blinking against the brutal sun until I was calm enough to pull my sunglasses from my bag.

I felt like such a fool, such a bloated, gassy, sweating fool. I'd actually been thinking romantic thoughts about Jack. I'd actually thought he might have romantic feelings for me. Idiot. Stupid hormones! They'd made me into someone I hardly recognized.

The air was thick; it felt dirty. I'd take a nice cool shower the moment I got home. I'd try to forget the awful scene that had just taken place.

And I'd think about the baby. At least I had the baby. And that made me very, very happy.

Part Two

59
Revolt

There wasn't time to wait for an ambulance. I just knew. Biting my lip against the violence happening inside me, I made it down to the entrance hall of my building, step by excruciating step. There was no sound at all from Mr. Audrey's apartment or from Katie and Alma's. Everyone, it seemed, was asleep. It simply didn't occur to me to wake them.

Once outside, I hailed a cab. Inanely I thought, I'm having incredible luck with cabs these days. Carefully, I got into the backseat.

"Emergency room, Beth Israel. And please hurry."

"Someone in an accident, lady?" the driver asked as he screeched off.

"Yes," I said, in a remarkably calm voice. "There's been an accident."

It didn't occur to me until I was standing just outside the doors to the ER that I should call Ross. Somehow I seemed to know that cell phones don't work in hospitals; I don't know why. The pain caused me to double over, but I managed to make the call on my cell phone before walking through those automatic doors.

Ross's recorded voice met my ears. "It's Anna," I told it. "I'm at the ER, Beth Israel. It's about eleven thirty, I think. Something's wrong, Ross. Something's very wrong."

60

Answers

Life is so much messier than art. At least in art there's a conscious creator, an identifiable author. And sometimes there's even a frame. But in life? Who knows? And even if there is an ultimate creator of life, a god or goddess or some non-anthropomorphic force, why should anyone assume that his or her or its motives and grand plan are transparent or at all knowable to mere humans?

Here's one of the things I like about art over life. You can sit down with a painter, face to face, and ask why she chose to paint a particular subject in a particular way, and you'll get an answer. The answer might be difficult to interpret, but it will be an answer. You'll hear it with your own ears.

But you can't sit down face to face with the master or mistress of the universe. Sure, you can send a question out into the air through prayer or chant or meditation, and maybe an answer will come whispering back, but how can you be sure the answer isn't your own attempt to fill the void? How can you ever be sure you're not playing God and hearing what you want to hear?

Give me art over life any day. I like things someone can explain.

61

Loss

There was no heartbeat. There was nothing.

62

Last Steps

Ross drove me home. Unspoken agreement had led us to my apartment, not the loft. We sat for a moment in the front seat of his Jaguar, silently.

"You go on up," he said finally, his voice even. He didn't look at me when he spoke, just stared ahead through the windshield. "I'll find a place to park and be up in a minute."

"That's okay," I said quickly. "I mean, I'm okay. I just need to sleep. Why don't you go on home. I mean, it's so hard to find parking here, and you have a spot at the loft."

Ross didn't spend much time thinking about his answer.

"All right. If you're sure . . ."

"I'm sure. Thanks for the ride," I said.

"No problem."

I eased out of the car. As Ross drove off, I flashed back to those awkward first and only dates of high school. I remembered how I felt as the unhappy boy drove away, leaving me at the bottom of our driveway. Very alone. Terribly aware that the evening had been a huge mistake. Relieved to be home, where I belonged.

I climbed the long flights of stairs to my apartment, conscious at every step of the doctor's words of caution. But the only way home was to climb those stairs. Past Mr. Audrey's door, decorated with a stark grapevine wreath. No sound from within. Past Katie and Alma's door. From their apartment I heard distant strains of classical music. For half a second the idea of stopping there crossed my mind, but I kept on climbing.

I opened the door to my apartment, and for the first time it seemed like an awfully lonely place. I'd been coming home to an empty apartment for years, but somehow, it had never felt really empty until that moment.

Not all the baby gifts we'd been given were stored in the loft apartment. A sterling silver piggy bank, still in its box, sat on the coffee table. A Lamaze infant play mat was spread out on the floor beneath the table. The hideous handmade sweater Mrs. Davis had commissioned was in a heap on a dining room chair. I picked it up and took it with me into the bedroom.

Sun streamed through the window; it was only one o'clock in the afternoon. I slipped into bed in the clothes I was wearing and pulled the covers to my neck.

I'd never felt so tired, so flattened and boneless. Under the covers I bundled the lumpy sweater to my chest.

"Goodbye," I whispered. "Goodbye."

63

Poking the Wound

Thus began the worst few weeks of my life.

What do you call a person who courts misery? A person who is most content being sunk in depression or self-pity?

A misanthrope. A cynic. A defeatist.

I don't like misery. I'm not happy being unhappy.

I woke to find the bedroom already dark. I reached over and turned on the light; my watch said it was eight o'clock. Carefully, I got out of bed; the hideous sweater was on the floor in a heap. I checked voice mail; no one had called. Not even Ross. I wondered if he'd told anyone.

Slowly I made my way into the kitchen where I realized I hadn't eaten in almost twenty-four hours. And I was ravenous. I spread peanut butter and jelly on crackers; I wolfed down a banana.

And still the phone didn't ring.

I went into the living room and pulled my college copy of *Roget's Thesaurus* from the bookshelf. I looked up synonyms for the words *miscarry* and *miscarriage*. There were many.

For example: A miscarriage was a failure. It was a non-success.

A miscarriage was a fruitless endeavor.

By miscarrying I had missed my mark.

To miscarry was to botch the job.

And then there were the more colorful turns of phrase. A miscarriage could be described as a slip 'twixt cup and lip. To miscarry could be said to roll the stone of Sisyphus.

For a project to miscarry was for it to come to nothing.

I tossed the yellowing paperback aside.

My accidental pregnancy had come to nothing.

Listlessly, I reached for the remote and began to flip through the nine hundred channels. Nothing was of interest until I reached Lifetime. The station was airing a movie about a young, kind-hearted, wide-eyed woman fighting her older, evil, narrow-eyed ex-husband for custody of their seven-month-old baby. I wept through the entire two hours.

Maybe, I thought, I'm a defeatist after all.

64

Well-Meaning

Spontaneous abortion. It's Nature's way of weeding out the imperfect.

Nature.

I was terrified. The world was full of risk; anything at all could happen at any time; this moment could be my last. My own body could rise up and rebel, destroy what it had created, and there was nothing I could do about it.

Nothing at all but recover.

And recovery was on everybody's mind. Everyone had ideas about how to move on. Everybody felt the need to express them.

Get pregnant again immediately, some said. At least, as soon as the doctor says it's okay.

Others said, Wait a year before trying again. Get married, go on the honeymoon, relax.

Put it all out of your mind, a nurse at my doctor's office told me. Miscarriage is common; millions of women have miscarriages; the fetus wasn't a baby yet, anyway. Not a real person. Me? I've had three, and you don't see me missing any sleep, do you?

Go to a therapist for counseling. Join a support group. Women grieving the loss of an unborn child. I'm sure the hospital can hook you up.

Get over it, go through it, ignore it, embrace it.

People I hardly knew sent me articles clipped from women's and parenting magazines. Ross's mother alerted me by phone to a weeklong segment on the evening news; it was devoted to, in her words, "women with hostile wombs." My own mother sent me a standard issue inspirational greeting card that assured me God was watching over me every second of the day. The card only made me feel paranoid.

Kristen sent me a flowery card reminding me that she was my "Forever Friend." Katie and Alma brought me homemade chicken soup—perfect, they swore, for soothing the wounded soul. Alexandra checked in with me every two hours on the dot, offering a delivery of groceries, wine, or magazines. Tracy came by with flowers and helped with my housekeeping.

No doubt everyone's intentions were good, but the clamor began to wear on my nerves. Why can't my grief belong to me, I wondered. How am I supposed to know how I feel if they all keep talking, yammering, shouting in my ear!

Everyone, I thought, should just shut up.

65

Don't Bring God Into It

"Can I get anyone something to drink?" I offered listlessly. "I haven't been to the store since last week but—"

Four days since I'd lost the baby and I wasn't feeling any less miserable. I warned them I was a mess, but they came anyway.

"Quit trying to play hostess," Alexandra commanded. "We can fend for ourselves."

"Do you know what my mother said to me?" I asked. "She said, and I quote: God only gives us what we can handle. If He didn't think you could handle losing this baby, He wouldn't have allowed it to happen."

"Since when did your mother get religion?" Alexandra snapped.

Tracy winced. "That's so wrong on so many levels."

"And that nonsense is supposed to make me feel better!" I said. "I'm supposed to be able to handle this miscarriage and I'm not handling it, I'm not able to handle it, so I'm screwing that up, too? I can't be a good mother and I can't be a happy fiancé, and now I can't stop crying . . ."

Kristen patted my shoulder gently. "A lot of that's hormones, you know," she said. "It's not really you. It's the chemicals."

I swiped tears from my cheeks. "Why is everything about the chemicals?"

No one had an answer.

"You need to stop blaming yourself."

Alexandra, too? Where, where did people get these notions? From the *Clichés in Times of Trouble* catalogue?

"I'm not blaming myself," I protested. "At least, not entirely. I know these things just happen. It's not like I went horseback riding over rough terrain or went bungie jumping at Great Adventure. It's not like I tried to end the pregnancy."

"Maybe what you need is—"

I cut Kristen off. "What I really need is to go to sleep. For a long, long time. I'm just so tired. So awfully tired. And no," I added, looking at each of my friends in turn, "I don't mean tired of living. My mother also reminded me that God helps those who help themselves. God, it seems, doesn't like losers."

There was a moment of charged silence; Kristen broke it.

"I know I shouldn't say it, what with the kids in Sunday school and all, but, well, sometimes the notion of God does more harm than good."

"That's the understatement of the century." Tracy sighed. "I'd be happy if God—or the idea of him—just went away."

"It's not God's fault the world is so horrid," Alexandra said. "It's people who commit idiocy. God and guns are not to blame. Human beings, the creators of God and guns? Now they're the big culprits."

Tracy nodded. "And there's no escaping our human nature."

I moaned and fell back against the pillows. "Please, I'm depressed enough as it is."

Kristen adjusted the shades and straightened the rumpled covers. "We'll let you sleep. Do you want anything before we go? A glass of milk?"

"Kristen," I said, "I haven't had a glass of milk since I was twelve. Maybe a glass of water. But I can get it. Thanks."

My friends gathered their bags. When they were at the door to my room I said, "Everyone?"

Alexandra, Kristen, and Tracy stopped and turned.

"Thank you."

66

Interference

Five days and counting.

"Hi," said Ross. "It's Ross."

"Yes," I said. "I know. I have Caller ID." It wasn't a gracious reply, but I wasn't feeling very gracious.

"Look, Anna," Ross said, "I know I promised I'd stop by later but something's come up."

Something's come up? Was he really pulling out that tired old line? And what about a few conversational preliminaries like, how was your day? Or, how is work going? Since the miscarriage Ross hadn't once asked if I was behind schedule, if I needed to hire some temporary help.

"What's come up?" I said.

"There's this guy I really need to meet tonight, for business purposes. I know I said I'd check in on you, see if you needed anything—"

"That's okay," I said, forestalling another lame excuse. "I'm fine. Katie was here earlier, and I talked to Tracy a little while ago."

"Good. Good." Ross sounded infinitely relieved that I hadn't made a scene. Not that I ever had. "Because this guy could be very important to us. To the family. He knows just about everyone there is to know both in Boston and New York."

"He must be quite a guy." I wondered if Ross heard the sarcasm in my voice. If he did, he chose not to respond to it.

"Oh," he said. "I almost forgot. My mother asked about you."

"Oh? She called you?" Mrs. Davis hadn't called me since the miscarriage. But then again, my own mother hadn't returned the call I'd made to her. Although maybe it was better she hadn't called, given that completely unsympathetic card she'd sent me.

"Yes, I spoke to her earlier."

Did I have to drag it out of him? "Well, what did you tell her?" Although how would Ross know how I was doing? I'd hardly seen him since he'd dropped me off that dreadful day. And our phone conversations had all been about as stiff as those between an employer and the employee he'd just fired.

"I told her you were fine."

I imagined my nerve endings fraying into nothing. "Look, Ross, I've got to go."

"Right, me, too. Wish us luck with this guy."

"Ross?" I said, suddenly not wanting to let him go. "How are you doing?"

He sighed. He sounded impatient now to be gone. "I just told you, work is crazy right now so I'm a little stressed. I've got a massage scheduled tomorrow so that should help and—"

"Ross. I mean about what happened. Losing the baby."

There was a long moment of silence. I tried to picture the expression on Ross's face as he struggled for something to say, but I couldn't. I couldn't see him at all.

"Anna," he said finally, brusquely, "I've got to go. This is the office, not a place for a personal conversation."

I took a deep breath before saying, "Right. Good luck with the connected guy."

We didn't actually say goodbye.

67

Honesty

The phone rang at nine the next morning, waking me from a deep sleep and the dreams. I was being choked. My mouth was full of grit. I crouched at the edge of a pond and saw in the water my own face in miniature.

Caller ID told me it was Tracy. I reached for the receiver. I didn't want to go back to sleep and those awful dreams.

"Did I wake you?" she asked.

"Yes. But it's okay. Really." I pushed the pillows up behind my back. I saw my reflection in the vanity's mirror and shuddered.

"So, is it okay if I come over for a bit?"

"Sure," I said. "Okay. But I'm warning you. I've looked better. This might be the worst hair day of my life."

"I promise not to grimace. I'll be there in half an hour."

I managed to put a robe on over my nightgown and to drag a brush through my hair. By the time Tracy arrived a half hour later I'd had a cup of coffee—oh, how I'd missed coffee!—and was semi-awake.

"How are you?" Tracy asked.

Oh, I was getting so tired of that question. "The doctor," I told her, "said that I'll probably be depressed and irritable and all sorts of nasty things for some time. So I've got that to look forward to."

"Think of the potential, Anna," Tracy said brightly. "You can get away with murder—in some states, anyway—because the hormones are responsible, not you."

"Can't anything I feel be real?" I cried. "Does it all have to be caused by hormones? Is every feeling suspect? I resent this. I resent being told I'm not the real owner of my feelings. Who I am can't be reduced to some stupid chemical formula!"

Poor Tracy. She was only trying to help.

"I'm sorry, Anna," she said softly. "Really. It was dumb; I shouldn't have tried to make a joke."

"No, I'm sorry. I shouldn't have gotten all crazy. See?" I tried to laugh. "I can admit I'm acting crazy so maybe I'm not a total mess."

"You're not a mess at all. You're a very normal woman going through a very difficult time. That's all."

"That's enough!"

Tracy gave a half-hearted laugh, then the words came blurting out.

"Anna, I have something to tell you." Suddenly she was agitated; she looked down at her hands and twisted her wedding ring crazily. "I'm embarrassed to admit this, but we're friends and I'm your matron of honor, and I feel uncomfortable not being totally honest with you."

I wondered, Had Tracy taken a hint from Alexandra's life? Was she having an affair with a married man? Or maybe, like Michaela, she had made a play for Ross! What, I wondered, was happening to my friends?

"Okay," I squeaked.

Tracy looked back up at me and folded her hands. "It's a terrible thing to admit, especially just after the miscarriage—"

"It's okay," I said, just a bit desperately. "Just tell me."

And she did. "Well, when you got pregnant . . . It was a

little difficult for me. It shouldn't have been, but it was. I wa happy for you, Anna, honestly, but I was also miserable. Fo me. For a while. Every time I think I'm fine with not havin children of my own, surprise, something makes me realiz I'm not fine. Not entirely."

"Were you jealous?" I asked, remembering Michaela' poisoning jealousy.

Tracy took my hand and laughed a self-deprecatin laugh.

"Oh, no, not jealous. But the truth is, Anna, that some times I feel left out. I feel as if I'm never going to be a full fledged, card-carrying woman because I missed out o motherhood. I know that sounds crazy, but not being a mothe excludes you from so many important experiences . . ." Trac shook her head as if to dismiss her troubled thoughts. "I'n sorry, Anna. I'm being all whiny and self-pitying. And be lieve me, I'm so, so sorry about what happened. I came ove this morning thinking I might be of some help but . . ."

Tracy still held my hand in hers. I squeezed it back.

"Let's say we're both here to help each other, okay? I'n so sorry, Tracy. I never knew you felt so bad about not hav ing a child of your own."

"Well," she said, "it's not something that rules my lif anymore. I've worked on that. It's bad enough I brought it u now. Talk about dampening a good mood."

"Friends have a right to dampen each other's good mood once in a while," I said. "I've certainly dampened my shar of good moods since that little pink stick told me I was preg- nant. And let's face it," I added. "I wasn't in such a good mood this morning anyway."

Tracy pulled her hand from mine and stood up.

"I know just how to get us both into a good mood." He voice was determinedly cheerful. "We need to go get a bi cookie. One for each of us. A big, dense, chocolate chi cookie."

"One you could eat with a knife and fork?"

"Exactly."

I got up from the couch and stretched. It felt good to move.

"I thought you didn't eat sweets," I teased. "Miss Whole Foods Tofu Girl."

Tracy smiled. "This is an exception. Now go and put on some decent clothes."

I took a few steps toward the bathroom and then stopped.

"You know," I said, "everyone but you had a suggestion about what to name the baby. Even Alexandra had an opinion."

Tracy grinned. "Oh, I had a suggestion. I just didn't think I should offer it."

"Why?"

"What you named the baby was your business, not mine."

"Tell me now," I urged. Now that it doesn't matter.

Tracy seemed to consider. "How about," she said, finally, "I keep my suggestion to myself. Until the next time. Okay?"

Tears came to my eyes again, but this time they weren't sad tears. What would I do without Tracy, I wondered. Without Alexandra, without Kristen. Who would I be?

"Okay," I said. "Until the next time."

68

Chance Encounter

I woke to a beautiful late May morning. The sun was shining through a few scattered puffy clouds. I opened the windows to a cool, refreshing breeze. And for the first time in what seemed like forever, I felt a surge of mental energy.

After a hearty breakfast—my appetite seemed to have returned, as well—I sat at my computer and got down to work in a serious way. It felt good to focus on something other than me. I made a few calls, wrote a few letters, worked up a few preliminary sketches, checked out a vendor's new web site.

Sometime after noon I finally stood, stretched, and glancing out at the vibrant green trees that lined my block, decided to get some fresh air. It was a major decision; since the miscarriage I'd left my apartment only once, with Tracy, and she'd acted as a buffer between the unpredictable world and me. I remember not even looking for traffic as we crossed Tremont Street. I just took her arm and, like a child, trusted her to keep me safe.

You can't be a child forever, Anna, I told myself, as a car cruised down the block pumping rap into the spring air. Anyway, what was so great about being a child? You got taken to places you really did not want to go and there was nothing you could do about it.

After wolfing down a frozen Lean Cuisine, I showered and dressed. At the door of the building, my hand on the knob, I halted. Did I really want to go out there into the maddeningly unstable world of muggers, of bricks falling from crumbling facades, of out of control city buses hurtling onto the sidewalk?

Somehow, miraculously, I opened that door, walked down the stairs, and turned left toward Washington Street. The first step is the hardest. Believe it.

By the time I got to the end of the block I felt a whole lot better. Three blocks later and there was a bit of a spring to my step. By the time I got to the corner of Rutland and Shawmut I was thirsty—I hadn't moved much in over a week—so I decided to stop for a cup of iced coffee. I'll drink it in Blackstone Square, I thought. I'll sit quietly and alone on a bench, sip my coffee, and watch people play fetch with their dogs.

The tiny bakery and sandwich shop was crowded with people needing a mid-afternoon pick-me-up. Jack Coltrane was two ahead of me on line. I hadn't seen him since that awful fight right before the miscarriage. Almost immediately, as if sensing my presence, he turned. I gave a little wave; I couldn't help it. Jack let the person behind him go ahead and joined me.

"Hey," he said.

"Hey."

I looked far from my best, but for once I didn't care. Well, not entirely. Sand-colored T-shirt, pale gray jacket, taupe chinos, and beige slides. Bland neutrals head to toe. I guess I wasn't quite ready for color.

"Do you have a few minutes?" Jack asked. "I want to show you something."

I touched my hair, which was pulled back into a ponytail, and was immediately aware that I'd just exhibited a common sign of self-consciousness.

"I just stopped by for an iced coffee to go," I said, not really answering his question.

"Please. I'd like your opinion." He gestured to the ubiquitous ratty leather bag over his shoulder. "About some photographs."

Somehow, I managed a smile. "You're asking for my opinion?"

"It's not my work," he said. "It's the work of a kid at some high school downtown. A friend who teaches there asked me to critique it, maybe advise the kid in some way."

I suppose I should have refused. I was still angry with him for his last brutal assessment of Ross, and thereby, of me. But what did I have to go home to? An empty apartment. A rumpled bed. My own grief and self-pity. No. I was determinedly on the mend.

"Buy me a brownie?" I asked.

"Deal. I'll order. Why don't you grab that table in the back?"

I left Jack at the counter and squeezed my way through the tiny, bustling café.

My feelings were still raw; my nerves overly sensitive to the crush of mid-afternoon snack seekers. Maybe this is a bad idea, I thought. Maybe I should just go.

But then Jack was there with our coffees and a brownie.

"A squirt of chocolate, right?" he said, placing a cup in front of me.

I nodded. Ross and I had been together almost a year and still he didn't know how I took my coffee, iced or hot.

Jack's an artist, I reminded myself sensibly. He notices things, people, details. He can't help it. He pays attention. It's what he does. That's why he knows my favorite flower. No big deal. All part of the territory.

Jack pulled a slightly battered folder from his bag and opened it so that I could see its contents. "The kid's name is Rasheed Kelly," he said. "He's fifteen. Maybe sixteen. What do you think?"

I looked down at the four black-and-white photographs

before me. They were shots of two or three kids hanging around on urban streets and in schoolyards.

Jack continued to stare down at the images. After a minute he said, "There's a consistency of vision here that's very unusual in someone so young."

"I agree," I said. "I think they're very good. But I'm not an expert."

Jack put down his coffee cup with a bang. "You don't need to be an expert. What does that mean, anyway? Someone with an advanced degree? You're a sensitive human being. And you know how to put your thoughts into meaningful words. Mostly."

I laughed. "Okay," I said. "Maybe that's where a degree comes in handy. When you have to verbalize your instinctual responses."

"Maybe."

"So, are you going to help what's his name? Rasheed Kelly. Be his mentor?"

"I don't believe in inflicting my so-called wisdom on anyone under the age of twenty-one. But yeah, I'll meet with him. I'll look at more of his work. I hope he's not a self-obsessed little jerk, though. I'm too old to deal with an egomaniacal kid."

Jack scooped the four photos back into the folder and replaced it in his bag. And I watched his hands. They were very different from Ross's hands. Not better or worse, just different. I like Jack's hands, I realized. They're strong and big, and yet he does the most sensitive things with them.

But that way lies madness, Anna.

"I think we should go," I said, nodding slightly toward the horde of hovering coffee drinkers. "People want our table."

Jack smiled. "Since when do I care about what other people want?"

"That's right. No social graces."

"But I'll be nice, for your sake." Jack hefted his bag and stood.

"What you really mean is that you're late for an appointment."

"Yeah. Come on."

And then Jack did something he'd never done in our entire professional relationship. Ever so lightly he took my elbow and steered us through the crush of hungry mid-afternoon folk. And something very strange happened to me. For the first time in my life I was suddenly, unexpectedly flooded with desire. It hit me hard. I felt sick. I felt euphoric. I felt dizzily alive.

Outside the shop Jack let go of me.

"I'll see you," I said, just a bit shakily. "Thanks for the brownie." I wanted to add, And thanks for asking for my opinion. And for listening to it. And thank you for touching me.

Jack nodded. "Right."

Reluctantly—what did I want to happen?—I turned toward Shawmut Avenue. Jack's voice called me back.

"Anna?"

He stood there on the corner, only fifteen or so feet from me. "I'm sorry," he said.

"You know about the miscarriage." I was pummeled by a riot of emotions—relief, fresh sadness, desire. Who, I wondered, had told him? Did it matter?

"I wanted to say something earlier. I should have."

A small, absurd laugh escaped my lips. "It's okay," I said. What did Jack have to apologize for? "Really."

And suddenly that riot of emotions was just too much, and I began to cry. I wanted to rush at him, fling my arms around him, beg him to hold me. But neither of us moved.

Jack's eyes held mine. "Things will be better, Anna."

I could only nod. And then I turned again toward home. I thought of the roses and knew in my heart that Jack stood and watched me go.

69

Mourning Becomes No One

Ross called later that afternoon to say he was stopping by on his way home from the office. Stopping by, not staying for dinner or spending the night. And while I waited for Ross, a strange little memory came to me.

When I was a child I thought that mourning doves were morning doves. Although I'm not sure I ever actually saw a mourning dove before noon, I thought, What a nice name for those beautiful gray-brown birds.

When I finally learned my mistake I felt so foolish. Of course "mourning" made sense. It perfectly describes the bird's plaintive call, what's often been described as its mournful murmur.

Mourning doves are monogamous maters. It's not unusual for the male to stay with the female through the winter. Oddly, especially given this fact, mourning doves are notoriously poor nest builders.

Mourning is the act of sorrowing.

I stood before the bookcase in the living room and scanned titles. I suppose, I thought, without much enthusiasm, I should buy a book on grief. I suppose I should read something by Elizabeth Kubler-Ross, and maybe that book about bad things happening to good people. Then maybe I'll better understand what's happening with me. And what's happening with Ross.

I'd done all that research on celebrating new life; why shouldn't I do some research on letting life go? On letting lots of things go.

I turned away from the bookcase and sat tiredly on the couch. Since the miscarriage, Ross and I had hardly spoken to each other; the conversations we'd had were stiff and cool. Suddenly, we were so very distant from each other. I knew that the days and weeks following a miscarriage were trying for any couple. I imagined that such a misfortune might bring a couple closer.

But I was mourning alone. Ross, I assumed, was, too, because we certainly weren't mourning together. We weren't even sympathetic to each other's grief. I had no comfort to offer him, and he had none to offer me. Whatever it was we had had together seemed suddenly gone. Just—gone. Just like the baby.

I heard the sound of familiar footsteps below and peered out the living room window. I saw Ross take a set of keys from the pocket of his suit pants just as he reached the foot of the stairs leading up to the building. A few minutes later there were three knocks on my door. Ross had chosen not to use his key to my apartment.

Suddenly nervous, I opened the door. "Hi," I said.

"Hi." Ross stepped inside and immediately opened his briefcase. "Here," he said, handing me a catalogue. "This came for you."

"Thanks." I took it; it was from L.L. Bean. I wondered why Ross hadn't just left it at the loft where I would find it soon enough, but I didn't ask.

"How's work?" I said.

"Fine. Busy." Ross didn't touch me at all, no gentle kiss, no soft squeeze—no comforting hold on my elbow.

"Me too," I said. Only a few days earlier I'd been dying to

ask if he'd confirmed the band's playlist for the reception. It occurred to me then that I didn't really care what the answer would be. So I didn't ask the question.

"Would you like to sit down?" I asked, as if Ross were a guest and not the man I was soon to marry.

"No," he said, "I can't stay long. Anna, I want to talk to you about something."

"Okay," I said. Hornets sprung to life in my stomach.

"Did the doctor say when it would be okay to try again? To get pregnant?"

"We never tried in the first place," I replied. Why did I find it necessary to remind us?

Ross rolled his eyes. I remembered reading a study about lasting relationships. Supposedly people who roll their eyes at each other are headed for divorce.

"You know what I mean, Anna."

"We can have sex now, if you want," I said, surprising myself.

Ross laughed bitterly. I'd never heard bitterness from him. "You don't sound very interested."

I wasn't at all interested.

"What about the pill?" he asked then. "You didn't go back on it already, did you?"

So he didn't want me to be on the pill?

"No."

"Well, are you going to?"

So he did want me to be on the pill?

"Not without discussing it with you, first," I said. "We're getting married, Ross. We're supposed to discuss things."

Ross threw his hands in the air. Huh, I thought, watching Ross as if from a great distance. I've never seen him so animated.

"Isn't that what we're doing now?" he said. "Come on, Anna, give me a break."

"We already decided we didn't want children."

I hadn't planned to say that. I hadn't planned to say anything.

"Yes, but everything's changed now," he said testily. "When you got pregnant—"

"When you got me pregnant," I snapped.

"I seem to remember you being there, Anna. It took the two of us. I never forced you to be with me."

No, I thought. You never forced me. I said yes to you. But why? When I still didn't reply, Ross demanded, "Are you mad at me?"

What did Ross want to hear? Was he spoiling for a fight?

I looked away. "Yes," I said. "No. I don't know."

Suddenly, Ross reached for the briefcase he'd set on the hall table. "Look, maybe we should talk about this some other time. I'm going home."

"Don't go, Ross," I said. "Stay with me. You haven't stayed with me since it happened."

"You didn't seem to want me to," he said.

So, he'd noticed. "Are you mad at me, Ross?" I asked, wondering if I was spoiling for a fight. Knowing I was desperate to feel—something, anything—with Ross. "Be honest."

"Not tonight, Anna. Not while you're in this mood."

I moved to block his way to the door.

"It's not a mood, Ross. It's me. It's better we talk about this now."

I don't, I thought, have any more time to waste being in the wrong life.

Ross looked at me closely and said nothing for a long moment. Finally, he took a deep breath.

"All right, you want to talk. We'll talk. I am mad, Anna. Maybe I shouldn't be but I am."

"At me?" I asked, afraid to hear the answer I knew was coming.

Ross's eyes shifted away from mine. "Yes."

There it is, I thought. At last.

"Do you blame me for the miscarriage?" I asked in a perfectly modulated voice.

Ross looked back to me. His eyes were blazing. "You never wanted a baby in the first place," he spat.

I recoiled. "Neither did you!"

"But I was excited when you got pregnant," Ross said, poking at his chest with his finger like some parody of a cave man. "When we got pregnant. You were never excited. You were never happy."

How little he knew me, the man I was supposed to marry!

"That's a lie!" I cried. "How can you say that, Ross! My God, I so wanted the baby. My baby."

I wondered, Our baby? I put my hands over my face. I felt so awfully alone.

"I'm sorry, Anna." Ross's tone was properly repentant. I didn't believe him for a minute. "I shouldn't have—"

I lowered my hands but kept my eyes focused on the floor. "You should go now," I whispered.

"I thought you wanted me to stay."

I shook my head. I couldn't speak the words that were crowding at my lips.

Ross left.

70

Glimpse

The confrontation with Ross left me too disturbed to sleep, which, in the end, was probably a blessing. I wasn't sure I'd survive the dreams that night.

How, I wondered, could things have gotten so bad so quickly? Could Ross and I ever get back to where we'd been before I got pregnant? That place seemed so very far away. I almost couldn't remember what it was like.

My mind was a dark whirl of fear and sorrow until morning.

Throw yourself into work, people advise. If you're busy you can't sit around worrying or being depressed. Take refuge in work, volunteer at a retirement home, keep moving to avoid anxiety.

Keep moving. Not bad advice.

Although I could have faxed Jack the revised layout for the Gott event, I told him I would drop it off. Keep moving. Walk the walk, climb the stairs.

A note was taped to the door of the loft. It read, "A. Had to run an errand. Leave plan on desk. J."

I found the key where it always was, atop the doorsill, and let myself into Jack's loft. Of course, I thought Jack was crazy to leave a key where anyone could find it. Of course, I'd told him that. There were thousands and thousands of dollars worth of equipment in his loft. But Jack does things his own way.

I'm not a snoop. I'd never set out to paw through someone's private space, to rifle through their mail, to examine their medicine cabinet. Really. But there it was, a yellowing piece of paper lying right there on Jack's desk, typewritten except for a signature in blue ink. How could I resist glancing at it?

The date on the top right corner indicated that Jack was eight or nine when this teacher's evaluation was written. It amused me that Jack had kept this artifact of his early childhood. I wondered if he'd had it for years or if someone had recently come across it in the old family home. Who was that someone? Did Jack have a brother or sister? Were his parents alive? It occurred to me then that Jack had never mentioned a family.

And I'd never asked.

The document began:

As a participant in the activities described on the previous page, John appeared to show the following characteristics.

I wondered, briefly, when John had begun to be called Jack. Maybe at home he'd been Jack from the start. Maybe he'd adopted the nickname in high school.

I scanned the list of categories and stopped on Cooperation. John, the teacher had typed, was "cooperative with adults though less so with children. At times," Ms. Sidler went on, "his intellectual interests override his thoughtfulness."

"They still do!" I said aloud, amused.

The sound of a door slamming somewhere in the building made me jump. Hastily, I put the paper back on the table and waited. But there was no other sound; no footsteps in the hall; no breathing just outside the door to the studio. With a final glance over my shoulder I picked up the report again.

Creativity? No surprises there, either. "John is a creative thinker and shows great creative ability in the arts."

I read on to the next category. Ability to Express Ideas.

"John," Ms. Sidler wrote, "has an excellent vocabulary and expresses ideas in an organized manner. However—"

"Ah!" I said to the studio. "Here it is."

"However," Ms. Sidler wrote, "he tends to hold forth as if in a courtroom and often cannot be silenced. On one occasion my teaching assistant clocked John as pontificating on the rising and falling of the tides for a full seven minutes."

Only seven minutes? When Jack got started on a topic he could easily go on for twenty or thirty minutes without a break. And then I remembered that the pontificator Ms. Sidler described had been only a child at the time, a child gearing up for a life of pontification.

Finally, I reached Participation in Planning and Discussions. Poor Ms. Sidler, I thought. How did she survive an entire summer with little Jackie? "John," she wrote, "is an active participant in group discussions and offers excellent contributions. However—"

And there it was again, the ubiquitous qualifier.

"However, he demands more than his fair share of turns and tends to interrupt others while they are speaking. John also has a tendency to criticize his classmates in an unproductive manner. For example, instead of pointing out a potential weakness in a classmate's argument, he makes strong statements such as, 'You're wrong' or 'That's stupid.' I would strongly suggest that John work on his people skills."

I burst out laughing. It sounded strange in the otherwise unoccupied studio space, a bit maniacal, like something you'd hear in a movie about an evil circus clown.

Jack was Jack and always had been. He was a brilliant, pain-in-the-butt, dyed-in-the-wool individual. I had to hand it to Jack Coltrane. He'd remained true to himself all his life.

Sure, maybe there'd been blips of compromise along the way, but at the age of forty-five, he was still—or once again—who he'd always been.

I laughed harder than I'd laughed in a long time. And I wished Jack were there to hear my laughter because I wasn't laughing at him, exactly. Okay, I was, but the laughter wasn't born of meanness. It was born of fondness. It was coming from a place of affection.

From a place of love?

Maybe, I thought, it's better that Jack isn't here. I grabbed my purse and made a dash for the door.

71

Nasty Truths

Alexandra came over bearing the latest issue of Italian *Vogue* and a large piece of German chocolate cake. I'd told her about my fight with Ross; this was her way of alleviating my posttraumatic stress.

For a while we sat quietly. Alexandra flipped through the *Vogue*; I poked at the cake with a fork and thought about losing the baby. I had suffered a miscarriage. That was what Alma had said the other day. That I had suffered a loss. I thought about the word *suffer* and about the act or the state of suffering. I thought about enduring. About bearing the burden, about tolerating the pain, about learning to reconcile myself to this new, stark reality.

The new and stark reality of being alone.

The fight had only confirmed what I'd sensed was happening between Ross and me. We were so alienated from each other. I felt as if he'd shoveled the tragedy onto my head, thrown it at me, and walked away. I felt as if I'd done something wrong and shameful and that that something now stood between Ross and me. The miscarriage hadn't bound us more closely. It had driven a wedge between us.

I wondered, Had the pregnancy started the process of tearing? Or had it simply accelerated a process already begun?

And if the pregnancy hadn't ended like it had, if the baby had been born at full term, healthy and strong, would the truth about Ross and me never have come to light? Would we just have gone on side by side, never really touching, until death did us part?

I'd never know, not for sure. And the fact was, I'd never really been able to imagine a family of three—Ross, a baby, me. I'd come to see me and the baby, the two of us, alone together and happy. But I'd failed to see Ross as part of the picture.

A failure of imagination. Just another one of my many failures.

"I'm the first bad thing to happen to Ross," I said abruptly.

"What a horrible thing to say!" Alexandra cried, tossing the big glossy magazine aside.

"No, it's true," I assured her. "Ross has never failed at anything."

"Maybe he never tried hard enough to fail."

I didn't bother to comment on Alexandra's observation. We both knew it was true.

"No one close to him has died," I went on. "His parents adore him. He's never been cut from a sports team or rejected from a club. Do you know he turned down the presidency of his fraternity's local chapter because he was too busy being president of some young businessmen's club?"

"And delegating his workload to his staff." Alexandra's tone was acidic.

"Does it matter? Ross never asked anyone to marry him before me. And I said yes, immediately, no hesitation. Even then he'd won. And now . . . I just know he sees my miscarriage as my failure. I'm tainted, and because I belong to him, he's tainted now in some way, too. And it's really upsetting him."

"And you still want to marry someone who finds you unacceptable because you're human?"

"Less than human. Damaged goods. A tarnished good luck charm."

"Answer the question." Alexandra's voice was tight.

I looked at my friend. I could be wrong, I thought. I could be loading my own confused feelings of shame and failure onto Ross. I could be inventing the awkwardness between us since the miscarriage.

But I knew I wasn't.

"I can't," I said, and my voice was weak.

Alexandra's eyes held mine. I wanted to look away, but I couldn't. "You can't answer the question," she said, "or you can't marry him?"

I thought of Jack. I thought of his hand around a coffee cup, of his hand on my elbow.

"I can't." It was all I could say.

72

The Unhappy Couple

"Are you giving me an ultimatum?"

I stood there, hands at my side, looking at the stranger who was my fiancé.

"It's not an ultimatum," I said. "I just think that maybe we should go to counseling together. Because we're not talking about what happened."

Because we're falling apart and I don't know what to do about it.

Ross had called earlier that morning. All of the fixtures in the master bathroom had been installed; the room was ready for painting. He wanted to know if I cared to see the mini marble palace. I told him that of course I wanted to see it. Hadn't we chosen the marble together at the stone yard?

He'd greeted me at the door to the loft with barely repressed hostility.

"You're late," he said.

"No, I'm not," I replied. And then I checked my watch. "Oh. I'm sorry, I am. My watch has slowed down. I'll replace the battery."

Ross stepped back to let me enter. "It's not good to keep people waiting."

"Yes," I said, wondering suddenly why I was really there. "I know."

I admired the marble. I admired Ross's final choice of paint color. And then I suggested that we see a therapist.

"The whole idea is ridiculous," Ross said dismissively. "Therapy is not for people like us. At least, it's not for people like me."

"What does that mean?" I demanded. "Don't you want to work things out between us? Grief doesn't just go away, Ross. You can't just pretend everything's okay. You can't hide—"

"I'm not hiding anything."

Looking at Ross then, at his blandly handsome and oddly closed face, I believed he was telling the truth as he saw it.

I shook my head in amazement. "My life," I said, "is becoming a soap opera."

"Only because you're letting it," Ross snapped. "Why are you doing this to me, Anna? Why are you ruining everything?"

"I'm not ruining anything," I cried. What was there to ruin? A fantasy? A construct? The notion of a perfectly fine life? "This is life, Ross. Bad things happen for no good reason, for no reason at all. Stop blaming me."

Ross stalked out of the master bathroom. I followed him into the kitchen. And for the very first time I wondered if I was the great love of Ross's life. Was I really loved? I didn't have the nerve to ask.

"Do you realize this is the first time we've ever fought? Ross, we never even really talked until we lost the baby. I mean, really talked. About the big stuff."

Ross slapped his hands on the shiny counter. "What was there to talk about? Everything was fine. Everything still would be fine if—"

Ross looked down at his hands.

"If what, Ross?" I said finally. "If I hadn't lost the baby? Or if I hadn't gotten pregnant in the first place?"

Ross continued to stare at his slim, manicured fingers. "Never mind," he said. "Look, my mother wants to have us for dinner this Sunday. Can I count on you to be there?"

"Can I count on you to talk to me about what's really going on between us?"

Ross said, "I'll pick you up at six."

73

Beauty

"Didn't your mother ever teach you not to snoop?"

I'd heard Jack come into the studio, but unlike the last time I was there alone, I didn't care. I continued to gaze at the darkly lit black-and-white nude studies spread out on the table before me.

"Jack, they're beautiful," I said. "And I wasn't snooping. They were right here for anyone to see. I'm sure the UPS guy who was just here thinks they're wonderful, too. By the way, I signed for the package."

Jack began to slide the prints into a rough pile. "You're not a professional critic," he said. "Not that I have any use for the majority of them."

"I never claimed to be a professional critic. And might I remind you that you sought out my opinion on that student's work that afternoon at the café. And don't tell me you did it out of pity, or I'll be furious."

Jack gave me a dirty look. "I don't do anything out of pity. I don't believe in pity. You know that."

I did know that.

"Why haven't I seen these before?" I asked. Jack was

now holding the stack of black and whites protectively against his chest. Did he really think I would make a grab for them?

"I don't show you everything I've ever worked on."

"These are new, aren't they? I thought you'd given up on personal projects."

Jack slid the photographs into a flat file and locked the cabinet.

"Time to go, Anna. I've got work to do. Heather-Marie Rich's Sweet Sixteen party shots are due to the wealthy spineless daddy and artificially ageless mommy first thing tomorrow morning."

Why did I have to push him?

"You know they're good, don't you?" I said. "There isn't a humble bone in your body, and you can't be so disingenuous as to pretend you don't know serious art when you see it."

There was a deadly silence. Jack's expression was dark.

"Okay," I mumbled, "I'm going. I'm sorry I think you're the most talented photographer I've seen." I snatched up my purse and headed for the door.

And still Jack said not a word.

Part Three

74

The End

The last of the baby gifts had been returned, with carefully worded notes of thanks. Even the awful sweater, the one that had afforded me some comfort just after the miscarriage, had gone back to Mrs. Davis. The childbirth books and parenting magazines—all were gone. There was nothing in my apartment to remind me of what had happened—nothing except me.

I checked the clock over the stove. Ross was due in half an hour. I wasn't looking forward to seeing him, not really—how sad!—but I had to. Once last time I had to try to reach him, try to make some connection to this person I was taking on as my life partner.

Life partner. Husband. Those words had come to sound ugly, confining, murderous.

I sat on the couch and opened one of the coffee table books, a collection of Ansel Adams photographs, but for the first time the images held no appeal. I went to my computer and checked e-mail; nothing but SPAM. The latest headlines from Reuters made virtually no impression on me: another car bombing in Palestine; another midnight wedding for another drunken starlet; another storm off the coast of Florida.

Twenty minutes. In twenty minutes Ross would be at my door and maybe, just maybe, this misery would be over. What did I mean by 'over'?

Our official engagement portrait, framed in Tiffany silver, stood on a small table by the couch. I picked it up and studied our smiling faces, Ross's and mine. And try as I might I just couldn't recognize either of us, not really. The woman in the portrait wasn't me, not now. And the man . . . With a rush of anger I realized I had never known the man because there wasn't much of a man to know. All along I'd wanted to believe that there was more to Ross than met the eye. But I'd come to know there was less.

Without care I set the portrait down; it fell glass first onto the floor. I let it stay there.

The dreams. I thought about the dreams. Increasing blindness, loss of voice, choking, abandonment. Even if I could ask questions of Ross, would he be able to answer? Was he even capable of listening?

I took a few deep breaths but my heart continued to race. Ten minutes. Ross would be at my door in ten minutes. And then . . .

Ross wanted to know when we could start trying to get pregnant. Why had he assumed I wanted to get pregnant? And even if I did, wouldn't I need time to mourn the loss of our child? What, what, what was Ross thinking?

I walked to the kitchen and poured a glass of wine. Ross was thinking nothing. Ross wasn't capable of real thought, not beyond what suit to wear to what function or what new diet fad to try next.

Why, I wondered, couldn't Ross ever admit to being confused or distressed? Why, I wondered, couldn't Ross ever admit to being human?

I put the empty wineglass in the sink. Five minutes. I held my left hand before my face and studied my engagement ring, the sign of my commitment to Ross, the sign of my retirement from life.

Four minutes. And everything was a mess. Ross blamed me for messing things up. He blamed me for bringing the sweaty chaos of life into his cold and ordered world.

How, I wondered, could I ever trust him to be there in the hard times? How could I ever trust him to be there for me if I got sick with cancer, especially a disfiguring kind, like breast cancer, something that would cause him public embarrassment? How could I trust him to support me if I had a nervous breakdown, if I lost my self-confidence, if I got fat?

I looked again at the kitchen clock. It was time. The doorbell rang. Calmly, I walked into the foyer; calmly, I opened the door.

"Hi," I said.

Ross hesitated a moment before stepping inside. "Hi."

We stood there in the foyer of my apartment, facing each other, too far apart to touch.

"What did you want to see me about?" he said. He wouldn't meet my eyes.

"Why did you stop having sex with me when I got pregnant?" I asked.

Ross didn't answer. His eyes darted back toward the door. I wondered if he was going to bolt.

"Was it because you found me disgusting?" I went on. "Or was it because you thought I was too precious? Pregnant women are women, Ross, they're people, but maybe that's the problem—"

"Anna," Ross said angrily. "Stop."

My voice became higher, thinner. "No, I won't stop. You don't like women very much, do you Ross? Not really."

"Don't be ridiculous, Anna."

"Then answer the question," I said. "Why wouldn't you have sex with me?"

"Look," he said, with some emotion, "I don't know, all right? Can we just drop it? What's done is done."

He was right. What had been done to us had been done to us. And this was what we were left with.

Suddenly, we both seem to have lost steam. Ross leaned against the foyer wall. I sat heavily on the couch.

"Everything's that happened, Anna," he said, shaking his head. "I just don't know—"

I looked at the fallen portrait. "It's okay, Ross," I said. "I understand."

But it seems that I didn't understand, not entirely.

Ross pushed away from the wall; his arms seem to hang loosely at his side. "It's just that I want a family. I can't be with someone who doesn't want what I want. I want a family, Anna." Ross said it simply, matter-of-factly, like what he was telling me was nothing more important than his saying, "I like my coffee black."

I shot from the couch; my skin was tingling; I wondered if I were having a heart attack. "Since when?" I spat. "When did you decide you were a family man?"

"I've wanted a family for a while now," Ross said, evasively. "I mentioned the pill. The other day. Remember? But you didn't want to talk about it. You just don't want to be a mother and I can't live with that."

I looked at his pretty face and wanted very badly to slap it. Ross was even more obtuse than I had imagined. "All this time wasted . . ." I laughed. Suddenly, it all seemed so ridiculous. "Why, Ross? Why the big change of heart?"

But to answer the question required more creativity and self-awareness than Ross could manage. "I want a family," he said again. "Can you tell me you want the same?"

"I don't know, Ross," I said, honestly. "I can't make any promises right now, not to anyone. You see, I'm suffering."

And that repulses you.

"Okay. Fair enough." Ross ran a hand through his perfectly groomed hair. It was something I'd never seen him do. "So, this is it, I guess. It's just—over."

It was just over. There was no way to negotiate such a

lack and white issue. There was no way I could forgive him or his gross lack of understanding.

"Ross," I said, "you should go now."

I slipped the engagement ring off my finger and took a tep toward him. Then I held out my open palm and offered im the ring.

Ross's face was drawn, unhappy, tired. "Anna, you don't—"

"It doesn't belong to me anymore," I said, and it didn't urt at all.

Slowly, Ross put out his hand and took the ring. When his ingers touched mine I felt nothing, no spark of desire or tenlerness, nothing to make me take back my ring and in doing o, my life with Ross—and his children.

When he was at the door I said, "Ross? I'm sorry."

He didn't turn; his hand remained on the doorknob.

"I'm sorry, too, Anna," he said. "I really am."

And then it was really over.

75

Revelation

You think you're living your own life and then somethin happens to jolt you into the awareness that all alon you've actually been living someone else's life.

The engagement was off. The wedding was off. The mar riage was off.

I wasn't unhappy, not exactly. But I wasn't happy, either. wondered, How do you define happiness? The absence o pain? Or the presence of—of what? The presence of a feel ing, a thing, a person in your life?

Maybe happiness is knowing you're right where yo should be, doing what you should be doing, sharing tim with the people you should be sharing time with. Mayb happiness is knowing that you're finally living your own life

And maybe the first phase of happiness is owning up t your own brand of heartache.

In those days right after the end, a line kept runnin through my head, a song lyric, and at first I couldn't place it And then I did.

"Nowhere you can be that isn't where you're meant to be.

But it isn't all that easy.

76

Breaking It Down

The dismantling of our lives began. Ross and I agreed that family would hear a brief, sanitized version of the truth. Our story was this: We realized we just weren't right for each other. The end.

Our intentions were good, but parents are parents. My father decided that Ross had left me cruelly and threatened to "have a talk" with him. By which he meant "punch him out." My mother lamented all the time and money she'd spent—now gone—on planning for various aspects of my life—wedding and baby—and in doing so made me feel even more like a dismal failure. What did I expect from her? Sympathy beyond a throw-away sentiment?

I never learned Mr. Davis's reaction to the news of the disintegration of his younger son's wedding plans. I assume he said something to the effect of "There are a million girls out there. Forget about her."

Ross's mother, on the other hand, was very vocal with her feelings. I don't know for sure if Ross kept to our agreement, but even if he did it wouldn't have mattered. Some evil woman had broken her baby's heart, and she wasn't about to take that lying down.

First, there were the phone calls. I was smart enough—or just plain scared enough—not to answer the phone when her name appeared on the Caller ID screen. But I did listen to the messages, afterward. They were largely incoherent and always angry. After a while there were letters, and the real shocker, e-mails. I didn't know Mrs. Davis had ever seen a computer up close, let alone knew how to use one.

Alexandra and I met for coffee late one afternoon a few weeks after the breakup. I told her about my angry ex-future-mother-in-law.

"Wow," she said. "I've never gotten hate mail. You'd expect someone like me would have, wouldn't you? I tend to make enemies."

I smiled weakly. "Nothing from Luke's soon-to-be-ex-wife?"

"Not yet. So, what does Ross's mommy say to you? You can omit the foul language."

"The worst she's called me is bitch. But it stings. Anyway, first she just yelled about how no one these days respects the sanctity of marriage."

"But you and Ross weren't even married yet!"

"I didn't say Mrs. Davis has been coherent. Eventually, she got around to telling me in no uncertain terms that God was punishing me for losing the baby by taking away Ross, who, she believes, is the best thing that will ever happen to me."

Alexandra's normally pale complexion darkened. "My blood pressure is dangerously high at this moment. I want you to know that in case I spontaneously combust."

"Anyway," I said, "in a bizarre new twist she's decided that Ross and I should get back together. I know she's upset but—"

"But nothing," Alexandra said firmly. "It wasn't her relationship that broke up. Mrs. Davis needs to get her own life, and pronto."

"Well," I said, "I doubt that will ever happen. You know, from this perspective I am so glad she's not going to be my mother-in-law. I used to think she was harmless, if a little annoying. But now I see that as Ross's wife I would have been at her mercy for the rest of my life."

"Tell Ross to call off his mommy," Alexandra commanded.

"I don't think I should mention it to him."

"The woman is harassing you. I think you have to mention it to him. And make it very clear that you'll take legal action if she continues to invade your home via telephone, e-mail, and angry notes under the front door!"

"I can't press charges against the woman who was going to be my mother-in-law!"

"Why not? She's behaving like a criminal."

"Because—because it just wouldn't be right."

Alexandra looked utterly disgusted with me. "Okay, okay. Fine. If you won't talk to Ross, then you have two choices left. Ignore the witch, but I don't see how you can do that when she's lurking in your hallway. Your second choice is to confront her."

"What if she screams at me and things get even worse?"

"Scream back. Things won't get worse if you scare the crap out of her."

"Could I send a letter?" I said, after some consideration. "A sternly worded letter?"

"Only if it's copied to your attorney," Alexandra snapped in reply.

"I'll think about it," I said.

In the end, Mrs. Davis backed off. Maybe it was seeing Ross getting on with his life that cooled her fury. Maybe it was learning that I'd returned the expensive diamond ring he'd bought me. Maybe she just got tired of coming into the city two or three times a week to stalk me.

Luckily, I hadn't yet sold my apartment. Ross owned what was to have been our love nest, so we each came out of the mess with a place to call our own.

The things we'd bought together for our new home caused some problems. What to do with the Eileen Gray reading lamp, the reupholstered 1930s art deco chair, the Eames coffee table? In the end, Ross returned what could be returned and gave me a check for the items he kept.

And then there were the gifts Ross had given me. There's something unbearably sad about a once cherished object suddenly devoid of personal meaning.

Like the beautiful gold bangle Ross had given me when I'd told him I was pregnant. I couldn't bring myself to wear it or to sell it. Finally, I brought it to the bank and tucked it into my safe deposit box, where it would rest along with my birth certificate, my passport, and the deed to my apartment—documents that represented the official Anna Traulsen. Artifacts of my life in progress.

We lost most of the deposits we'd put on wedding venues and services. I halted work on my dress and had it put in the shop's storage.

We hadn't bought the wedding rings yet; that was a relief.

In short, it was a divorce without the marriage.

I wouldn't have wished it even on Michaela.

77

Sympathy From an Unlikely Source

"My dear," Mrs. Kent said, "you seem in low spirits today." I looked up from the notes I was jotting. "Oh," I said, "I'm fine. I'm sorry though. I didn't mean to—"

Mrs. Kent cut me off. "No need to apologize. You haven't done anything wrong. Not like that ridiculous thing of a housekeeper the agency sent over this morning. Why Rose had to go to Detroit to attend her niece's wedding is beyond me. Rose has been with me for twenty years, my dear. Her loyalty should be to me above all others." Here Mrs. Kent sniffed like a properly offended grande dame. "At least she might have invited me along. Don't you agree that would have been the right thing to do?"

Mrs. Kent's purposefully outrageous sentiment made me smile. "Oh, of course," I assured her. "I'm sure Rose is regretting her decision at this very moment."

"And I don't believe for a second that you are fine," Mrs. Kent went on imperiously. "I know I'm a terribly nosy old woman and that perhaps I have no right to press you to reveal your personal affairs. But as I have pointed out at an earlier time, I am old and often quite bored. I am interested in the lives of the young even if they are not interested in mine. Besides, I am one of the few people of my acquaintance who has learned a thing or two from my own mistakes. If something is troubling you, perhaps I may be of some help."

Perhaps, but I doubted it. In addition to Ms. Butterfield, personal assistant extraordinaire, Beatrice Kent employed a full-time, live-in housekeeper and butler. She had been born into an old-money Brahmin family and had married into another one. She had come of age during World War II; I was born during the Vietnam era. We occupied two very different worlds. How could she possibly understand my life?

"Well, you are my client," I pointed out reasonably. "I really shouldn't bother a client with my personal affairs."

"My dear," she answered impatiently, "it is true that I am your client but I am also old enough to be your grandmother, and age takes precedence over the formalities of the workplace."

"Oh?" Mrs. Kent's argument might have been faulty, but I knew where she was heading.

"Yes," she declared. "In my house we follow my rules."

I tried to hide my smile. I really tried. "Are you commanding me to tell you what's on my mind?"

Mrs. Kent tried to hide her smile. She was about as successful as I'd been. "I am strongly suggesting that you do, yes."

Well, I thought, why not?

Mrs. Kent ordered tea to be served and when we each had a cup, I told her about Ross and me breaking up. And about my losing the baby.

"Ah," said Mrs. Kent, nodding. "I see. Poor Anna. Men come and go, my dear. It's best simply to accept that fact and soldier on."

"Yes," I said, though I wasn't sure I could ever accept that fact. If I fell madly in love, if someone loved me madly in return, how could I survive the end of that? How could anyone survive the end of true love? I thought of Alexandra. I thought of Jack.

"You thought," Mrs. Kent said, "that you were in love."

"Yes," I said automatically. And then, "No. No, I never pretended to be in love, even to myself. That makes me sound horrible and cold. I'm not, it wasn't that way."

"I think I understand," Mrs. Kent said. "I think many women would understand."

I wondered. Were that many women marrying for reasons other than love? "I'm ashamed to admit," I said then, "that I don't even miss him."

"But you do miss the child. The loss of a child is a terrible thing."

I felt compelled to say, "I was only a few weeks along."

"Don't minimize your grief." Mrs. Kent put her hand on mine and squeezed. Her rings dug into my skin. "And don't ever apologize for it."

"Okay," I said. My voice was shaky. I tried not to cry.

Mrs. Kent looked closely at me with her sharp, intelligent eyes. "I, too, lost a child. A daughter. She lived for three months."

"Oh," I said. "I didn't know. I'm so sorry." I felt ill. To have seen the face of your child and then to have that precious face taken away . . .

"My husband," she went on, in a remarkably neutral tone, "would not give me another child after my Vanessa was gone. Not that another child could have replaced my dear daughter in my heart, you understand. But another child might have helped ease my grief. No matter. My grief is old, as am I. Your grief, dear Anna, is still fresh. But so are you. You will survive this sadness."

I fervently hoped so.

"My fiancé and I never even discussed the possibility of an abortion," I told her. "I thought about abortion, of course, in the very beginning. But I just couldn't imagine going through with it."

"And that came as a surprise?"

"Yes," I admitted. "Maybe it's my age. I felt like it might be my last chance. And then suddenly, I was happy. I realized I did want a child. And then—then I wasn't pregnant anymore. My friends say it's not too late. My friend Kristen, she has three children, she says she knows I'll have my own some day. But how can she know?"

"She can't," Mrs. Kent replied shortly. "Your brief pregnancy might well have been your last chance. And it might not have been. I wish I could be more assuring, my dear. I wish I could tell you that everything will work out wonderfully, just the way you want it to. But I can't."

"That's okay," I said. "Honesty is best in the end. I'm finally learning that."

Soon after, I went home to my apartment. I felt comforted. Yes, Beatrice Kent was almost forty years older; yes, she had lived a life quite different from mine. But she was a woman, and that, at bottom, was all we needed in common.

78

The Big Day

The phone rang at six o'clock that evening. I didn't recognize the phone number, but the call was coming from my parents' area code.

The caller loudly announced herself as Mrs. Brown; she was one of my mother's cronies.

"Oh," I said. "Hello Mrs. Brown."

"Your mother gave me your number, I hope you don't mind, dear."

"No, of course not," I lied. Did Mrs. Brown want to hire me to organize a party? How would I refuse graciously?

"So, Anna, this is why I called. I was thinking that maybe Howard could get a diet plate at the wedding. Something low-carb and low-salt but not too much fat. But not vegetarian. Howard hates vegetables."

I felt as if someone had stabbed me in the stomach. "Um, Mrs. Brown," I said, "you see, the wedding is off. I thought my mother told you."

Mrs. Brown made a sound like a dog's bark. "She didn't mention a thing about it, and I just talked to her a few days ago! Oh, you poor thing, I'm so sorry. What happened? You can tell me."

I faked an important business call coming in on my nonexistent second line and got off the phone. I was furious. It figured my mother wouldn't have bothered to tell her friends that the wedding was off. Why should she inconvenience herself? So what if one of her bridge partners called to ask me about her fussy eater of a husband, forcing me to revisit the trauma? Why should my mother start thinking about my feelings at this late date?

And of course, it would never have dawned on my father to make the bitter announcement. Family maintenance was woman's work.

Anyway, let me tell you a bit about the wedding that never happened.

Ross and I had chosen a Unitarian minister to officiate, a friend of one of Ross's colleagues. Neither of us are churchgoers, but our parents attend church on the holidays so choosing this minister seemed like a good compromise.

Ross chose his brother Rob to be his best man. My decision was a bit more difficult to make.

Kristen is the friend I've known the longest and so a clear choice for matron of honor. But being matron of honor involves a hefty expenditure of time and money, expenditures I didn't feel comfortable asking Kristen, with three kids and one income, to make.

At heart I really wanted Alexandra to be the legal witness to my marriage. But Alexandra had made it very clear she thought Ross wasn't the right man for me. If I asked her and she said no, well . . .

In the end I asked Tracy to sign my marriage license. She was a dear friend; had the disposable time and money; and though she didn't exactly love Ross, she was very, very subtle in her disapproval.

Both the service and reception were to be held at the Tuxedo Hotel, starting at six o'clock in the evening. After the brief ceremony there was to be a cocktail hour with passed appetizers and, at Mr. Davis's insistence, an open bar. A champagne toast was to precede dinner and dancing. We never got to finalize the menu. We never got to choose a special song.

The wedding was to be an adults-only affair—elegant, sophisticated, and pristine. Not sticky. That was Ross's big concern, sticky fingers on his expensive tuxedo or my one-of-a-kind dress.

Ross and I were to walk down the aisle together.

And that's what it would have been like.

79

Nothing Ventured

Butter pecan ice cream. Reddi Wip. It would be so easy to reach for that container and that can, curl up on the couch, and vegetate until a sugar coma sent me to dreamland.

Too easy.

Anna, I told myself, you are not going to eat a pint of ice cream for dinner. You are not going to spend another minute in front of the television watching lame sitcoms and lamer local news broadcasts. You are getting out of this apartment. You are going somewhere for dinner, and you are going to eat a healthy, well-balanced meal that will include vegetables.

I dressed with more care than I'd taken for several days and headed for a small neighborhood bistro. The bar was empty but for another woman at the far end, engrossed in a hardcover historical novel and an order of steak frites. We caught each other's eye as I pulled a stool away from the counter and shared a brief smile. I wondered, Would an order of French fries be considered a vegetable?

And then Jack Coltrane walked through the door.

Jack was the last person I wanted to see. And the only person. That was hard to admit.

And then he was standing next to me. "Hi," he said.

"Oh. Hi." I could hardly believe my tone was so neutral.

Jack grinned. "Your lack of enthusiasm speaks volumes. I know. I keep turning up, like a bad penny."

"I don't know what that means," I admitted, with slightly more animation. "I don't know why we say that when we do."

"Me, either," Jack admitted. "I'll pull out my *Bartlett's* when I get home and let you know."

"You have a *Bartlett's*?"

Jack gave me an odd look. "I have a dictionary and a thesaurus, too. Why does that surprise you? I am literate."

"I've never seen you read," I explained. "A book, I mean. I've seen you read memos. I've seen magazines in your studio, but I've never actually seen you reading one."

"You don't see me taking a shower but I do. Every day. I have a life even when you're not around."

"I know. Sorry." I wanted to add, What's that life like, Jack? Would I want to be part of it? Would you want me to be part of it?

Of course, I said none of that. Craziness.

Jack gestured at the stool next to mine. "Mind if I sit here?"

I shook my head. "Of course not."

"Good. I'm starved."

"And there's nothing in your fridge but rolls of film and batteries."

"Pretty much. But you forgot the one beer and a moldy burrito. Really should throw that thing out."

Jack ordered, but suddenly I didn't feel hungry anymore. Well, I'm sure the hunger was still there; it was just temporarily buried under a layer of adolescent fluttering.

"You're not on a diet, are you?" he asked. "Everyone is on a crazy diet these days."

"No," I said, "I'm not on a diet. I'm just not very hungry."

I wondered if Jack knew that Ross and I had broken up. I figured he probably did. Someone had told him about the miscarriage. Why not about the breakup?

"So," I said jauntily, once Jack's dinner had arrived, "I suppose you heard the news?"

Jack chewed vigorously then swallowed before he said, "What news? What's happened since I last checked the Internet? How many children have starved this week in Sudan? How many people have been infected with the HIV virus in Africa? How many people have been poisoned in the subway systems of a large European city? What major monument has blown up since lunch? How depressed or enraged should I be?"

Ah, yes. There were more important events than Anna's broken engagement.

"My life," I said. Nothing major. Not really.

"What?"

"My life has blown up." I held my left hand in front of my face.

Jack shook his head. "What am I supposed to be looking at?"

Mr. I-Notice-Everything didn't notice the lack of iceberg on my finger? Well, I reminded myself, there are other things on Jack's mind than me.

"No ring," I said. "No fiancé. Ross and I broke up. We're not getting married. In fact, I'm pretty sure we're not even speaking. We're not doing anything together anymore."

I watched Jack's face. His expression was inscrutable. "That's why you're here alone," he said finally.

"I do have a life when you're not around."

"Sorry. For all I know you spend every evening sitting alone at a local watering hole."

"Apology accepted," I said. "I kind of thought you already knew. About Ross and me."

"Are you okay?" he asked after a moment or two. "Life's been giving you a tough time lately, hasn't it."

"I guess so. It could be worse." I could be a starving child in Ethiopia. Nothing like a world news report to put one's troubles into perspective. "And no, I'm not okay, but I will be."

"Regrets?"

I looked Jack right in the eye. "None," I said. "The relationship just wasn't right. We just weren't right. You know?"

Jack took a sip of his beer and set the bottle back down before answering.

"Do you really want me to reply to that? Because I'm going to have to say, Yes, I do know. I knew all along."

I wondered, Was I the only one who hadn't known all along?

"At least you haven't said, 'I told you so.'"

Jack grinned. "I think I just did. Seriously, Anna, I'm sorry."

I smiled brightly, falsely. "Better now than after the wedding, right?"

"It's still got to hurt."

I abandoned the smile. It certainly hadn't fooled Jack. "Oh, yes. It hurts. And, well, I'm also a bit embarrassed. How could I have been so wrong?"

"That's a waste of time." Jack's tone was final. "Being embarrassed about being human just proves how ridiculous human beings really are."

"That's what Alexandra says."

"You should listen to Alexandra. Since you don't listen to me."

I did listen to Alexandra. She found Jack inappropriate. She thought he was good for me.

"I do listen to you," I said. And for the first time I realized just how true that was.

And then the air around us was filled with sexual tension. At least, I thought it was.

Jack tossed some bills on the bar and got up from the bar stool. "I've got to go."

"Oh," I said. "Are you sure? Can't you stay for just a bit?"

"I can't," he said brusquely. "I still have some work to do before tomorrow. We've got that Gott debacle in a few days."

"I'll get it all done," I said, with a touch of annoyance. "You'll have the final seating plan and layout. Don't worry."

"I never worry."

"I don't believe you."

"At least about you doing your job."

"Thanks," I said, but I don't think he heard. He was already at the door, then out on the sidewalk.

I watched as Jack loped off into the evening. Always moving, never still. Except when he looked. To really see requires stillness.

I wondered, Had anyone ever pinned down Jack Coltrane, even for a little while? Yes. Leslie Curtin had done something of the kind, I was sure of it. Female intuition. Womanly instinct. Jack's former girlfriend had made some big mistakes.

Maybe Jack couldn't be pinned down. Maybe it would be unfair of anyone to try.

Anyway, that's not really what I wanted, to pin Jack down.

The bartender nodded toward my empty wineglass. "Another?"

"Sure," I said. "And I'll take a menu, please."

I glanced once again out the window but Jack was long gone. So, Anna, I asked myself, What is it you do want with Jack?

80

With Friends Like These

"Your hair! You got it colored. It looks fabulous."

Kristen was sitting at the table, the first to arrive at Boucle that Friday evening. She beamed. "You really think so? I just felt like I needed a change, something to perk up my look. You know, I've been wearing my hair the same way since B.J. was born."

I sat across from her and beamed back. "Really, it looks great. What does Brian say?"

"He likes it."

Confirmation: Every one of my girlfriends was in love.

"This place is nice, isn't it?" I said, apropos of nothing. "The food is very good."

Kristen glanced around the main dining area. "Well," she drawled, "it's not The Cheesecake Factory."

"Alexandra refuses to eat there," I explained. "Something about it being mobbed with commoners."

"Alexandra doesn't know what she's missing. How are you, Anna?"

"I'm okay," I told her. "Some days are worse than others. Some days are better."

"Have you talked to Ross?"

"Not since last week. We've pretty much finished apportioning everything we owned in common. There's really not much reason to talk, I guess."

How strange that is, I realized. One minute we're engaged and expecting a baby. The next minute we're apart and have nothing to say to each other.

"I suppose I could call him," I said, musingly. "Just to see if he's all right."

"Do you really want to know?" Kristen asked and I wondered, If Ross told me he was unhappy, what would I say? What would I be obliged to do?

"Well, I don't want him to be miserable," I said. "But the truth is I don't really need to know how he's doing. That sounds so horrible, doesn't it? Ross and I were planning to spend our lives together and now I don't even miss him."

"It wasn't meant to be," Kristen said, with that all-too-familiar air of wisdom everyone seemed to have adopted since the breakup. "It's all for the best. You and Ross just weren't in the cards. The relationship was ill-fated. Ross and Rachel, yes; Ross and Anna, no."

"I guess it wasn't," I said.

The waiter came by, and I ordered a glass of wine. Kristen, I noticed, was suddenly very interested in her napkin.

"Stop fiddling," I said, "and tell me what's on your mind."

Kristen put her napkin on her lap and laughed. "It's nothing, really. Just something I was thinking about. Something concerning you and Ross."

"Oh. Okay. What?"

Kristen waved her hand dismissively. "Forget I said anything, really."

I wondered, What could she possibly have to say about Ross and me that hadn't already been said? "Come on, Kristen, tell me."

"Well . . . okay. It's just that it occurred to me last week that maybe Ross is, you know."

I laughed. Kristen can be so charmingly maddening. "No," I said, "I don't know. Ross could be what? A spy?"

"No!" And then her eyes widened and she leaned in. "Is he a spy? That might explain some—"

"No, Kristen, Ross is not a spy. And if he were a spy, would I tell you he was a spy? Would I even know he was a spy?"

"Oh. You're right." Kristen folded her hands on the table. "Okay, Anna. I'll just say it. It occurred to me that maybe Ross is gay."

It was the very last thing I expected Kristen to say. The very last thing I expected anyone to say.

"What!" I cried. "Why? Because he's thin and well groomed?"

"Well, there is that. But—Oh, I'm sorry, Anna. I shouldn't have said anything. It's stupid."

Yes, it is stupid, I thought angrily. And you're stupid. But of course I said nothing.

"Anna?" Kristen grabbed my hand across the table. "Are you all right?"

I smiled gamely and withdrew my hand. "Fine. I'm fine."

But I wasn't fine at all. Kristen was a lawyer. Okay, an out-of-practice lawyer, but someone good at putting evidence together to build a case. Why would she think Ross might be gay unless she had some real clue?

"You didn't hear anything, did you?" My words came out in a hiss. "Any rumors?"

"Oh, God, no! Of course not."

"Because I assure you that Ross is not gay. I'll admit he doesn't have a huge sexual drive. Pretty much none after I got pregnant. But—"

I stopped. But what? It had occurred to me before: Maybe Ross had met someone else, another woman, someone far sexier than me. Someone far less inhibited. And her lack of inhibition had enticed Ross to shed his own inhibitions . . .

"I know about the loss of sex drive," Kristen reminded

me gently. "You told us, right before Michaela made a play for him."

Which, I remembered with a shock, had repulsed Ross, but maybe not for the reason he had claimed. Maybe Ross was sickened not as much by Michaela's unseemly advance but by Michaela herself. Michaela, the epitome of sultry female sexuality.

Frantically, I tried to remember if Ross had ever exhibited any behavior that could be called gay. But what did that mean, anyway? Did he swish around the apartment in a pink chiffon robe? Of course not. And neither did most gay men! Anna, I scolded, how prejudicial! What horribly stereotyped thinking! You've been watching far too many sitcoms.

"Um, let's order." Kristen smiled too brightly at me. "Okay?"

I nodded and reached for my menu. The words were meaningless. All I could think about was Ross and his interesting sexuality.

A giant portabella mushroom studded with crabmeat and cheddar. Crab cakes. Scallops wrapped in bacon with a maple glaze. Who cared? I'd lost my appetite. All that mattered at the moment was the answer to the following question: Had Ross ever had sex with a man? Bravely, I reminded myself that in some cultures it wasn't at all unusual for an otherwise heterosexual man to have a youthful affair with another man. Right? So what if Ross had had an affair in college? So what? How did that affect me, his former fiancée, today?

Sexually transmitted disease. HIV. It was all over the news. Bisexual men routinely brought home all sorts of nastiness to their unsuspecting wives and girlfriends.

I gripped the menu more tightly. I felt slightly dizzy. Calm down, Anna, I told myself. Ross is the most cautious person you know. He's obsessively clean. He's ultraconcerned about his health. The last thing Ross would ever do is have dangerous sex.

Unless, of course, he were very young and very drunk and maybe very in love.

"Anna? Anna!"

I dropped the menu to the table. Kristen was staring at me, eyes wide.

"Are you okay? You look terrible!"

"No, I'm not at all okay. Please, Kristen, tell me why you thought Ross might be gay!"

Kristen fiddled with her napkin. She realigned her knife and fork. She took a sip of water. And then, she said, "Well, I was watching Jerry Springer the other afternoon and—"

"A talk show! You're basing your judgment of Ross on something some piece of trash said on Jerry Springer!"

"She wasn't a piece of trash," Kristen said hastily. "She was a sexologist."

I groaned. "Oh, that makes it all better!"

"Anyway," Kristen went on, "she was talking about lack of sex drive in heterosexual men, and one of the other guests told her story, which was that her husband stopped having sex with her, and eventually she found out it was because he realized he was gay."

"I'm still processing the fact that you, a Phi Beta Kappa, watch Jerry Springer. And that you admit it."

Kristen politely ignored my scorn. "Anyway, it got me thinking about Ross."

"Ross and I didn't break up because of a bad sex life," I reminded her. "He didn't find me repulsive. I didn't find used condoms in his car or receipts from cheap motels in his pants pockets."

"I know that." Kristen glanced around for eavesdroppers. "Anyway," she went on, her voice a bit lower, "I should clarify. I don't mean 'gay' as in Ross actually, you know, does anything about it. I mean gay as in maybe he's in denial. Like maybe he's never come out of the closet."

"Oh." I was stunned. "Is that supposed to make me feel better? Ross wasn't actually cheating on me with a man. It's just that every time we made love he imagined he was in bed with, I don't know, some guy with a big black mustache and an even bigger—I can't even say it!"

Kristen's face grew very red, and she reached for her water. As she took gulp after gulp, I wondered, Why hadn't Ross gotten married long ago? With his looks, charm, and money he could have had his pick of the single women in Boston. It wasn't as if he'd been wildly playing the field all those years. Boston is a small town. I knew all there was to know about Ross's romantic past.

At least about his romantic past with women.

Kristen lowered her empty glass and waved. I turned to see Alexandra making her way toward us.

"Oh, look, Alexandra is here!" Kristen said brightly. "Has it only been twelve minutes?"

"You're not off the hook," I told her.

Alexandra arrived and by way of greeting said, "This day is sucking."

"Well, mine isn't any better," I said, before she was fully in her seat. "Get this. Kristen thinks Ross might be gay. In denial, but gay nonetheless."

Alexandra sat and shrugged. "I can see how she might think that. Ross's affect is oddly sexless. Like maybe he's hiding something."

"That's it, exactly!" Kristen said excitedly. "I just didn't know how to put what I felt into words. He's so handsome and well dressed and all, and he's in perfect shape, but he's not at all sexy. What I mean," she added hastily, "is that I don't find Ross sexy. But I'm happily married. So I don't count. Now, Michaela is single and she made a pass at Ross so maybe I'm totally wrong and that sexologist was just crazy and—"

Alexandra put a finger to Kristen's lips. "Haven't you learned that backpeddling just intensifies the insult?"

"I'm going to have a heart attack," I stated with false brightness. "I'm serious. If I think Ross is sexy, and if Ross really is gay but just can't admit it, what does that say about me? What does that say about me as a woman? Am I an emotional freak? A psychological disaster?"

"We're dropping this subject right now," Alexandra said sternly. "Come on, Anna, Kristen's right. What does she know about sexual affect? She's been married to the same guy for years."

"Hey! I—"

But Alexandra cut her off. "And me, well, why would you want to listen to my opinion? I'm just a loud mouth. Now, come on. Let's order. I'm starved."

One more sharp-edged piece to the miserable puzzle that was my life. Why, I thought, can't people keep their suspicions to themselves? What good does it do me now to wonder if Ross is a gay man lodged in the back of a deep, deep closet? Now, in addition to questioning my ability to sustain a long-term relationship, I could doubt my sexual appeal. I could obsess about my own worth as a woman!

I wondered, What if the only reason I'd found Ross physically attractive was because my own sexuality was so repressed I could only handle being with a closeted gay man. One whose libido—at least the libido he could reveal to me—was lukewarm at best.

And to further complicate everything, there I was, falling in love with Jack—or maybe I'd been in love with him the whole time, how would an idiot like me know?—a man who didn't seem to care a bit for me in the romantic sense.

Life wasn't looking very bright. Numbly I ordered, and while Kristen and Alexandra chatted about something or other, I wondered, Was my romantic life effectively over? Had I become a classic urban single-woman failure, unable to tell gay men from straight, unable to sustain a long-term relationship, unable to have a baby the old-fashioned way?

I wondered, When was the last time a man had shown any romantic interest in me? I thought back to the months before I'd met Ross and came up with nothing. Was it true I'd been experiencing a dating dry spell when Ross came along?

And here I was, almost thirty-eight years old. Almost

forty. Would anyone, I wondered, ever find me attractive again? Maybe I'd lost the glow of youth, that was inevitable, but had I also lost the more mature appeal that was supposed to come after?

I was brought back to the moment when our meals arrived. "Fresh ground pepper, ma'am?" asked the smooth-cheeked waiter.

Ma'am. It was official. I was not only a grown-up. I was old. I was an old woman with no fiancé and no baby and no—

"Ma'am?"

Kristen eyed me with concern. Alexandra frowned.

"Yes, thank you," I told the waiter. I flashed him what used to be a winning smile. I thought of how pepper had been bothering my digestion of late. "But not too much please."

81

Slam

Alfred, Lord Tennyson wrote, "In spring a young man's fancy lightly turns to thoughts of love." Unfortunately, so does a woman's.

The next morning around eleven I decided quite out of the blue to stop by Jack's studio to see if he wanted to grab a cup of coffee. Why not? Two colleagues sharing a brief break in their busy work schedules. What could be more normal?

No excuses. No hand delivering what could have been e-mailed, no books to loan or articles to share. Just an invitation to share a cup of coffee.

The door to the loft was unlocked. I knocked lightly as I pushed it open. "Hi, Jack," I said. "I—"

And then I saw that the person sitting at Jack's desk, the person using his precious computer, was not Jack at all.

The person turned and gave me a calm but suspicious look. She had slim shoulders and a delicate neck and a short choppy haircut that perfectly topped a perfect, pixie-like face. She was no older than twenty-five.

"Yes?" the pixie said.

I stood frozen for a moment, one hand still on the doorknob behind me.

"Oh," I finally said. "I'm sorry. I came to see Jack . . ."

"He left early." The pixie offered no further information. She didn't offer to take a message. She was not Jack's employee.

I wanted to say something, but what? I didn't have the nerve to ask the girl if she knew where he was. Or with whom.

Her wide blue eyes narrowed just a bit. "Do you need something?" she asked.

"No, no," I said, backing out through the door. "I'm fine. Thanks. Bye."

The pixie turned back to the computer screen, and I closed the door behind me. I didn't dare linger; what if Jack came back and found me there? I raced down the stairs and out onto the sidewalk. The sunny sky seemed to mock me. Without breaking my pace I headed for my office.

The image of that petite pretty thing haunted me all the way. Was this Jack's latest girlfriend? Was Jack at her place now, waiting for her to come home so they could spend the lunch hour having hot and steamy sex?

I reached my office just as the tears came. What had I been thinking, assuming Jack would be in his studio, assuming he would want to spend time with me? The stark reality was that Jack did have a life and I was only a tiny, insignificant part of it.

82

Ladies' Night In

"How can a cookie be healthy?" Kristen peered dubiously at the plate of homemade no-fat cookies Tracy had just placed on the table.

Alexandra grimaced. "Don't tell us. I don't want to know when I'm eating fern spores and acorn shavings."

"Just try one," Tracy said. "Aren't you supposed to be the adventurous one here?"

The Chinese food arrived before Alexandra could reply.

"What more does a girl need?" Kristen said as we unpacked the three large white bags. "Look at all this scrumptious food. Brian's not big on Asian cuisine. I don't remember the last time I had dim sum! Let's go to Chinatown some Sunday morning, okay?"

"A day at a world-class spa," Alexandra said suddenly. "That's what else a girl needs. No, make that a week, but not at one of those places that serves a lettuce leaf and a boiled brussels sprout for dinner. A place that serves croissants for breakfast, truffle omelettes for lunch, and bouillabaise for dinner."

"Speaking of things French," Tracy said, "a girl could use

a month-long trip to Paris, with all expenses paid by a wealthy benefactor she never has to meet, let alone sleep with."

Alexandra laughed. "Now that is a fantasy beyond the realm of ordinary fantasy. No sex in return for a fabulous meal of coq au vin, foie gras, and Grand Marnier souffle?"

"What about you, Kristen?" I asked. "You must think a girl needs something beyond sesame noodles and beer."

Kristen considered. "Can I say a wonderful husband and kids she adores?"

Suddenly, everyone's eyes were on me.

"You can say anything you want," I said, but I wasn't able to stop tears from springing to my eyes.

Kristen grasped my hands in hers. "Can I also say that even more than sesame noodles and beer a girl needs her girlfriends?"

"Ugh, this is so disgustingly maudlin and we haven't even begun to drink! Quick, hand me the corkscrew."

"What about you, Anna?" Tracy asked, tossing the corkscrew to Alexandra.

"Stick to fantasy," Alexandra advised, handing me a glass of chilled Pinot Grigio.

I shrugged. "I think a girl needs all of it. Chinese food, girlfriends, a spa, and a trip to Paris. And when she comes home, a wonderful husband and maybe even adoring children waiting breathlessly for her at the airport."

"Hear, hear!" Tracy raised her glass and we toasted.

Alexandra grinned. "Our former so-called friend Michaela would say a girl needs wild sex and lots of it."

"What do you mean by wild?" Kristen asked.

"Passionate," Tracy said. "And yes, I've certainly had passionate sex."

"With your husband?"

"Alexandra!" Kristen exclaimed. "That's so personal!"

"That's okay," Tracy said. "Yes, I have had passionate sex with Bill. But there were a few other special men in my past.

In case you're wondering, I wouldn't trade Bill for the world, let alone one more night with the others."

"Well," Kristen said, "if Tracy can admit to having passionate sex with her husband, then I can admit to having passionate sex with mine. Brian is the love of my life."

"But not your first and only lover?" Alexandra asked.

"No. There were two before him but neither really meant anything. And I never, you know, felt anything. And that's all I'm saying about that!"

"Alexandra?" Tracy asked. "Wild sex?"

"Oh, my, yes. Once upon a time."

"That's it?"

"That's it."

"Oh, come on, Alexandra. Tell us about him," Kristen pressed. "Were you in love?"

Afraid my face would give away Alexandra's secret, I pretended to find a California roll deeply interesting. Alexandra let everyone wait while she poured herself another glass of wine.

"I've said," she finally announced, "all I'm going to say. Anna? What about you? Have you ever had wild, crazy, nothing's-off-limits sex? The kind of sex that makes you feel like you've died and gone to heaven. The kind of sex the angel has with Prior Walter. Otherworldly. Astounding. Addictive sex."

"I get the picture," I said dryly. "And the answer is no. Okay, everyone can feel sorry for me now. My life is an empty shell. My romantic life, at least."

"Oh," Kristen said. "You know, Anna, there's more to life than sex."

I sighed dramatically and put the back of my hand to my forehead. "So I've been told. But alas! I've yet to find satisfaction anywhere."

"I'm not surprised," Tracy said. "I always thought Ross's affect was kind of flat. He's very handsome but he's just not very sexy."

Alexandra and Kristen burst out laughing.

"What's so funny?" Tracy demanded.

"It's just that these two clowns have said the exact same thing. Kristen has even suggested that Ross is gay. In the closet, but gay."

"Well, that's just ridiculous," Tracy replied. "If anything, Ross might be asexual."

"Please," I said, "you're destroying what's left of my self-esteem!"

"Ross and his dubious sexuality have nothing to do with your self-esteem," Alexandra said forcefully.

I thought for a moment before saying, "Ross has nothing to do with me at all. He never really had. I think that's why I didn't want to have a baby with him. I think I knew we couldn't sustain that level of intimacy. And that still scares me. Why was I going to marry him?"

"Don't be so hard on yourself, Anna," Kristen said. "You and Ross might have had a fine marriage if the issue of a family hadn't, well, hadn't been thrust upon you."

Maybe, I thought. But then I wouldn't have Jack. Not that I really had him. What I did have was the realization that I was falling in love with a man who didn't have any feelings for me in return. Wonderful.

"I know this question is unanswerable," Tracy said, "but I'm going to pose it anyway. If having a baby with someone is so monumental, why are so many men able to leave their wives and kids?"

"It isn't always easy for a man to leave a marriage." Alexandra shot me a look I took to mean, My secret is still safe with you, right? I reassured her with a nod. "Sometimes," she went on, "the marriage just isn't working. Divorce doesn't necessarily mean abandonment. It can be the healthiest thing for everyone involved. It can be the end of a destructive dynamic and the opportunity for a fresh start."

"Of course," Tracy said. "But I'm talking about those men who just walk away from their family without trying to make the marriage work. I can't imagine how a woman gets over that. I just can't."

"It happened to a friend of mine," Kristen said as she reached for another spring roll. That made four; Brian really needed to learn to like Chinese. "Her name was Joyce. Her son and B.J. were in playgroup together. Anyway, she was pregnant with their third child when her husband just moved out. He didn't even give her a reason."

"Maybe he had a nervous breakdown," I said.

"Or maybe," Alexandra added, "he was just a bucket of slime. Go on, Kristen."

Kristen shrugged. "Well, that's it, really. Funny. I met her husband once and he didn't seem like the type to do something so—violent."

Alexandra rolled her eyes. "He was a nice man. A quiet man. Who knew he had an ax under his pillow? Oh, please."

"None of us who knew Joyce and Bob could believe it," Kristen said, ignoring Alexandra's remark. "She had to wonder if he'd ever felt any tenderness for her, or if all along he'd been disgusted by her. It's almost too awful to think about. To be so vulnerable with someone and then to be discarded like an old shoe."

"What happened to Joyce?" I asked.

"I don't know," Kristen admitted. "She took the kids and moved to New Jersey. Her parents live there. She just couldn't stay in that big house all by herself. Anyway, I haven't heard from her since. I think maybe she just wanted to erase everything connected to her life in Wakefield."

"For some reason sitcoms would like us to believe otherwise," Tracy said dryly, "but in the real world, eligible men aren't exactly beating down the doors of single mothers. Kristen's friend might be single for the rest of her life."

"Maybe she wants it that way," I remarked. "Maybe she's through with men. At least, through with marriage."

For a moment or two no one spoke. I poured myself a bit more wine. Tracy seemed lost in thought. Kristen added more duck sauce to her plate. Finally, Alexandra broke the silence.

"There's another scenario we're not considering."

"What's that?" Kristen asked.

"A scenario in which the man is the victim or the long-suffering party. What if the wife has made her husband's life miserable?"

"I suppose it happens," Tracy said.

Alexandra nodded. "You bet it does. Maybe the marriage was a mistake from the start but the husband stuck it out for all the so-called right reasons. Maybe his love for his wife was more a duty than a passion. And then maybe he just couldn't do it any longer. Maybe he broke down or maybe, incredibly, he met the love of his love, the woman he should have married, the woman he would have married if she'd been around when all his friends were getting married and he figured he should get married, too. You know, to fit in, to be grown up. To prove something to his parents who never thought he'd amount to much of anything. To prove something to himself. To—"

I caught Alexandra's wildly gesticulating hand in mid-air.

"I think we got your point," I said quietly.

"Oh," she said. "More wine, anyone?"

"Love dies," Tracy said abruptly. "Not always, but it does die. Sometimes two people who were in love come to hate each other. Or to feel indifferent about each other. I think that happens a lot more than anyone wants to admit. It's so terribly depressing to accept the death of love as a fact. I mean, if you accept that love can die, how can you ever make a forever-after commitment? And yet, people do it all the time. Over and over again, just hoping the next love will outlive them. Just hoping that only physical death will part them from their loved one."

Kristen sighed. "It's all so sad."

"Or all so wonderful," I said. "Isn't it a testament to the human spirit that we keep reaching for love?"

"That we keep struggling for survival," Alexandra corrected. "Maybe it's all a biological urge at bottom."

"It can't be. Can it? I don't want it to be," Kristen said urgently. "I want to believe there's something noble and fine about romantic love."

"I don't know if I could stand my love for Bill dying." Tracy sighed. "Or his love for me dying. Just imagining that possibility makes me overwhelmingly sad."

"Then don't imagine it, Tracy," Alexandra said fiercely. "Block it out. Live for today, carpe diem, be in the moment. And in this particular moment you and Bill are in love and your marriage is fine."

"Thank my lucky stars. Knock on wood and all that."

"I'm sure your marriage to Bill has nothing to do with superstition or luck," Kristen said. "I'm sure you guys work to stay in a good place."

Tracy shrugged. "Sure. But don't you think luck or fate plays some part in everyone's life? The day Bill hobbled into my office started out like any other day. I had no idea I'd meet my future husband at 2:15 that afternoon. How did that come about? Luck, fate, serendipity? No one set us up. No one played matchmaker, which, I suppose, is also a form of fate. Fate personified."

"Maybe fate explains why some people never find true love," Kristen wondered. "Maybe they have bad luck. Maybe they have bad karma."

"I think," Alexandra said, "that most people who never find love don't find it because they're not looking for it. Or they're not open to experiences that might put them out in the world where luck and fate happen. I find it hard to believe that every single woman in this city is single because of bad luck. Or because of something bad she did in a former life!"

"So," I said, "therapy or a self-help program will guarantee finding a soul mate? Or at the very least, a summer fling?"

"Well, therapy might help dislodge some unhealthy mental and emotional habits."

"Like?" Kristen said.

Alexandra considered. "Like, for example, the tendency to date significantly older, powerful men because they remind you of your father, whose love you never achieved because he thought you were an airhead. Or whose love you never achieved because you thought he thought you were an airhead and so you actually were the one to sabotage any attempts at building a relationship he initiated."

"But what if dating older, powerful men makes you happy?" Kristen said. "What if you meet a man who really loves you, and supports you in your work, and who wants to marry you?"

"You have a point," Alexandra conceded. "Sometimes our neuroses work for us, not against us."

"In such cases a neurosis becomes a coping mechanism," Tracy said. "A survival strategy. A means to a healthy life."

"Speaking of a healthy life," Kristen said, "and I mean that with irony, has anyone heard anything about Michaela's adoption quest?"

"Now there's a woman who should not be a parent!" Tracy declared. "She's got absolutely no maternal instinct. I bet you couldn't even train it into her. I shudder to think what a child of hers would turn out to be like. At the very least he'd be an emotional cripple."

Alexandra snickered. "More likely a long-term resident of a state penitentiary."

I refrained from commenting. Let Tracy and Alexandra have their opinions about the bleak future of Michaela's adoptive child. Would the child that was so briefly mine have been any better off? Would she have been an emotional mess or a hardened criminal, too? Since losing the baby I didn't feel I had the right to judge other people's parental possibilities.

"Anna," Kristen asked, "have you heard anything?"

"After she tried to steal Ross out from under my nose at

that awful party I haven't talked to her. Except for one very unpleasant moment just after the party."

"What happened?" Kristen asked breathlessly.

I sighed. "I said, 'Our friendship is over as of right now.' Very cutting, don't you think?"

"So, what did Michaela say back?" Tracy asked.

I didn't miss Michaela in my life and I'd never loved her like I love my other girl friends. But let's face it. No one likes rejection.

"She said, and I quote, 'Like you matter to me?' And then she laughed. The end."

"Bitch," Tracy said.

"Whore." Alexandra grinned. "Tramp."

"I think she's pitiful," Kristen said. "I feel sorry for her."

"You're wasting your time feeling anything for her. She probably never even registered your presence."

"Alexandra!" I scolded. But I was pretty sure she was right.

"You know," Tracy said, "now that you and Ross are no longer a couple, I wouldn't put it past Michaela to make another move on him."

"Well, she's welcome to him," I said. "He's single, he's wealthy, he wants a family. They'd make the perfect couple."

Although I didn't really believe that. Ross, for all his flaws, wasn't a harsh person.

"Yeah," Alexandra said, "they're both egotistical, shallow, and morally ambiguous. The only problem I see is that Michaela is so much smarter than Ross. She'd be bored with him within a month."

"Hey!" I protested. "What does that say about me? I was with Ross for almost a year and I wasn't bored. Entirely. Are you saying I'm not as smart at Michaela?"

"No, honey, of course not. But you are an awful lot nicer than she is. You give people the benefit of the doubt. You see the good in them. I'm sure you kept thinking that someday Ross would wow you with—well, with something."

She was wrong. I'd never expected anything spectacular, from Ross or from me.

"I think Michaela might do well with Ross," Tracy said then. "I think she needs a man she can easily manipulate."

"Ross isn't as pliable as he looks," I muttered. "Look, can we stop talking about my ex-fiance? I'm getting depressed, and that wasn't the point of the evening."

Kristen gasped. "You don't regret breaking up with him, do you?"

"No, no, of course not. And I didn't really break up with him. We broke up with each other. But the point is that if I'm going to move on I shouldn't be dwelling on my past, right?"

"Right," Kristen agreed. "You should be focusing on your future. You should be thinking about falling in love again."

"I have a feeling," Alexandra said slyly, "that Anna's already working on it."

Kristen's eyes went wide. Tracy cleared her throat.

"Falling in love is the last thing on my mind!" I protested.

And I knew that none of my friends believed me.

Truth: Falling in love was the only thing on my mind.

83

The Scene

"So, how about it? Can I give him your number?"

"Ginger," I said, "I just don't think it's a good idea."

The last thing I wanted to do was go on a blind date. But Ginger Matthews, that suspiciously enthusiastic lady, was not to be deterred.

"Anna, listen," she said. "Tom and I have known Russell for five years now. He's a great guy. Trust me."

"It's too soon," I said.

"You know what they say about falling off a horse."

"I don't ride."

"Anna, you need to get back into the dating scene."

"Why?"

"Because you're not getting any younger. If you want to get pregnant again you're going to have to find a man first, and the clock is always ticking. Tick, tick, ticking!"

Maybe, I thought, Ginger had a point.

I didn't need a therapist to tell me that I was making little or no progress in my personal life. I didn't need a therapist to tell me that I had been crazy for quite some time. All on my own I'd realized that the real reason I'd been afraid to tell

Jack that I was pregnant was because on some deep, unexplored level, I felt as if I'd betrayed him by sleeping with another man.

I know. It's insane. How can you cheat on somebody you've never even been involved with? Someone you've never even kissed? Someone you don't even know you're in love with?

Someone who clearly isn't in love with you.

"Okay," I said. "Give him my number."

Three times in the days before the date I picked up the phone to call Russell and cancel. Each time I called on every ounce of determination in my being and resisted the urge. Look at this as a job, I told myself. Be your own client. Your client needs something; she needs to get over a man she can't have. She's hired you to provide that service for her. Step 1: Go on the date.

Russell Hill met me at Tundra. Maybe, I thought, there's more to Ginger Matthews than meets the eye. Russell was well educated (Harvard undergrad and Columbia journalism); a good conversationalist (he spoke easily of politics and of pop culture); athletic (he told me he rode his bike to work every day); funny without being crude or nasty (he admitted to knowing every episode of *Seinfeld* almost verbatim); and handsome in a sort of boyish, blond way (he reminded me of a young Robert Redford).

He paid for everything. He was a gentleman at the end of the evening. He promised he'd call. And I hoped he wouldn't because the date had been a failure.

Russell Hill, bachelor extraordinaire, wasn't Jack Coltrane.

84

The Morning After

Russell did call. I turned him down. He sounded surprised. I explained that it was me, not him. And I prepared to receive a scolding from Ginger.

I thought about the night I told Jack that Ross and I had broken up.

I thought about the afternoon I stumbled upon the report written by Jack's teacher Ms. Sidler.

I thought about the extravagant bouquet of flowers.

I thought about the time Jack and I ran into each other at the café and he'd asked me to stay for a while. It wasn't because he needed my opinion on the student's work. It was, I knew, because he wanted to help distract me from my grief. I remembered his gentle touch that day. I remembered wanting him to touch me again.

And I remembered the fury Rowena and the pixie raised in me.

What sane woman falls in love with a man who infuriates her?

I needed help.

"This is on me," I said. We were in the bar at Polar. "Consider yourself my therapist for the next hour."

"Fine." Alexandra picked up the menu. "Hmm, what's most expensive?"

"I don't care. Order everything. Order two of everything. What I've got on my mind outweighs any concern about my entertainment budget."

Alexandra lowered the plastic-coated menu. "Tossing away your hard-earned cash? You've got my full attention," she said.

I took a deep breath, as if preparing for a dive. In a way, I guess I was.

"I like Jack Coltrane," I said, looking her right in the eye. "*Like* as in—"

Alexandra raised her hand to stop me. "I know what you mean. Well, all I can say is it's about time."

"I don't know what you mean," I lied, utterly relieved.

"Anna," Alexandra said with false patience, "it's been obvious to me for some time now that you 'like' Jack. I'm not blind."

"Then why didn't you say something?"

"Anna, dear, I did say something. I said several things, on several occasions. At times you chose not to understand what I was hinting at—"

"See, that was the problem! You just didn't come right out and—"

"—and at other times you took offense at what I was implying. Anyway, it wasn't my job to break up your engagement. That was your job."

"Hey—"

"You know what I mean, Anna."

I did know what she meant.

"What if he's seeing someone?" I asked.

"He's not."

"How do you know? He was at that horrid party with some person in a dress a Victorian fairy would wear. Rowena. I think she's a witch."

"I think you meant to say bitch."

"And there was some pixie chick in his studio the other day."

"They all mean nothing."

"They all?" I suddenly felt sick. "How many are there? Wait, maybe I don't want to know the answer to that."

"There are a few," Alexandra said, matter-of-factly. "Not that many. He doesn't even sleep with them all. And none of them are special."

Well, I thought grumpily, what does that say about Jack? Was he a cad, a heartless seducer, a lothario, a Don Juan, a Marquis de Sade?

"And no," Alexandra said. "He's not any of the things you've been thinking. The women he dates are intelligent adults, even if some of them look like refugees from Renaissance fairs. He's very upfront about not getting involved. And don't underestimate his taste in women. It just might turn out to be a reflection on you."

"How do you know all this personal information, anyway?" I demanded.

"I have my ear to the ground. And Jack and I talk. Sometimes. And no, I'm not going to play matchmaker for you. You're going to have to deal with this situation on your own."

Okay, I thought. I'm used to doing things on my own. I can handle this. "So, he's never . . ."

Alexandra smirked annoyingly. "Never what?"

"You know. Has he ever said anything about me? About being interested in me?"

"Of course not. He's not in high school, Anna, and neither are you, which is why I'm staying out of this. I'm not cut out to be a messenger of love. Can you picture me in Cupid's wings?"

I sat silently for a moment or two. My emotions were rioting.

"What if Jack is just a rebound?" I asked suddenly. "What if I'm only interested in him because I'm upset about breaking up with Ross? What if I'm into Jack just because he's there?"

Alexandra sighed dramatically. "Anna, you have got to stop thinking so much and just act. Talk to Jack. Jump him. Do something. Besides, your feelings for Jack are real. They have nothing to do with a rebound."

"How can you be so sure?" I demanded.

"Because there has to have been something against which to bound. What I mean is, you and Ross had nothing. Not really. How can you react against an experience you never experienced?"

"That's a horrible thing to say," I said, "and yes, I do know what you're getting at, even if your language skills seemed to have failed you. Ross and I were a couple for almost a year. We were engaged. Of course we had something! We had a relationship."

"Not much of one," Alexandra said. "Admit it, Anna. You were sleepwalking through that so-called relationship. It never really touched you. Not where it counts. Look, you're so much more than Ross. It might have worked if he'd known that and appreciated it. But Ross never could see you for all you are. It's just not in him. And because of that the relationship was, well, it wasn't much of anything."

I knew Alexandra had a point. And it infuriated me.

"I can't believe you're dismissing a year of my life!" I cried. The bartender shot me a look, which I ignored. "How dare you. Did I ever tell you that you were wasting your time waiting around for some married man to dump his wife and appear on your doorstep? Wait a minute. How could I have? You never told me about Luke, not until I dragged it out of you. You were lying to me about your love life."

"I was keeping a secret," she said. "That's not a crime."

"Well, maybe it should be," I said, petulantly. "Friends shouldn't have secrets from each other. I thought you were one person, and then I found out you were someone else entirely."

"You've conveniently gotten away from the topic,"

Alexandra said calmly. "Look, I'm sorry about what I said. Yes, you and Ross had a relationship, and it was real. Fine. But my original point still stands. You're overthinking this thing with Jack. You're not trusting your feelings, and how can you? You've never done it before, you have no practice. Your decision to marry Ross was made with your head, not your heart."

"I loved Ross," I lied. I knew Alexandra wasn't fooled.

"You knew all along I didn't think Ross was the one for you. So what? Nothing's changed. Why get mad at me now?"

Why, indeed? Because now that Ross and I were over there was nothing tangible in the way of my reclaiming my life—or maybe claiming it for the first time. There was nothing tangible in the way of my pursuing a relationship with Jack Coltrane. There was nothing in the way of my future but my fears. And they seemed very tangible.

"I'm not mad at you," I mumbled.

"Yes, you are," she said. "But that's okay. I can be horrible." Alexandra reached for her bag. "Look, honey, I think I'll just go straight to Luke's now. Do yourself a favor and think about what I've said."

I watched as Alexandra left the restaurant, on her way to meet her lover. I almost hated her at that moment. Almost.

85

Blow

"Anna."

"Hmm?"

"Remember I told you about the San Francisco offer?"

"The what?"

I was at Jack's studio. We were reviewing the success that had been the Gott event.

"The San Francisco offer," he said. "I told you about it last month."

I thought for a moment. "Vaguely." There had been so much going on in my life; some days I didn't trust myself to remember my own name. "You did mention something. Why?"

"Well, it's going through. I'm going through with it."

I felt my stomach drop, my world bottoming out. I leaned back against the worktable and gripped its edge with both hands.

"Going through with what?" I said past the sudden roar in my head. "What are you talking about?"

Jack attempted a grin. "And you accuse me of not listening. I'm moving to the West Coast in about three weeks. I'm joining up with a small photography group. Look, I can hook you up with a good photographer in Boston so you won't be left high and dry."

"I know other photographers," I snapped. "I don't need your connections. Why, Jack? Why are you leaving?"

"It's not so much that I'm leaving Boston as that I'm going to San Francisco. I'm starting over."

"Midlife crisis?" I spat and immediately regretted my words and their tone.

"If it makes you happy to think so," he replied coldly.

"It doesn't. I'm sorry. I just don't understand."

"Do you have to?"

"I'm your friend. I would like to understand."

Jack sat at his desk and swiveled around to face me.

"Maybe there is nothing to understand," he said. "Maybe I'm just going. No big motivation. Just time for a change of scenery."

I said, "I'll believe that the day I get a tattoo of George W. on my forehead. Don't be an ass, Jack."

For a while the conversation went dead. Jack swiveled back to his computer; I stood and stared at the wall. Why, I thought desperately, hadn't I told him how I feel? Maybe it would have made him stay in Boston. But maybe it wouldn't have. If Jack didn't have feelings for me in return—and it was clear he didn't, since he was planning to move across country in just over two weeks!—what would I have gained by revealing my secret? Nothing except embarrassment.

I looked then at the back of Jack's head, his dark wavy hair, his strong shoulders. I could tell him now, I thought. I could ask him not to go. I could beg him . . .

Jack swore under his breath, damning Photoshop, which had just crashed again. And then I thought, Face it, Anna, it's too late. You missed your chance. You can't tell Jack now that you're in love with him. It would be totally unfair. He's made his plans. Don't make a mess of everything.

"What about your work?" I said, suddenly. "Your own work. What about that project you're working on, those nudes I saw?"

"What about them?"

"Don't be obtuse. I thought—"

Jack looked over his shoulder at me. "You thought what?"

I threw my hands in the air and groaned. I think it was the first time I'd ever done that. "I don't know what I thought," I admitted. "I guess I thought you might be spending more time on your own work and less on the business. But I guess you can't do that when you're starting up with a new group."

Jack swiveled around to me again and shrugged. "I guess not."

"What is it then?" I challenged. "Do you have friends in San Francisco?"

"No."

"Family?"

"No. I've never even been there."

I put my fingers to my temples as if I had a headache. It was another unfamiliar dramatic gesture. Where were they coming from? "You're relocating to a city you've never even visited! Jack, that's insane!"

Jack waited a beat before replying. "Anna," he said calmly, "people in San Francisco speak English. California is part of the United States of America. It's not as if I'm moving to some remote Maui village."

"But what if you hate it? What if you get out there and start the new job and buy an apartment and then, suddenly, you find yourself pining for the Northeast?"

Jack laughed. "First of all, I'm not the pining type. Second, if I hate San Francisco, and I don't think I will, I'll either suck it up or move on."

I think I might have gone temporarily insane.

"I get it," I said, with the same conviction as if I'd just discovered, without a doubt, that the Earth was round. "There's an old girlfriend. That's why you're going to San Francisco. You're having an early midlife crisis and you're running off to California to dye your hair blond, buy a red convertible, and win back the only woman you ever loved."

Jack looked at me with a strange expression on his face. "Nothing," he said, "could be further from the truth."

Once again he turned back to his computer.

"Don't ask me to be supportive of this, Jack."

Without looking away from his work Jack said, "I'm not asking you for anything, Anna."

I left shortly after. Jack had made it perfectly clear. It didn't matter what I thought. He was going whether I liked it or not.

86

Leap

Maybe, I thought, I should get an aquarium. The companionship might be nice. Or maybe even that small, nondestructive dog Ross and I had considered adopting. Someone to greet me each morning. Someone to love.

But it wasn't in me then to make the commitment. Face it, Anna, I told myself. The fish will up and die and the dog will up and run away, and you'll be left all alone to mourn. Again. And I was so, so tired of loss.

Loss. I had to come to terms with the fact that Jack was leaving or go insane.

Desperate times call for desperate measures.

I burst into the studio. The door swung back against the wall with a metallic crash.

"You used to call before you came by," Jack said laconically, over his shoulder.

I did used to call, I realized. I used to do a lot of things differently.

"I have an idea," I said, "and I want you to hear me out before you say no. Okay? Please?"

Jack saved whatever it was he was working on and

swiveled around in his chair to face me. "Fine. What's your idea?"

"I'd like to mount a show, something small but important."

"And?" Jack grinned up at me annoyingly. "What does that have to do with me?"

"Don't be dense," I snapped. "I want to mount a show of your work. Some older works, some new; I'll leave the content up to you, and I don't know a lot about hanging photographs, but I'll learn or I'll hire someone to hang the show. I want to do this, Jack. A show before you leave Boston. Think of it as a farewell if you want, I don't care. What do you think?"

Jack was unnaturally still. It almost frightened me. I continued to stand before him, although it was tempting to collapse into a chair.

"I leave in two weeks," he said, finally.

"I know. It won't be easy. I have to get a space first and—"

"I'm not good at being the center of attention."

I smiled. At least he hadn't said no. Yet. "So be the socially awkward artist and stand in the corner."

Jack twisted the mechanical pencil he held in his hands. "Anna, look, give me some time to think about this."

My enthusiasm deflated. The adrenaline just flooded from my body. "You mean, no thanks."

"I mean, give me some time to think about this."

"We don't have a lot of time—"

Jack cut me off. "I'm aware. And I know you're aware of the fact that if you push me you'll only damage your cause."

"I know," I said. "I'm sorry." I checked my watch, unnecessarily. I had no other place I needed to be. "Look, I've got to run. Just—just let me know."

Nothing ventured, nothing gained, I thought as I clumped down the metal stairs to the lobby. Only weeks ago my life was all planned out. Now? I had no idea what was to become of me or of my life.

The phone rang at eleven o'clock that night. It was Jack.

I hesitated to take the call. Why not let voice mail record Jack's negative answer for me? And then I lifted the receiver.

"Hi," I said, flatly.

"Okay."

Truly, it took a moment for this to register.

"What?" I finally snapped. "You mean yes, you'll let me do this? You'll let me put together a show for you?"

"That's what 'okay' means. Yes. Go ahead. Just answer this one question for me."

"Okay."

"This show is partly for you too, isn't it?"

"Yes," I admitted. "It is." I waited for Jack to mock. He didn't.

"So," he asked, tone brisk, "what's next?"

"You mean, what's first. I've got so much to do!"

"Leave me out of the details, okay? Like should we have beer and wine and should we have a fruit platter or just cheeses. You make the decisions."

"You won't be sorry, Jack."

Finally, he laughed. "Yeah. I've heard that before."

"I mean it."

There was a beat of silence before Jack said, "I know you do."

87

In Action

Some people are at their best when busy. Some people flourish under pressure. Some people produce their best work when a deadline is barreling toward them. Some people rise to the occasion when their budget for a project is tight—and coming out of their own pocket.

By the following afternoon I'd rented a space in Teele Square, Somerville, from a friend of a friend of a friend; talked to the caterer; put together a preliminary guest list; enlisted Rasheed Kelly as Jack's assistant for the show; considered where and how to advertise; and begun to draft a press release.

By seven that evening I was exhausted and happy and eager for Alexandra to arrive with the Thai food. When she did, I told her about Jack's plan to leave town and about the show I'd decided to mount.

Alexandra carefully patted her mouth with a napkin before responding. "Why are you doing this?" she asked. Her eyes betrayed her concern.

I poked at the remains of my dinner and contemplated an answer. Did I really think Jack would be so grateful for my belief in him as an artist that he would fall madly in love with me and decide to stay in Boston?

Yes. No. Mounting the show was a scheme, though not a very complicated one. I just didn't have the nerve to tell Jack how I felt. I just didn't have the nerve to hear what he might have to say in return.

I pretended nonchalance. "I thought you were the one who told me I should tell Jack how I feel."

"Tell him, not trick him."

"I'm not tricking him," I protested.

"But you're not being honest with him. And your motives aren't entirely altruistic. Not that anyone's ever are. Still, Anna, I'm worried you're setting yourself up for heartache."

"I don't have any illusions," I said. "Really. I know this is silly. But it's all I can do, Alexandra. It's all I can do."

She leaned over and gave me a one-armed hug. "I'll help you in any way I can, of course. I'll tell my clients they just can't miss this show. Whatever you need."

"Thanks," I said. I fought to hold back tears.

Alexandra left. It was only eight o'clock and there was plenty of work to be done, but suddenly I felt drained of all energy. I crawled into bed and pulled the covers up to my chin. I was asleep within minutes.

88

News Flash

"Rasheed is really a sweetie," I said. "He's so excited about helping out with the show. I told you he's coming by at three, right?"

Jack didn't respond.

"Jack? Did you hear what I said?"

"What?" Jack shoved his thick dark hair back from his forehead. I made a mental note to remind him to get a haircut before the show. "No, sorry."

I shook my head. "I wonder if there's a way to feed you information intravenously. Maybe a shot directly into the brain. I said that Rasheed is excited to be your assistant for the show. He'll be here at three today."

"Good. He's a good kid."

I looked more closely at Jack. He seemed worried or preoccupied or maybe sick. "Do you feel okay?" I asked. "Are you getting a cold? I have some ibuprofen in my bag and—"

Jack cut me off. "Look, Anna," he said, "there's something I've been wanting to tell you. No, wait, that's a lie. I never wanted to drag you into my life, but now I think that maybe I need to drag you into my life. My personal life."

My heart began to race. This was a step in the right direction, a step toward closeness. Unless, of course, Jack was about to tell me he was getting married to Rowena or the pixie.

I attempted a carefree smile. "I guess I've dragged myself into your artistic life, haven't I?"

"Is that how you see it?" Jack looked at me musingly. "I'd like to think I welcomed you. Albeit begrudgingly."

"Let's say it was a little of both. I pushed, you pulled, and here we are, preparing this show. We still have a lot to do, you know."

"An unnecessary reminder."

"Sorry. So, what is it you want—I mean, what is it you need to tell me?"

Jack perched on the edge of a worktable. "I'm hoping it will explain some things about me. I don't know if it will."

I'd never heard Jack being so hesitant, so equivocal. It frightened me.

"Let me be the judge of that," I said. "What is it, Jack?" Please, I thought, I can handle his getting married. Just don't let him be sick. Don't let him be dying.

"About three months ago," he said, "I got a call from a friend, a guy I haven't seen in a few years. We keep in touch sporadically. Mostly through e-mail. Anyway, he called from L.A. He was visiting some college friends when he ran into Leslie Curtin."

Jack looked at me steadily, waiting.

"Oh," I said, pretending some indifference. "The woman you were once involved with."

"Yeah. Her. Long story short, my friend found out through some other people in her circle that she has a kid. A boy, eight years old."

I didn't get it at all. My brain felt all foggy. "Oh," I said. "So?"

"So, Leslie and I broke up eight years ago." Jack looked at me as if willing me to put it all together. "The boy could be mine, Anna."

"He could be yours," I repeated stupidly. "Or he could not be yours."

Jack's eyes held mine. "It's likely," he repeated, "that I'm the boy's father."

It was terribly important at that moment for me to play devil's advocate.

"But you have no proof," I insisted. "Right? It's entirely possible you're not the boy's father. I don't mean to imply that Leslie cheated on you," I added hurriedly.

"Don't freak." Jack smiled ruefully. "It's entirely possible Leslie did cheat on me. It's also entirely possible that she hooked up with another guy as soon as we broke up. Of course some other guy could be the father. But so could I."

"What's his name?" I asked, as if that bit of information would tell me something significant. How, how, how did an eight-year-old boy fit into my scheme to make Jack fall in love with me? Why was life always so messy?

"Heath. I don't know, I guess it has some special significance to Leslie. Her father's name was Albert, and she hated him. She hated most of her family. There's no way she'd ever name a kid after a Curtin."

"Heath is a nice name," I said.

Jack shrugged. "Yeah. It's all right. Funny, when I was young I used to think that if I ever had a kid I'd name him after my father."

"What's his name?"

"His name was James. Pretty standard stuff, not like some of the things people call their kids today. But he was a great guy. He deserved the honor of having a kid named after him."

"But he didn't get it?" I asked, touched by Jack's respect for his father.

"He died when I was eighteen. My sister had a boy years later but she named him after some actor she had a crush on. Leonardo."

I had to find some levity in the moment. "I think Leonardo is also the name of one of the Ninja Turtles."

Jack frowned. "The who?"

"It doesn't matter. I'm sorry about your father."

"Yeah," he said shortly. "It's been a long time now."

Clearly, that part of the conversation was closed. "If you are Heath's father," I said, "why would Leslie keep the truth from you for all these years? And I don't understand how you didn't find out before now that she had a child. What about your mutual friends or your colleagues? Wouldn't someone have known? Wouldn't someone have told you?"

Jack got up from the worktable and began to pace slowly.

"As for why Leslie would keep Heath from me," he said, "I don't know. I'm surprised she didn't tell me just to make me suffer. And to get some money to help pay for school, at least. Which, of course, I would have given."

"Of course."

"And about why no one else found out . . ." Jack shook his head. "When Marc called with the news I almost didn't believe it. I wondered where she'd been hiding the boy. But then I thought about it. The few times I've seen Leslie's name or picture in an industry journal there's been no mention of her personal life. And when she left me—let's just say my friends, although few, are loyal. They cut her out of their lives. And then Marc ran into her a few months ago. When he put the facts together he began to wonder. So he gave me a call."

I thought of Alexandra's past returning in such an unexpected way. Nothing, I thought, is ever really over. Everything we do has unending consequences.

"You must be glad he came to you with his suspicions," I said.

"Yeah, I am. This is not easy, but no one ever said life would be."

Maybe, I thought, ignorance isn't always bliss. I remembered the conversation Alexandra and I had about Luke's wife knowing or not knowing about the real state of her marriage.

"Now," I said, "you have a chance to be part of Heath's life."

"Yeah."

"You don't seem very enthusiastic."

Jack laughed bitterly. "Because I'm not very enthusiastic. This is not a simple situation, Anna."

"Give me some credit, Jack," I snapped. "I know it's not a simple situation. But how can you stand not knowing if Heath is your son? My own head feels like it's about to explode."

Jack shoved a chair in my direction. "Sit down. I shouldn't have told you."

I remained standing. "It was only an expression. Please, Jack, I'm fine. I'm a lot tougher than I look."

"I guess so."

"I know so. You've been underestimating me. It's a bad habit you have, Jack. It's part of your superiority problem. You assume you know all the answers and—"

"Please," he said firmly. "There's no need to enumerate my flaws and foibles. I feel shitty enough as it is."

"Oh. Sorry." And then, "Jack, what happened with Leslie?"

Jack hesitated a moment before answering my impertinent question. "Leslie and I had been together for five years when we both applied for the same grant, only I didn't know Leslie was applying. She pretended to support me while all along she was schmoozing her way into the winner's circle. Some would say sleeping her way into the winner's circle, but I never had any hard and fast proof of that. Anyway, when she got the grant she walked out on me. I mean, just packed up her stuff and was gone. All that was left was a two-line note on the back of a grocery store receipt. And no, I'm not telling you what the note said."

"Okay," I said.

Jack shrugged. "So, there it is. Poor Jack Coltrane. Stabbed in the back by the woman he loved and left all alone. After that I lost steam. I lost the passion I'd had for my work. In short, Anna, I crapped out."

"Don't say crapped out. You chose to retire from the world of art photography."

"Same thing. And that was no one's responsibility but my own. All Leslie did in the end was leave. I chose how to handle it. Not so young and stupid."

Not so young and heartbroken, I thought. One woman had destroyed Jack's faith in his work. Another was helping to restore it. One woman had broken his heart. Another woman . . . But what did it matter? Jack was still leaving for San Francisco right after the show.

I struggled to bring my mind back to what was most important. Jack's relationship with this boy.

"You have to find out if Heath is your son," I said. "And if he is, you have to tell him."

"Why?" Jack challenged. "Why do I have to tell him? If I find out I'm Heath's biological father I'll figure out a way to offer some financial support. I'll set up an account in his name, something Leslie can't touch."

"So you'd pretend to be a long-lost uncle, a modern-day fairy godfather? Jack," I said, "you just have to find out, and if Heath is your son you just have to tell him. You owe it to yourself. You owe it to the boy."

"Do I?" Jack challenged. "Assuming I am his father, how do I know Heath won't be better off without me? Marc told me Leslie's been with some guy for about five years now. As far as I know he hasn't officially adopted Heath, and I don't know if he and Leslie plan on getting married. But this guy, I've heard nothing bad. For all I know Heath loves him like a father. Now why would I want to crash in and screw that up?"

"Oh," I said. "Is it also about Leslie? Are you afraid of having to deal with her?"

"Afraid?" Jack laughed. "No. Looking forward to it? Again, no. But don't accuse me of wimping out on the boy who could be my son because I despise his mother. I want this to be about Heath, not about me or about Leslie. I just don't know how to do that yet. I don't know how to get close enough to the kid and not destroy any stability he's got in his life."

"I'm sorry," I said. "I didn't mean to accuse you of anything cowardly. Really, Jack. And I understand your concerns. You're right. It's a tough situation. You have to tread cautiously."

"The problem is I've never been very good at treading cautiously."

How true. "One more thing," I said. "Did Marc see the boy?"

"Yeah." A quick, spontaneous smile flashed across Jack's face. "He caught a glimpse. Said he looks like my Mini-Me. Without the gray hair of course."

"Oh," I said eloquently. I knew then for sure that Jack was the father. I just knew.

Jack looked at me carefully. "So. I told you."

"Thanks," I said. "I'm glad you did."

"Really?"

"Yes, really." I checked my watch. Jack and I had been talking for almost an hour and a half. "Oh, I've got to go," I told him. "I've got an appointment with the dentist."

Jack grinned. "Better a guy with a drill than a guy with a closet loaded with skeletons?"

"There are more?" I asked, with some trepidation. Did Jack have a secret identity, an alias? Was Jack a member of a witness protection program? Was he the incognito leader of a crazy neo-Nazi cult?

"Actually, no," he said, pretending regret. "People are surprised to know how clean a life I've lived."

Twenty minutes later I was on the Red Line headed for Downtown Crossing and the dentist's office. As the train rattled along, I wondered how this new and startling piece of information would affect my life. I asked myself if my feelings for Jack had altered. No. They hadn't. I loved him, I was in love with him, and short of his revealing he was a mass murderer, those facts were not going to change.

I realized then that Alexandra was right when she said that love was simple. It was just there. It just was.

As if it mattered. I stared blindly at the row of ads across the car: adult education courses, laser surgery offers, domestic abuse hotlines, requests for volunteers for clinical trials. For all I knew, Jack Coltrane saw me as nothing more or less than a friend. Not as a lover. Not as his soul mate. Just a sometimes pushy, always reliable friend.

It was something. It was better than nothing. It was breaking my heart.

89

Sink or Swim

"I just might have a skeleton story to top yours."

Alexandra opened her eyes wide. "You have a murky past? You've been lying all along about your spotless reputation? I don't believe it."

We were having drinks at Lemur, Alexandra's pick of the week.

"No," I said. "I mean, the story isn't mine. It's Jack's. Just promise me you won't tell anyone. He didn't ask me to keep it a secret, but I think it's safe to say he doesn't want just anyone to know."

"Thank you for considering me not just anyone. Now, what is it?"

So I told Alexandra about Heath, the little boy who was possibly—possibly, I repeated—Jack's son.

"Wow," she said when I had finished. "Let me guess. It doesn't make a difference in how you feel about him. Right?"

"Right." But then I considered. "Only it does make a difference. I feel like now I want to protect him from more hurt. I don't know. If it's possible, my feelings have intensified."

"It's always possible to feel more," she said, matter-of-factly.

Yes, I thought, it certainly is.

"I'm mad about him, Alexandra. I'm mad for him. I feel like a rabid animal. I want to tear at him, I swear, it's the most awful feeling. And the most wonderful. Except that if I don't get to be with him I don't know how I'll stand it. Can you believe this is me? I can't believe I'm saying these things but . . . I just feel so desperate. I have to be with him."

"You're in love."

"Hah!" I said. "If this lunacy is being in love . . . But what if it's not love? What if it's just lust? What if I'm just having a delayed adolescence? That's sickening."

"Why should you be above passion?" Alexandra challenged.

"I didn't mean that!" I knew I sounded angry, and I was angry, although I wasn't sure why or with whom.

Wait. I'd lost my baby. I'd lost my wedding, my fiancé, my marriage. I'd lost what I'd thought I wanted my life to be. Of course I was angry. I was angry because I was bereft. I had nothing left, not even a vague idea of what I really wanted my life to be.

And now I had to start all over, create my life anew, and I resented that. I was tired. Suddenly, the idea of starting another relationship seemed overwhelming.

Why did I have to tell Jack how I felt about him? I'd put this show of his work in motion so of course I'd have to see it through. And then what? Be realistic, Anna, I told myself, suddenly feeling very foolish, too. Jack's not going to declare his love for you. In less than a week he's going to get on a plane and head for the West Coast, and then you can grow old with your pathetic secret, a picture of Jack under your pillow, a scrap of his handwriting hidden in your underwear drawer. Life will be empty but calm.

I don't have to do anything, I assured myself. I don't have to reanimate myself. I can just stay put and rot away like the macabre Miss Havisham. It's my life. I can do what I want with it even if that means wasting it magnificently. Even if that means avoiding love. My friends might not like it but there's nothing they can do to make me get up and start over. Nothing.

"So," Alexandra said, calling me back to the irritating moment, "what are you going to do about your life?"

I had no answer. Maybe Jack's revelation had affected me more than I'd first assumed. Maybe I was afraid that Heath—if indeed he was Jack's son—would stand in the way of Jack's realizing I was the woman he loved.

Jealous of a child. How pathetic.

"This love business," I said, "is wearing me out."

"You'll toughen up. Either that or you'll fall apart. It's your choice."

I looked at my friend. I realized I didn't want to waste away. I realized I wanted to have what she had. Love. Great big love.

"Is there some magic potion that will help me toughen up?" I said with a smile.

"Yes," Alexandra said. "It's called a martini."

90

The Time Is Now

"Everything's in place for tomorrow night. At the risk of jinxing the show, I think it's going to be a success."

Jack grimaced. "You're not superstitious, are you?"

"No," I said. "It was just something to say. I'm tired." Jack and I had worked on the show until ten; now we were sitting at a corner table in the almost empty bistro, finally ordering dinner.

"You should be exhausted. Have you slept at all in the past week?"

"Surprisingly, yes," I admitted. The bad dreams were temporarily in abeyance; also, I'd come to better terms with the notion of Jack's possibly having a son. Since the day he first told me we'd talked through the situation again, solving nothing but, I hoped, helping Jack to come to better terms, too.

"By the way," I said then, "have you ever given an interview?"

"Who would want to know about how I like my eggs or what brand of detergent I use?"

"You don't use detergent. You take your laundry out. And

don't be silly. I mean, have you ever given an interview about your work?"

Jack considered. "Yes. I think so. There was some small rag and I was just out of college. I don't remember."

"You don't have a copy of the interview?"

"I doubt it."

"Oh. I have a clippings file that dates back to when I was in the Girl Scouts and my troop put on a play at the local senior center. Does that sound pathetic?"

Jack laughed. "Only slightly. But why the sudden interest in interviews?"

"There's going to be a reporter at the show tomorrow night. And I'm working on setting up a full-length interview with the arts editor of an important magazine. I'm not telling you which magazine until I've got the interview nailed down, so don't ask."

Jack took a long swallow of his beer. "Fine," he said. "I'm not looking forward to any publicity, but I'll do as you command. So, have you ever given an interview?"

"No," I said. "Not really. Just silly quotes about an event. Like, the reporter from the society pages says, 'How do you think the party is going?' And I answer, 'It's just wonderful, everyone is having a marvelous time, the food is just great, and the music has everyone on their feet.'"

"That's disgusting."

"I know. I'm ashamed of myself. But it's my job. A dirty business but somebody's got to do it and all. Pour me more wine?"

Jack did and then said, "So, would you want to be interviewed by some serious publication?"

I laughed. "Oh, no! Besides, who would want to interview me? I've done nothing noteworthy."

"In this day and age you don't have to do anything even remotely noteworthy to make the cover of *People*."

"Well, that's true. But is *People* a serious publication? I'm sure it makes serious money but it isn't exactly the *New Yorker*."

"The *New Yorker* isn't exactly the *New Yorker* anymore," Jack noted. "Great, the food's here."

Neither of us spoke until we'd eaten enough to take the edge off.

"I feel human again," I said. "Almost. And stay away from my fries."

Jack withdrew his hand from my plate. "How about I interview you right now?" he said. "Just for fun."

"Whatever. As long as I can chew while I talk."

"Deal. Okay. Tell me about your expectations."

I frowned. "I thought you were going to ask me questions like, what's my favorite movie?"

"I'm not pretending to work for a dating service. I'm pretending to work for a serious publication. So, talk to me about expectations."

"I don't know what you mean by expectations," I replied. "Do you mean the things everyone expects without realizing they're expecting them? Like enough food to eat and a roof overhead, the things everyone takes for granted but shouldn't?"

"Do you really expect a roof over your head?"

"No," I admitted. "Not since I've had to earn my own living."

"I didn't think so. I don't think you take much for granted. That opinion is the reporter editorializing, of course."

"Of course."

"Okay," Jack said then, "what about hopes and dreams?"

"You're sure you don't want to know my favorite color? My favorite flavor of ice cream?"

"Pink and butter pecan."

I felt weak with desire. Jack's hand on the table was inches from mine. I couldn't take my eyes off it. "Oh," I said with a croak. "Oh. I mean, I don't know. I had fantasies, when I was a little girl."

"This reporter," Jack said, "would like to know about those fantasies."

I raised my eyes to his face. Had he moved his chair closer to mine? "They're pretty silly," I said.

"Tell me."

"Okay. Well, when I was a little girl I fantasized about living in a big castle on a windswept moor. Or on a cliff overlooking the sea. With a stable of horses." Jack hadn't laughed. He was looking at me with . . . "It was all stuff from the books I was reading," I said dismissively. "I'm sure lots of little girls were fantasizing about castles and horses and princes landing on the shore in beautiful ships."

"So," Jack said, and he leaned back, away from me. "Do you think the fantasies were really about romance?"

How, I wondered, had we gotten to this wonderful, dangerous topic?

"I don't think so," I said. "I think they were mostly about escape. Escape from my real world."

"Was your real world so terrible?"

"No." I laughed. "It wasn't at all dark and menacing. But that was the problem. My real world was boring. I fantasized about a world that was dark and menacing, in a romantic way of course. So maybe the fantasies were about romance at heart. I'm embarrassed to admit I fantasized about a life of difficulty and distress."

"Why should you be embarrassed?" Jack said. "You were just a kid."

"I know. But then you grow up and realize that too many little girls are living real nightmares and that they'd give anything to live in a safe and boring world. If they can even imagine a world without mayhem and murder."

"This is a side of you I haven't seen before. Do your thoughts always turn to darkness?"

"Of course not," I protested. Did they? "At least, I don't think so. I guess I'll have to monitor my thoughts for a while and find out."

"What makes Anna tick. Now that would be a fascinating documentary."

"Don't mock me."

"I mean it," Jack said, and I felt my cheeks flush.

"This wine," I said brightly, "is making me warm."

Jack crossed his arms in a matter-of-fact, professorial way. "So," he said, "what do you do for drama in your adult life? Where do you find the spooky castles and wild moors and guys on mighty steeds? I'm asking as a reporter, of course."

Was Jack's question really meant in a serious way? Or was he flirting with me? I was too overwhelmed to know.

"Oh," I said flippantly, looking at a spot on the wall over his head, "I rent movies like *Rebecca* and *Wuthering Heights* and *Possession*. You know. I'm always so busy I don't really have time for . . ."

"So, what did you want to be when you grew up?" Jack's sudden change of nuance put me back on more even ground. Maybe I'd been imagining the erotic charge between us. Did it matter?

"Nothing in particular," I said. "I wasn't sure I had the brains for law or medicine or banking. I stumbled on event planning, really. I like to see people enjoy themselves, and I like to know I had some part in making them happy."

"That's it?" Jack's tone was kind.

I shrugged. "That's it. I'm a pretty simple person, really. Either simple or very dull."

"You're not dull, Anna. But at the risk of pissing you off, let me just say this. You can't live on the fumes of other people's lives. In the end you'll still be left with your own life. You'll be all alone, just you and yourself. Other people don't owe you anything; they're not responsible for filling up those empty spaces inside. You are."

"Are you trying," I said boldly, "to convince yourself of that, or me?"

Jack grinned. "Both."

The waiter appeared, put the check on the table, and glided away.

"They're throwing us out," I said, reaching for my bag.

"This is on me." Jack tossed a credit card onto the table.

The night was almost over. Jack would pay the bill and we'd each go home to our separate apartments.

"What about the one you marry?" I said boldly.

"What *about* the one you marry?"

"You were talking about being all alone with your life. So what about your life partner? Aren't you responsible to each other? Aren't you supposed to complete each other? Isn't that what *soul mate* is all about?"

Jack looked first at the table, then up to me. "I don't," he said finally, "think you're 'supposed to' do anything or 'supposed to' be anything in particular for anyone else. Love is a gift; it has no reasons, it just is. You love someone—that's it, you can't help it. That's fact. Love isn't hard to do. Liking someone all the time, now that can be hard."

I thought of the things about Ross that had driven me crazy, like the way he peeled an apple before eating it because he didn't want apple skin getting caught between his teeth. Would that habit have bothered me less if I'd been in love with Ross?

Jack went on. "You can get pissed off at her for spending too much money or hate the way he picks his nose when he thinks you're not looking, but you still love the one you love. Love is big. Still, it's not big enough to be someone else's soul. The term is soul *mate*, meaning companion, best friend for life, buddy. *Mate* implies two people. Two complementary people."

I looked down at the bag in my lap. "Alexandra says much the same things about love."

"You know what they say about great minds."

I laughed and looked back to him. "That's lame. Even for you."

"I know," he said. "I'm tired, too."

We left the bistro and without consultation began to walk in the direction of Jack's studio.

Ross, I thought, was not my complement. He was not my soul mate. He was not the great love of my life. But it didn't matter anymore, did it? Because Ross and I were history, we were the past.

Jack's arm brushed mine.

I didn't want to be a Miss Havisham. I didn't want to rot away. I wanted to grasp my present.

I stopped. Jack stopped, too. We stood face to face. And then I kissed him, right on the mouth, and he kissed me back.

"Hello," he said when we pulled away.

"I want you to come back to my apartment," I said. "Or I'll go with you to yours, it doesn't matter. I want us to be together, Jack, just tonight, just this once. And look, if you don't want to, okay, fine, just don't, don't, don't tell me you're too tired or I really think I'll go medieval on you. I really do. No stupid excuses, just a simple *no* will do."

Jack put his hands on my arms and pulled me closer again. "Of course I want to, Anna. I've wanted to for a long time. Believe me. But . . . you've been through so much lately . . . I don't want you to—"

"Jack," I said, "I know what I want and what I can handle. How many times do I have to tell you not to think for other people. You act so mind-numbingly superior sometimes—"

Jack grinned. "And you still want to have sex with me?"

"Yes."

"Then I'd better stop arguing and just do it."

"Just do it, Jack."

He did.

91

Opening Night

"Looks like the show is quite a success." Alexandra was smashing in a silk sheath in lime green. "Congratulations, Anna."

If turnout was any indicator, the show was a success. The space was jammed with people; some were even waiting outside to squeeze in when others left. Best, it was a varied crowd, well-heeled suburbanites and art school kids—people from Back Bay, the South End, and Somerville.

"I think you should be congratulating Jack," I said, "not me. It's his work that brought people here."

"Don't be so modest. I can't stand false modesty in a friend. You know you're the one responsible for this show. Without you, Jack would be off shooting a retirement dinner in Framingham right now."

I laughed. "Okay, okay. So I'm partly responsible for the crowd. But let's not count our chickens before they hatch."

"Dear, sensible Anna. Has he made any sales yet?"

I nodded. "A few. But the night's young. Anyway, the sales aren't as important tonight as the exposure."

"Never underestimate the importance of sales," she said. And then she looked at me closely. "Are you okay?"

"Fine," I lied.

"You look, I don't know, different. Jack's still leaving tomorrow?"

I nodded. I didn't trust myself to speak.

Alexandra took my hand and gave it a squeeze. "Hang in," she said. "I've got to go and join Luke."

For a moment I stood alone, listening to the excited talk and exuberant laughter of the crowd. I imagined the good reviews in the next day's paper. I thought of the interview I'd set up for Jack with an important art magazine out of New York, an interview he'd be doing via phone. Because the next day Jack would be on a plane to San Francisco and his new life. My heart constricted. It seemed wrong that we wouldn't be sharing his triumph, his time in the sun, his fifteen minutes of fame.

His first fifteen minutes of fame. Because I was sure that with hard work, inspiration, and a little luck, Jack was going to go far.

And I wouldn't be there with him. My plan had failed. In truth it hadn't been much of a plan. Still, I'd had hopes. I thought of the previous night at Jack's loft and was flooded again with desire.

At least, I thought, I have one spectacular night of passion to savor for the rest of my life. The trick would be to prevent an ecstatic memory from decaying into a bitter one. It would be a very difficult trick to pull off.

"Hi!"

I whirled to see Tracy smiling up at me.

"Oh, hi!" I said. "I'm glad you made it."

"Actually, Bill and I have been here for about a half hour. It's such a mob scene it took me forever to find you."

"Do you think people are enjoying themselves?" I asked.

Tracy swatted my arm. "You know they are. So, how long has Alexandra been seeing this new guy? She just introduced Bill and me."

"Um," I said eloquently, "I think she knew him a long time ago. But things just got romantic. I guess."

Tracy nodded. "He seems nice. I'm happy for her. I mean, she seems somehow, I don't know, lighthearted. Well, as lighthearted as Alexandra will ever be."

"So, what do you think of Jack's work?" I asked. "Be honest but not too honest."

"I like it, Anna. And Bill's working up the nerve to spend a thousand dollars on the piece in the far corner, the big one of the ancient glass jar."

"Oh," I said, "he's not buying something just to be nice, is he?"

"Bill?" Tracy laughed. "The man who considers the pros and cons of every major purchase for weeks before acting? No. He wants the piece as a gift for me. For us, I suppose."

"Ah, I knew I liked Bill," I said. A financially responsible man who also liked to give his wife gifts? Bill was every woman's dream. "What's the occasion?"

Tracy suddenly looked uncomfortable. "Anna," she said, "I know this is not the right time to tell you this, I know that you're busy, but . . ."

"Tracy," I said, "look around. Everyone's having a fine time. No one needs me, for the moment at least."

"I'm going to try to get pregnant."

"Wow," I said. "I just assumed . . . I don't know what I just assumed, exactly. Maybe that Bill didn't want to start another family."

Tracy smiled ruefully. "He didn't. He's sixty years old, Anna. But he loves me enough to do this. I just have to try."

"What if—" I began, and then changed course. "There are so many options today for women our age."

"I know. So, if I don't get pregnant the good old-fashioned way, Bill and I will explore other ways of getting pregnant. I've already talked to my gynecologist. He's hopeful we can make this happen."

Hopeful but not certain.

I thought of the expense and the possible heartbreak. I'd read somewhere that only about forty-four percent of women who wait until they're forty to try to conceive for the first time will be successful. I'd also read that assisted reproductive technologies like in vitro fertilization just don't make up for the loss of fertility women experience as they age.

"There's always adoption," I said. I thought of Michaela's quest for a child and wondered how many of her horror stories of endless red tape and incompetence we could believe.

"I'm not sure I'm cut out for adoption," Tracy said matter-of-factly. "I'm not sure that's what I want. I'll have to wait and see. I'll have to see what I learn from this experience. Whatever happens, I know it will change me. I know it will change everything."

"Change is exhausting," I said. "But I think I'm learning to accept it as an inevitable part of life."

"What choice do you have?" Tracy said with a dry laugh. "What choice do any of us have? Roll with the punches, bend in the wind; she who adapts, survives. By the way, speaking of someone who easily adapts, where's Kristen?"

"The whole family is down with a stomach virus," I told her. "I can't imagine how horrible that must be."

"She has my sympathy. Look," Tracy said, "I should get back to Bill. Congratulations, Anna."

Tracy moved off and I wondered, If Tracy wanted a child so badly, why hadn't she gotten married in her twenties; why hadn't she married a man closer to her own age, one without a family behind him?

Because maybe she just hadn't been ready for marriage or for motherhood in her fertile twenties. Or maybe she had been ready but just hadn't been able to find the right man. There were a million possible reasons for Tracy being in the place she was in. There were a million possible reasons for my being in the place I was in. How do we wind up at any given point along the way? How does life get away from us? Those are questions with no easy answers.

And it was not the time to be contemplating those questions.

Because suddenly I was confronted with my former fiancé, perfectly groomed, masterfully coiffed, gorgeously dressed.

"What's wrong, Anna?" he said by way of greeting. To be fair, I think my mouth was hanging open.

"Nothing," I said, with only a bit of a squeak. "I'm just a bit surprised to see you here."

"Why?" he asked, ingenuously.

Why? Where should I begin? With the fact that he thought Jack Coltrane not worth serious consideration as a person, let alone as an artist?

"I thought you weren't interested in art photography," I said neutrally.

Ross shrugged. The gesture was elegant. "I'm not, really."

"Then why . . ."

I wondered, Did Ross know I was going to be here? Did he come to the opening to talk to me? And then anxiety struck. Did Ross, I wondered, know about last night? Was he here to accuse me of having been in love with Jack Coltrane all along?

"A business associate," Ross said. "He's over by that big picture of a fence. Or whatever it is. He's really into this sort of thing. We're just stopping by before dinner at Shantung."

I smiled, relieved. Of course Ross didn't know about last night. "Well, then," I said, "I hope your business associate enjoys the show."

Ross glanced around at the crowded room. "This place is mobbed."

"I did it," I said. "This is my event."

"Oh." Ross seemed genuinely surprised. "I assumed you were here because you had to be. I mean because you work with Coltrane." Ross then scanned me from head to toe. "You look great, Anna. Is that a new dress?"

"No," I told him. "I wore it once before." Just after you and I announced our engagement, I told him silently. We went to dinner and the symphony. Remember?

"Ah. Well, it looks new. Unfamiliar. You look different. You're probably wearing your hair differently."

It wasn't really a question so I didn't bother to answer. Because I would have had to point out that a French twist was something Ross had seen many times before. Nothing on the outside was different. Something on the inside was. And Ross couldn't identify it.

"So, you're feeling okay?" he said suddenly. "I mean, health-wise?"

"I'm fine," I told him, wishing he'd move on and join his colleague. "I'm perfectly healthy. Thank you for asking."

Suddenly, the expression on Ross's face grew serious. "Anna," he said, "I've been thinking. Maybe we gave up too easily. You know, everything happening so fast . . ."

"Ross," I said. "Please. It wasn't going to work. We both know that."

And suddenly I knew that Ross didn't completely know that.

"We were good together, Anna," he said, reaching for my hand. "We had fun."

I extricated my hand from his light hold. "Until the big stuff came along," I said. "And then look what happened. Instead of turning to each other we turned away. If the pregnancy hadn't happened, something else would have come along soon enough and we'd be filing for divorce. It was better in the end that things ended when they did."

Ross shook his head. "Then why do I feel so bad?"

I smiled ruefully. What could I say?

"I miss you, Anna," Ross said then. "Do you miss me?"

I wondered, Why, oh why, is he doing this? Why at Jack's big show? Why on Jack's last night in town? I glanced around the room but didn't see Jack anywhere. None of my friends. Not even a distant acquaintance glancing back at me. No one to come to my rescue.

I looked back to Ross. "No, Ross," I said evenly, "I don't miss you. At first I missed some of the fantasy we built around our relationship. You know, the glamorous life we were going to lead. The spectacular loft. Month-long vacations in Europe. The best restaurants. But not you, Ross. I don't miss you. I never really had you. How can I miss what I never had?"

It was bold to say what I said. But I thought Ross deserved the truth. Clearly, in Ross's case, ignorance was not bliss. It was giving him false hope.

The expression in Ross's eyes hardened. "I see," he said, coldly. "I shouldn't have bothered saying hello tonight."

I thought, He asked a question. I gave him the answer. Now he's mad at me?

"I'm leaving," he said, and immediately walked away from me.

"I wish you happiness, Ross," I said.

He didn't wish me anything in return.

I spent the next three hours circulating among the guests; answering questions about the work and referring people to Jack for more information; making sure the caterers were doing their job; and sending Rasheed off on necessary errands. I spoke to Jack only once, near the end of the party.

I caught his eye from across the emptying room. He smiled and came to join me. I wanted so badly to fling my arms around him. Of course, I didn't.

"I haven't seen you all night," he said.

"That's a good thing. It means you were a hit."

"Not me. The work. And I wouldn't assume it was a hit just because there were a lot of people gawking at it. I'm sure some of them hated it."

"Okay, okay," I said with mock annoyance. "Can't you just accept a compliment?"

Jack grinned. "Obviously not."

"Look, you need to say goodbye to this final wave of admirers."

"Do I have to? I don't even know that bunch." We both looked at the small group of people gathered near the door, clutching the last plastic glasses of free wine, and looking with hope back at Jack.

"Don't crap out on me now, Jack," I warned. "Just another half hour or so."

"Okay. You're right. I'm going."

I watched as Jack greeted the well-wishers; I watched as they touched his arm and leaned in close, eager to have a part of him. Oh, I thought, now I know what it means to be heartbroken.

92

New Day

"I'll lock up. Go home, get some sleep. You've got to catch that flight."

Jack hopped up onto the empty drinks table. "No, I don't."

"What?" I was bone tired; it was two o'clock in the morning. It was understandable that I questioned my hearing.

"I cancelled it."

"You what?"

"I cancelled my flight to the West Coast."

"What does that mean?" I asked stupidly. "That you're not going today but you're going next week? And why are you grinning like that?"

"No, Anna. It means that I'm not going at all. And I'm grinning because I'm happy. Is that all right with you?"

I shook my head but it didn't clear the fog that had settled there. "Yes, fine, of course," I said. "But what about your new job?"

Jack's grin got even wider. "I quit yesterday morning. Well, as soon as it was morning in San Francisco. The partners weren't pleased, but I have a good lawyer. He'd built in a sort of escape clause in my contract and—enough of the boring details. I'm out of the agreement."

"Oh. So . . ." So, last night, I thought, last night, when we were together, Jack knew he wouldn't be leaving town . . .

"And I cancelled the moving company. They weren't going to ship my stuff out until next week anyway, so it was no big deal."

"It's not like you'd even packed," I said automatically.

Jack laughed. "How did you know I hadn't packed?"

"Good guess."

And something Alexandra had said weeks earlier came to me then. Life, she'd exclaimed, was deliciously uncertain. At the time I'd thought she was being overly dramatic. But now?

Look before you leap, Anna.

It was too late for that, especially after the previous night at Jack's. It was time to throw every last bit of caution to the wind.

"Jack," I said, "I love you. I'm in love with you, and I have been for a long time only I didn't understand what it all meant. My feelings, I mean. I've never been good with feelings."

Jack hopped off the table and took a step toward me. "Anna, I—"

"Wait. You don't have to say anything you don't mean. Not that you would, of course, but I'll be okay. I mean, I never assumed you felt the same way about me. You don't have to feel any obligation to me or—"

Jack took another step toward me. "Anna, will you shut up, please?"

"All right but—"

And then he was just a foot away from me, and then less. "Why the hell do you think I'm staying here in Boston? Because I love the Red Sox?"

"Because of your work?" I whispered. I didn't dare to believe what I thought might be happening.

"Right." Jack laughed. "People get married in every city,

nna. People have birthdays and retirement dinners and weet Sixteen parties." He kissed me then, and I knew. Anna, I'm staying here because of you. I need to be near ou. I love you. Why do you think I was skipping town in the rst place? I couldn't stand to see you every day and know I ouldn't be with you."

"And that I was married to Ross," I said.

"Oh, yeah, that, too."

"You just said you love me."

"I did. Anna, you don't let me get away with being the uy who avoids his own life. I know it sounds selfish; it is elfish. I get so much from you. What do you get from me? I ean it. I'm not fishing for compliments here. But really, ive me a clue."

I grinned. "Let's see, where should I begin? You don't let e get away with being the woman who avoids her own life. ou're never boring. You've got a gorgeous face. Your hands re magic. You make me feel things I've never felt before. ou—"

"Stop," he said. "You're embarrassing me. I mean, I'm a uy and I've got a guy's big delicate ego, but enough is nough. I'll be unbearable."

"You're already unbearable. It's part of your charm." And en I began to laugh. The enormity of what Jack had done nally hit me. "You didn't know if I felt the same way," I aid. "And yet you quit your job just like that. You took a uge chance, Jack. You're crazy."

"Look who's talking. You're getting to be more of a loud ushy broad every day. First you demand I have sex with ou—"

"I never demanded. Exactly."

"Well, you presented a pretty irresistible argument."

"What if I get too loud and pushy?"

"Won't happen." Jack kissed me again, then said, "You're till Anna. You'll always be Anna. You're changing, but ou're still and always Anna."

93

Wonder

Later that night, early morning really, we lay in Jack's be
looking at the ceiling, looking at each other, talking.

"Why was it so hard to get together?" I asked.

"I don't know," Jack said. "I'm a little rusty in the lo
business. Anyway, I enjoy a challenge. I'm not complai
ing."

"We got what we wanted so what difference does it mal
how we got it. Is that it?"

"Sure. That sounds okay."

"And it doesn't matter," I said, "that we didn't even kno
what we wanted until we almost lost it?"

"Correction. You didn't know what you wanted. I kne
all along what I wanted."

"Oh, yeah?" I challenged. "Then why didn't you just gra
it? It would have saved us an awful lot of time and miscon
munication and loneliness."

Jack raised an eyebrow at me. I must, I thought, learn th
trick.

"Yeah. That would have worked just fine. I'm not a pirat

Anna. I don't see something—or someone—I want and proceed to pillage, plunder, and rape."

"I guess I wouldn't have liked a strong-arm approach," I admitted. "But when Ross and I broke up . . ."

Jack stroked my hair and looked me right in the eye. "What kind of a man would I be if I'd swooped in for the kill when you'd just gone through so much grief?"

I thought about it for a split second. "Not much of a man."

"Besides," he said, a sly smile creeping across his face, "I was pretty convinced you had no feelings for me. Other than contempt and scorn, that is."

"That's not fair!" I protested.

"I know. I'm just teasing. But you didn't give anything away, Anna. I figured that even if I waited a decent amount of time before saying something I'd still be rejected."

I thought about all the miscommunication and said, "Do you think our coming together was so hard because we're both so damaged?"

"No," Jack said definitively. "Maybe it took some time because like all human beings we can be stupid and pathetic. But not damaged. I think both of us have a hard time believing we can be happy. Happiness smiles right at us, and instead of smiling right back we turn our heads."

I rolled over and threw my arm across Jack's chest. It felt so good to hold him.

"Maybe we won't do that any longer. Maybe we've finally learned that we can be happy."

"I damn well hope so, Anna, because I'm not getting any younger."

"Well, neither am I. But thanks for not pointing that out."

"I'm not entirely stupid when it comes to women. I know you don't talk about a woman's age."

"Not entirely stupid, no. But you still need to learn the social graces." And then I considered. "You probably never will learn, will you?"

Jack shook his head. "Probably not. I'm an old dog Anna. No new tricks. Well, at least regarding manners."

We were quiet for a time and then I said, "They say tim ing is everything."

"It's something," Jack agreed. "It's important."

"I saw that report," I blurted. "From a summer progran you went to as a little boy. I read it."

Jack laughed. "I'd better watch what I leave around. O second thought, you can see everything. I have nothing t hide. So, it sounded like I was a real pain-in-the-ass kic huh?"

"Yeah," I said, "it did. Nothing much has changed, yo know?"

"I'd argue if I could. My mother sent that report to me She was cleaning out the attic and found that and a bunch o other stuff. She said it gave her a real laugh. My mothe never lets me get away with anything, either. That's one o the reasons I love her. And yes, you'll meet her."

"I didn't ask to meet her," I said, all innocent.

"It was all over your face. She'll like you. As long as yo continue to be you."

"Deal."

I wondered, Was our story the kind you could tell th grandchildren? Probably not, at least not until they were ol enough to be embroiled in wrong-headed love affairs of thei own. Miscarriage, a broken engagement, an unknown child betrayal. And all the while the right person right under you nose.

No, I thought. Our story was not suited for the ver young. Besides, who said there would even be children, le alone grandchildren?

Suddenly, Jack leaned up on one arm and looked down a me. "Look, Anna," he said, "I don't like talking about m feelings. But there's something I just have to say. This migh be the last time you'll ever hear me talk this way."

"Okay," I said.

"Anna, you're like . . . It's like you're my air. You allow

me to breathe. Because of you I can breathe. You're my soul or my spirit. You're something ethereal but at the same time absolutely necessary. You're vital to me."

I used to resent the body. I used to wish for it to go away. But not anymore.

"Can I tell you what you are for me?" I said. "You're like my stomach. Something solid and essential and not at all ethereal."

"Your stomach?" Jack grimaced and fell back onto the bed. "Well, at least you didn't say your small intestine."

"Okay, then," I said, laughing, "my heart, but not in a goopy, Valentine's Day kind of way. You're my heart for what it really is. A vital organ. The thing that works for me, the thing with weight and presence. You ground me."

"Are you saying I hold you down?"

"No. Grounding isn't repressing. You're like an anchor, something that keeps me from floating away and avoiding the real stuff of life."

"Okay," Jack said. "Now can we end this conversation before Hallmark offers us a writing contract?"

"Deal."

"And we'll never speak of this again?"

"Speak of what?"

Jack pulled me onto him. "That's one of the things I like about you, Traulsen," he said. "It might take you some time, but when you finally get something, you really get it."

94

Checking In

Alexandra was right all along. You just don't walk away from love.

Jack stayed in Boston and gradually cut back on his event photography business so that he could spend more time pursuing his own work. Within a week he moved his personal belongings from his giant loft into my apartment. As soon as my lease was up I moved my office into the loft. There's plenty of room in each place for our accumulated possessions. (Jack even likes the badly gilded horse with the clock in its stomach; he's got it on his bedside table.)

Anna's Occasions is still going strong. I've taken on an intern, a young woman still in college. Her help has allowed me to act as Jack's manager. He's had a few shows already, one in New York and another in Connecticut. Sales have been strong, but the money isn't why Jack does what he does. He does it because he loves it; he does it because he has to. And most of what he earns from this work goes into a college fund for Heath.

Jack, it turns out, is indeed Heath's father. How we came to learn the truth is a long and messy tale. Suffice it to say that together we faced down Leslie Curtin, Heath's mother, and won.

Jack and I spend days and nights together, working, sleeping, eating, arguing, laughing, being in love and loving each other.

Marriage?

We're in no rush to tie the knot. We're entirely committed to each other; we'll make our union legal someday. The word *elopement* has been spoken, and I think it's a good one. Maybe we'll get married in Ireland. Both Jack and I have always wanted to go there. I'll be sure to send my parents a postcard.

Children?

I would love to have a child with Jack, but sometimes we just don't get what we want. And sometimes we get it when we least expect it. The traumatic experience of discovering Heath's existence in the way he did, and the struggle to be allowed access to his son, has wearied Jack. For now, at least, we're committed to each other and to getting to know Heath and our family seems whole.

Did I mention that family now includes a ninety-pound, very messy black Lab named James?

Katie and Alma continue to thrive. They bought a building in Dorchester, made some minor repairs, and flipped the unit for a very nice sum. Emilio is off to preschool and loving it. Although they never met Ross, Katie and Alma declare that Jack is a million times the better man. I suspect one reason for their enthusiastic approbation is Jack's skill with the grill. Yes, I finally bought a charcoal grill, and Jack has proved he possesses yet another valuable manly talent. I don't know how the neighbors on either side of us feel about our boisterous year-round grill fests on the roof deck, but we certainly enjoy them.

My brother and his wife continue to live their hectic lives. I wish Paul would meet someone, fall in love, maybe even get married again, but I don't see any sign of that happening for a long, long time. It makes me sad. Bess and I have gotten past most of our post-divorce awkwardness; my own troubles helped me to understand something of what Bess has gone through. Now, at least, Bess and I have something in common. Painful experiences that seem to have left us smarter people. For my part, I've made a conscious effort to get to know Matthew and Emma better; Bess has been open to that. Maybe someday I'll even be brave enough to babysit.

Kristen is starting to prepare for a return to work—paying work, that is—once B.J. goes off to daycare six months from now. Job hunting is going to be a logistical hell; adjusting to the life of a career woman with three young children is going to be almost as difficult. But she'll make it work. I have a lot of confidence in my friends.

Jack, it turns out, is quite handy with a hammer. He and Brian spend one Saturday afternoon a month working away on the old Victorian. Afterward, while the men sit in front of the TV, grunt, eat pretzels, drink beer, and probably scratch, Kristen and I sit in the kitchen and chat over a glass or two of wine. This part of our life isn't exactly glamorous but it is entirely wonderful.

I can't resist reporting that Michaela finally gave up her quest for a child. I'm not sure why, exactly. Rumor has it that she was turned down by every legitimate adoption agency as "unfit," but I suspect that particular rumor was started by one of her many enemies. Like the twenty-something DAR member whose boyfriend Michaela dramatically stole while the entire guest list of a black-tie fund-raiser watched in titillated embarrassment.

I don't know how Michaela feels about losing the fight for a child, but I have no doubt that no matter how many enemies she makes, she'll survive to fight another battle another day. I just won't be there to witness her triumphs or failures.

Which leads me to the struggle I am witnessing. Tracy and Bill haven't been able to get pregnant, yet. They've pursued a few of the most common therapies but without any luck. I don't know how much longer they'll continue to try to have a child. I don't quiz Tracy on every little step she takes on this difficult road. I do, however, see that the process is taking a toll on her; she doesn't smile as often as she used to, and her face is bordering on gaunt.

Sometimes I wonder if it would have been better if she'd never tried; I wonder if she should just have let it go. Maybe, I think, Tracy should have resigned herself to not giving birth to her own child; maybe she should have learned to be satisfied by what she already had—a good marriage, a career, friends. And then I take myself to task for forgetting, even for a moment, that at some point or another every single one of us is compelled to pursue what we really and truly need to be happy.

Or what we think we need.

And Alexandra? My dearest friend is still blissfully happy. Well, as blissfully happy as it's in her to be. She and Luke are weathering his divorce and all the emotional horrors that go along with the legal proceedings, but they're together, finally, and that's all that seems to matter to them.

Of course, they get on each other's nerves and fight over the things every couple fights over. "It took me about a month," Alexandra told me once, "before I remembered in full-blown detail all the things about Luke that drive me crazy. Anna, I swear I want to kill him at least once every three days. But isn't it fantastic that now I actually have the opportunity! I mean he's right there next to me in bed. I can reach right over and strangle him. I am a very lucky woman."

I hope she is. I like Luke, really, but I still harbor, maybe unfairly, a small doubt about his character. I suppose he'll have to prove to us that he's a good man. He did give Alexandra a lovely antique engagement ring as a token of his renewed devotion. That's a start.

Did I mention that Alexandra is now always on time?

Ross Davis. Well, Ross got married not quite six months after we broke up. I hear his wife is very sweet, very blonde, and currently very pregnant. She's only twenty-four. She is not wearing the three-carat emerald cut diamond ring that once was mine, but she is living with Ross in the apartment I once thought would be mine.

Which is fine because the life I'm living now is my own. Totally and completely my own real life, and Jack is an integral part of that, as I'm an integral part of his own real life.

The small reunion party I arranged for Mrs. Kent was a success. Occasionally, Mrs. Kent sends me a handwritten note on her personalized stationery. The note always ends with the same phrase: "Carpe diem, my dear Anna. Carpe diem."

I think sometimes of Mrs. Kent's lost daughter. I think a lot about my own lost child.

One last note. Those awful nightmares, the ones about not being able to speak, about choking, about not being able to see, are becoming just nasty memories. Someday, I hope, I'll be free of them entirely, but I suppose they still have a few lessons to teach me before they retire.

So, that's it. That's my story, so far. Life, as you know, is deliciously uncertain.

First comes love. Then comes marriage. Followed by boredom, infidelity, nasty surprises, and divorce.

In this wickedly funny, tender and true novel, bestselling author Holly Chamberlin introduces four Boston divorcées looking for love, sex, fun—and themselves . . .

Jess Marlowe didn't mean to fall out of love with her husband. It just happened—kind of like the passionate affair with a grad student. Oopsie. Now her marriage is over, so's the affiar, and Jess? Well, she feels like she's just beginning. And the only thing scarier than being in a boring, doomed marriage is the strength of her passions now that she's free . . .

Nell Keats had it all: money, marriage, two grown children . . . until the day her husband announced he was leaving her—for another man. Now, Nell's diving back into a whole new dating pool (since when did "Let's do it doggie style" become a romantic pickup line?) and feeling her way around. And once she breaks out of her shell, there's no going back . . .

Laura Keats, Nell's younger sister, wanted a baby; her ex-husband didn't. No problem. Like a general mounting a war campaign, Laura's on a mission to find out that P.F.M. (Perfect Father Material), a quest that will take her through outrageous chat rooms, singles' clubs, parenting groups, and other disasters, and into the arms of the one guy who should be off-limits . . .

Grace Henley is still financially—and emotionally—supporting her ex, a promising artist whose greatest talent was in bed . . . mostly other women's. She can't seem to stop listening to his tales of woe, letting him crash on her couch, even lending him money. No more. It's time for Grace to learn to live her own life and produce her own work. But letting go is even harder than holding on . . .

Nobody said life was fair. That love was forever. Or that getting back in the game would be easy.
Then again, nobody said they had to play by the rules, either . . .

Please turn the page for an exciting sneak peek at
BACK IN THE GAME
coming next month in trade paperback!

Jess

So he left you for a younger, more beautiful woman. It's a fact; accept it. No one respects a whiner.

—*What Now? How to Pick Up the Pieces and Save Your Pride*

"Hi," I said, tossing my bag on an empty chair. "It's been ages. Why are we all so busy?"

Nell smirked. "Contemporary society tells us we have to be busy. If we're busy, our lives must be important. Busyness, I am told, helps fill the emotional and spiritual void most of us find ourselves condemned to. Hello, Jess."

"Aren't you in a chipper mood," I commented.

Nell just shrugged.

She'd arrived at the restaurant before any of us; she's always just a bit early. She says she was punctual even as a little girl, punctual and in charge.

I met Nell a few years back at a charity event she was co-hosting. We hit it off when a particularly rude woman at our table was told off by the waiter she'd been abusing. Nell and

I spontaneously applauded and met for lunch later that week. Though our lives were playing out very differently—Nell was married and I wasn't; Nell has kids and I don't; I teach sociology at Northeastern while Nell has chosen a more traditional manner of career as a full-time mother and volunteer—we had enough of the important things in common to make a friendship grow.

A love of reading, an interest in the arts, a sometimes wry approach to life, and a tendency to applaud when justice is served.

I never really got to know Richard, Nell's husband, the man she'd been with since college. I saw him rarely and my general impression was of a quiet, intelligent, well-mannered guy, a tiny bit hesitant or secretive, or maybe just private. It was clear to me from the start that Nell adored him; they were best friends, really, and for a brief time I was almost jealous of their union. I remember thinking: that is what marriage should be. Somehow, Nell and Richard got it right.

Grace arrived at the restaurant just after I did and took the seat against the wall; she always does. She likes to people watch; she can hold an intense conversation with someone while at the same time noting minute details of passersby. I imagine this ability to focus on one thing and yet observe another is essential when you're a teacher of nine-and ten-year-olds.

Grace and I met almost eleven years ago when I was seeing a guy named Carl, a jazz saxophone player. One night Carl introduced me to his friend Simon, and to Simon's wife, Grace. Simon was a painter, supposedly gifted—not that I would really know; I appreciate art but don't really know what I'm looking at—and sexy in that charming, bohemian kind of way. While Simon was charismatic, prone to dramatic gestures and a roaring laugh, his wife was more guarded in her behavior, self-contained. For a while I wondered if Grace was intimidated by her show-stopping husband, but when I learned she taught art at a prestigious, private middle school, I figured the discipline her job required informed every aspect of her life.

The long story short is that Grace and I became close and the guys didn't last. Carl and I broke up—he was far too carefree for me—and Grace, finally tired of Simon's infidelity and other costly antics, divorced him.

Around the time Grace filed for divorce, Nell invited me to a cocktail party at her beautifully appointed apartment on Marlborough Street. Temporarily single, I brought Grace along. That night we both met Nell's younger sister, Laura, and her husband, Duncan. Duncan seemed a nice enough guy and made a nice enough impression on me. Laura and Duncan seemed well suited, as did Nell and Richard.

Well. It wasn't the first time I was wrong and it won't be the last.

Laura finally arrived at Café Alice. Her tendency to be late or to slip in just under the gate is only one of the ways in which she's different from her older sister.

Nell is tall and slim, aristocratic in her bearing though certainly not in her attitude. She has a delicate beauty, with fine features, sapphire blue eyes, and sleek blond hair. Laura also has blond hair but it's thicker and darker than Nell's. She's medium height and slightly plump in a way that might be a problem later but which suits her perfectly now. Laura's eyes are wide and blue green and somehow innocent.

Grace is small and slim. Her hair is dark, almost black, and she wears it in a bob reminiscent of Louise Brooks. Her eyes are brown and doelike; her style, urban sleek.

As for me, at five foot nine inches I tower over Grace. I've never been shy about my height; I like being tall, though it can be difficult finding pants that fit properly. The rest of me is unspectacular. Brown hair to my shoulders, brown eyes. End of story. Well, I have heard that I have a good smile.

"Well," Nell said when we had ordered a round of drinks, "I don't know about you gals, but I've had quite a week."

"What happened?" Grace asked.

Nell told us about the wedding invitation from the Smiths.

"That's awkward," I said. "So, did you ask Richard to respond?"

"I didn't ask him; I told him to respond. And to explain to Mr. and Mrs. Smith that he now prefers the company of men. Rather, that he has always preferred the company of men but was too scared to admit it. So, what's new with you, Jess?"

I related the sad tale of my conversation with Matt.

"So, it's official," I said. "We're divorced and I'm single and Matt is miserable."

Nell, not terribly demonstrative, patted my hand. "I still think we should raise a glass to the whole nasty business being over."

It had been a nasty divorce, though it could have been worse. Much worse. My lawyer was very good and very expensive. The settlement was fair and equitable; my personal finances hadn't taken too bad a blow, but my insides, my heart and soul and sense of myself as a decent person, felt crushed.

We raised a glass. The toast was restrained.

"Well, I've got some news," Grace said then. "I've cut Simon off and before you say 'again?' let me assure you that this time it's for good. No more taking him back, no more lending him money, no more help of any kind."

Laura frowned. "I'll believe it when I see it," she said. "Seriously, Grace, sometimes I think you'll be dragging Simon around like a bad smell for the rest of your life."

If Grace was stung by this remark, she didn't show it. "You'll see," she said. "This time he went too far." And she told us about the outrageous charge on her credit card.

"How did he get the card in the first place?" Nell asked.

Grace blushed. "I let him use it. Once. Maybe twice. I suppose he assumed he was free to use it any time he liked. It's my fault, really—"

"No," I said fiercely, "it's not your fault! Simon is a bum!"

"How did he get away with it, anyway?" Nell asked. "What happened to security measures like a picture ID? Who would believe his name was Grace?"

"Simon is charming." Grace smiled ruefully. "He always gets what he wants."

"Until now."

Grace nodded at me. "Right. You know what the worst part is? The bauble he bought was for his new girlfriend. I swear in all the years we were married he never spent even a fraction of that amount on me!"

"Good riddance to bad rubbish," Laura pronounced.

"Well, I wouldn't call him rubbish—"

Laura cut Grace off with her own news update. "Duncan was served the divorce papers," she said.

The three of us just sat there; even Nell, quick-witted Nell, had nothing to say.

"Well, aren't you happy for me?" Laura demanded.

Grace and I mumbled something incomprehensible; I certainly didn't understand us.

"Well, I'm happy." Laura looked pointedly at her sister. "Not happy like I'm jumping up and down, but I'm glad the divorce is moving along. The sooner I'm free, the sooner I can start my new life."

I thought for a moment that Nell would have to be restrained. It was no secret she thought her sister's divorcing Duncan was a huge mistake. We all did.

Nell's continued silence was bothering Laura.

"Do I have to explain it all again?" she said plaintively. "It's just that I see myself as a mother. It's what I want more than anything. Why should I give up my dream? What do I get in return?"

Nell pretended to consider. "Well, let's see. How about the love of a good man?"

"If Duncan loved me, he'd make me pregnant. He'd give me my baby."

"Laura," I said, finally finding my voice, "if you loved Duncan, you wouldn't force him to do something he didn't want to do."

"I didn't force Duncan. I gave him an option. Either give me a baby or we're through."

"That's harsh." Grace shrugged. "I'm sorry. It strikes me as harsh."

"Becoming a father isn't like sitting through a chick flick," I said. "The flick is over in two hours. The paternity lasts until the day he dies. Maybe Duncan just needed more time to think things through. Most people don't respond well to ultimatums."

Laura frowned down at her Cosmo. She always orders sweet, colorful drinks.

"I don't know why you just didn't get a dog," Nell said. "You could have dressed him in little outfits and carried him around with you. Besides, dogs are a lot cheaper than kids. No college tuition, for one."

Laura looked up. "I don't want to talk about Duncan and me anymore."

"Fine," I said, eager to restore some peace.

"So," Nell said with false brightness, "here we are, four single women. Back in the game. Back on the market."

Grace frowned. "We're commodities?"

"Yes. Whether we like it or not, we're commodities on the market and players in the game."

"What ever happened to romance?" Laura mused.

I figured Duncan and Matt were probably thinking the very same thing.

"It died a slow and agonizing death some time around the turn of the nineteenth century." Nell paused before adding, "Maybe earlier."

"Romance is still alive," I said, though I wasn't entirely sure I believed what I was saying. Was romance just a pretty word for lust? If so, yes, romance was alive and I'd encountered it recently.

Nell finished her glass of wine in one long draught. "If I'd :nown my marriage would end in the way it did," she said hen, "I would never have gotten married in the first place."

Laura gripped her sister's hand. "What about Colin and Clara? If you'd never married Richard, you never would have ad the children."

Nell removed her hand from Laura's death grip. "I know, know. I'm just venting. You always take everything so liter-lly."

"No one goes into marriage thinking, hey, what the hell, f it doesn't work, I can get a divorce, no big deal. Not even ne." I laughed; no one laughed with me. "It's so much work even to get to the point of talking about marriage, let alone planning a wedding and a life together. You have to believe hat marriage is forever. You just have to, in spite of all evi-lence to the contrary."

Nell smiled ruefully. "So, everyone who gets married is n idiot?"

"Blinded by visions of lacy veils and lush bouquets?" Grace suggested.

"Naive?" Nell said.

Laura drained her Cosmo.

I shrugged. "Maybe. Or maybe just hopeful. To be human means to be weak and hopeful. Though hope, I suppose, is a sort of courage."

"Weak, hopeful, and newly single. Or in my case," Grace went on, "not so newly single. Just newly committed to get-ting on with my life post-Simon."

"You know," Laura said suddenly, "divorced women with young children are really at an advantage."

Nell shook her head. "Excuse me?"

I hoped there weren't any single mothers within earshot. But of course there weren't. Single mothers were at home paying the bills, cleaning the toilets, and helping the chil-dren with their homework.

"No, I mean it," Laura said. "Because they can meet divorced men with children through school activities and soccer practice and Boy Scouts and Girl Scouts. Children are even better than dogs when it comes to attracting attention.”

“Maybe,” Grace said carefully. “But life isn’t exactly rosy for single parents of little kids. Even if they do manage to get remarried, there’s a good chance they’ll have to deal with a blended family. And that has to be exhausting.”

Laura rolled her eyes. “Duh, remember *The Brady Bunch*? Blended families can work just fine.”

Really, at times I wondered if Laura’s already tenuous grasp on reality wasn’t beginning to weaken.

“Sure,” Nell said, “on television anything can happen. Aliens can be fuzzy smart alecks and astronauts can keep genies in their living rooms.”

“By the way,” Grace added, “in real life the actor who played Mike Brady, all-American dad, was gay.”

“You know, I always thought he was the only character on the show with half a brain.” Nell turned to Laura. “So, as a single mother of college-aged kids, I’m out of luck?”

“Not necessarily,” Laura said, missing, as she often did, her sister’s sarcastic tone.

“Speaking of kids,” I said to Nell, “how are they faring? I’m sure they have opinions about the divorce and their father’s new life. And I’m sure they’re not shy about voicing them. Kids that age don’t seem to be shy about anything.”

Nell shrugged. “Remarkably, both Colin and Clara have been pretty quiet about the whole thing. I know Richard’s coming out and our divorce must have shaken them up, but so far, I haven’t seen much fallout. We’ll see. Maybe they’re having a delayed reaction. Maybe when they’re thirty or forty they’ll go after Richard with an axe.”

“Colin and Clara love the both of you,” Laura protested. “They understand.”

“Kids never understand their parents’ divorce,” Nell said. “Not really. They have to blame someone. With my luck they’ll probably decide I’m the one they hate for breaking up the family.”

"But, Nell," Grace protested, "Richard is gay. He's in love with a man. You had no choice. You had to get divorced. You're not to blame."

Nell's face took on a hard look. It was a look I'd seen too often since Richard's bombshell. I looked forward to the day when it would go away for good.

"I could have figured things out a long time ago," she said. "I could have been smarter; I could have been not so embarrassingly stupid. I can easily imagine my kids having no respect for me. I mean, what kind of example did I set for them? Why would either of them ever want to get married after the debacle that was their parents' marriage?"

"Richard was very deeply in the closet, Nell," I said carefully. "You couldn't have known."

"I should have known," Nell replied fiercely. "I was his wife, for God's sake! How could I not have known? I was so wrapped up in my own life I never really saw the person on the other side of the bed. And yet, I loved Richard; I thought I was being his true partner."

"You were his true partner," Grace said. "Don't blame yourself for his choice of secrecy."

Nell ignored her and ranted on. "I swear I still don't know when he was having all this anonymous sex because we spent almost every night together, from dinner through Jay Leno. Sure, sometimes he had to work late, but when he came home, he never smelled of anyone else's cologne! I'm furious with myself for being so blind. I'm furious with Richard for tricking me so thoroughly. And I'm furious for having wasted twenty years of my life as Mrs. Richard Allard. Who was she, anyway? Who was that sorry woman?"

I wished I had an answer to that question, something smart and also comforting, but I didn't. Neither, it seemed, did Grace or Laura.

"Um, I have a date next weekend," Laura said.

Grace rolled her eyes.

Nell poured more wine into her glass from the bottle on

the table. "In spite of my sister's freakish success in the dating game," she said, "I believe that the four of us are at a disadvantage. We've been off the market for too long, and yes I know I'm mixing metaphors. Single women our age who've never been married or who've never been in a long-term relationship know the rules. And you can bet they're not going to share insider information with us. They'll view the four of us as an additional threat. We're swelling the already swollen population."

"Why thanks, Nell," I joked lamely. "You've really lifted my spirits."

"Sorry. Anyway, I have no interest in dating just yet. Not much interest, anyway. God, it's not like my dating someone is going to make Richard jealous!"

Grace looked troubled. "I've been wondering. What kind of man is available to women our age? And to women the age we're going to be in a few short years? Men in their thirties and forties—if we can find them—are either married or looking for younger women."

"Some younger men are really into dating older women," Laura said. "You know, because it's hip."

"Dating is the operative word," Nell pointed out. "Most young guys aren't going to stick around for marriage and menopause."

"And older men?" I said. The oldest man I'd ever been with was twenty years my senior. I was just out of college. I thought I was being terribly adult, about to embark on an affair with an 'older man.' Visions of foreign cigarettes and dry martinis and expensive lingerie danced in my head. And then we had sex and I discovered that the reality was far less interesting than the fantasy. He wore faded boxers. Alcohol made him break out in hives. His smart suits hid a significant roll of fat around his middle. When he called me a few days later, I told him I'd gotten back with an old boyfriend. It was a lie."

"Well, that depends on the man, I guess," Nell conceded. "If he's tired of life's nastiness, if he's learned the value of ıe companionship, he might be interested in meeting a ntemporary."

"It's all so unfair." Laura pouted; it made her look about teen. "Women have the advantage for such a short time. ıe minute we hit thirty we, like, stop being desirable to a ıge part of the male population. Men grow into the advan- ge. A man in his fifties—even if he's not filthy rich—can ll get a woman in her early thirties. If he is filthy rich he n get a woman in her twenties. It's ridiculous!"

I wondered how carefully Laura had considered this fact hen she dumped Duncan.

"But, consider the mature man," Grace said. "I mean, meone not looking for a trophy wife, someone looking for ve. If I met a man in his fifties who wanted to go out with e, I'd say yes. Assuming, of course, he seemed nice. And ıd a job. And wasn't an artist."

Nell laughed. "Yes, you've had more than your share of e creative types. Still, think about the baggage an older an is sure to be lugging around. Like bitter ex-wives and eedy kids. And, if he's been living alone for some time, ısty bachelor habits."

"Everyone has baggage, " I said. "We'd be terribly boring we didn't."

"True," Nell agreed. "But with age come health prob- ms. Once a man reaches fifty the illnesses start coming on st and thick. Heart problems are almost guaranteed. eight gain. Prostate troubles. Erectile dysfunction. Then a an reaches his sixties—if he reaches his sixties—and it st gets worse. Before you know it, you're a forty-five-year- d with an invalid on your hands."

"That's not always true," I protested. "The general popu- tion is healthier than ever."

"Except for the obese," Laura added, nodding none too screetly toward a table at which sat a hefty couple. There's an epidemic, you know."

"People live longer lives. Medical care is available." race paused before adding: "For those who can afford it."

Nell shrugged. "I'm just trying to make a point. Sur older men are appealing in a way, but in another way, they' simply not."

"Well," Laura said, "older men aren't an option for m anyway. I need a man who's young and virile, someone wh wants to start a family. I don't want my children to have doddering old man for a father."

"Heaven forbid," Grace murmured.

"He needs to be able to help with midnight feedings an take the kids to soccer practice. He can't be falling asleep the dinner table and in bed by eight."

"Here's a news flash, Laura." Nell leaned close to her sis ter, as if about to impart a vital piece of information. "A parents fall asleep at the dinner table and yearn desperatel to be in bed by eight. You have no idea what you're in for."

Laura made a dismissive motion with her hand. I notice her empty ring finger and wondered what she'd done wit the set Duncan had worked so hard to afford.

"I remember when Colin and Clara were little," she sai "It didn't seem too bad."

Grace and I shared a look. It was hard to know if Laur was truly dim or just besotted with the notion of having cute, cuddly baby of her own.

"Because you went home at night and left the demons t me!" Nell laughed a bit harshly. "You were the fun, youn aunt. I was on the front line; I was the mean, crabby mommy I was the one who cleaned up vomit and went to borin teachers' conferences and made the rules the demons strug gled mightily not to follow."

Laura looked deeply distressed. "How can you call Coli and Clara demons? They're your pride and joy! Aren't they?

For a second, only a second, Nell's eyes glimmered wit tears. "My children," she said, "are my life. Now that Richar isn't."

I called for the check.